PENGUIN BOOKS

If I Should Die

ABOUT THE AUTHOR

Matthew Frank lives in Kent with his wife and three young sons. *If I Should Die* is his first novel, and the first of a new crime series featuring Detective Joseph Stark.

If I Should Die

MATTHEW FRANK

PENGUIN BOOKS

PENGUIN BOOKS

UK | USA | Canada | Ireland | Australia
India | New Zealand | South Africa

Penguin Books is part of the Penguin Random House group of companies
whose addresses can be found at global.penguinrandomhouse.com.

Penguin
Random House
UK

First published by Michael Joseph 2014
Published in Penguin Books 2015

001

Text copyright © Matthew Frank, 2014

The moral right of the author has been asserted

Typeset in 12/13.75pt Garamond MT Std by Palimpsest Book Production Ltd, Falkirk, Stirlingshire
Printed in Great Britain by Clays Ltd, St Ives plc

A CIP catalogue record for this book is available from the British Library

ISBN: 978–1–405–91751–3

www.greenpenguin.co.uk

For Vanessa

GLOUCESTERSHIRE COUNTY COUNCIL	
9934988313	
Bertrams	22/12/2015
AF	£7.99
GHE	

Soldiers will be called upon to make personal sacrifices – including the ultimate sacrifice – in the service of the Nation. In putting the needs of the Nation and the Army before their own, they forgo some of the rights enjoyed by those outside the Armed Forces. In return, British soldiers must always be able to expect fair treatment, to be valued and respected as individuals, and that they (and their families) will be sustained and rewarded by commensurate terms and conditions of service . . . This mutual obligation forms the Military Covenant between the Nation, the Army and each individual soldier; an unbreakable common bond of identity, loyalty and responsibility which has sustained the Army throughout its history. It has perhaps its greatest manifestation in the annual commemoration of Armistice Day, when the Nation keeps covenant with those who have made the ultimate sacrifice, giving their lives in action.

From Introduction to 'Soldiering – The Military Covenant', published by the Ministry of Defence, April 2000

Prologue

The denizens of Combat Outpost McKay had that end-of-tour look: worn desert-camo, seams bleached and salt-rotten from sweat; dust-ingrained faces staring blankly at the stranger in their midst. The faces of men worn thin with sleep-deprivation and danger. They'd been under sniper and mortar fire day and night for five months, then foot patrols with IEDs on top. Even the major, Collins, looked like a scarecrow, shrunken in his clothing. They had three weeks to go until the next roulement arrived, and they needed a sergeant. Until then Corporal Stark would wear a third stripe.

'Acting Sergeant Stark?' demanded the major.

'Sir.'

The officer looked him up and down. 'Private Walker here will show you where to bunk down. Get some kip. We're on foot at zero six hundred sharp. Get yourself dusty – stand out and the snipers will target you for an intelligence officer.'

Walker led him wordlessly through the maze-like compound, the old police station and civic buildings of a tin-pot town linked with Hesco and razorwire, windows re-glazed with sandbag gun slots. Another combat outpost, another Helmand hellhole – surrounded and marooned. Walker showed him the latrine, a chemical loo sheltered on three sides with corrugated iron and sandbags – someone had sprayed 'SHIT FROM ABOVE SHIT FROM BELOW' on the olive-drab canvas curtain that stood for a door – then a bare concrete room with bedrolls and belongings strewn in three corners. Walker pointed to the fourth. 'Doonan's spot.' His dull tone said Doonan no longer had need of it; home on a Hercules, wrapped in bandages and blanket or box and flag. 'Cheer up, Sarge.' He chuckled. 'No mortars tonight. Maybe the bastards've run out!'

Stark didn't try to sleep. He stripped and cleaned his weapon, reloaded magazines, wrote a letter home and tucked it into his bedroll. At 0530 a private led him to the briefing room. Objective: to clear a back road of IEDs. The briefing was short and to the point, same shit, different day – crack on, job done, home in time for tea and medals.

It was still cold as they stepped out. Walker, accompanied by another private, was driving a dusty old Snatch Land Rover at walking pace behind them, two other privates with Vallon metal detectors scanning every inch of road and path as they advanced. It took two hours to reach the objective, by which time it was far from cold. A handful of locals led by a town elder appeared and were greeted by the major. They crouched and conversed awhile in broken phrases, gesticulation and maps scratched in the dust. Their last interpreter had been beheaded and dumped in the local well, a corporal called Gaskin told Stark.

Those were the snippets you didn't tell your mum. Stark was going to have a hard enough time explaining this little detour when he should've been on a transport out of Kandahar today. Scanning the rooftops, he felt the familiar tingle of exhilaration.

Eventually the Afghans led them to the road in question, pointed at various locations and withdrew. The street was eerily abandoned. No wonder, if the locals thought the Taliban had been at work here.

Progress was even slower. Several times the scanners called

a halt while the bomb specialist, a sergeant named Tyler, checked out yet another bit of scuffed earth or discarded tin can.

Then the real thing. They all kept watch while Tyler disarmed the device. A simple bent-metal pressure trigger taped to batteries and explosive, all wrapped in a plastic bin liner. Small, aimed at maiming the foot soldier, buried in the verge with dry turf carefully replaced over it. Batteries removed, Tyler carried it back to the Snatch as if he were doing no more than taking out the rubbish, then stripped off his blast helmet and shared water and laughs with Major Collins.

Stark felt himself relax and checked it. They moved forward again, slow, careful. A hundred metres on, another device. Another taut half-hour while Tyler inspected, described aloud, planned and disarmed the bomb; another just like the first.

Onward again, Stark and the others taking up covering positions as the scanners and vehicle progressed, then moving on past the next covering man. Another halt. Standing beside the vehicle, Stark listened through the open window as Walker cracked up his mate with the filthiest of jokes. The boy noticed Stark chuckling and traded smiles. He passed a plastic bottle out of the window.

'Thanks . . .?'

'Private Smith, Sarge,' announced the boy – what was he? Eighteen, nineteen? 'No relation to all those other shites. Everyone just calls me Danny.'

'Joe Stark.'

'Shite 'ere, innit?' commented Danny.

Stark chuckled and glugged the blessedly icy water just as the explosion slammed into the far side of the Land Rover.

PART ONE

I

May 2009

Stark sat bolt upright, choking off a scream. Agony gripped him, like a fist tightening around his heart. Then reality shuddered back, the desert heat burning to ice as cold sweat ran down him in the chill bedroom darkness.

The first heartbeat came, then another, and another, and the pain faded, like so much mist in the night air, leaving only grief and the blurs and echoes of unwelcome recollection. Of blood, shouting, explosions and gunfire.

He swept the duvet aside, limped to the bathroom, stiff hip easing with each step, went into the shower and let icy water drive out lingering vestiges of the dream before he turned up the heat. He leant against the wall as the stinging cascade brought mind and body alive, then wiped water from his eyes and looked at his watch. Four forty. Great. Just what he didn't want for his first day.

Stepping out, he wiped steam from the mirror and ran fingers through his thick whiskers for the last time. Taking up the scissors he began cropping them short, watching the remnants collect in the basin, relic of a former life. His first decision after the stitches were removed was to begin growing back the beard they'd shaved off him somewhere between Bastion and Selly Oak. Vanity, denial or both. His mum would rejoice to see it gone. Massaging in foam he inspected the new razor, its multiple blades glinting in the LED bathroom

7

spotlights. Then, methodically, he scraped off the desert soldier.

Staring at his clean-shaven face for the first time in months, he ran a finger down the longest scar and shivered.

He pulled on some baggies and creaked half-heartedly through his exercises, grimacing and cursing, then hobbled into the tiny kitchen of his tiny flat and drank orange juice straight from the carton while he whipped up an omelette. *News Twenty-four* was still showing mostly yesterday's news but he let it drone on in the background. He dressed with the sunrise and paused to assess his reflection. Another day, another uniform. It was almost a year since he'd worn this one and a different man stared back. It looked wrong now, alien. Would he feel the same about the plastic-wrapped regimentals now consigned to the back of the wardrobe? 'Can you take the man out of the uniform?' he wondered aloud. He'd find out tomorrow, of course. But for now, for today, this was him. Not British Disruptive Pattern Material but camouflage of a different kind. His gaze lingered on the stranger in the mirror, the damaged doppelganger of the proud fool who'd stared back nine months and a lifetime earlier.

Ready early, he checked the phone but, despite days of promises, the phone company still hadn't connected the line. At the allotted time he limped down the stairs to wait for his prearranged lift to his first day in his new job; his new life. His letterbox contained the usual barrage of takeaway menus and junk mail, an appointment letter from the hospital and one other. The sight of the Ministry of Defence frank shook him, as had the previous two, the notification and the warning. Would this one contain the verdict? Surely not . . . The CO had said he'd call first, but with the phone still dead . . . He ran his thumb over the seal in trepidation. Procrastination costs lives, he reminded himself. He tore it open and scanned the contents, as terse and abrupt as before.

He sat on the stairs and read it again. It didn't get any better.

He dropped his head into his hands, nausea and shame twisting his stomach.

Detective Sergeant Fran Millhaven peered out of the window as a uniform vehicle pulled into the car park. The driver and passenger got out and stood talking briefly, then shook hands; warm, friendly. The car left and the passenger looked up at the building before entering. Chauffeur-driven to work on his first day. In his shiny uniform too, rather predictably. He'd probably been up since four polishing boots and buttons.

Trainee Investigator Constable Joseph Peter Stark. She'd been shown his photo in cuttings from his hometown paper, courtesy of the super in his old nick. 'LOCAL BOBBY WAR HERO!' How the rags loved their hyperbole. As if police work wasn't public service enough, the idiot had signed up for the Territorial Army. Weekend warrior. Did the regular army look down on the Territorials in the same way regular coppers did on Specials?

He'd been posted to Iraq or Afghanistan and got himself blown up or shot, or both. Fair enough, patriotic exploits and all that, give the man a medal. But there was altogether too much homecoming-hero talk for Fran's liking. It wasn't even as though this *was* his home. He was transferring from Hampshire. Glowing reference, apparently, but who'd dare offer less under the circumstances? Why not return to the force on his own turf? There had to be a reason and Fran suspected something was off there. That's what detective sergeants do after all: suspect.

Now he aspired to be a detective constable. She sipped her coffee thoughtfully. 'Ease him in gently,' she'd been told. Like they had her, she thought sourly. She abandoned the bitter coffee and stalked down to the small meeting room. Groombridge was already in there with the super when she knocked.

'Francine, have a seat,' said Superintendent Cox. 'This is Constable Joseph Stark, our shiny new war hero.' Stark had the

9

decency to wince. 'Joe, this is DS Fran Millhaven. She's recently joined us from the far-flung reaches.'

Croydon, thought Fran, eight miles away. And I've been here a year, you arse!

'DCI Groombridge and DS Millhaven are going to be looking out for you while you ease yourself in. No cotton wool, mind, just keeping a friendly eye out. We're aware of your rehabilitation needs. We all know what you've been through for Queen and country. Your old super said you were a bright spark. Fran will introduce you to the masses. Soon have you up to speed. So, any questions?'

'Thank you, sir, no.'

'Good. Good. Well, the door's always open. Glad to have you. Well done, lad.'

He wasn't as tall as she'd imagined he'd be, she mused, as they walked to the canteen, the best place for a scattergun introduction, probably only about five-ten. Maybe it was the hero crap: you expected someone taller, stockier. And older. He was only twenty-five. He'd clocked up some miles in that time. He was good-looking, though. Not aftershave ad, but handsome, or had been before the scars, still livid and ragged. One ran from his neck hairline below his left ear and down behind his collar, another along his left jaw, smaller ones on his right cheek, and there was a nasty one on his right temple. Both his hands showed evidence of burns. The right was missing half of the little finger. He'd been in the wars, all right. He limped too, carrying his left leg slightly. His pink chin looked like he'd shaved three times before parade. His shoes and buttons positively gleamed.

'I'll bet you wore uniform to school even on non-uniform days,' she said, by way of an initial probe. He didn't rise to it. 'Didn't they issue you with a cheapo demob suit when they hoofed you out?'

'It's at home with my ration book and moustache,' he replied, deadpan.

So there was a little bite there. 'Everyone, this is Constable Stark, joining CID today after a sunshine holiday in Iraq. Got himself a bit blown up and this is his first day back on the job so we've all got to be nice to him – to start with, at least.' Everyone nodded in a friendly way; a few came over and introduced themselves.

- 'It was Afghanistan,' said Stark, as she led him down to the custody desk and control room for more intros.

'Not Iraq?'

'Not this time.'

'But before?'

'Three years ago.'

'Didn't get blown up that time?'

He smiled. 'No, thanks for asking.'

'Pleasure.' A nice smile, wry but genuine, she thought. 'Right, this is Custody Sergeant Mick Day. Mick, Constable Joseph Stark, new today.'

'Yeah, I heard. Welcome aboard, Constable. Well on your way to putting a D before your C, I understand. Fancy a peep round the cells? We've got a couple of D-and-Ds in but nothing more exciting, I'm afraid. Perhaps you can help collar whoever's been kicking ten bells out of our local domestically disadvantaged demographic?'

Stark accepted the tour, failing to sense Fran's impatience. Maybe he felt it his duty to know his way around, even down here with the drunk and disorderly. Fran didn't miss uniform.

'Someone been assaulting the homeless?' he asked, as she led him to the control room.

'That's an understatement. We think we know who – local youths of questionable parentage – but we've nothing incriminating. Victims too scared or distrustful to help with enquiries. Morning, Maggie, this is Constable Stark, Joseph, he's new. Hands off, he's fragile. Keep away from this one, new boy, you'd be little more than a snack.'

'Don't let her put you down, sweetie. I'm sure you're the full three courses,' said Maggie, sizing him up and poking her tongue out at Fran. The assorted crowd in the control room greeted him with varying degrees of interest.

Fran always wondered how regular people imagined this room. They probably pictured dimmed lighting, wall-to-wall high-tech, banks of uniformed officers. The reality behind those calm, professional 999 voices was a small room with a tiny window, cluttered with obsolete computers and varying shapes and sizes of civilian, in their navy polo-necks with logo and 'civilian staff' stitching. They took fag breaks, left coffee stains, bantered, gossiped and complained, just like anyone else. They did a vital job well. Still, Fran thought, regular people would be horrified.

'That's most of the usual suspects,' she said. 'You'll catch up with everyone else as you go along. They've all been told your sob story.' He looked at her sharply and she regretted her tone. 'Right. Well, come on, you owe me a coffee.'

Stark had hardly taken a sip when the interrogation began. 'So, Joseph or Joe?' Fran demanded.

He blinked. A perfectly normal question, yet one he'd not been asked in a while. For the last few years his superiors in both careers had almost only ever addressed him by rank and surname, from 'Constable' to 'Private' to 'Lance Corporal' to 'Corporal'. In military hospital he'd remained 'Corporal', in the NHS he'd reverted to 'Mr', and when he'd begun his CID training he'd become Trainee Investigator Constable Stark. His mum called him Joseph. A smattering of old friends called him JP. Everyone else called him Joe, but that sounded overly intimate from strangers now. 'I don't really mind.'

She didn't accept this. 'You must have a view. What do mates call you?'

'Either.'

'Okay, why transfer?' She'd changed her angle of attack. 'Surely your old nick would've been easier. And family, friends? Don't you need the love and support and all that crap?'

'All that crap wears thin,' he replied, watching her carefully.

She seemed to consider this, perhaps waiting for him to expand. 'That's it?'

'That's it.'

'Hmph,' she said, evidently dissatisfied. His new sergeant seemed to think asking personal questions wasn't rude but refusing to answer them was. Maybe it was a CID thing. Maybe she thought she was being tough, establishing superiority. Either way he quite liked it. Rule number one, after all: no fucking sympathy.

Despite her frown she had a pretty face, attractive, an everyday lived-in face, mid-tone brown skin, flattish nose, high forehead, hair scraped back into a frizzy ponytail. Caribbean, maybe. Her skin suggested thirtyish but her dark-brown eyes said more. Average height, a little overweight, smart in her charcoal trouser-suit and white blouse. Flat shoes. No wedding ring. She gave the distinct impression of not liking him much but he couldn't decide if that was personal or simply her default position. Time would tell, he supposed. Fending off her questions, however politely, only served to bolster this impression. Giving up, she showed him around the Territorial Policing areas, introducing him to the senior uniformed officers and the attached CID team, led by DI Graham. Then up to the CID floor and the MIT.

'And this is our little nerve centre, for our sins. DCI Groombridge's office is through there. He's not bad. DS Harper is off with flu.' She rattled off names of the DCs present but most fled Stark's memory instantly. 'Everyone else is out and about somewhere.'

'No detective inspector?'

'Early retirement and not replaced. Cutbacks,' she answered, without rancour, though it must've added significantly to her and DS Harper's workload: promotion and responsibility without rank or reward. 'That's yours.' She stabbed a finger towards a tiny desk wedged uncomfortably into a corner between filing cabinets and a photocopier. Stark considered asking which poor sod had occupied it before him but thought better of it. She'd probably give him some bollocks about the last trainee resting in a shallow grave for giving her cheek.

So, this was to be his home. The Major Investigation Team, often called the Murder Investigation Team or Murder Squad.

'The DCI suggested you start by familiarizing yourself with the happy-slappings.'

Stark frowned. 'What makes them MIT? No one's been killed. Has intent been established?'

'No, but the sodding risk assessment suggested substantive risk to life so uniform punted it upstairs to us. It's as good a place as any to cut your teeth and I don't want you underfoot with anything serious. DC Dixon will show you where to find the files.'

'Yes, Detective Sergeant.'

'"Sarge" will do. Any questions?'

'No, thanks.' This didn't seem the right time to ask after the mobile phone he'd been told to expect. He'd cancelled his own in anticipation, prematurely as it turned out, with his landline still not connected. It might have given him a nice break from his family but he was still an army reservist, if pending discharge, and required to provide a valid number.

'Good. Read those files. There'll be questions later. And stay out of everyone's way.' And that was that, his introduction. No cotton wool.

The DCs all said hello and asked a few polite questions. Stark carried the files to his excuse for a desk and got stuck in. They didn't make pretty reading. There had been four assaults reported in the last three months, though there might have been more.

Homeless folk weren't always in a hurry to report things to the police. Stark felt rising anger prickle his skin as he read on. All the attacks had taken place late at night in secluded places, always on a single victim, outnumbered and defenceless. Broken bones, cuts, contusions, concussion – helpless middle-aged men and women, beaten and humiliated, and for what? The level of despicable cruelty was only matched by the cowardice.

Unsurprisingly, suspect descriptions varied, but they overlapped enough to lead the local officers' suspicions to a particular group of nasty young thugs. A gang, led by one Kyle Gibbs and his girlfriend Nikki Cockcroft. The word 'gang' was often misused. Greenwich might endure its share of drug-gang turf disputes but this was just the common teenage tribal affiliation, another ASBO-generation epicentre. Gibbs and his coterie sprang from the Ferrier Estate – which, Dixon informed Stark, was the borough's least desirable postcode – a loose aggregation known as the Rats. From what Stark knew so far, the name was too good for them.

Dixon invited Stark to lunch with him and the two passed the time in polite conversation. He seemed a decent enough bloke, of similar age to Stark though ahead in career. Hadn't wasted time playing in the sand. Maybe that was why he seemed unsure of himself with Stark – people often reacted strangely when they knew you were a veteran. Being a veteran of two unpopular and misunderstood wars was worse. It wouldn't be long before someone here got hold of that ridiculous *Gosport Herald* article, if they hadn't already. Stark asked him about DS Millhaven but he wouldn't be drawn, saying only that she was all right once she got used to you.

Towards the end of the day she reappeared and offered to drive Stark home via the Ferrier Estate. It was a couple of miles as the crow flew and she used the time to quiz Stark on what he'd read earlier, as if trying to emphasize his inexperience.

If anything, the estate was worse than Dixon had described, a late-sixties carbuncle bisected by a main road, each half a series of large courtyards that were all but enclosed on four sides by six-storey blocks of flats and ramped walkways with the occasional twelve-storey tower thrown in for extra misery, all in cheap brutalist concrete panelling; the culmination of decades of ever-cheaper bastardizations of the thirties' modernist ideal.

Tucked in one corner, Telemann Square had once held a series of inward-facing shops. Most were boarded up now, including the once-notorious Wat Tyler pub and a community centre that had never looked its best. All that clung to life were a pharmacy, a doctor's surgery, a dentist, a tiny library and the Holy Spirit Church Centre, surely the C of E's most desperate outpost, and an off-licence/convenience store so covered with security grilles that it had to display a 'WE ARE OPEN' sign behind the glass.

Almost everywhere you looked there was graffiti. Not Banksy-esque satire or hip-hop street art, just the usual anatomical diagrams, four-letter words and throwaway tags – stylized nicknames sprayed, gouged or etched, like a tomcat pissing on a post.

With its war-zone chic the 'shops' area was the hangout of choice to the 'local scumbags with little better to do'. Looking around, Stark saw there *was* little better to do. The embattled offy probably ran a fine line, peddling two-litre bottles of cheap white cider to all ages more out of self-preservation than greed.

The few people he saw hurried along in a manner Stark recognized all too well but had not seen outside Basra and Helmand. Fear, in broad daylight, in London. Stark felt bile rise in his throat and swallowed hard. Looking down, he found his fists were clenched.

As they drove out of the estate Fran pulled over and pointed out a lean, pale, shifty-eyed teenager leaning against a wall, smoking. 'That's him, Kyle Gibbs, local hero, several convictions for burglary and shoplifting as a minor, served three months' youth custody. Suspected of dealing wraps and pills at the cockroach level. Cautioned for possession of cannabis, but usually has the nous to drop his stash if a stop-and-search looks likely. Cocky little shit. *De facto* leader of the rudderless scrotes because he's older and marginally more vicious.' Gibbs glanced their way and, sitting in the unmarked car, Stark was acutely aware of his uniform. Gibbs smirked, stubbed out his cigarette and flicked it in their direction, spat on the pavement and walked off round the corner with the bow-legged, bent-arm swagger of the wannabe hard-nut, the ape trying to look big. 'He and his girlfriend Nikki Cockcroft rule the roost and, for sure, they and their hangers on are behind the happy-slappings.'

'Always on the homeless?' asked Stark.

'So far. They're not above jumping some poor sod outside a pub and there's no shortage of muggings on the estate, but I guess the homeless are less likely to fight back. One of the attacks even turned up briefly on YouTube. The spiteful little shits like filming their exploits on their phones. Nice to know who you were fighting for, I'm sure,' she huffed. 'No offence,' she added, watching him out of the corner of her eye.

Stark didn't bite. 'You pulled him in?'

'And her, and half a dozen others. Waste of a perfectly good Sunday. Cocky little shits just clam up, laugh at us.'

'Forensics?'

Fran laughed. 'Perhaps if they beat someone who mattered.'

She dropped him at home. 'Demob suit tomorrow,' she said, by way of farewell. 'Moustache optional.'

2

The bad dreams when they came could be bright, hot and painful, but the degree varied. If there were some way to predict or control them, going to sleep might involve less trepidation. They'd begun a few weeks after he was evacuated, when body and mind began to accept his survival. They'd escalated fast but he'd had help, medicinal, cognitive and peer-oriented. It was understood, expected, manageable. That night they wandered erratically from warm surreal twists on recollection to darker, hotter places but without the searing hyper-real intensity of the bad ones. He awoke more with relief than terror, tired but not exhausted. He did his exercises, like a good boy, ate like a horse, then shaved and showered in swift order, acutely aware of the military conditioning grinning through.

Reaching into the wardrobe, his hand hovered between green and blue, then slowly withdrew charcoal grey. Mufti to work. Stark stared at his reflection and tutted at the odd insecurity he felt without uniform to define his role. He reflected on his first day in the Metropolitan Police Service. Everyone had been nice enough, though DS Millhaven wasn't a barrel of laughs. If she warmed up, great; if not, he'd known worse. Right now he had bigger worries.

It wasn't until Stark was halfway through breakfast that he noticed the answerphone blinking a red number two. He jumped up and lifted the receiver. A clear tone greeted his ear. Finally.

The first message was his mum, predictably – the usual

mixture of worry and accusation. She also said his CO was trying to get hold of him. I'll bet he is, thought Stark, glancing at the offending MoD letter. The second was from Colonel Mattherson himself. 'Sorry to do this with a message but I've been trying to reach you for days. Felt you should hear it from me, not some ministry oik. I think you'd better sit down . . .' Mattherson had that senior-officer quality of delivering all information, welcome or otherwise, without the slightest modification in tone. He had junior officers to do the shouting. If anything, that made it worse. Stark hit delete.

When he arrived Fran was perched on the end of Dixon's desk, halfway through a warm pastry. 'MoD spared no expense, then,' she said, looking Stark up and down. The sarcasm was implied rather than expressed, and he ignored it. It was a decent enough suit, smart enough to pass muster, cheap enough to chase a suspect over a wall if required. And he was close enough to NATO Standard to make off-the-peg look made-to-measure. 'Good morning, Sarge.' He smiled.

'If you say so.' She glanced at his gleaming shoes. 'Right, get the coffees. There's a team meeting in ten and I'll be buggered if I'm going in there without another caffeine hit.'

The meeting was as dull as Fran's tone had suggested it would be, not least because Stark knew nothing of the cases discussed. He wasn't about to drag it out for everyone else with questions, so pieced together as much as he could. He was introduced to several more new faces, and surreptitiously began jotting down names.

Afterwards there seemed little for him to do. DS Harper had been leading the happy-slapping case but he was still off sick and his DC, Bryden, was out. Rather than just get in the way Stark suggested he went out in one of the patrol cars for the day to start getting a feel for his new patch. Fran agreed with an uninterested shrug. Maggie helped find him a ride, calling him 'sweetie' again, and soon he was being driven around by Sergeant Ptolemy and WPC Peters, two decent uniforms, no apparent axe to grind with his CID aspirations. He bought them lunch from a local sandwich bar and they gave him an overview of their manor, warts and all. They seemed quite fond of the place, proud almost, in that learnt-rather-than-felt cynical tone used by coppers before the shine had worn off. You saw the same thing in the army.

The first thing Stark did after they'd dropped him home was call the base. It had been on his mind all day and he needed it off. The adjutant put him straight through.

'Corporal Stark! About bloody time!' Colonel Mattherson's rapid-fire delivery.

'Constable Stark now, sir.'

'Ah, yes. Thought you'd dropped off the bloody world!'

'Comms were down, sir, logistical misunderstanding.'

'Situation normal et cetera. Now, you got my message?'

'Yes, sir.'

'And the letter?'

'Sir.'

'Well, then, what have you got to say for yourself?'

The next day DS Harper had failed to recover so Stark re-read the file before sitting down with DC Bryden to talk it through. In essence the investigation was at a halt awaiting new leads, meaning fresh assaults, so Stark tidied his desk and ordered a cab. Though University Hospital Lewisham was only two miles away across Deptford Creek, it was outside the borough. Greenwich's Queen Elizabeth Hospital was four miles over in Woolwich, and Stark had no idea how to get there by public transport.

'Going somewhere?' frowned Fran, noticing him pull on his jacket.

'Hospital appointment, Sarge.'

'This was in the schedule you submitted?'

'Yes. I'll be back after lunch.'

She pursed her lips. Maybe she wasn't a fan of people getting special treatment but there was little he could do about that. The force had made it clear he was free to work around his recovery needs. Maybe resentment would build up in others if it went on too long. He also got the impression she was fishing. The schedule he'd submitted didn't say what each appointment was for, though Superintendent Cox had full details, and Stark wondered if she'd got wind that Wednesdays were psychotherapy.

He found the right department with little difficulty but they kept him waiting. He'd never been in one of these sessions that was allowed to overrun by a millisecond yet they still contrived to keep him waiting every time. It was some kind of institutional fourth-dimensional phenomenon. It shouldn't make him angry or anxious but it did.

He wasn't looking forward to it, he never had, and the thought of starting with a new therapist, someone with no military affiliation or experience, made him feel sick. At least the military ones had got straight to the point. Nevertheless Stark had never balanced the pain with any alleged gain. There was a joke they used at Headley Court – *PTSD: it's all in your head*. Post-traumatic stress disorder; symptoms manifest in various ways and severity. Stark's were mild at most, so mild he felt fraudulent accepting treatment. But until the dreams left him alone he'd never persuade the shrinks to do the same. In theory this new one should have reviewed his notes in detail, prepared, planned. In theory he shouldn't have to cover too much old ground. In theory.

So much for theory, he thought an hour later. Few people leave you with a true impression of imbecility, but Dr Hazel McDonald made his head throb. It was like wading through treacle or, worse, like talking to a wall – every statement echoed back at you with a question mark on the end, every fact queried, every frustration seized upon. Nothing went in, nothing. He had a dreadful feeling the next session would start where this had and get no further.

And it was past lunchtime. If they were just honest about appointment times he'd have been able to eat beforehand. He didn't like being hungry. Army life was regular except when it wasn't, teaching you to associate regular meals with safety and rest. Selly Oak and Headley Court had reinforced the point by associating mealtimes with respite from torture and, despite what people might say, food in the army and in hospital was plentiful and nutritious. It didn't matter if you liked it, you ate it: fuel, fuel, fuel, for fighting or healing, shovel it in. All was well when the food came like clockwork. Right now his stomach told him all was not well. The thought of speaking to that woman again made him feel all the more sick.

He found what passed for a sandwich in the hospital canteen and spent the cab ride back dispelling the unpleasant thoughts rattling around in his head. Talking of which, he ought to phone Margaret Collins. He couldn't keep his head in the sand for ever. There didn't seem much way he could hope to avoid what was coming and she deserved to hear it from him first.

Fran made a point of peering at the wall clock when Stark reappeared well after lunchtime, but said nothing. He didn't apologize; if this was how long his appointments were going to take, better she got used to it now. It wasn't as if she'd given him anything else to do. Ptolemy and Peters had offered to show him more that afternoon and evening and, with apparently no plan for him, Fran waved her consent wordlessly as she took a call.

This tour covered more of the borough, all the way out to Abbey Wood and Thamesmead, with its iconic riverside Flat Block Marina, immortalized by the film *A Clockwork Orange*, returning to Greenwich town by the evening. Around pub closing a call came over the radio requesting response to trouble brewing at the Meridian pub.

Ptolemy picked up the handset. 'Control. Car Eleven responding, ETA two minutes.'

The Meridian turned out to be one of those chain McPubs popping up in every town like aggressive weeds, strangling traditional pubs. Trouble had already brewed, boiled and spilt over. Outside, two groups were posturing and yelling abuse at each other.

Both sides fell back at the arrival of the blue lights. Ptolemy and Peters leapt out and strode into the gap. The shouting and posturing barely diminished as they tried to make themselves heard and establish coherence if not order. Out of uniform Stark hung back by the car, ready to assist if required.

Perhaps it was situation normal at this establishment. A big doorman peeped out to observe the blue lights and ducked back inside, content to have pushed his mess out for someone else to clear up.

The more aggressive group was led by a gobby chavette, hair scraped back in a council face-lift, big hooped gold ear-rings, mauve velour tracksuit and the latest must-have accessory: a gold clown on a gold chain. She was incensed about something. Her eyes were wild and there was saliva on her lips as she spat startling vitriol. It was only when she paused for breath that he recognized her. The infamous Nikki Cock-croft from the assault files. Others too. Stark couldn't recall names but this was them, including Kyle Gibbs, hovering near the back. Stark's eyes rested on Gibbs. It took a second to work out why but then he had it – Gibbs had one hand in a pocket.

There was only one reason someone on the brink of a fight would keep one hand in his or her pocket. Gibbs watched the police nervously, backing away slightly. Stark began moving cautiously to flank him. Suddenly, among all the commotion,

Gibbs glanced his way. That was just how it went some days, the army taught you – be as sneaky as you like, but sometimes the enemy just looked your way.

There was a slow-motion dawning of realization. The hand withdrew from the pocket but it was too late, too obvious, and Kyle knew it. They stared at each other for a moment. Anger flared in the boy's eyes. Stark took a step towards him but he turned and fled, like a scalded cat, across the main road into a narrow lane. Stark gave chase but the boy had ten years and one good leg on him. The lane turned almost immediately right but Stark arrived at the corner only in time to see the boy leap up a metal gate and disappear into darkness beyond. The gate was six feet high and spiked but Stark made the attempt. He pulled himself up but couldn't gain any purchase with his bad leg and dropped down with a curse, kicking the gate in frustration. The darkness inside looked like a small park, suggesting other exits, one of which Kyle was surely scaling at that moment. Stark cursed his weakness for the thousandth time and returned to the fracas.

Improbable order was emerging. Ptolemy had Nikki and her side corralled into the narrow pedestrianized passage, dampened down, perhaps, by the unexpected disappearance of their leader. Peters had the quieter ones lined up meekly around the corner. It was amusing to hear both officers trotting out the same tried-and-tested phrases, the same deadpan measured tone dripping with unspoken sarcasm. More cars arrived. Names and addresses were taken and the opposing sides sent packing in opposite directions under orders to calm down, piss off home and sleep it off.

'What was it about?' asked Stark.

'Sweet little Nikki decided a girl from another table had looked at her,' replied Ptolemy. 'What was that all about?' He nodded in the direction Kyle had fled.

Stark told him.

'Kyle Gibbs? Knife probably. Not sure any of the Rats have moved up to guns yet. I'll see if Control can put someone outside his block for a stop 'n' search. Anyway, it's not him you should worry about,' Ptolemy added. He pointed after Nikki Cockcroft. 'That's the source of the vile, right there. Been pulling her claws out of people since she was thirteen.'

'You're limping.' Fran frowned, the following morning.

'I'm fine, thanks, Sarge,' replied Stark, though there'd been no concern in her statement.

He explained his antics the previous evening, and Fran made a mental note not to rely on his assistance in any kind of chase. 'Did uniform pick Gibbs up?'

'No. They put a car in the estate but . . .'

'It's a Rat warren.' She nodded. 'Well, never mind that. Here . . .' She scooped up the stack of paperwork she had ready on her desk and slapped it into his hands. 'You'll need to keep a log of your daily activities, so read this lot and fill in the PDP forms for signature. Don't let it build up. I won't sign anything half-arsed or fictitious. No one likes having their time wasted.'

'Sarge.'

Fran studied him a moment, trying to discern sarcasm in the flat monosyllable. It was her job to supervise him and she meant to do it, but he was hard to read. 'Okay then, get a good feel for the dull end. Nothing much happening up the sharp end anyway.'

At the end of that week Fran bumped into Superintendent Cox on the stairs. 'Good afternoon, Fran!' He'd greeted her in his usual effusive manner. DCI Groombridge seemed to have a lot of time for the man but he grated on Fran. 'How's our new boy getting on? Living up to all our expectations, I trust?'

'Too early to tell yet, sir,' she replied.

'Ah . . . uncompromising as ever, eh? Fair enough. But you might want to grant him a little grace, special circumstance and all that. The lad's done his bit, after all.'

'Yes, sir.'

'Good, good. Carry on.'

There was more than a little of the clichéd moustache-puffing army officer about Cox. Perhaps he harboured fantasies in that direction. Maybe he idolized Stark in some infantile manner.

It shouldn't irritate her so much, she was sure, but it did. Cotton bloody wool, whatever Cox said to the contrary. It wasn't that she'd had a particularly hard time of it. She hadn't, really. It was just a matter of principle. You didn't ask for favour and you didn't give it. Policing wasn't about compromise. And there was something in Stark's manner that niggled, a self-contained imperviousness. She was sure it was just a front, and fronts bothered her. Something was going on under there, something serious. Whatever it was, if it interfered with his work or, worse, hers, he'd regret it.

Perhaps she should've given him more time in his first week but she was busy helping CPS with an old case that was finally coming to court so she'd lent him to Dixon to go through some closed-case files, preparing them for shipping out to a data-input company so that they could be scanned into the digital world. If she was arse-deep in paperwork he might as well be too – on-the-job training and all that.

At five thirty on the dot she slipped on her jacket. 'Right, I'm gasping. Come on, you miserable lot. You too, Williams, it's your round.'

The Compass Rose was a dingy little pub with ceiling beams older than time and lower than comfortable, considering half of its clientele came from a profession where it used to be compulsory to be six foot tall. Friday night was Rosie's, no excuses. If you weren't on duty, you had a drink. More and more officers opted for something soft, these days, but that wasn't the point.

Williams bought the first round with good grace and gradually the place filled with bodies and noise. Stark sipped at something short, she noticed, whisky by the colour. At least he wasn't on orange juice. In every other way he seemed buttoned up and out of place. It wasn't long, though, before he seemed to relax and join in. Dixon and Hammed, both of whom she noted were in some kind of awe of him, visibly relaxed too. There was conversation and laughter. When she next looked he was playing doubles pool, partnering Dixon against a couple of uniforms, the ones Maggie had sent him out with earlier in the week. She watched him interact with ease. She was always suspicious of good-looking lads with their effortless charm.

Groombridge slid into the seat opposite and put a fresh glass in front of her. 'What do you think of him, our anointed one?'

'I'm not one for messiahs, Guv.'

'Me neither, but all that nonsense is hardly his fault. You've been watching him. What's your opinion so far?'

'Impenetrable, non-compliant, haughty.'

'*Fran!*' laughed Groombridge. 'Be fair.'

'Honestly? I don't know, Guv. I've not had as much time with him this week as perhaps I should. But I get the impression he's coasting – here in body but not in mind, not in heart. I've tried picking at the edges but he either avoids answering questions or gives answers so simple you're left with little or no more information than you started with.'

'Some people are just private,' suggested Groombridge.

Fran didn't buy it. 'It's more than that. I get the impression he enjoys the avoidance, but I can't shake the feeling that he's hiding more than his privacy.'

'Given what he's been through, maybe that's understandable.'

'If you say so.'

'You might try cutting him some slack.'

'Not you too!' cried Fran. 'Cox bent my ear on that earlier. Frankly I think he's getting enough slack already.'

Groombridge looked at her strangely, as if he were considering something. 'Even so,' was all he said, sipping his pint.

3

Technically Stark wasn't obliged to work Saturday – he wasn't on the unsociable hours rota yet – but he was conscious that his hospital appointments would eat into his forty hours. Dixon was down to work so Stark offered to help him finish off what they'd been doing. Once it was done they had lunch together in the canteen. The previous evening had narrowed the chasm between them somewhat. On the subject of DS Millhaven, however, Dixon wouldn't budge. Stark had been aware of Fran glowering at him over her drink the previous evening and had had the impression that she and DCI Groombridge had been discussing him. He was still far from sure about his new career choice and his first week had done little to alleviate his doubts; the last thing he needed was the dislike of a senior officer. He didn't relate any of this to Dixon, of course, restricting himself to a few basic questions. He recognized loyalty in Dixon's answers so let it drop. If she was all right once she got used to you he'd either have to be patient or let down his own barriers a little.

After lunch he went home and spent the rest of the day rearranging the little flat he'd taken for twelve months, moving things from where he'd unpacked them to where they ought to be. Try as he might, though, he couldn't occupy himself enough to avoid thinking about the next day. It had taken all his determination to phone Margaret Collins. She'd sounded happy enough to hear from him but it had to have been forced, especially when he asked to see her in person. God knew, she probably dreaded seeing him too, though she'd remained polite despite his unwillingness to explain himself. He regretted arranging the meeting now. He hadn't had the first week he might have hoped for, his wounds ached and he would've liked a day free to recover at leisure. But it had to be done.

The crunch, crunch, crunch of your boots, your laboured breath, wafts of acrid black smoke from the burning Land Rover, the jangling of your kit, quiet as the regimental band, for fuck's sake! The crack of the AK47s and the surreal whine of bullets tells you Terry Taliban's overcome his surprise.

Jump down the low wall and stagger, nearly fall, turn and help one of the others down. Collins points at the house, if you can call it that. Set off, heart pounding, kit killing your shoulders, rubbed raw – at least Terry won't get his hands on any of it. Not today. The whoosh of an RPG; detonates well behind. Nearly there, expecting muzzle flash from that window any second. Never comes, and you're there, slammed against the wall, gasping for breath. Check the safety's off for the tenth time. A nod, Collins kicks the door and you pile in, weapon raised, Collins behind you. Movement in the corner! Collins shouts. Swing, SHOOT!

Stark twitched so hard his body left the mattress, the sickening crack of shots echoing in his ears. Limbs tangling in the sheet, trapping him, panic rising, dust and cordite choking him, he fought to free himself in the dark; and all the while the mother's eyes stared up at him as she crouched in the corner cradling her child, stared right along the barrel of his gun. He choked off a sob, kicking free of the tripping sheet as he staggered out into the living room where the orange streetlight streaming in drove her face from his mind.

He snatched up the bottle and downed long slugs of burning whisky. Gripping the bottle, he came within an inch of hurling it at the wall but fought down the frightening anger, the loathing. Instead he screwed the top back on and slammed it down on the table. Next to it sat the phone with an accusatory red blinking three. He'd been in no mood to listen to his voice-mail last night. He yanked the lead out and threw it into the corner, then slumped on to the sofa, face buried in his hands, rocking forward and back.

Her face came flooding in, imploring, defiant, terrified. And the child, small, maybe three, a boy, just one dark, peeping eye visible through his mother's protecting hands. A millisecond, frozen for ever. Stark opened his eyes wide before the memory drove him mad. He could still hear Collins's shout, echoing down through time.

Standing, he limped to the window and scanned the calm, cool urban night, the thick vegetation, the lush deciduous trees struck orange and black in the familiar sodium light. Helmand in August could have been Mars compared to this, the Taliban and Afghans some weird alien creatures, light years away. But the mother and her child, human, so very human, brought the whole thing to your doorstep. He could have been looking out on the boy, playing, laughing with the soldiers, entreating them for boiled sweets, bottled water, NATO bloody ballpoints.

Your decent movie hero would punch his ghostly reflection now, bloody knuckles a token penance. Stark grunted through his exercises instead, showered and fell asleep on the sofa.

Later, as he was pulling on his shoes to leave, he noticed the phone still lying where he'd thrown it. He plugged it back in and pressed play. His mum sounding worried and cross, then his sister sounding cross and stressed out: the standard tag-team guilt trip. Last but not least, a female captain shiny-arse, Pierson, asking if he'd received the MoD letter, and if so why he'd not responded. Another woman voicing disappointment in him. Well, it was Sunday and they could all wait.

He'd done the tourist thing the previous weekend and *had* been looking forward to more, before Monday's letter. He'd always enjoyed learning; a trait inherited from his father that had just about survived the mire of mediocre comprehensive schooling. He'd left with decent A levels, but with his little sister struggling at school and his mum's solitary wage already stretched, university was impossible. They needed income. So he'd settled for a library card and joined the police. Only the force was duller than he'd imagined. It had its moments of excitement but spread out in an eternity of lost hours. Lost walking streets, standing with his back to football matches, filling in paperwork, locking up drunks, stopping-and-searching dodgy wasters, standing outside the crime-scene tape while others went in.

Girls came and went. Mates got on with their lives. He needed something else. So, at the end of his two-year probation, he'd decided to hedge his bets.

The Territorial Army was everything he'd imagined. One night a week, one weekend a month and a two-week training course each year. Weapons, demolitions, engineering, strategy and tactics: what wasn't to like? More than once he'd seriously considered transferring to the regulars, but staying a weekend soldier gave him the best of both worlds and breaks from both.

He was in good shape going in and kept up with the kids around him. The great thing about the TA: it wasn't just kids around you: there were guys and girls younger and older, from different backgrounds and levels of qualification. The TA prided itself that this enabled them to learn quicker, to go from reserve to combat-ready in short order. They tried to talk him into going Red Cap, Military Police, but he'd politely declined. The best of both worlds.

That was enough for many. Others, like Stark, sought deployment. You didn't come out of training shy of a fight. Scared or otherwise, you wanted deployment. Not to look back and say, 'Yes, I served, but I stayed at home.' You wanted to serve your function and, as an infantryman, that meant boots on the ground. There were plenty whose function kept them from front-line duty and were no less crucial for it. PONTIs, some called them, Persons of No Tactical Importance. The expression infuriated Stark. You put yourself in harm's way when you enlisted, full stop; whatever role you were assigned was vital and there was no telling where you would end up or in what danger. It was all too easy to forget that when you were being shot at, but if you were hunkered down with an empty belly or no ammunition you'd soon remember. Or if you were relying on the person at the other end of the radio to correctly relay the co-ordinates of a nearby enemy position to the American aircraft about to drop a bloody great bomb, you should be hoping they were having a very comfortable, stress-free day back at base following a good night's sleep and that their hands, as they typed, weren't trembling like yours.

Deployment. Three weeks' intensive training, six months in theatre. It could've been any number of benign places but there were only two truly hot tickets in town and Stark was both happy and apprehensive when he had drawn Iraq.

Operation Telic. Telic, meaning 'directed towards a definite end, goal or purpose'; the understated British name for what the Americans called Operation Iraqi Freedom. Fifteen-hour shifts, seven days a week, boiling in the day and freezing at night, bored shitless ninety per cent of the time, scared shitless the rest. He'd walked patrols, driven patrols, guarded things, smiled at the locals, won hearts and minds, helped officers wipe their arses and on several occasions been shot at. Most of the time it was impossible to see where it was coming from. If anyone could confidently see where it *was* coming from, you shot back. Stark couldn't say whether he'd ever hit anyone, most likely not. Contacts like those were exhilarating, terrifying, surreal and not a little sickeningly pointless, the only way in which it was anything like a video game. Of the company Stark augmented, seven were wounded, two killed. They were lucky. Luckier than the poor people of Basra, that was for sure.

Then had followed two months' 'Decompression & Normalization', army speak for making sure you were safe to let out of the box. This was particularly important to TA veterans who, not having army 'family' close through living on or around a base, were twice as likely to suffer mental-health issues, through drink, depression or domestic disharmony. Stark had read that nearly 6 per cent suffered PTSD symptoms compared to 2.5 per cent of regulars. The TA downside. Stark got ten days in Cyprus on the way back, sitting on the beach with occasional lectures on stress followed by twenty-four hours' family leave, then straight off for a week on the Brecon Beacons, hiking up and down in the rain, and the rest on barracks guard duty, still in the rain. Then he was back on Civvy Street, the same but not the same. He'd done his bit, but it wasn't enough.

A lot had happened since then. If not, he'd probably still have been sitting on the fence between two vocations. But here he was, career copper, and finding the lack of alternative uncomfortable. He'd give it a year, see how he felt about it then, see how he healed, see what was left.

All these thoughts bounced around in his head whenever he looked up from his book to stare at the countryside and townscapes flitting past the train window. Two changes and a taxi ride later he stood before a white plastic front door in a generic brick house in a cul-de-sac in a development of dozens like it. His hand hesitated, then pressed the bell.

'Mrs Collins,' he said stiffly, as she opened the door.

'At ease, Corporal,' she replied, forcing a smile. 'You'd better come in and tell me what's so awful you had to come all this way.'

4

Fresh dreams chased him awake. The intensity of recollection seemed to be increasing rather than diminishing with time. He had pushed fear aside, he thought. But it pushed back hard, so hard it still racked him here in this cold room, conscious, whole, alive, nearly nine months later.

How long could this go on? Why some nights and not others? The shrinks at Headley Court might tell him, the door remained ajar, but he was damned if he'd go back. It was a limited resource and some other poor sod needed it now. Besides, his papers were due soon – Honourable Discharge. Tell that to the guys with no legs, no arms or no eyes. It was wrong to call it bitterness: you took the coin, you knew this could happen. But a discharge might as well have come with a boot in the behind and the door slamming shut behind you. Suddenly you belonged to the NHS, but 'Don't worry, priority treatment, military covenant and all that. Great to have you, honour to have served and all that, good luck!' And the NHS was too cumbersome to notice those drifting away from treatment in droves. Those most in need, those with combined physical and mental damage, were too often those least able to meet the NHS halfway. That left the charities, but with the state abdicating responsibility to them so heavily, they were already stretched to breaking. No, thought Stark, struggling to his feet, he would make do with Doc Hazel, ineffectual as she might be, and with the physical treatment he knew he was lucky to receive.

Dawn was well under way and there was little hope of more

sleep. As he ate he stared hard at the whisky and pills on the coffee-table. Little blue OxyContin pills, 5mg, the smallest dose available. An opioid nonetheless, a loathed, all too frequently necessary crutch, both masking and highlighting his physical state. Not to be mixed with alcohol, they proclaimed – unless you're an insomniac who thinks he knows better than a consensus of informed doctors and expert pharmacologists, thought Stark, with a minor twinge of guilt. Very minor. Needs must when the devil drove. He'd done without both last night; it would be ridiculous to start either now. The pain wasn't too bad and the sleep was already lost.

After exercises and shower, he studied his reflection as he shaved, studied the scars, not for the first time feeling a strange, chilling, detached ambivalence creeping over him. He made himself look harder, past the marks to their causes, groping for the warmth, however burning. Maybe his mind had decided it was just too tired today, he thought, giving up.

When the uniform car pulled up he was feeling discernibly less motivated than he'd felt a week earlier. He'd have to start walking it soon; being a burden didn't sit well. The very thought made his hip twinge but he wasn't ready to buy another car, not until the physios said a manual was okay: with his hip as it was, they insisted it was an automatic or nothing. You had to draw the line somewhere. Besides, walking would speed things up.

He didn't know the two constables. 'DS Millhaven asked us to drop you in town,' said the passenger. 'There's been another homeless assault, bad one.'

'How bad?' asked Stark, shaking off his lethargy.

'Don't know much. An old fella, I think, in the hospital.' The two talked about the string of attacks and what they'd like to do to the culprits in a cheerfully righteous manner until they turned and parked in the grounds of the large town-centre church, St Alfege. There was police tape across a substantial pedestrian gateway that opened into some kind of park beyond.

Uniforms were deflecting public curiosity while Fran stood talking to a man Stark didn't know. He might have said arguing with, from their body language.

Stark took a moment to get his bearings and realized this must be the other side of the dark space into which Kyle Gibbs had climbed the previous week. Fran spotted him and impatiently beckoned him over. 'DS Harper, this is the new boy, Trainee Investigator Constable Stark. He's been tasked to the investigation since he started last week.'

Harper was a tall, solid, thick-set man in his thirties with one of those broken-nosed, hard-bitten but handsome faces, like a rugby flanker; he even had a fat lip and freshly healed cut over one eye. He looked more post-match than post-flu. He glanced at Stark without comment and returned his attention to Fran. 'You still haven't answered my question.'

'It was DCI Groombridge's decision. We didn't know you'd be back today and I've been boning up on the files to quiz Stark here. It's nothing personal. I'm sure the DCI will take me off it once he knows you're back.' Fran smiled reassuringly.

Harper nodded unsmilingly. 'What's the vic's condition?'

'Intensive care at the Queen Elizabeth, stable but hasn't regained consciousness. Churchwarden found him after he opened the gates,' continued Fran. 'Thought he was just asleep till he noticed the blood. Apparently knew he was here, said that the homeless sometimes come here during the day, a quiet refuge of sorts, and he lets the elderly or frail stay overnight if they want to. He's not really supposed to. He said the old boy'd been "beaten like an animal".'

Harper nodded. 'I'd put money on Gibbs and Co.'

'Working hypothesis,' agreed Fran. 'The shops will be opening now so I've sent Bryden and Dixon to see if any have external CCTV we might use.'

'SOCO got anything yet?'

Fran lifted the tape. 'Let's find out.'

Harper ducked under and Stark took the tape for Fran to do the same. He hesitated, then passed through with a guilty thrill, a wholly inappropriate excitement that made it hard not to smile. He stood at the other side of the tape and took a deep breath.

The open space proved to be the old church burial ground, but at some time the headstones had been relocated against the perimeter walls; only the small stone sarcophagi remained in their original positions. Now it was St Alfege Park, a pretty little space despite its visible history. To his right he saw the gate Gibbs had scaled to evade him, now unlocked and open. In a far corner there was another, offering Gibbs two exit options. It was futile to speculate on which he'd used. With all three gates taped off, the whole park was now the outer cordon. Inside, figures in disposable white hooded overalls, blue overshoes and gloves were painstakingly preserving the scene. Several areas had been taped off to form inner cordons, scene-of-crime officers only. Fran beckoned over a man holding a clipboard, the crime-scene manager. 'What have we got?'

The CSM pointed to the old brick public convenience near the headstone-lined perimeter wall. 'The assault took place behind there, a narrow passageway open at both ends. A dirty, tatty, bloodstained sleeping-bag, some cardboard and a knitted bobble hat. The victim's limited belongings in a plastic bag, kicked away, items strewn, nothing to identify him.'

Stark felt a chill. This was suddenly a lot more real than it had been reading it from the files. He listened closely as the man continued: 'Also a condom packet, open but with the condom still inside. Lubricant still wet.'

'Perhaps indicating an amorous couple retreated this way for a quickie knee-trembler and found it occupied,' said Fran.

The CSM shrugged and pointed across the park to one cluster of sarcophagi. 'Over there we found the grass littered with empty lager cans, Tennent's Super.'

'Ferrier Rats,' growled Harper.

'If we come across anything significant we'll pass it on, but for now that's as far as we've got. After that it's down to the forensics.' The CSM excused himself and went back to work.

'Did they finally beat someone who mattered?' Stark asked Fran rhetorically.

'We're not talking broken bones this time. The guy's probably in his seventies and the paramedics didn't rate his chances above fifty-fifty.'

'What's his name?'

'Unknown. Perhaps you'd like to be the one ringing round to see if anyone's missing a dirty old tramp,' she replied, with a hint of anger, pulling out her phone. 'Why don't you two go and see if the poor sod's fit for a statement?'

As he drove, Harper asked Stark how he'd found his first week, but Stark sensed he wasn't really listening to the answer. He thought he'd detected tension between Harper and Fran, a minor power struggle. Fran seemed to hold some kind of seniority. Perhaps she'd been a DS longer; that was how it usually worked in uniform.

They were shown the victim in the intensive-care unit, bandaged and horribly bruised. He looked old and frail. A machine next to him was monitoring his vitals. He was being kept unconscious so they had to settle for a photo on Harper's phone. The poor old sod didn't exactly have a best side right now.

A doctor appeared. 'Police?'

Harper flashed his warrant card. 'How's he doing?'

'Not good. Half-a-dozen broken ribs, cheekbone, collarbone. One of the ribs requires surgery to reposition, as will the cheek in time, but there's nothing we can do till his vitals improve.'

'Will they improve?'

'Maybe. There's a risk of internal bleeding and kidney damage. Scans also indicate possible swelling on the brain but we won't know unless he wakes up. If he was ten years younger, better nourished, I'd be more confident. Do you know his name?' Harper shook his head. 'I don't know whether this will help, then – it was tucked into a pocket.' A faded black-and-white photograph in a palm-sized tarnished silver frame: a young woman, smiling, in her prime.

Stark carefully opened the back but found no name or dates written anywhere. 'Should we leave it with him, Sarge?' suggested Stark. Harper shrugged, uninterested, and took a photo of it.

'I'll call you if his condition changes,' said the doctor. 'We'll just have to see what fight he's got left in him.'

What fight he's got left in him, thought Stark. Not much, by the look of him. What fight had he been able to put up last night? Had they even let him out of his sleeping-bag or just kicked him halfway to death like a badger in a sack? The thought made Stark so angry he had to force his mind elsewhere. It was an irrational anger, way beyond proportion. He'd experienced it many times before, been coached in how to step away and dial it down. Even so, he was still simmering dangerously when they got back to the station.

None of the shop CCTV had much to offer. The traffic camera at the nearby junction picked up kicking-out time at the Meridian and one group crossing the street into the lane leading to the park, but it was too far away for any hope of identification. Fran sent Dixon and Stark to question the landlady, who picked out photos of several Ferrier Rats, including Kyle Gibbs and Nikki Cockcroft. They were regulars, she admitted, and Sunday nights were relatively quiet. No she wasn't aware some were under age. They'd been in all evening and reluctant to leave, becoming abusive. She'd had to threaten to bar them, for the hundredth time.

Stark glanced at the notice on the bar declaring that company policy was to demand identification from any customer who might appear under age. And any landlord worth their salt would not just threaten to bar repeat troublemakers – they would do it. 'Why didn't your door staff just throw them out?'

'Doormen? In this quality establishment?' The landlady smiled at her own irony. 'Our area manager says it's not right for our corporate image. Or his financial spreadsheet, more like.'

Stark frowned. 'My mistake.' Then he recalled that some of the group on the traffic camera had been holding carrier-bags. He asked if she sold takeout beer; she said not. That made it more likely the bags had contained the lager cans. She didn't recall whether the gang had brought bags in with them.

Outside, Stark asked Dixon where the nearest off-licence was. A quick survey established that of the handful of nearby mini-supermarkets only one sold Tennent's Super, but they had no recollection or footage of Gibbs and Co.

'Let's start from the beginning,' suggested Stark. 'I'm still learning my way around. Presupposing Gibbs and Co. are our perpetrators, that they fled the park after the assault and that they would have headed for home, which way would they have gone?'

Dixon got out his phone and opened a maps app to show him a number of routes they might have taken up to Blackheath, where they could cut across towards Kidbrooke.

'But the most direct route must be across Greenwich Park,' suggested Stark.

'It's surrounded by walls, and the gates close around nine thirty this time of year.'

'If they were willing to climb into St Alfege Park why not Greenwich Park? The darkness would shield them from sight.' The huge park would save them time and cover their escape.

Dixon shrugged. 'Some of the gates have CCTV, I think. The Royal Parks Police are stationed up the top end. We can go and ask them.' He phoned the office to say they were running down a theory and drove up to the main gate off Blackheath. Inside an RPP sergeant sat them down at the CCTV bank and showed them how to work it. Shortly before midnight a group could be seen climbing in at the gates nearest the town centre. They had hoods, caps or both and the camera was on a high pole. It was possible to guess at some of the clothing but little more. All of the gates had cameras but none showed the group egress.

'They wouldn't use this gate because we're right next door, and the Vanbrugh Gate on to Maze Hill has a high wall arched over, with no room to squeeze over the gate. But we've had problems in the past with vandals in the nursery at the top. They might have cut through there,' said the sergeant. 'I'll show you, if you like.'

The Flower Garden in the south-east corner, separated from the main park by low railings, boasted manicured grass, a picturesque duck pond, paths edged with deep thickets of flowering shrubs and beds alive with colour. The gate from it into the nursery was not spiked. Neither was the gate from the nursery on to Maze Hill. There was no evidence anyone had passed through but it fitted the theory. Stark suggested they walk the short distance up to the heath.

At the road junction a curved bite had been taken from the park wall to accommodate a large stone war memorial. The left panel was carved with a large 1914, and the right with 1918. The central panel read 'IN GLORIOUS AND GRATE-FUL MEMORY OF THE MEN OF THIS BOROUGH WHO GAVE THEIR LIVES IN THE GREAT WAR'. Below, the horizontal stone had later been carved with the words 'ALSO IN GRATEFUL REMEMBRANCE OF THOSE RESIDENTS OF THIS BOROUGH WHO

GAVE THEIR LIVES TO THE COUNTRY DURING THE WAR 1939–1945'.

The remains of a vodka bottle lay smashed against the foot of the monument, and a giant pack of cheese puffs had burst its contents across the ground among a number of lager cans – Tennent's Super, like those at the crime scene. Over all hung the acrid stench of urine. Stark's hands curled into fists.

'I think I'd better call DS Millhaven,' said Dixon.

Fran found Dixon and Stark guarding the memorial with an RPP sergeant. She set a couple of uniforms to take over and phoned for SOCO. Aside from fingerprints, the lager cans and the neck of the bottle would probably have DNA, and several of the gang were on the database for previous infractions. There probably wasn't any money for testing, but if the old boy died that would change. Better to have the evidence in the bag just in case. Dixon talked her, again, through the rationale that had led them there. He was a good copper, thorough and honest; too honest to take credit for uncharacteristic initiative. She looked at Stark but he said nothing, which, it seemed, *was* characteristic. Fran was mildly impressed but if he wanted to remain reserved she would reserve praise. 'Reserved' was just another word for 'aloof'.

She let him stay while the SOCOs came and did their work. SOCOs were civilians rather than CID officers but Fran didn't hold that against them. They were a good crowd, professional, dedicated and, most importantly, content with the tedious task of gathering forensic evidence so she didn't have to. Stark paid close attention to what they were doing, she noted, still new to life on this side of the police tape. She studied him for a moment.

Stillness, she thought. He had a way of appearing motionless as the world moved around him, a rock in a stream, unaware or unconcerned for the turbulence it cast. Eventually the stream would wear it down. She looked for outward signs of anger but saw little. He had to be angry, she thought, looking at the mess, furious. From his perspective this was desecration. Perhaps there was a kind of frozen sternness; it was hard to tell. She shook her head. Pity the Juliet to his Romeo. Perhaps aloof was unfair: he could be friendly enough, in his way. He *was* an oddity, though. Perhaps her prejudice against all the homecoming-hero nonsense was getting in the way of figuring him out.

She asked Dixon and two more uniforms to walk the route to the Ferrier Estate to look for more evidence of the gang passing. From the memorial they could cut across the heath and zigzag along a few roads to the estate. Thinking about Stark's initiative, she also asked Dixon to speak with the estate's embattled off-licence.

Her phone rang. She answered and listened with rising annoyance. 'Yes, I'll tell him.' She beckoned Stark over. 'That was Hammed. Apparently a Captain Pierson has been pestering the switchboard for you. Could you please return her calls ASAP, et cetera.' Stark looked awkward, but also something else – annoyed? A chink in the armour. 'We don't encourage private calls at work,' said Fran, pointedly. She didn't like being his messenger girl. Admin had yet to supply him with a phone. It wasn't his fault, but calls from a neglected Juliet were. 'Need to use my phone?' she offered.

'It can wait, Sarge,' he replied levelly.

Fran caught Stark checking his watch at the end of the day. 'Somewhere you'd rather be?'

'Hospital appointment, Sarge. It's on the schedule,' he added, as her frown deepened. They were expected to do overtime in the crucial early stages of an investigation. She could demand he stay.

'What is it this time?'

'More physio.' Two half-truths.

44

She paused. 'Clear off, then.'

The Gosport physios had referred Stark for hydrotherapy but the nearest facility had closed. The same proved true in Greenwich. The Carter Orthopaedic Hospital in Dulwich was a private charity and more than happy to mop up NHS overflow. The cabbie was honest and Stark arrived early, so the friendly receptionist directed him to the well-stocked tea and coffee machine, free, with a selection of biscuits. 'You're not in Kansas any more,' he said to himself, as he settled into an armchair with his book.

'Mr Stark? They're ready for you now. Turn right down the corridor and follow the blue signs.' She smiled. You got the odd smile in the NHS but mostly harassed exasperation. This one smiled because she was nice and had time. It was almost disconcerting.

He was greeted by a short, round, grey-haired woman with an easy grin that wrinkled her whole face. 'Lucy,' her badge declared. 'Hop in there and change, dear. Just your gym kit for the moment so we can do our initial assessment. Pool work later. I'm off now but Kelly will be through in a mo. Good luck.' It was a cheerful farewell rather than a 'you're doomed', but Stark still felt an odd tweak of trepidation. He stepped out of the cubicle, expecting another Lucy, but was pleasantly surprised to see a girl his age or younger with dark-brown hair, blue eyes, a pretty face and a figure to make anyone with a clinical-uniform fetish die on the spot.

'Something the matter?' she asked, glancing up from some notes. He shook his head and managed a smile. 'Quite the rap sheet you've got here, Constable. Or are you still a corporal?'

'Yes and no. Joe will do fine.'

She continued scanning through the file, occasionally glancing up at him, or parts of him. 'How did you find hospital physio?'

Oversubscribed, underfunded, impersonal and frustratingly

non-military after Headley Court ... 'It hurt, if that's any guide.'

'You've had worse, I expect,' she replied. 'Most of what they've had you doing seems appropriate. They say they've done all they can, thought hydro might move things on. Been doing your homework?'

'Religiously,' he lied.

'Good boy. Right. Let's see what you can do.'

He was accustomed to running through his routine barely supervised in a gym full of other invalids or alone at home. Close, direct scrutiny added a hesitant self-consciousness combined with boyish bravado, no doubt exacerbated by her attractiveness, that made the whole thing slightly uncomfortable.

'OK, I'm getting a view of your limitations. Hop into your trunks and we'll run through some basic pool work to finish up. There's a clean dressing-gown in the cubicle.'

He changed again, slower this time, grateful there was no mirror. He emerged to find her also in a gown, which he supposed he should've expected but hadn't. She led him through to the pool and slipped off her gown to reveal a sensible one-piece swimsuit, not skimpy by any means. On a figure like hers it didn't need to be. She paused on the steps, halfway into the water. 'Come on, don't be shy.' She smiled. 'I promise this will hurt you more than m—'

Her eyes widened in shock as she took in his scars. Then she blinked, realizing what she was doing. 'Sorry. I'm sorry. I had no idea . . .'

'It's OK.' But Stark found he'd already tugged the gown back on to hide the worst; it was too late to disguise his embarrassment, only its depth. 'I should've warned you. I'm sorry.'

'No, I'm sorry. I just wasn't expecting . . . The file said, but . . .' She was making herself look him in the eye now, professionalism reasserting. 'Let's start again. Why don't you describe the scars to me, cause and effect?'

46

Stark caught his fingers feeling the rough scar down the left side of his face and pulled them away. He nodded, wishing now that she wasn't so pretty. You stared into the mirror, alive, whole, healthy, but scarred. You mourned the old you, the unblemished you, and in your heart you dreaded this moment. He'd been lucky: no girl back home to speak of, not counting Julie, no one to say she didn't mind while her eyes screamed otherwise, only his own revulsion to face. Unlike many of the lads, he'd had time to heal a little more, physically, mentally, to ready himself. Even so, it stung. Kelly was the first young, pretty woman to see him like this and it was painfully clear that physical attraction couldn't have been further from her mind. At least her interest was clinical; she was only obligated to be kind, not dutiful, deliver platitudes rather than pity.

He peeled off his gown, relating the nature of each scar in turn, trying to sound matter-of-fact. The ones on the right of his face, neck and head and the missing finger were all from the initial IED explosion, but they were cosmetic, irrelevant to this process, so he didn't mention them.

The same went for the burns on the backs of his hands and fingers where he had gripped the wheel while the dashboard caught fire. Second degree mostly, they'd healed slowly, painfully, but the docs had decided they weren't bad enough for skin grafts.

Of the rest, rocket-propelled grenade shrapnel was the most common, peppering him down his left side, back and neck. He pulled down the hem of his shorts to show the left hip where a small piece had caused so much damage. Interspersed were the contrastingly neat surgical scars with their rows of dots to either side.

Lower still was the skin graft from his relatively undamaged right thigh to his left. Even days later, back in the UK and stabilized, it had looked as if that piece of RPG casing might still cost him his leg. The donor-site scar was a vertical rectangle with horizontal red striations, the recipient site an irregular dented mess, though surprisingly more healed-looking and less red.

Worst of the bunch unquestionably was the bullet. It had struck him in the upper chest just above the ceramic front-plate of his Osprey body armour, piercing the Kevlar, slanting down through his right shoulder blade and crumpling against the inside of the back-plate.

The surgeons had performed miracles putting bone fragments back together and his shoulder hurt less than his hip, but the exit scar, or cluster of scars, was appalling. As well as going through the top of the right lung it'd nicked his aortic arch and if the medic hadn't quickly got a drip into him he'd have died on that dusty stretch of waste-ground.

He realized he'd stopped talking. Kelly's expression had remained one of composed observation throughout. 'Well,' she said levelly, looking up into his eyes with a slight smile, 'you're a bit of a mess!'

5

There was a message on Stark's machine when he got home – Captain Pierson checking that he'd received her previous one and reminding him that a response was expected. He couldn't ignore it much longer: they were clearly determined to pursue him. That thought kept him awake into the night.

Tuesday began with tangible tension. Fran had been assigned the case, effectively placing her above DS Harper in the overall investigation. Harper had obviously not taken it well and sat stone-faced in the team meeting.

Fran appeared unperturbed. 'The victim is still sedated. Forensics called to say that key clothing and footwear collected from the suspects' homes had clearly been washed overnight. They're still looking but the chances of finding anything useful have greatly diminished. Gibbs and Co. may be smarter than they look. Perhaps they realize they've crossed a line this time.

'On a happier note, fingerprints at the scene and the war memorial match several of the gang, including both Gibbs and Cockcroft. If required, DNA testing will probably confirm. SOCO at the crime scene also found empty cocaine wraps. Following TI Stark's line of enquiry we questioned the proprietors of the Ferrier Estate off-licence. They were defensive – probably as worried about visibly assisting the police as being charged with serving the under-aged. After some reassurance they confirmed that two of the gang, Colin Messenger and Paul Thompson, bought lager and crisps early that evening, not vodka, but that they often stocked up on all three. Sadly their decrepit black-and-white CCTV feeds a prominent monitor but it's just for show. The recording VCR died years ago.'

'Okay,' said Groombridge, from the back. 'All this puts the gang at the scene but so far we've nothing to prove when. CCTV is inconclusive. All they have to do is claim they were there the night before instead. We'll need to trip them up. So, before we round them up for questioning, let's talk MMO. Means and opportunity are obvious, but what about motive?'

'They were pissed,' said Harper. 'And they saw an easy target.'

Lazy thinking expressed as certainty, thought Stark, shaking his head.

'Have you something to add, Stark?' asked Groombridge.

All eyes turned on Stark. 'Nothing, Guv.'

'Come on, something's on your mind.'

He was cornered. 'Being pissed is not an excuse, Guv.'

'Well, I think we all agree with *that*, Trainee Investigator,' replied Groombridge, coolly.

Stark thought about quitting while he was behind, but . . . 'Not a motive, I mean. Testing has demonstrated that people's behaviour is not altered by alcohol – '

'Bollocks!' scoffed Harper. 'Tell that to my missus when she's had a few!' He chuckled. A few people joined in but Stark suspected politeness. He'd overheard furtive speculation suggesting this wasn't the first time Harper had returned from a sudden 'illness' with a bruise or two.

'Go on, Stark,' prompted Groombridge.

Stark glanced at Harper, wishing he'd concealed his thoughts better. 'Repeated experiments show that alcohol impairs physically but its behavioural effects are dictated by culture rather than chemicals. In many cultures it is merely a social norm, as behaviourally neutral as coffee. But in many, like Britain, it's perceived as a disinhibitor. People act according to their preconceptions.'

'Meaning?'

'Meaning it doesn't cause aggression or promiscuity, it merely enables them.'

Groombridge nodded. 'Drinking makes relaxed people relaxed and violent people violent.' He'd known all this and put Stark on the spot anyway.

Harper wasn't laughing now. People were avoiding looking at him.

'So,' continued Groombridge. 'Motive. Why did this lot start attacking people? Why the homeless in particular, aside from the obvious vulnerability? They've a taste for violence, but is there something more, something we might use?'

No one had any answers. Harper repeated his view that they were just vicious little cowards, at one point staring at Stark as if daring him to contradict. Stark voiced no opinion, and was glad when Harper and Bryden set off with uniform to see who could be found. 'What shall I do, Sarge?' he asked Fran.

'Dixon.' She beckoned him. 'You and Stark, take the victim's photo and see if you can get a name out of social services.'

The local-authority social workers just winced and shook their heads. They had better luck with the homeless charities, where several people recognized him. Alf was the closest they got to a name, but one worker rummaged through his files and found a better photo.

They got back in time to watch through the glass while Gibbs was interviewed. In a set of police overalls, his clothes confiscated by SOCO, he didn't look as cocksure as he had on home turf. Even so, he remained defiant, sullen and contemptuous, flatly denying all knowledge of the assault, insisting he was at home in bed. As feared, he claimed that he and his mates had been in both locations the night before and he knew nothing about the cocaine. He was dismissive of the memorial.

Groombridge and Fran emerged far from happy. 'Enjoying the show, Lover-boy?' asked Fran.

Lover-boy? Stark frowned.

'Your neglected sweetheart's been on again. The girls on switchboard are starting to talk and Maggie's bordering on huff.'

'Sarge.' Stark kept his eyes front and centre.

'Rumour has it your Captain Pierson sounds far from happy with you,' pressed Fran. 'There's a lesson there, about wasting the time of your superiors in rank and gender.'

Stark accepted the dig without comment.

'Perhaps you'd like to do the honourable thing,' suggested Fran, pointing to the nearest phone.

'I'm sure you'd rather I got on with some work, Sarge.'

Fran huffed. 'Find anything?' Stark showed her the photo. 'All right, get your popcorn. It's going to be a long day.'

That's five hours of my life I won't get back, thought Fran, watching from the canteen window as the last of the Rats swaggered from the building to the disgusting cheers of those already released. Some were under eighteen, juveniles in England and Wales, and couldn't be searched or questioned without an 'appropriate adult' present to ensure they 'understood what was happening'. Few of their parents wanted to know, organizing social workers had slowed everything down, and when questions were eventually put they regurgitated identical answers.

The cluster of horrible little specimens jeered and gesticulated rudely at the station before oozing away up the street. They understood what was happening all too well. There were times Fran wished she lived in one of those banana republics where you could bang scrotes up because you knew they were guilty rather than because you could prove it. Not an uncommon sentiment in her line of work, she suspected, however PC the party line.

But the baseline said no more than twenty-four hours without charge. In this case the super probably had the 'reasonable grounds' to extend that by twelve while the investigation was 'being conducted diligently and expeditiously'. And assault was an indictable offence, of course, meaning they could then apply through the Magistrates' Court for another thirty-six and again after that for yet another thirty-six, ninety-six hours altogether without charge, even the minors, as they were all over ten and therefore legally responsible under UK law. A formidable power. Fran considered this magisterial oversight to be just one of those hoop-jumping inconveniences above her pay grade. You worked with what you had. The guv projected the same, though he'd confided in her that he thought things had gone just about as far in their favour as was reasonable, and perhaps a little more. In truth, it rarely came up anyway. Only for the big, complicated cases, the dangerous suspects. For the rest, the everyday humdrum crimes, you either had evidence to charge or you didn't. If you didn't, maybe you would tomorrow. In this case they didn't, and Royal Hill had too few cells to have that many clogged up. There was little gain in holding on to disruptive delinquents when they could be brought back if and when new evidence emerged. So long as the little sods didn't do a bunk.

She swallowed her frustration and went back to her desk. There wasn't much in the way of new evidence. Ferrier Estate residents reported hearing a disturbance at just after one in the morning, but none had looked outside. The estate lighting was regularly smashed with stones anyway, the CCTV cameras had been vandalized so often they'd been abandoned years ago, and even if they'd been able to reference clothing from other footage it would be circumstantial at best. They needed more. They needed blood.

Stark was cataloguing all the footage they did have, a menial job but someone had to do it. His limp seemed more pronounced and once she'd noticed him suppress a wince. On closer inspection he was sweating a little too. For a moment she allowed herself to imagine how hard this might be for him. Nonetheless he had a job to do, just like everyone else.

Alf's photo appeared on the next day's local news but no one phoned in to claim him. Fran sent Dixon and Hammed out on foot with shelter workers to speak with the local homeless.

Before midday she looked up to see Stark pulling on his jacket.

'Where are you going?' she demanded, but then she rolled her eyes. 'Not another one.'

'Sorry, Sarge.' He did seem contrite but made no offer to stay. It was on the schedule he'd submitted and that, Cox had decreed, was that. 'If I miss it they can bump me off the list. Failure to engage, court-martial offence.'

'People don't like having their time wasted,' agreed Fran. 'Which department today? Detox massage or hot-stones therapy?'

He ignored the question. 'I'll be back in a couple of hours.'

Fran thought for a moment. 'Wait, I'll give you a lift. Alf's sedatives were withdrawn this morning but he didn't regain consciousness. I want to speak to his doctors and see for myself.'

She watched him out of the corner of her eye as she drove. He looked tired. Clearly he was struggling physically. Whether he'd cope, time would tell. Despite herself, she hoped so. Much as he grated on her, he might have the makings of a decent copper. Whether he'd cope mentally was another issue. From the schedule's lack of disclosure she suspected that one or both of his weekly appointments might be for mind rather than body. She'd given him opportunities to confess but he'd overlooked or ignored them. It bothered her that she couldn't always tell which. Sometimes you knew he was taking the piss, others you were left guessing.

The old boy looked like he had nine toes in the grave already.

His darkly bruised and stitched face was sunken and yellowed. The doctor on duty put his chances at less than fifty-fifty now.

Fran seethed. Looking at the poor old sod, imagining his last waking moments, made her angrier than she could ever remember. If he died she was going to make it her personal mission in life to hound Kyle Gibbs to his grave. Stark's face betrayed nothing.

'What time's your manicure?' she asked outside.

'Ten minutes, though they have a rather quantum perspective on time around here.'

'Need someone to lean on?' She grinned, nodding at the complex hospital map. 'Help you find the right department?'

'I can make it from here, thanks.'

'Clear off, then.'

She watched as he limped in, waited a few seconds and followed. Stark was standing right inside, pretending to read the signs. 'Forget something, Sarge?' he asked innocently.

'Yes. Don't be late!' She spun on her heel and walked out, cursing under her breath.

Stark smiled but didn't laugh. He'd been on his feet more in recent days than in any given month since his discharge from Headley Court and his hip ached. He'd finished the previous day with OxyContin and a double, drugged himself asleep with a cocktail of opiate and alcohol. The good folk of Headley Court would not approve. They'd spent weeks getting him ready for the real world and that didn't include substance abuse. But needs must . . . He'd slept like a log but woken groggy and, with nothing more than digital filing to stimulate his attention, he'd struggled through the morning on coffee. Fran's trip to ICU had killed his hopes of eating before his session, and Doc Hazel kept him waiting.

The sight of Alf had set a fury in him that the shrink predictably pounced on, spending disproportionate energy delving into his anger about something that should make anyone's blood boil. He fought a constant urge to clam up, but he wouldn't be accused of failing to engage. It made a change from prodding old wounds, perhaps, but it missed the point, as usual.

Having exhausted the irrelevant, the good doctor finally asked a pertinent question. 'Why do you call it "taking the coin"?'

'It's from the Napoleonic wars, or before. Taking the King's shilling meant enlisting as a soldier or sailor. A shilling was your daily pay before stoppages.'

'So it's about being paid,' said Hazel, making a note.

Stark sighed, trying not to get angry. Regardless of how it might have been in Napoleonic times, a modern soldier did their duty for the *privilege* of taking the coin, not the payment. It represented the reciprocal covenant between the soldier or sailor and the monarch they fought for, but the thought of trying to explain that in a way that might be understood was too daunting to attempt and he was relieved when Hazel moved on.

'Tell me about IEDs.'

'What do you want to know?'

'Everything, I suppose.'

'The clue's in the name – improvised, so they vary enormously, though on three themes. Most are pressure triggers, often two bits of springy metal held apart at either end with wood or plastic. Push them together in the middle and you make a contact, the battery or batteries send a current along wire to trigger the explosive, which is either strapped on or hidden in something innocent-looking nearby, such as a cooking pot or plastic container. Sometimes they're buried, sometimes just under an object you might knock or kick aside. Bigger, stiffer triggers can be buried for vehicles. Those are all plant-and-forget, by far the most common. There's self-detonation 'suicide' devices – they're more commonly used against civilians – and finally remote-detonation devices, operated with two mobile phones or a radio-controlled servo, usually in line of sight.'

'Which kind did you encounter?'

'Encounter?' asked Stark. He'd encountered plenty, seen them disarmed, seen or heard and felt them detonate, witnessed the aftermath from small anti-infantry to massive car-bomb.

'Okay, which type were you injured by?'

'Remote-detonation. There was no phone coverage, so it was operated by radio nearby, part of the ambush.'

'Was this unusual?'

'Yes and no. In Iraq it was mostly plant-and-forget, and contact was usually just incoming fire from some distant tree-line or compound. You hardly ever saw the man shooting at you. We shot back, but even if we made it to their firing point we rarely found bodies. Either we missed or their mates hauled them away. Or we called in an air strike. Either way they were gone. Afghanistan was different. Closer-quarters contact and remote-detonation devices were common. But a close quarters, three-sixty ambush . . . that took planning.'

'You saw faces.'

'Not really, no. Not that I remember. Too distant. Too . . . hectic.' In his dreams they often did have faces – who knew whose? People he'd met, Afghan civilians, just people off the street? 'It was a determined assault at close quarters. They pursued when we tried to escape, changed location to keep firing on us, never more than two hundred metres or so away, to begin with right over our heads on the rooftops.'

'More personal, then, than your previous experiences.'

'There's nothing impersonal about kinetic contact. Even if the arseholes shooting at you are invisible it's hard not to take it personally,' Stark joked ruefully.

Hazel just nodded and made a note. 'Talk me through it.'

Stark hesitated, reluctant. 'All right. Well, it's hot. Your kit's heavy and starting to rub. You're standing in the open in clear sight of numerous buildings, any of which may contain people eager to gun you down and, apart from those with you, the only living thing in sight is a skinny dog too stupid to know better. But it's going well, you're getting the job done. Then some shit presses his radio trigger. But his timing is off, inexperienced or over-zealous, he's impatient and fails to get the vehicle broadside.'

'You were lucky, then.'

Lucky? Another fine choice of word. Luckier than Walker and Smith, certainly. 'I truly hope that fuck with the trigger didn't live out the day,' he said, with sudden ferocity. At least, he felt the ferocity, but it remained inaudible, as if the anger was being stripped from his words as they left his lips, as if it were somehow remote from him. 'What does that say about me?'

Hazel seemed unprepared for direct questions. It was almost fun to see that momentary look of panic. Mostly it added to his sense of futility. She made a contemplative face, playing for time. He was starting to spot her tools. 'I should say it was understandable to focus thoughts of retribution on the man who struck the first blow, killed your colleagues.'

'Comrades,' corrected Stark, not for the first time. '"Colleagues" whine about wives nine to five, then go home and whine about colleagues.'

'You're not married.'

Here we go again, thought Stark.

'Your girlfriend split up with you while you were in hospital.' She pretended to read this from his file, as if it was just occurring to her, but to Stark it seemed she was more comfortable pulling this string than the others. 'And now you've moved away from home, family, friends, to start work at a new job in a strange city. Perhaps we could talk about that for a while.'

'It's your dime.' It wasn't, but she didn't seem to get that. She waited.

'Julie wasn't my girlfriend. We'd been out a couple of times, shagged a few times more. She came to see me in the hospital because she thought she ought to. I let her off the hook.'

'Did she say that or did you put the words into her mouth?'

'What's the difference?'

'Maybe she-wanted to be there. Maybe you pushed her away for your own reasons.'

Maybe he had. Then again, maybe the barely concealed relief on Julie's face as she left was as real as his relief in watching her go. 'You think I pushed her away. That I've deliberately distanced myself from anyone who might care about me, that I'm fearful of intimacy, friendship, love, that I'm scared of getting close to another human being in case I have to watch them succumb to some invisible IED fallout.'

'Isn't that what you've done?'

Stark considered telling her about Kelly, but that would further misdirect her. 'Perhaps I'm just ashamed of my physical disability.'

'Are you?'

'Or maybe it's the mental scars I'm hiding. Perhaps I'm afraid of letting someone love me, lest the monster inside ever slips its leash.'

Hazel frowned. 'I can't help you if you don't take this seriously.'

'I don't think you can help me all that much either way.'

'Why do you think that?'

'Look, Doc, I'm tired and tetchy. I'm tetchy because I'm tired. All I want is to be able to sleep at night without waking up screaming. I want to dream about something else.'

'And I want to help you with that.'

'Then stop changing the subject just because you can't handle it. I don't wake up screaming about imaginary girlfriends or my mother's passive-aggressive cotton-wool act!'

'Now you're getting angry.'

'This isn't angry. Angry is how I feel about the spiteful fuck with the remote trigger. Angry is how I felt when those fuckers kept shooting at me even when I was running away with a wounded man over my shoulder. This isn't angry, but it's starting to get there.'

'Perhaps we should call it a day.'

'Perhaps we should.'

Stark stalked back into the station, hungry and vexed.

Fran glanced at the clock. 'Your manicure and facial overrun again?'

'Something like that. Is it okay if I grab some lunch?'

She rolled her eyes. 'Go on then, but don't dawdle.'

Stark brought a sandwich to his desk and went back to his filing. Fran went out and he soon found his concentration wavering. He was half asleep when his phone rang. Switchboard announced a Captain Pierson for Constable Stark and put her through before he could respond.

'Hello?' said the voice to Stark's silence. '*Hello?*'

'Who's calling, please?' he asked, stalling.

'Captain Pierson for Corporal Joseph Stark, is this he?'

Stark hesitated.

'It's a simple enough question!'

Her accent was that clipped kind of posh, every word shaved bald, upper lip genetically inert. That was okay, but the cold, hard certainty in her tone spoke of privilege at its worst. Stark took an instant dislike. 'We have a Constable Stark,' he suggested levelly.

'Put him on, then. I don't have all day,' said the voice, frostily.

'Can I take a message?'

'He's not there?'

60

'Perhaps I could take a message.'

'I'll wait,' said the voice.

Stark considered putting her on hold for ten minutes but decided he was being childish enough already. Besides, he'd have to talk to her eventually; winding her up further wouldn't help matters. 'I shouldn't like you to waste your time. I'd be happy to take a message.'

'I've left several already, for days in fact.'

'Perhaps one more will do the trick.'

Cold silence flowed from the receiver but stubbornness trumped impatience. She tutted. 'Very well. Please tell him, for the umpteenth time, to call me at his *very earliest opportunity*.' Stark dutifully repeated the number back to her and she hung up without another word. It was a shabby thing to do but Stark was shabby in condition and mood, and with that tone she could wait another day.

6

The IED explosion and the sight of the Land Rover teetering above him on two wheels before it crashed back down on to four snapped him awake.

Lying on his back, waiting for his heart to slow and the phantom tinnitus to fade, he let the memory roll on in his conscious state. So much confusion, shouting, screaming, and cutting through it a cold, lightning certainty of purpose. He remembered feeling absolutely awake in those minutes, utterly conscious, instantly decisive in a way he'd never imagined possible. It was easy to understand how people became addicted to adrenalin, if that was what it was. It was also easy to understand how dangerous it could be, to you and those around you, to let that intuitive purity take over, caution and restraint be damned. How different that day might have been.

The luminous hands of his watch read 04:10. He swore quietly. So now not only was therapy not suppressing his dreams, it was trawling them up from the foetid depths. He grunted, forcing himself off the bed and away from another round of futile what-if. Save that bollocks for the next show-and-tell with Doc Hazel.

Later that morning Stark and Dixon were sent back to the council offices to speak to a key officer returned from sick leave. Judy was prematurely middle-aged, heavy-set, both chirpy and slightly defensive in the brittle manner Stark thought stress-induced. She'd seen Alf's face on TV and come in to work to delve back into her files – she was sure, but she wasn't, she had found him, but it might not be. She opened a worn, faded file and turned it on the desk to face them. A man, perhaps in his sixties, stared out. 'Is it him?' she asked tremulously.

Dixon looked at Stark, who nodded. There was no mistake. 'Alfred Thomas Ladd,' he read. 'Born Deptford, 1932. First appeared on Greenwich social-services homeless radar in August 1996. Previous address unknown. No known living relatives.' There were several pages of assessment forms filled in by varying hands. He'd been admitted to a care home in 1999 but discharged himself. Hospitalized with pneumonia March 2005, admitted to care again and again refused to stay. A competency assessment at the time described him as fully cognizant and physically able. The scrawl also described him as obdurate, irritable, wilfully independent to the point of irrationality and rude bordering on abusive. Stark smiled.

There was no further record. Judy's orbit stabilized once hunch became fact. She happily copied the whole file while they waited and waved them off cheerily. They returned to the station well pleased with their morning's work.

Their smiles shattered against Fran's icy reception. She scanned the name beneath the photo. 'Alfred Ladd. Well, at least we'll have a name for the death certificate if he doesn't survive surgery.'

Alf's condition had worsened sharply and the doctors feared internal bleeding. He'd been rushed into theatre.

Stark felt like he'd been kicked in the stomach. If Fran noticed she made no sign, unless, perhaps, there was a softening in her tone. 'Get yourself up there and wait. Call me when he gets out.'

He almost thanked her, taken off-guard by the strength of his reaction. He rushed off and found Maggie, who dropped the play-acting and found him a car. Twenty minutes later he stood at the operating-theatre department reception desk being told he'd have to wait up on the ward. His response was short and to the point. The nurse yielded.

He had plenty of time to reflect on the irrational investment he felt in a stranger's well-being. This was just the kind of thing he should probably discuss with Doc Hazel, dread the thought. It was more than three hours before a grey-haired man in scrubs emerged at speed through the theatre doors. Stark jumped to his feet, startling him. 'Nurse Adams, why is this person loitering here?' demanded the doctor.

Stark held up his warrant card. 'Are you the surgeon operating on Alfred Ladd?'

'Finally came up with a name, did you?'

'Yes or no?'

'I am the chief of surgery. Mr Ladd, if that's his name, is alive and not well. He's being closed as we speak and will likely remain in post-op recovery for an hour or so before returning to Intensive Care. If you wish to speak with him you're in for a long wait, possibly still a futile one. Now, please step aside.'

'I'm not here to interview him.'

Maybe something in Stark's voice betrayed him. The surgeon contemplated him for a moment, weighing him up, or weighing his words. 'We've had to remove a kidney. The other is damaged but salvageable. We've realigned the right posterior tenth rib but there was local damage to be patched up. We nearly lost him on the table but he rallied.'

'Will he live?'

'For now. Whether he recovers is out of my hands. I suggest you leave your number with ICU and get some sleep, in which you appear deficient. Now step aside, young man. I have work to do.'

When he got back, Fran said, 'Maggie's looking for you. I do believe she's moved from huff to strop.'

Before Stark could wonder why, Maggie stuck her head round the door. 'Constable, there's a *woman* loitering downstairs for you.'

'I'm not "sweetie" today, then?'

'Not while you're entertaining *other women*. I've had it with your sort,' said Maggie, suppressing her grin with limited success. 'She's been waiting ages. Won't leave. You must've been a very bad man.'

Stark reddened. The smirks of his colleagues didn't help, especially Fran's. He went quickly downstairs to the public entrance.

Maggie's 'other woman' was wearing a uniform. It wasn't blue.

'Corporal Stark,' she said, without preamble or pleasantry.

'It's "Constable" now,' he said flatly.

'Captain Pierson.'

'I'd guessed.'

'Dial down the attitude, Corporal. The only reason I'm not standing here with a pair of Red Caps is out of courtesy to our civilian counterparts.'

Perhaps she'd recognized his voice from the phone. Too bad. Stark was happy to match her spiky for spiky. 'I don't work for you any more.'

'You're not discharged *yet*, Corporal. Now, I trust you've kept this matter confidential.'

'I *can* read.'

'Have you, or have you not?'

'I have.'

'You still know how to follow *some* orders then. So, are you going to co-operate, as ordered, or not?'

Her voice carried and the desk officers were paying far too much casual attention for Stark's liking. He glanced at the cameras too. 'Can we talk outside?' he asked.

'"Can we talk at all?" should be the question, given your obstinate refusal to return my calls.'

'Please,' said Stark, desperately, conscious that the desk officer was now grinning.

'If you insist.'

*

Peering between the canteen window's vertical blinds Fran waited. As expected, Stark and his visitor emerged into view . . . The public lobby was altogether too public for a private conversation. So this was Captain Pierson. Stark's lady friend was trim, attractive and possibly not Stark's friend at all. Fran watched the conversation below grow more and more animated, heated, even. Right now she'd kill for one of those pointy dish microphones they always had conveniently to hand on TV cop shows. What was really going on here? Not a lovers' tiff, surely nothing so banal. She could imagine Stark throwing taboo to the devil in some sordid affair with a senior officer, but she could equally imagine him stubbornly resisting advances. The problem was, she didn't understand him. His momentary distress on hearing of the old boy's decline was probably the first emotion of significance he'd manifested. It was good to care, but in a man so dammed-up, cracks might be evidence of worrying pressure.

Maggie's love rival turned and marched away. Stark just stood and watched her go. Intriguing. Of course the public lobby had CCTV, with audio. Perhaps she'd saunter down there later and find out whether the pair had said anything . . . *important* that a dutiful supervisor should know.

Stark stormed into the office, steaming. No one said anything, but to avoid the sideways glances and smirking he flipped through the forensic reports. Something struck him and he opened the CCTV footage on DC Dixon's computer. His jaw tightened.

He found Fran nursing a coffee in the canteen. 'Who decided what clothes and shoes to take from Gibbs's house?' he asked.

'SOCO, why?'

'The only trainers listed are the cheap white Asda two-stripe he was wearing when he was picked up. But correlating the confiscated clothing with CCTV, the figure we think to be Gibbs is wearing dark with three stripes.'

'Adidas?'

'Looks like. And I'm not sure but I think Gibbs was wearing blue with yellow stripes when we saw him last week.'

'Bugger!' Fran looked pained. 'You're right! I can picture the little thug. If SOCO didn't find them . . .'

'Perhaps he couldn't get the blood off.'

'Come on, Smarty Pants.' She sighed. 'Looks like we've got bins to rummage through.'

An hour later Fran was placating Kyle's mother with decreasing patience while a uniformed constable was placing two bulging bin bags on a plastic tarp outside the front of her ground-floor flat. Neighbours were gathering to gawp and Kyle's mum moved from remonstration to abuse until Fran stepped smartly into the woman's personal space and said something Stark couldn't hear. The woman shut up immediately.

'All yours, Trainee Investigator.' Fran smiled darkly and tossed Stark a box. Disposable gloves. 'The council, in their infinite wisdom, dropped the collections to every other week. I expect they're a bit ripe.' The uniforms chuckled. Without a word, Stark pulled on a pair of gloves; it couldn't be worse than latrine duty.

There were no trainers. It had been too much to hope for, of course, but that was police work for you. He pored over the contents anyway, but there was nothing out of the ordinary, just the predictable poverty of freezer-food, ready meals and take-aways. He noticed a cutting from a magazine, about ten centimetres square, clearly once folded geometrically in on itself. Then he found four more. 'Sarge,' he said, holding them up. They were classic drug wraps, grams of cocaine most probably.

Fran turned to Kyle's mother. 'Tina, Tina, Tina . . . Yours? Or Kyle's?' Tina scowled, tight-lipped. 'Five wraps in under a fortnight, and that's just the ones we've found!' Fran shook her head. 'And you with nothing but income support to feed you.'

One of the onlookers laughed. Tina Gibbs stabbed a murderous glance at them.

Fran nodded to Stark. 'Bag those up, Constable. They may be of interest to Tina's parole officer.'

Tina looked sick. Fran turned to her and said quietly, 'Right, Tina, how about you let me have another look round upstairs? And while I'm doing that, you can have another think about what might have happened to Kyle's nice blue-and-yellow Adidas Gazelles.'

It was a good effort but, anxious as she was, Tina either knew nothing about them or wasn't ready to tell. And there was no sign of the shoes inside. Stark was left to re-bag the rubbish and the uniforms helped him carry it back through the flat to the bin.

'Foot search, Sarge?' asked one of the constables.

Fran's lips twisted in frustration. 'We can ask, but this isn't a murder case.'

'What did you say to calm her down?' asked Stark.

'I reminded her that the oldest profession is still illegal in this country,' replied Fran. Stark detected no judgement or cynicism, just a sort of world-weary sadness. She didn't say much on the way back to the station. The only good news for the rest of the day was that Alfred Ladd was back in ICU, stable and being kept unconscious for now. Tension that Stark had not noticed in himself eased.

That night, however, he woke in the darkness to the faint ringing of the living-room phone. Disoriented, he grappled the silent handset from his nightstand. It was Fran. 'Sarge?'

'The old boy died at three fifteen this morning.'

7

Stark closed his eyes. For any other news he might have been grateful for a call that tore him from another nightmare. On another night without whisky and pills, he noted.

'Stark? *Stark?*'

'Sarge.'

'Get your arse up. There'll be a car outside in ten minutes. We've got a few hours' head start to put a shine on this before the super talks to the press.' Fran barely paused for breath. 'DCI Groombridge is leading this now. Are you getting any of this?'

Christ, how many cups of coffee had she already consumed? 'Understood.' The army taught you how to go from asleep to clean, shaved and dressed in minutes. He was standing outside as the uniform car pulled up. Strangely, considering his previous emotions, he could summon no anger. He felt numb, detached, beyond. No doubt a textbook reaction.

Fran and DC Dixon were already poring over the case notes when he arrived. 'Well, don't you look shiny?' she said. Dixon gave him a limp smile.

A few minutes later, Groombridge rolled in. 'Right, where are we?'

'Cause of death to be determined, but liver and general health were poor. Possible failure of the remaining kidney or brain haemorrhage from the recent physical beating or blood clot from subsequent surgery.' Fran read off her notes efficiently. 'If that's confirmed, it's enough for the CPS to call it murder, though no doubt the defence would test the point. I'll get FSS to process the physical evidence for DNA to back up the fingerprints. The landlady of the Meridian pub remembers the core of the Ferrier Rats leaving around the time we see the group on traffic camera cross the road towards St Alfege Park. What appears to be the same crowd are seen climbing into Greenwich Park. The war memorial was desecrated with more physical evidence. A matching can was found in Blackheath on the way to the Ferrier where the crowd had earlier bought supplies from the off-licence. The magazine pages used for the cocaine wraps found at the memorial and at Gibbs's house matched. Fingerprint and DNA will probably confirm some or all were his, but he'll just say he bought them *from . . .*'

'A bloke in the pub,' chorused half the room.

'All this leaves us exactly nowhere. The CPS won't lift a finger unless we have blood – so we need a foot search to find those shoes. DS Harper will organize it. I'll go through the interviews again with Stark to see if any of the little shits said anything we missed. I'm assuming you don't want them all pulled in again until we've got more evidence behind us.'

Groombridge nodded. 'We've got their bullshit statements already. Maybe a day to sweat after the news gets out will open some holes. Can we spare some bodies to watch the estate?'

'Already got some uniforms out of bed,' Fran said, 'all happy to sit in unmarked cars for overtime.'

'Good. Right.' He clapped his hands together. 'The super's going to face some awkward questions about the lack of progress and, politically speaking, it doesn't do to hide behind funding shortfalls and resource priority. We need to turn something up quickly. So get to it.'

The interview recordings were painful to watch. It was truly shocking to think that, just a few precious years earlier, these kids had been smiling innocents, children with as much potential as any other. Now they were every *Daily Mail* reader's fear and delight. Watching them, Stark was inclined to join the chorus demanding boot camps for young recidivists; a lick of real authority would do them the world of good.

Worst among them were Kyle Gibbs and his girlfriend Nikki Cockcroft. He posed, feigning indifference, silent and sneering; she hissed like a cornered snake, spitting venom. They all trotted out their rehearsed alibis and clammed up like old pros. 'How do kids like this get so savvy?' Stark wondered despondently.

Fran said nothing. They'd both served enough time in uniform to know the answer, having endured the ceaseless tide of youth offending from the depressingly dim to the needle sharp. Kids like these had been in and out of interview rooms half their lives. The sharp ones learnt the system, learnt that keeping your trap shut really did work. You saw them changing, blooming from amoral youth into full-blown adult sociopath. But the dim ones . . . 'It's like they've been coached.'

'Or threatened,' said Fran. 'Probably both. And if they're not scared enough of Kyle, Nikki has her big brother to wave around.'

'Gary Cockcroft.' Stark dragged up the memory. He'd read about Gary in Nikki's file.

Fran nodded. 'Knocked over a security van full of cash. Killed three guards. The guv'nor worked the case.'

'I remember. Gary and another guy, Ben something, went down but a third suspect walked. Liam . . . Dawson?'

'They never got the cash back either. I was warned not to ask the guv'nor about it – a bit touchy? Anyway, Gary's doing life-minimum-twenty in Belmarsh but that doesn't stop little sis using him as leverage, I'm told.'

Stark thought about that, and about Fran's tone regarding Tina Gibbs's profession. They probably all had their hard-luck stories and unstable upbringing. Now they were the Ferrier Rats, busy repaying the fear, abandonment and abuse of their childhoods tenfold. Did their pitiful backgrounds excuse their delinquency? There but for the grace of name-your-deity go we all? Stark didn't know the answer, but he'd seen kids their age overcoming worse day in day out, and kids not much older fighting in the name of democracy. He resolved to call his mum and sister when he got home. The star of the last recording, Stacey Appleton, was at least less gobby than the rest, though no more co-operative. 'Wait,' he said suddenly. 'Do you mind if I replay that?' On screen the interview had concluded and both Fran and Groombridge had left the room. Just as the clip ended Stacey wiped a finger beneath both eyes. Stark paused the image. 'Is she *crying*?'

Fran pushed out her lower lip. 'Hard to say. I doubt it. The guv'nor pressed them all quite hard. None of them cracked.'

'Did she seem more frightened than the others?'

Fran shrugged. 'They were all crapping themselves behind the bullshit.'

Stark stared at the frozen image. 'We should talk to her again.'

'We'll be talking to them all again.' Fran sighed wearily. 'Come on, let's finish this up before I get any more suicidal.'

Harper was just wrapping up the foot-search briefing as they rejoined the team. 'Everyone clear? Right, then, you lazy sods, time for a stroll.' He spotted Stark and Fran. 'You too, Trainee. Time you learnt life out of uniform still has its muck 'n' bullets.'

The search was organized into teams, each taking a section of the most likely route from the war memorial to the Ferrier Estate. Harper and Bryden led the first line of uniforms across Blackheath. Stark and Dixon joined the second, assigned the first few residential streets beyond: wide streets lined with large houses in large plots, some divided into flats, some not. As well as lifting drains and picking through verges, this demanded knocking on doors, asking if anyone had found, seen or heard anything, and obtaining permission to search front gardens and bins.

It was a long and tiresome process, and when he guessed they were only about halfway, Stark had to rest on a wall. A treadmill was one thing, reality another. He'd passed the combat fitness test God knew how many times, completed the Fan Dance (fifteen miles in full kit up and down Pen y Fan) in under four hours, the Long Drag (a forty-mile yomp across Brecon in full kit in under twenty hours), and hacked his way through miles of Borneo jungle, yet here he sat, defeated by a stroll. It was pitiful.

It wasn't a particularly popular process either. They'd been met with everything from ambivalence to hostility. At most of the large houses, though, it was alarm, residents leaping from 'fatal incident' to vicious murder to killers in their gardens. Stark was struck by their exaggerated incredulity, at the paper borders between pockets of a city. People locked their doors and windows, set the intruder alarm and closed their minds to the darkness. In the end, though, what other way was there? Keep your head down and trust it won't happen to you, the burglary, assault, murder, the bullet or bomb.

'You okay?' asked Dixon.

'Hanging on my chinstrap.'

'Huh?'

Stark chuckled. It was an army line, which suggested that the only thing holding you upright was your helmet. 'Just waiting for my legs to catch up.'

'You look a little pale.'

Stark looked up into Dixon's earnest, innocent expression and suddenly felt a hundred years old. 'What's your name?'

Dixon looked confused.

'I was always deployed with strangers,' explained Stark. 'Everyone had surnames on their tunics. I only learnt first names when there was time.' He nearly said 'if'. 'I'm sorry, it's a bad habit.'

'John.'

John Dixon, a good man. 'OK, John.' Stark forced himself up. 'Let's crack on.'

The search produced bags of 'evidence', crap for some poor sod to sift through, but no blood-stained Adidas. The debrief was a downbeat affair. Afterwards, Fran followed Groombridge into his office. 'Something on your mind?' he asked.

Fran hesitated. Backing someone else's hunch was fine, but it implied a level of trust she didn't yet share with Stark. 'Stacey Appleton, Guv. Did she seem . . .'

'Seem what?'

It was too late for second thoughts. 'Frightened? On her interview tape, she looked as if she started crying after we left.'

'Really?' Groombridge raised his eyebrows, interested, and waved her to sit. 'There *were* a couple of moments when I thought we might be getting to her. Crying, you think?'

'Maybe. The tape cuts out. Here.' She handed him a memory stick.

Groombridge plugged it into his laptop and fired it up, skipping to the end. He watched the final frames three more times, pursing his lips. 'Mm, could be. Inadmissible, of course. Technically we shouldn't even be looking at anything after interview termination.' He sat back thoughtfully. 'You think we should get her in early, lean on her a little?'

Fran shrugged. 'The old boy's death's been on the news all day, so we can't hope to shock her tongue loose, but even if she doesn't crack I suppose it might rattle the others if we bring in her and not them. You never know.'

Groombridge was nodding slowly. 'Yes. OK, send Dixon with a couple of uniforms to pick her up. Nice work, Fran,' he added, as she was leaving.

74

Fran paused in the doorway, but left without saying anything.

Stacey Appleton looked nervously around the room for the hundredth time. Groombridge was letting her stew for a while before the interview, but Stacey wasn't the only one stewing. In the dimmed observation room Fran stared at her own ghostly reflection in the one-way mirror window, silently berating herself for not correcting Groombridge's misassumption. It wasn't her way to take credit for someone else's ideas and she wasn't sure why she'd not spoken up. It hadn't been deliberate, but –

'Is this going to take much longer, Sergeant?' asked the legal-aid lawyer, impatiently. 'I have other work to –'

'DCI Groombridge will be here presently,' replied Fran, a touch brusquely.

Stark had said nothing while they waited. Patient as stone. She clicked her tongue in irritation. She felt indebted to him, didn't like it, and couldn't even blame him. She returned her gaze to Stacey. A pretty sort of girl, trying too hard to be older than she was. Epicanthic folds to her eyes indicated some East Asian blood. Naveen Hussein was Indian or Pakistani, Tyler Wantage, West Indian. If you could say one thing for the Rats, they appeared colour-blind. Multicultural Britain at its feral worst, united in colour and creed against all comers. Was that why they'd begun picking on the homeless? Had they needed an outsider, an alien tribe too weak and unaffiliated to withstand attack?

Groombridge arrived and glanced around the silent room, perhaps sensing the chill radiating from her. 'Ready?'

Fran pointed at the social worker with her eyes. The local-authority youth-offending team's finest. An earnest girl in her mid-twenties, fresh-faced, freshly qualified and ready to do her bit. It wouldn't last. Give her ten years of this shit and she'd quit, sign off with stress or hide up the management ladder as far from the stinking scum as she could possibly get.

Groombridge nodded discreetly and turned to the girl with a winning smile. 'Lauren?' he read off her visitor's badge. 'Thanks for coming at short notice. You have Miss Appleton's file. Sixteen, only child, father abdicated his responsibilities when she was three. Mother drinks morning till night and has entertained a long line of unsuitable live-in boyfriends, some of whom may have taken an unhealthy interest in young Stacey. This is a delicate interview. I understand that Stacey has endured a lot, but we believe she has fallen in with the wrong crowd, got herself mixed up in things beyond her control. We need her help.'

'I understand.' Lauren smiled, responding to his warmth like a flower opening to the sun. Fran could only look on in admiration and try not to laugh. The lawyer silently rolled his eyes.

Stark watched from the dim observation room. Fran stayed out too. They didn't want to scare Stacey with too many people, she said, though Stark wondered if she also doubted her efficacy in a reassuring-female-presence role. Stacey bit at her thumbnail, eyes darting. She knew Alfred Ladd was dead all right.

'Stacey, I'd like to ask you again about last Sunday evening,' began Groombridge, kindly. 'You were seen drinking in the Meridian public house, non-alcoholic beverages, I presume, along with Naveen Hussein and others, including Nikki Cockcroft, Kyle Gibbs, Colin Messenger, Tyler Wantage, Harrison Collier, Martin Munroe, Paul Thompson and Tim Bowes.' Stacey shrugged. 'In your previous statement you said that you all drank up at closing time and were home by midnight.' Groombridge noted Stacey's nod for the tape. 'Both you and Naveen claim Naveen arrived home with you and stayed the night at your flat. Unfortunately your mother has no recollection of this.'

Stacey rolled her eyes. 'Can't remember her own name half the time.'

'She was drunk?'

Stacey shook her head. 'She's only *drunk* in the afternoons. By evening she's unconscious. In the mornings she's a bitch.'

'So you and Naveen have the flat to yourselves in the evenings, technically.'

Stacey bristled. 'It's not like that.'

Groombridge smiled. 'I was merely pointing out that you may come and go as you wish. That you and Naveen have no real alibi for the night you and your so-called friends kicked a defenceless old man to death.' He delivered these words warmly, but with such calm surety that Stacey blinked in surprise.

The lawyer placed a hand on her arm. 'You have no evidence to back that assertion, Inspector.' He wasn't to be as easily bamboozled as the social worker, but it wasn't him whom Groombridge needed to charm. The legal could only fend off questions; the social worker could slam the door on proceedings.

'We can match Stacey's clothing with that seen on CCTV not far from the scene of the brutal murder. Naveen's too, and the rest of her so-called friends.'

'We're hardly talking one-off catwalk lines or bespoke tailoring, Inspector. You can't build charges on high-street clothing.'

'Individually, no. But juries do love the coincidence of an ensemble outfit.'

'If all you have is coincidence, why are we even here?'

'Because Stacey has been told to lie, threatened most likely, by her so-called friends, to protect themselves. They're hiding behind you, Stacey.'

Stacey just stared at the desk.

'Did you happen to notice anyone desecrating the war memorial on your way home?' asked Groombridge.

Stacey looked up sharply. The legal's confused frown suggested Stacey had neglected to mention this titbit.

Groombridge pressed on: 'We erected an incident board there asking for witnesses. We have three independent sightings of a gang of youths drinking at the memorial around one a.m. We also took fingerprint and DNA samples from the lager cans, et cetera. The results are due anytime. I wonder if they'll throw up any names I recognize?'

A touch of panic crept into Stacey's eyes. Fear, too.

Groombridge smiled sadly. 'I've been doing this for a long time, Stacey. I can tell when someone's lying and I can usually tell why. Some people can't help themselves. Some lie for fun. Most to avoid the repercussions of their own selfish actions. Many to protect the people they love, or are loyal to. And sometimes people lie because they've been told to and they're scared shitless. You're scared, Stacey, I can tell. Just as I can tell that you're sorry for what happened, and that none of it was your idea or your fault. You never laid a finger on those poor homeless people. You don't have a vicious bone in your body, do you, Stacey, not really? But you're afraid if you tell them to stop they'll turn on you, your so-called friends.'

He let that sink in. 'I can help you. I can stop you being scared. I want to. But I need your help to do it. I need you to help me stop this happening again.' With that, he began sliding photos on to the desk in front of her, one by one. The victims, bruised, battered, bleeding, terrified. 'Or this,' he added, sliding a picture of Alfred Ladd across, cold and lifeless. 'I need you to help me stop this.'

Her eyes were drawn to the pictures in growing horror. Tears welled, but she said nothing.

'Bring in the goody-goody,' whispered Fran next to Stark.

As if on cue, Groombridge shared his best sympathetic look with the social worker.

'Here it comes.' Fran smiled.

The social worker gently placed a hand on Stacey's arm. The lawyer reached out, too late, to prevent it. 'It's OK, Stacey,' said Lauren. 'It's OK.'

Crumbling in slow motion, like the calving of a glacier, Stacey burst into tears. Sobbing, she pushed the photos away. The social worker murmured supportively, passed tissues and held her around the shoulders until the crying subsided. No one spoke for a good minute.

'Will you help me?' asked Groombridge.

Stacey finally looked up into his eyes, her own red and racked with remorse.

'I can't,' repeated Superintendent Cox. 'That's all she said?'

'All she would or could say,' replied Groombridge. 'After more tears she clammed up. The social worker made us call it a day and the legal reminded us we had little grounds to hold her. Uniform gave her tea and a biscuit and dropped her home.'

Cox sighed. 'Do you ever get tired of the lies?'

'They come with the job.' Groombridge dodged the question. It would be nice if every guilty suspect confessed but most did not. Perpetrators lied, suspects, witnesses too, even victims. Testing who was lying about what and why was at the heart of investigation. Lies were essential. To say you were tired of lies was akin to saying you were tired of being a copper, which was not something to admit lightly to your boss. It was best not to take Cox's cheerful bumbling or moments of introspection at face value. The man had agendas. 'I still think we have a good chance of turning her, sir.'

'Softly, softly . . .' Cox agreed. 'Good. How's your team?'

'Sir?'

'How's our new man settling in?'

When Cox had first placed Stark's application before him Groombridge had sniffed the air for the odour of public relations, but the application had merit and Cox seemed genuinely taken with it. They both understood the potential downside, should Stark not cope physically or, worse, mentally. 'Well enough.'

'I got the sneaking suspicion he might be a deal smarter than he lets on.'

'I'm sure we'll find out, sir.'

Cox nodded. The twinkle of amusement said he appreciated their game. 'See if a few drinks loosen him up a little, eh?'

'Care to join us, sir, you're always welcome.'

Cox laughed. 'If there's one thing I'm quite sure of it's that my presence in the Compass Rose on a Friday evening would not be welcome.'

Cox needn't have worried. The atmosphere in Rosie's that Friday evening was muted anyway. It had been a frustrating day. Groombridge sat with Fran and Harper, but she could be little deterred from shoptalk, while his sour mood had returned now that the low-priority case, once his, had escalated into murder. The rest of the team had joined with all the other coppers to put the day behind them and enjoy themselves. Groombridge noted Stark among them, but not long later saw him quietly slip away.

Stark limped down to the cab rank in town and rode home. He was tired, and sore, and the effort of smiling with his new colleagues had quickly proved too much of an effort. Faced with either pills, whisky and a Saturday hangover or an early night and some chance of recuperation he had taken the coward's way out. He didn't think anyone had noticed him leave. It was the weekend, and he was glad of it.

He swallowed a couple of pills and collapsed on to his sofa with a deep sigh of relief, feeling the tension in his aching muscles finally relax. He didn't even know he was falling asleep until the phone woke him with a start. 'What?' he managed, sitting up stiffly, blinking at the fresh dawn light.

'Stark?'

Fran's voice? He rubbed his face, still confused. 'In theory.'

'Dixon is on his way to pick you up.'

'Where are we going?'

'Ferrier Estate. We've got a body.'

8

Stark thanked his lucky stars he'd left the pub early. Dixon looked positively green at the gills.

They arrived moments before Fran pulled up with DCI Groombridge. Even at this hour a respectable crowd of morbid gawpers had assembled. Uniform had strung tape across an entrance to one of the main courtyards and people were craning their necks to glimpse something gruesome. The sun was rising, but the rectangular arrangement of tower blocks would keep swathes of their courtyards dim and cold till mid-morning.

Groombridge greeted the sergeant standing guard. 'Nice boots, Tony.'

Stark remembered the stocky Sergeant Clark from his first-day introductions – something of a legend among the uniforms, Ptolemy and Peters had said later.

Clark looked down at his blue wellingtons. 'SOCO's finest, sir.' His uniform shoes were, no doubt, in a sealed evidence bag.

'What have you got for us, then?' Groombridge gestured towards the weighted blue plastic tarpaulin at the foot of one of the ugly blocks.

'Female, late teens. Looks like she took a tumble from up there,' replied the sergeant, pointing up the brutalist façade. 'Resident found the body on his way home from the night shift and called it in just after five. SOCO got here a few minutes ago.'

'ID?'

'The poor girl is not at her best, facially speaking, and you know how SOCOs get if you go rooting around.'

'Mm,' agreed Groombridge. 'Young Jones looks a bit peaky.' He jerked his head towards the blue-booted constable guarding the tape.

'We all remember our first body, sir,' replied Clark, sagely.

'Even grizzled old campaigners like us,' added Groombridge. 'Relief is on its way. Take Jones for a cuppa on me, and a bacon roll, if he can stomach it.' He handed over a tenner.

'Thank you, sir.'

'Remember *your* first body, Stark?' asked Groombridge.

'No, Guv.'

The momentary embarrassment on Groombridge's face left Stark cursing his careless honesty. Perhaps lost for words, Groombridge turned to scan the SOCOs. In their white disposable overalls and blue rubber boots, they were proficiently establishing the inner cordon with its common approach path of raised steel chequer-plate stepping stones. Aside from the crime-scene manager, busy directing them until the scene was ordered to his satisfaction, another man in overalls watched over them, like a general. The pathologist, Stark guessed. Groombridge waved to catch his eye but the man just held up a hand. 'Ten minutes, Chief Inspector. Hop into some blues.'

The impatience of Stark's superiors was apparent, but it was vital Forensics got the first look. One of the SOCOs supervised as they passed through the transition area, a cheap plastic pergola tent full of cheap plastic crates. They ripped the plastic off blue disposable overalls and over-shoes, then pulled them on over their own clothes and stepped over a low bench into the clean area. Stark recognized the set-up from the surgical area of Camp Bastion field hospital.

All the SOCOs froze while the pathologist examined the area and the body alone, occasionally talking into a Dictaphone. When he had finished, he spoke to the CSM, then came to meet them.

'Marcus,' said Groombridge.

'DCI Groombridge. And DS Millhaven,' he smiled, 'always a pleasure. Who's your new friend?'

Fran answered. 'Marcus, this is TI Stark, latest CID victim. Stark, this is Marcus Turner, senior forensic pathologist and crime-scene nerd.'

Turner indicated his gloves by way of apology for not shaking hands. 'Grist to our ever-grinding mill, Constable, muted congratulations.' In his early forties, verging on plump, with a receding hairline and greying temples, he might have been mistaken for a very ordinary man, were it not for his occupational attire and the amused twinkle in his eye.

Groombridge gestured at the corpse. 'Cause of death?'

'Deceleration,' replied Turner, deadpan.

They all looked up at the concrete block. 'How high?' asked Groombridge.

'Sufficiently. Top-floor balcony probably.'

'Fall or pushed?'

Turner offered a Gallic-style shrug. 'Too soon to say. There are some anomalies. You'd better come and take a look.'

They followed him carefully along the stepping-stone path. Marcus had pulled the tarp back over the body but one hand protruded. Young, slim fingers, bloodied –

Stark's head swam. Dehydration, exhaustion and the afternoon Basra heat were beginning to tell. He crouched beside the hand, a child's, slim-fingered, grey with dust and dried blood, protruding from beneath some buckled corrugated iron. He dug away bits of rubble to expose the wrist. No pulse, but that might only be restricted circulation. He called out but heard no reply.

The hand felt warm, but in this temperature bodies didn't cool. Hours now since the car bomb had torn into the crowded market. They hadn't found anyone alive in a while.

Such a small hand, soft, almost weightless in his . . .

The fingers twitched.

Yelling for assistance, he began tearing at the rubble. The corrugated iron was burning hot in the merciless sun and his fingerless combat gloves offered little protection as he tried to bend it up.

Marcus pulled back the tarp.

Stark wiped sweat from his eyes and realized it was tears.

Now he blinked, new reality snapping away old.

Jesus! He glanced around but everyone appeared too fixed in the present to have noticed his brief absence. Christ, as if the dreams weren't bad enough ... When was the last time he'd had a flashback? Damn it! Another tear ran down his cheek and he wiped it away hurriedly, angrily, fighting to bring his breathing and heart rate under control.

He stared down at the body before him, lying on its front, limbs twisted and broken. Blood had congealed into clothing and hair, and into the cracks of the concrete paving slabs fractured by the impact. The downward side of her skull was similarly shattered and the girl stared along the ground through one lifeless, blood-clotted eye. Not for the first time Stark was struck by the surreal stillness of life extinguished, the repellent, baffling polarity between the animate and ex-animate.

Dixon put one hand over his mouth and turned away, his face now white.

'Shit.' Fran sighed.

Marcus winced sympathetically. 'Someone you know?'

Groombridge closed his eyes and let out a long sigh. 'Stacey Appleton.'

Fran swore again, then turned to Dixon and Stark. 'Right. You two work with uniform door to door. Someone saw something. Someone heard something. Someone *knows* something. Go.'

According to uniform, the proprietor of the embattled off-licence had heard a scream around midnight, so Stark went to talk to him first. A Sikh man with large calloused hands, he answered his questions in imperfect English scattered with jarring South London idioms and studied brevity. He had heard the noise, gone downstairs into the shop to check all was well and, finding no intruders, had gone back to bed. He had seen and heard nothing else until the blue lights arrived in the morning, he said emphatically. His wooden smile and anxious glances at the door suggested he could not wait for Stark to be gone. His wife hovered timidly behind him, saying nothing. Stark tried a smile. 'Did you see or hear anything?' he asked.

Her husband barked something in his native tongue, Punjabi most likely, and the wife retreated from view. 'My wife speaks little English, forgive us.'

Something in these words made Stark doubt them but he thanked the man all the same. Outside he glanced up at movement in the window above the shop. The wife's face stared down for a moment, before she let the net curtain fall back. They were frightened.

And they were not alone. Other residents also reported hearing the scream around midnight, but they had long given up peering out into the night at disturbances. No one had yet reported seeing anything, and if they knew anything they weren't letting on. Fear hung over the estate, like smog. It was truly depressing.

At least it corresponded with Marcus's preliminary time of death estimated from body temperature. Suicide, accident or foul play, at around midnight the previous night, while officers of the law revelled or slept, one of their suspects, their best potential witness, had met her end.

'How'd the mother take it?' Williams asked Fran.

'Not well. It's a shame we couldn't tell her in the afternoon when she'd be drunk. Stacey was right. Her mother is not at her best sober.'

Informing Stacey's mother: Stark was heartily glad to have escaped that particular duty during his on-the-job training. He stared up at the tower, wondering which window hid the grief-stricken woman.

'Did we get her killed?' asked Dixon.

Stark noticed Fran glance his way. She was wondering the same thing. And bringing Stacey in had been his idea.

Groombridge finished a phone call and waved them over. 'OK. Stacey's mobile phone was found smashed a few feet from her body. The memory chip survived. She sent a text at six minutes past twelve last night – "Goodbye Nav I'm sorry". That's it. Not much of a suicide note. Let's go see what Naveen Hussein has to add.'

'What about the rest of them, Guv? Shall we round them up?' asked Fran.

Groombridge shook his head. 'I can't face another round of their bullshit posturing yet. Not until we know more. Harper, you and the others knock on doors and get the occupants' whereabouts last night. Let me know who you think is lying.'

'I can tell you now, Guv,' muttered Harper. 'They all are.'

Fran glanced at Stark as they trudged up the concrete stairs and traversed the open balcony corridor to Naveen's front door, wondering why she'd dragged him along. She had resolved overnight to confess to the DCI that it had been Stark who had suggested speaking to Stacey again, not her. Now, of course, it would look like she was trying to shift blame. If Stacey had been killed as a result, it was Fran's fault, not Stark's. She had brought it to the DCI. Christ, she had even said it might rattle the others. Either they'd driven the stupid girl to suicide or made someone kill her.

'It's not our fault,' said Groombridge, out of the blue. His knack for guessing her thoughts was as disconcerting as it was maddening. 'We deal with people on the edge, but we don't put them there.'

'And sometimes they fall,' said Fran.

Groombridge glanced at her but said nothing more as he

knocked firmly on the door. A plump-faced Asian woman wearing a black hijab answered. 'What's he done now?'

They were shown into the living room, a space barely large enough for the *faux*-leather three-piece, over-large television, cluttered keepsakes and photographs. They declined the offer of tea and were told Naveen would be through soon. It was impossible not to overhear the hissed tirade she unloaded on the teenager from the hallway, though for the most part it was delivered in her first language. At one point Stark chuckled quietly.

'Something funny?' demanded Fran.

'My Pashto is sketchy,' said Stark, wincing at the next broadside. 'But I think she blames the father.'

Fran rolled her eyes.

Moments later the mother shooed Naveen in, clearly stirred unwillingly from his bed and worried to find three police sitting in his living room. 'Well! Go on, then!' prompted his mother, in accented gunshot English. 'Tell them where you were last night.'

'Here,' said Naveen, sullenly.

'And for once it's true!' cried the mother. 'Good-for-nothing layabout. Does nothing but sleep, muck about on that computer with the door locked or he's out and about with that cheap little harlot from block seven!'

'Mum!' protested Naveen.

'Her mother is a drunk! What does that girl know? I ask you! Fifteen years old and her mother lets boys stay all night long!'

Never mind that it's your boy she's letting sleep over, thought Fran.

'And now there's girls being murdered right outside our windows!' railed the woman, breathlessly. 'Where are their mothers? I ask you!'

Fran held up a hand. 'Mrs Hussein! Forgive me, but are you confirming Naveen was here all night?'

'Yes! Tapping away on that computer. Playing games or masturbating to pornography –'

'*Mum!*' cried Naveen, desperately.

Fran held up her hand again. 'Naveen, can we see your phone?'

'No!' He was automatically defensive. 'Why?'

'Did you receive a text message just after midnight?'

'I don't know, why?'

'Could you check?'

He stomped out of the room, glaring at his mother, and returned with his mobile. He thumbed through some content, then frowned. '"Goodbye . . ."?'

'From Stacey Appleton?' asked Groombridge. Naveen's frown deepened, but he stared at the message in silence. 'We know that text was sent from her phone to yours last night. And I'm sorry to have to tell you that we found Stacey dead this morning.'

Naveen looked up sharply, clearly shocked to the core. 'Bullshit!'

'*Naveen!*' barked his mother.

'I'm sorry for your loss,' said Groombridge. 'At this stage we think she died in a fall. Had she been depressed, or worried about anything?'

Naveen glared back. 'Only about you lot! Pest'in' us when we done nothin'! But this ain't right, man, this ain't right! Stace didn't do this.' He waved the phone angrily. '*This is bullshit!*'

That was too much for the mother. Launching into another incomprehensible barrage, she scolded her errant son from the room.

'Some of them seemed, or acted, surprised,' reported Harper. 'Kyle Gibbs wasn't around but his mum said he was at home all night. Nikki Cockcroft acted like she didn't give a shit. Her mum said she was at home.'

'So they all claim they were at home,' said Groombridge, not that he'd expected anything else.

'And they're all lying,' said Harper.

'Hard to prove until we get forensics. Find out if any of the pay-as-you-go numbers they coughed up last week are still active, or even real. I'll get on to HQ about warrants for call-location traces. Check with uniform whether any of the gang were seen out and about. Talk to any residents we missed this morning and any we've spoken to who looked frightened or edgy.'

'All of them again.' Harper chuckled to himself.

It proved an unproductive day. Stark was glad he got to spend it sitting at his desk instead of traipsing around the estate. His hip had been looking forward to a day off, but his mind was restless to know what had happened.

'Stark?' Groombridge was peering at him from his office door.

'Guv?'

'Seen many post-mortems?'

'None, Guv,' replied Stark, with a sinking feeling about the rest of his so-called weekend.

'Then tomorrow's your unlucky day.'

Groombridge picked Stark up early and drove to the mortuary. His intention was to get a feel for Stark on the way but something in the young man's silence made it curiously hard to strike up conversation, and when he did, the responses he received were appropriate, friendly, and so concise they often brought the topic to a close. Groombridge smiled, imagining the effect this might be having on Fran. But that hadn't been the reason for her mood yesterday, or that of the whole team.

'It really isn't our fault,' said Groombridge. 'People make their own decisions. All we can do is ask the questions we're duty bound to ask.'

'Guv.'

A monosyllabic ambiguity. Groombridge gave up for now. It hadn't been their fault; it was *his*. As DCI it had been his call to press Stacey, to drive a wedge into her weakness and expose that weakness to her tribe. He'd not expected this result, but that was his fault too.

Stacey lay on the mortuary slab, naked, blue-black and broken, the huge Y-shaped incision in her torso closed with oversized stitches. It seemed wrong to find her alone like that. An irrational sentiment. Groombridge watched Stark for any discomfort but saw no more than he had the previous day. The first time he himself had been in this situation he'd thrown up.

Groombridge remembered his first corpse all too clearly. An accidental drowning: the body had been in the water for several days. How many had he seen since? He might list them if he sat down to it but he doubted he'd remember them all. But not to remember your first? It was easier to believe Stark was just repaying a thoughtless question. Easier, not necessarily true.

'I had a feeling you'd be hovering,' said Marcus Turner, wandering in, drying his hands on disposable blue paper. 'Our concerns appear justified, I'm afraid.'

'Murder, then.' Groombridge raised his eyebrows, unsure what he'd been hoping to hear.

'A fall from height masks much, Chief Inspector, but in this case not enough. Look, the cut on the temple I showed you. It was fresh. It had only minutes to bruise *ante mortem*. I found the victim's blood on what's left of her mobile phone and the shape is consistent.'

'She was hit with her own phone?' asked Groombridge.

'Indeed. But the real smoking gun is round the back, here.' He pointed to several skull X-rays on the illuminated viewer. 'Here, bordering the shattered side, this edge, do you see? This semi-oval shape missing, and these surrounding pieces ...'

91

Marcus looked at them expectantly but when neither copper was willing to speculate, he continued, 'The skull shattered across this point, in part, because there was already a hole here.'

'Created by?'

'Blunt instrument. Heavy, rounded tip. Egg-shaped, perhaps.'

'So she was hit from the front with her phone, then from behind with something else. Multiple assailants?'

Marcus shrugged. 'Nothing from the scene to say one way or the other. There's too much post-mortem contusion pooling from the impact to find any defensive bruising on her arms, but there are bloody scrapes to the fingertips and split nails, which I fear will match samples SOCO found on the balcony of the derelict top-floor flat.'

'Suggesting that even with her skull stove in she resisted going over,' concluded Groombridge. The reports of the prolonged scream also suggested she was conscious all the way down. What a way to go. He shook his head to dispel the image, but it was instantly replaced with one of Stacey crumpling into tears before his questioning.

'Was there anyone else's skin or blood under her nails?' asked Stark.

'Sadly not. We'll swab the phone and clothing, too, of course, but any foreign DNA found will likely be everyday transference from family and friends.'

'Or so-called friends,' said Groombridge, coldly.

'I can confirm at this time that the deceased's name was Stacey Appleton, fifteen years old. We would ask you to respect her mother's wish for privacy at this difficult time,' said Groombridge, sternly.

Fat chance, thought Stark, watching his boss on TV.

'In light of early evidence we are treating this fatality as suspicious.'

'Inspector! Inspector!' A woman's voice made itself heard above the clamour. *Chief* Inspector, thought Stark, crossly. If Groombridge resented the shoddy informality he did not show it, merely beckoned for the question. 'Is it true that you think this death is linked with that of Alfred Ladd and the assaults on other homeless persons?'

Where the hell had they got that? thought Stark. On screen Groombridge blinked, twice. 'I can confirm that both cases are being dealt with under the purview of my team. That is all I can say at this time.'

Groombridge brought the briefing to a swift conclusion and the news moved on to the next item. Stark turned it off and poured himself a double. Half a day off had not made up for sleep squeezed between tumbling thoughts of guilt and death. The flashback had rattled him. It was the first he'd experienced in many months and the first time he'd thought about the marketplace bombing in years. An earlier wound. Iraq. They'd heaved off the debris to reveal a girl, perhaps ten years old, with crush injuries and a thready pulse. Stark had tried to stop them moving her until the paramedics returned, but shouting locals shoved him aside, snatched her up and rushed her away in the back of a tatty Hyundai. He'd made enquiries later but could not discover her fate among all those wounded. A day spent bagging bodies and body-parts of men, women and children while screaming bereaved threw shoes and stones at you, like it was your doing. A day best forgotten.

And if the sight of Stacey sprawled dead on cold ground had triggered unwelcome memories, the sight of her laid out on the slab had tested his composure to its limit. Groombridge had hardly blinked. Would he, too, be drinking tonight to forget?

Monday did not like Stark. The whisky had helped him begin the night but had done little for the morning. A hot shower had barely driven the dreams from his thick head. Pills were his only hope today, for hip and head, if not heart.

Kyle Gibbs was up first, shuffling into the interview room, looking about as resentful as it might be possible for a teenager to look. He said nothing during the preliminaries, barely nodding at his name and date of birth.

'Where were you on Friday night?' began Groombridge.

'Home,' grunted Kyle. 'My mum already told you.'

Groombridge returned Kyle's stare for several seconds. 'I would remind you that you are being interviewed under caution. That if you're lying, and I pretty much take that as read when speaking with you, it will harm your defence.'

The legal leant towards the microphone. 'Have you anything in the way of evidence, Chief Inspector? My client wishes to help and has confirmed his whereabouts.'

'I have considerable evidence. And I'm sure Forensics will tell an interesting tale. I sometimes wonder at how easy it was for criminals to get away with things before DNA comparison. Thank goodness for technological progress.'

'Is this relevant?' asked the legal.

'Oh, I do hope so.' Groombridge smiled.

In all likelihood, probably not, thought Stark. As Marcus had said, unless it was from blood, DNA was only really helpful in establishing a link between criminal and victim: everyday transference was all but inevitable between family and friends. Or so-called friends. Stark did not like Kyle Gibbs. This was his first time in close proximity to the young man and for once he would happily have stayed behind the glass. But for whatever reason Groombridge had had other ideas.

The call-location traces had drawn a blank too. They only worked if a phone was switched on and a call or text was made or received. The Ferrier Rats knew to turn them off when they were up to something, and to replace SIM cards on a regular basis.

Kyle did not look worried. Not on the surface, anyway. Perhaps there was something in his eyes, but he was not about to confess and at this stage that was just about all they could hope for. As if reading his thoughts, Kyle glanced at Stark and huffed, a small sneer appearing. Groombridge probed him a while longer but everyone in the room knew they were here to tick a box. The sneer returned as he left.

Nikki Cockcroft came next. A different piece of work: coiled like a spring, not wound tight with fear or guilt but with malice and a mouthful of venom. She did not keep silent through the preliminaries, but sniffed and swore at every opportunity. The questioning did not go much better.

'Are you at least sorry?' asked Groombridge, wearily.

'For what?'

'For the death of your friend, Stacey? She was the only other girl in your little gang. Was she not your friend?'

Nikki shrugged.

'That's it? You've known each other since childhood and she gets a shrug, nothing more?'

'I didn't kill her,' snarled Nikki. 'Why don't you finish your questions and fuck off?'

Groombridge did just that. In all honesty Stark could hardly wait to get out of the room. If Kyle had made him want to lean across the table to slap him, Nikki had made his skin crawl.

'I could use a shower,' said Groombridge. 'Who's next?'

'Colin Messenger, Guv,' replied Fran, who had been watching through the glass.

'The brains of the bunch,' observed Groombridge. 'Remind me why we do this.'

'Because no one else would for the pay,' replied Fran.

'What do you think, Stark?' asked Groombridge. 'Should we chuck it all in?'

'No one else would have me, Guv.'

Now Groombridge laughed. 'Great. We're the only drinkers

in the last-chance saloon. How long till we can go to the pub and wash the bitter taste of despair from our mouths?'

'At least six hours, Guv,' Fran replied despondently.

'How about you, Stark? I'd say you're earning a pint today.'

Stark made a pained face. 'Busy tonight, Guv, sorry.'

'Hot date?' scoffed Fran.

Stark laughed. 'Only with pain.'

'Ah,' she nodded knowingly, 'the laying-on of hands. Or is it the one when they plonk red-hot stones on your back? You've the look of the masochist about you. Or one of those massages when they walk on your spine? I hope your masseuse is a thirty-stone hirsute Samoan called Trevor.'

Behind their amusement Stark knew they were watching for clues. Maybe half of the truth would keep them happy, for now. 'Hydrotherapy.'

'*Hydrotherapy!*' Fran threw her head back, laughing. 'Oh, *bless*! Aquarobics without the music! Tell me it's a class of chubby old ladies in swimming caps!'

To Stark's amazement, she resisted the chance to share this nugget gleefully with the office, but when he put a call through to her later she couldn't resist saying, 'Cheers, Bob.'

As she listened to the caller, all amusement fell from her face and her head dropped. 'OK, thanks.' When she looked up, Stark was struck by her uncharacteristic sadness. She got up wordlessly and knocked on Groombridge's open door. 'Guv, Stacey Appleton's mum was just found dead.'

9

Karen Appleton lay on her back on her stained sofa, vomit on her cyanotic lips. One empty bottle of budget vodka lay on the floor nearby. Another looked to have rolled from her dangling hand, spilling some of its contents into the filthy carpet. The room stank of booze, urine and despair.

'Family Liaison called round yesterday to see how she was doing and got no answer,' said Fran. 'Today they had a peep through the net curtains. Looks like she choked on her own vomit.'

'A logical conclusion.' Marcus nodded. 'Doors and windows locked, no indications of a struggle, no pills in the vomitus. Dead at least twenty-four hours, probably longer. We'll check for physical evidence, of course, and I'll confirm cause of death, but at this stage I'd hazard accidental death at best, suicide at worst.'

Groombridge said nothing. Stark could imagine what he was thinking. Another death to chalk up, pointless and, above all, preventable. Tragedy squared. It hardly mattered whether Karen had drowned in bilious despair or died merely because her carer, her long-suffering daughter, wasn't there to roll her into the recovery position before going to bed; accident or suicide, this was little short of double murder. Whoever killed Stacey had as good as killed her mother too.

Stark turned away and went to look in Stacey's room. If anything, it was worse. Peeling, mould-stained wallpaper in some hideous seventies pattern, a faded child's princess duvet cover and pillow on the bed. There were no boy-band posters, no teen magazines, no make-up or hair products. Just a child-sized wardrobe with a limited array of clothes, begged, borrowed or stolen, a solitary My Little Pony toy and a heavy-duty slide-bolt screwed to the inside of the door to keep her mother out or, worse, her mother's gentlemen friends.

'Not much to show for a life,' commented Groombridge at his shoulder.

Stark had seen too much poverty to be shocked but that didn't make it any less depressing.

Karen's death photo joined her daughter's on the board next to Alfred Ladd's. There was no office banter that afternoon. Three deaths in as many days were no laughing matter. The team retreated into their own thoughts, unwilling or unable to look each other in the eye. Stark could have used that pint. His anticipation about seeing Kelly again now seemed flip. Just as he was pulling on his jacket to leave, his phone rang. He had to overcome temptation not to leave it. 'Stark.'

'Constable, this is Sergeant Ptolemy. I've got someone in the car I thought you should talk to, just out front. Can you come?'

Intrigued, Stark wandered down. A girl in her late teens or early twenties, with dyed purple hair, multiple facial piercings and a glorious black eye, puffy and fresh, was sitting in the back of the car. She was holding a half-finished burger and a milk-shake and appeared torn between these riches and her present company.

'This is Rachael. She got into a row with a shopkeeper in the covered market. He didn't like her begging outside and she's got a bit of a gob on her. Probably what got her the shiner. But it wasn't the shopkeeper that gave it to her. She doesn't want to make a statement about who did but we "negotiated terms" by which she will now repeat to you what she told us.'

'Go ahead, Rachael. He doesn't bite. That I know of.' Peters winked at Stark.

Rachael looked at Stark, clearly reluctant. But she'd taken the food. 'It was that lot that've been beating us up,' she began defensively. 'You lot won't stop them.' Ptolemy coughed meaningfully and she altered her tone. 'Those arseholes from the Ferrier. That wanker and his slag and the rest.'

'Kyle Gibbs and Nikki Cockcroft?' Stark couldn't quite believe his ears. Surely they weren't so stupid as to carry on their antics while the police were looking at them so hard.

Rachael shrugged. 'Don't know names.'

'The description she gave us sounded all too familiar,' said Ptolemy.

'When was this?' asked Stark.

'Saturday night,' said Rachael. 'Shit night for begging. I was just having a quiet one out of the way, but they wouldn't leave off. Why won't they leave us alone? You lot should stop them,' she spat, 'but you don't give a *shit*!'

Stark clenched his jaw against a harsh rebuke. On deployment he'd been confronted with angry, often grief-stricken nationals on more than one occasion, people overcome with bitterness and fury, people with genuine cause or pain, who had to be placated or faced down. This clueless chit, with her belly full of fast-food and her thoughtless accusation, should never have got to him, but after today . . . He crouched to her eye level, speaking with all the quiet calm he could muster. 'I *do* give a shit. If I had concrete evidence, those vicious little fuckers would be locked in our cells right now and half the building would be dancing and pouring drinks. But I don't have the evidence. Yet. Perhaps you could help me with that instead of venting blind assumptions while you devour the payment you extorted for doing your civic duty.'

Despite his effort to conceal his anger she shrank back as he spoke, hardly able to meet his cold gaze. Both officers were looking at him askance. 'Tell him what they wanted,' prompted Ptolemy.

Rachael glanced nervously between them. 'They were looking for someone. A girl, with pink hair.'

'A homeless girl?' asked Stark. Rachael nodded. 'Do you know who? Or why?'

She shook her head. 'Can I go now? Please.'

Stark couldn't shake off the sheer lunacy of Kyle and Nikki. Were they so sure of themselves, so sure of police impotence, so shameless? It beggared belief. The cab journey to the Carter Orthopaedic Hospital slipped past unnoticed and, arriving with time to spare, he settled into a comfortable reception armchair and shrugged off unwanted thoughts the best way he knew, with a book: one of a series of twenty naval tales set in the Napoleonic wars that a navy lad had once recommended to him. The first had started so innocuously that it was only halfway through you realized you were hooked. The story was at a particularly gripping juncture, deep in the heart of an engagement, and Stark was soon engrossed, tea cooling on the small table beside him, a biscuit poised halfway to his mouth. It was only the sense of someone standing next to him that startled him into the present.

'That biscuit hasn't moved in minutes.' Kelly slid into the opposite seat. 'We called your name, you know.'

A glance at the chuckling receptionist said it all. 'Sorry, miles away,' he said, flushing a little.

'Somewhere sunny, I hope?'

He showed her the cover. 'Bay of Biscay, winter of 1802, at night.'

'I'm sure it had its delights. How are you? Any new acts of recklessness to report?'

'Fictional only.'

She looked at the blurb. 'Boys and their toy soldiers. I thought you'd have had your fill.'

'Actually it's about a friendship.'

'In war.' She shook her head. 'Are you looking for validation or thrills?'

'Perhaps just distraction.' The part of his nature that too often revelled in the funny side of confrontation was keeping quiet. He was knackered, and the last person in the world he wanted to argue with was her. That thought was new and disconcerting.

She studied him for a moment. 'You OK?'

Stark frowned. 'OK?'

'You've the weight of the world on your shoulders.'

Uncomfortable, he half nodded, half shrugged, and wholly avoided.

Kelly smiled. 'I'd like Lucy to sit in on this session. I'd value her opinion. But I'll understand if you'd prefer her not to.'

Prefer not to parade your disfigurement in front of yet another stranger, she meant. 'I've been nursed by enough motherly types to abandon dignity long ago.'

'Poor you.'

It was a surprising riposte, said with warm sarcasm and a twinkle in those pale-blue eyes. It threw him slightly and made him regret his touchiness. The care he'd received had indeed left few refuges for dignity, but often enough it was the indifference with which it was administered that eroded dignity rather than the physical imposition. He retained an unflattering opinion of nursing that might or might not have been fair.

The military wards at Selly Oak hadn't been too bad. The patients were young soldiers, fit, aside from injury, and most still had that early-stage determination. But once you'd made it to the general wards with the elderly and infirm, poor sods who needed more, far more, it exposed a lack of empathy in some nursing staff that at times bordered on shocking. The doctors were OK generally but it was easier for them: competent or otherwise, they could breeze in on rounds, be cheerful and reassuring, then breeze off to the next bag of bones. But the nurses ... There were gems, of course, a handful who remained amused and engaging as they went about their work. Perhaps their warm light cast shadow on the rest. Nights were the worst.

It was the one topic you could never broach with a medical professional and perhaps it was an understandable reaction to their daily grind of suffering and tedium, how they had to be just to cope. They had a hard bloody job, that much was obvious. Who would want their hours, their duties? Who but a service-person. Nurses too often displayed a 'poor me' attitude, which infuriated the soldier in Stark. God help an army of whining soldiers. That was the whole purpose of rule one: no fucking sympathy. It wasn't that you didn't feel sorry for yourself, you just didn't seek affirmation from your fellow sufferers. What would be the point? They knew just how shit it was; they already empathized to their core. It was a given.

'Quite right,' he agreed. Besides, it wasn't the motherly types who unsettled you, it was the beautiful, clever girls who saw straight through you. And a girl prepared not to hide it was positively terrifying. He tried to summon something clever, something flirtatious, but was relieved when nothing came.

'Come on.' She led him to Hydro, walking just far enough in front to afford him an absorbing view. To his – mild – shame he used his limp to advantage.

'Evening, dear,' Lucy greeted him cheerily. 'Don't mind me. I'm just here as a second opinion.'

'We'll run through your homework routine first for Lucy,' said Kelly. 'Not those tracky bottoms again, though, if you don't mind, and those big swimming shorts cover too much as well. We want to assess the musculature. Try these.' She held out a pair of hospital-branded swimming shorts, much briefer than his own. He stared at them. 'Just be thankful we replaced the old Speedos.' She grinned. 'No top either. Off you go.'

Stark suspected he was being played with, but what could he

do? He could hear their muffled voices deep in some conspiratorial conversation. He emerged from the cubicle with his gown on, looking at Lucy.

'Don't be shy, dear. I've seen my share of car-crash rehab.' He slipped off the robe and she didn't flinch. 'Give us a twirl,' she said. Their eyes remained coolly professional. 'OK, let's see what you can't do,' said Lucy.

It had been a long week. He was impatient to get better and felt he must be improving, but tonight it seemed he was getting worse, although he tried fiercely to prevent it showing. It was all the more excruciating in the skimpy shorts. Aside from the scars, he wasn't the specimen he'd once been. He'd always been lean, but pain and rehab-focused exercise had robbed him of some of the natural muscle he'd always enjoyed.

'Hm,' said Lucy. 'OK, shower that sweat off and we'll see how you are in the pool.'

Kelly ran him through the routine she'd begun teaching him the previous week. It hurt, and the sight of her in her swimsuit, which had allowed him to ignore this before, failed this time. If anything, it hurt more, and his earlier thought of flirtation seemed all the more foolish. As foolish as the expectation that swapping uniform patrol for CID would involve less time on his feet.

His torturers spent an age closely inspecting and manually articulating parts of him while discussing him in cold medical jargon, much of which he understood all too well. Back on the poolside they put on their gowns but had Stark stand on the spot doing about-faces on command in his wet shorts, humiliated and rather depressed.

'I concur,' said Lucy to Kelly. 'He should move up to two sessions a week.' Addressing him directly she added, 'I have to agree with Kelly's initial assessment. You really *are* a bit of a mess.'

Kelly covered her mouth to hide her amusement, while Stark prayed for the earth to open up beneath him.

'Cheer up, though.' Lucy grinned. 'She was right about you having a great arse too!'

Kelly's laughter gave way to a crimson blush.

Six in the morning and still Stark presents himself with disgustingly impeccable dress and grooming, thought Fran, only a faint redness around his eyes giving him any semblance of humanity. Were it not too precious she might've spilt coffee on him as she drove. Groombridge had drowned his sorrows with a pint and gone home to his wife. Fran had continued her self-saturation at home, alone. There were days when her tiny flat seemed cavernous. 'Physio going OK?' she asked, for something to say.

'Fine, thanks.'

Another brush-off, though she caught an odd expression on his face when she glanced over. He said nothing more until they were in the office, with the team muttering over their caffeine of choice. They had a long day ahead, collating and cross-referencing statements, looking for slip-ups and incongruities. The usual summons from Scotland Yard meant Cox wanted all his ducks in a row before he faced the brass.

'Anything else?' asked Groombridge, after the summing-up.

Fran held up her phone. 'Text from my contact in Pathology, Guv. Karen Appleton died of asphyxiation, almost certainly accidental.'

Stark raised his hand. 'I had a strange conversation as I left work yesterday, Guv.' His news that Kyle and Nikki's escapades against the homeless were still ongoing caused visible consternation among the team. 'I don't really know what to make of it.'

Fran did. 'Little shits! They've got some front! They know if we had any real evidence we'd have arrested them.'

'Maybe they'll get cocky and give us something we can really use,' said Williams.

'It's odd, though, don't you think?' said Stark.

Dixon nodded. 'Yeah – all their previous victims were old.'

'Careful with that word "old",' chided Groombridge, closest in age to the victim profile.

'Sorry, Guv.'

'More importantly, who are they looking for and why?' said Stark.

Groombridge looked at Fran. 'All right,' she said. 'I'll have a word with the local authority and charities when the rest of the world wakes up, see if anyone knows about a girl with pink hair.'

She was still vaguely blaming Stark for this addition to her workload when they sat down to a canteen breakfast a couple of hours later. She gazed at Stark's traditional English plateful. The boy had hollow legs. It was hard not to think of him as a boy – twenty-five seemed a lifetime ago. Yet at the same time he came across as so serious. He'd seen things, she supposed. Sometimes you glimpsed it in his eyes, like the moment they'd pulled the tarp from Stacey's corpse.

She was pondering this, taking her time over her coffee and Danish, when Maggie hurried in. The control-room matriarch rarely left her fiefdom for less than hot scandal or breaking news. Spotting them, she pulled up a chair. 'Am I right in assuming you'll be wanting another chat with Kyle Gibbs at some point soon?' she asked, pinching a sausage from Stark's plate and taking a semi-suggestive bite.

'Why do I think I'm not going to like this?' wondered Fran.

'Because you're a classic glass-half-empty personality. Rather than being relieved that our streets might be rid of one nasty little oik, you're more inclined to be peeved at the death of your prime suspect.'

10

Fran put down her half-empty coffee mug. 'He's dead?'

'As the proverbial doornail,' confirmed Maggie, with unseemly pleasure. 'Assuming Sergeant Clark knows a stiff when he sees one. Manager at the Pavilion teahouse spotted the body behind the bandstand about twenty minutes ago. Clark recognized him, of course. SOCO are already on the way. DCI Groombridge took the news stoically but I thought you'd like to know before he comes in here with that dark look of his. Nice sausage, sweetie.' She winked at Stark and sashayed off.

Groombridge's look was indeed dark. They took the stairs rather than wait for the lift, and the speed of his gait and the way he thrust the doors aside gave further evidence of his frustration. As they crossed the lobby a heated exchange was taking place between the desk officer and a dishevelled drunk with a thick, greying beard, old army boots and a burgundy bobble hat. It seemed to revolve around whether or not he should be allowed to bring the shopping trolley containing his worldly possessions into the lobby or leave it outside.

'There's no need for bad language, sir. I'll be happy to listen to you, but we can't have that in –' The desk officer was trying to guide the man out without touching him.

'Do you wanna 'ear about this or not?' slurred the man, angrily.

'Sir, your belongings will be perfectly safe outside.'

The tramp saw Stark staring. 'Oi! You a blue top? I wanna report a crime.'

'Sir!' persisted the desk officer.

'I'm a wanted man. I'm 'ere to turn m'self in!' He held out his hands, wrists together to be cuffed. 'Oi, come back!'

St Mary's Gate was just a few hundred metres away so they left on foot, Stark struggling to keep up and silently cursing. For some reason he looked back in time to see the tramp being ejected into the street. The man sighed visibly, shoulders slumped. Maybe it was the lack of ranting and gesticulation, the resignation, that caught Stark's eye or perhaps it was something else: the man just didn't behave quite like your average street drunk.

'Keep up, Constable,' called Fran.

'Can I catch you up, Sarge? I just want to see what this is about.' There was something familiar.

'Take your time,' meaning 'Don't'.

Stark stared towards the station as the man pushed his trolley back down the ramp. An articulated lorry trundled thunderously past and a nearby car tooted its horn. A knot of kids shrieked and yelled. The sun broke through the clouds and reflected dazzlingly off a half-open window. Something about these overlapping sensory inputs narrowed Stark's focus. Not a flashback, more a merging of worlds. He could smell the sharp tang of age-old desiccation. The hairs on the back of his neck stood up.

'Stark!' Fran. Impatient. The moment slipped from Stark's grasp, like a cheated memory. Shaking his head, he hurried after his masters.

It was a climb to the upper plateau of Greenwich Park, past the Royal Observatory, to where the bandstand stood, a short distance off one of the main paths. Sergeant Clark and the same young constable stood guard over the outer cordon, tape flapping loosely between trees and traffic cones. SOCOs were busy inside. The sergeant's face was grim as he stared at the corpse on the small strip of tarmac at the back of the bandstand. Kyle Gibbs stared back through lifeless eyes.

Groombridge sighed. 'Nice boots, Tony.'

Clark looked down at the blue wellingtons. 'They'll have to let me keep them if this carries on. I'm down to my third best shoes now.'

'The price of being the legendary Sergeant Clark, the first man they call when they find a body. What have you got for us today, then?'

'Face battered and bruised, knife poking out his back, sir. An ugly end to an ugly life.'

'Poetic injustice,' suggested Groombridge. 'Jones again?' He jerked his head towards the blue-booted rookie.

'Not his lucky week,' muttered Clark. 'To his credit, he wasn't sick this time.'

Groombridge glanced at Stark, who pretended not to notice. 'All right, Clark, take Jones for a cuppa in the Pavilion, and get a statement from the manager.'

'Got a preliminary statement here, sir.'

'Tea plus cake for you both, then, on me.'

'Thank you, sir.' Clark took the proffered tenner, winked at Stark and beckoned to the unfortunate PC Jones.

Marcus Turner was already passing through transition and took his time looking over the body with the CSM. When he was done he wandered over, his face grave. 'Ah, DCI Groombridge. Which should sadden us more – young life truncated or Lady Justice cheated?'

'Marcus.' Groombridge nodded.

'DS Millhaven. And young Stark. Three murders to investigate now, in at the dirty end.'

'Darkness dogs our steps indeed,' said Groombridge. 'First impressions?'

'Preliminary, of course.'

'Of course.'

'At this stage suppositions are few. There's a wallet in his inside jacket pocket, suggesting this wasn't a mugging, unless the killer spooked and abandoned their spoils, and the grass around appears scuffed as if by multiple persons. The only blood appears to be the pool beneath the body but I'll let you know. Body position suggests it hasn't been moved. Cause of death probably stabbing but marks to the face and throat suggest at least the possibility of other fatal trauma. Body temperature places time of death between one and five but I'll narrow that down. I'll remove the knife during autopsy but from the handle it's clearly a modern flick-knife, one of those with the index-finger hole for better grip. If I had to guess I'd say multiple persons left the scene diagonally across the grass there towards the Flower Garden. I'll wander that way with the CSM for a look-see.'

'Look out for lager cans – Tennent's Super,' said Stark, earning a look from Fran – speak when spoken to.

Turner smiled, polite enough to be told how to suck eggs by a fool. 'All too common a poison, I fear.'

Fran watched him go. 'Internal gang squabble?'

'Or inter-gang,' mused Groombridge.

'We stopped a fight between them and another group when I was patrolling with uniform in my first week,' said Stark, and described the incident. 'Names were taken.'

'Really?' Groombridge pursed his lips. 'And you think Gibbs was carrying a knife?'

'Just a hunch, Guv. I didn't see one.'

'There's only one knife at the scene,' said Fran. 'So far,' she added, gesturing at Turner's receding form.

'Too many possibilities as usual.' Groombridge looked at Stark and forced a smile. 'Don't worry, it always starts like this, flapping in the wind. Don't let yourself get used to it. Frustration is the detective's sustenance.'

'Shall we round up the usuals, Guv?' asked Fran.

'I suppose.' Groombridge didn't sound enthusiastic. 'What's left of them. Get Harper on to it.'

'Maybe one or all of the faithless little shits will finger Kyle for everything now,' she offered cheerily, 'while continuing to deny involvement themselves.'

'If only . . .' Groombridge responded. 'Stark, get one of the DCs and go to Lewisham A-and-E. Ask about admissions or treatment for knife wounds or fights, and tell Harper to send someone to the Queen Elizabeth. Fran, wait and see if Marcus can give us anything else.'

'What about you, Guv?'

Groombridge stared at the body. 'Get someone from Family Liaison to pick me up here. I'd better break the news to his mother.'

Dixon volunteered to go with Stark and they got chatting on the way. 'Why does the guv'nor keep giving Sergeant Clark money?'

Dixon laughed. 'They go way back, started as constables the same day. The way I've heard it the guv'nor wanted to go career uniform like his dad, but Clark reckoned CID would find a way to poach him.'

'And they bet on it.' Stark grinned.

'It's been their tradition ever since. Last one to the body buys tea and cake. It's for the rookies, really.'

The A&E receptionist was as unhelpful as she was casually uncaring to the walking wounded queuing before her throne. 'Wait over there.'

'This is an urgent police matter,' insisted Dixon.

'Someone will help you as soon as they're free.'

And that was that: her attention was gone. Stark was feeling the effects of an early start, interrupted breakfast and too much walking, and had already met all the self-anointed hospital deities he could stomach. 'Excuse me,' he called politely to the amassed host looking busy behind the goddess. 'Would one of you mind taking over from your colleague here? She's about to be arrested for obstructing a murder investigation.'

A little shockwave of silence expanded from him. Dixon froze. The goddess looked indignant, then slowly her faith buckled. 'How can I help you?'

'By telling us who was sitting in your chair between one and five this morning.'

'That would have been me,' said a woman, coming out of a side door pulling on her coat.

She looked dog tired but amused, and listened intently. 'Yes, we had some last night, we almost always do. I'll get the list but that injury-type give false names as often as not.'

'I have some photos,' said Stark, pulling out photocopies he'd made.

Nothing matched. They scanned reception CCTV but Stark didn't recognize any faces from the Meridian pub altercation.

'I'm not sure we're allowed to threaten people like that,' said Dixon, on the way back to the station.

Stark smiled. 'Ignorance is bliss.'

Harper came up blank too, but didn't let that smother his glee at having most of the gang back in the cells. 'Couldn't find Tyler Wantage. Colin Messenger is at his granny's house in Dartford according to his mum, and there's no answer at Naveen Hussein's flat. I'm trying to track down his mum.'

'Did you tell them why they're here?' asked Groombridge.

Harper grinned. 'Saved that for you, Guv.'

Groombridge puffed out his cheeks and blew. His lack of enthusiasm proved justified. The interviews progressed at the usual monotonous pace. Ordered to sit in once more, Stark was in awe of the guv'nor's patience.

'Once we got past the usual monosyllabic posturing and whining about police harassment they all stuck to their earlier statements regarding the assault on Alfred Ladd and the killing of Stacey Appleton,' Groombridge reported to the team. 'And they all have parent-clad alibis for last night – they went drink-ing in Greenwich, supped up at eleven, went straight home and were all tucked up asleep by midnight, like good little girls and boys. When I asked about Kyle they all said he'd got separated somewhere.'

'Nikki again?' suggested Fran. 'She's had all night to put the frighteners on them.'

Groombridge was clearly already thinking this. 'She never shed a tear for her boyfriend. The rest maintained some sem-blance of shock when confronted with the news of Kyle's death but she just lapsed into indifference.'

'She's a cold little bitch,' agreed Fran. Others nodded.

Groombridge clicked his tongue in irritation. 'I should've had them all locked in the cells days ago. We'd still be looking at *one* death instead of *four*.'

'Don't beat yourself up, Guv,' said Harper. 'You couldn't have known.' Stark couldn't decide if the man was being syco-phantic or merely stating the obvious. Groombridge just grunted. 'No one's going to give much of a shit about this lot, Guv,' added Harper. 'They obviously don't even give a shit about each other.'

'Naveen seemed to,' said Stark, 'about Stacey.'

'Crocodile tears,' said Harper, who'd not been there.

Groombridge stood and looked at his watch. 'Well, maybe a night in the cells will shake their resolve. Owen, nip down the Meridian and talk to the landlady, see if they really were in there,' he said to Harper. 'Then come and find us in Rosie's.'

There were groans from those left to man the graveyard shift. Stark suppressed his own, knowing he couldn't excuse himself a second time. Even the walk up the hill to the Com-pass Rose made him grit his teeth. Christ, was this what he'd come to?

Harper swaggered in while they were still being served at the bar. 'The landlady of the Meridian confirmed that the

Ferrier Rats were in, Guv, or some of them, but she wasn't sure when or for how long.'

Groombridge didn't look all that surprised.

'We could try phone traces again,' suggested Harper.

Groombridge nodded disconsolately. He and Fran soon retreated to their regular table, deep in conversation. Harper propped up the bar with DC Bryden and a handful of cronies, while Stark and the remaining DCs waited to play doubles pool. People made the effort to put a dark day behind them, but it *was* an effort, you could tell. Stark managed to nab a bar stool but he was struggling. When faces began slipping away early, he quietly did the same.

His route took him back downhill past the station. On the far side of the street a tramp limped in the opposite direction, pushing his trolley and muttering drunkenly. It'd been such a long day that Stark almost failed to associate the shuffling, rattling shape with the ranting madman in the station that morning. Poor old sod, he thought, wondering where the man was going, where he would be sleeping tonight. He stopped, fished in his pocket and pulled out a ten-pound note, plus change. It would have to do. He saw the old man bump the trolley up the kerb outside the station and push it determinedly up the ramp – looking for a quiet night sleeping it off in the cells, Stark thought, and Mick seemed just the kind of custody sergeant to offer shelter. Then he frowned: the tramp was struggling, favouring one side . . .

The cheated memory from earlier crashed back into his consciousness, mocking his stupidity. The cash dropped from his hand as he began to run, sprinting across the road, holding out one palm to the car that screeched to a halt, the shocked driver thumping his horn furiously, and across the station's small front car park. The tramp had stopped near the top of the ramp, grasping the railing with one hand. Stark charged at the point where the ramp dog-legged halfway up and vaulted the railings unthinkingly, landing on his left leg and driving a jarring jolt of pain through his bad hip, which sent him tumbling. The tramp turned and looked down at him, perplexed. Stark rolled upright with a grunt just in time to catch the old man as he fell, guiding his weight safely to the ground.

'Where is it?' Stark demanded.

'Piss off!'

Stark could have kicked himself. He should've seen it that morning. The pallor, the sweat, the stiffness, the boots, the clothing, the vocabulary. 'Don't fuck with me, soldier, you're no good dead! Where are you hit?' He felt round the man's limbs and torso.

The tramp's feeble struggling subsided. 'Little prick was quicker than he looked.'

'Here?' A squeeze of the man's upper right arm elicited a wince. Not enough for the way he'd moved, despite the drink. 'Where else?'

'You ain't no medic.'

The desk officer was standing over them now. 'Ambulance, now!' barked Stark.

'Don't want no fucking ambulance!'

'Too bad.' Stark's hand pressed against the man's lower left abdomen and this time the wince came with a groan. There was a slash in the jacket, unnoticed among the general disintegration. They locked eyes. 'Show me!' The man tried to roll away but Stark pinned him. 'Show me or bleed out. It's your choice, soldier!'

'All right, all right!' The tramp lifted his jacket. The various layers beneath were stained with blood. He pulled them up to reveal a yellowing medical dressing held in place with black gaffer tape. Blood was leaching through. 'Kept me old field kit, just in case. Can't be too . . .' He belched. 'Behind enemy lines. Stitched 'em up myself. Arm's just a nick, but little fucker got the point in here.'

'This needs looking at now.'

'I ain't going to no fucking hospital!'

'We'll let the paramedics decide that, shall we?' said Stark. 'What's your name?' The man tried to get up, but Stark held him down. 'Name, soldier!'

'Maggs, Harry Maggs, corporal, serial number five nine seven . . . something. Now piss off and let me –'

'Lie still.'

'Piss off!'

'Who was quicker than he looked? Have a little run-in with some delinquents in the park last night, did we?'

'At last!' cried the tramp, holding out his hands, wrists together, just as he had that morning. 'A blue top with ears!'

Stark sat near the ICU nursing station at Lewisham University Hospital, yawning and rubbing his eyes. God, he hated hospitals. Footsteps clipped to a halt beside him and he looked up.

'Dinner,' said Fran, handing him a packet of crisps. She must've come straight from the pub. She sat in the next chair and opened her own. 'Bit tasteless, reading him his rights in the ambulance?' She smirked. 'I like it.'

'He actually seemed relieved,' said Stark, opening his packet and staring at the meagre contents.

'Feather in your cap. The guv might not be so happy, though. Nice juicy murder and he doesn't get his name on the arrest sheet.'

'It won't go to murder, though, will it?'

Fran shrugged. 'Knife in the back is pretty suggestive of intent.'

'But Maggs has two knife wounds himself. He's in surgery.'

'Did you get a statement?'

'The paramedics and doctors shut me out before I could get anything coherent.'

'Probably for the best. Gives the defence less chance to argue duress.'

'But CPS will call it self-defence, though, don't you think?'

Fran shook her head. 'Manslaughter maybe, but they do love reaching for the stars ... He really stitch himself up?'

'Not very well. I've never seen angry paramedics before.'

'They teach you that in the army too?'

'Up to a point. Field dressing, tourniquet, compression,

CPR and the rest, but you're supposed to leave the needle-and-thread stuff for the field hospital unless you have to.'

'Have to?'

'If the helicopters can't get you to the field hospital quickly.'

'Not enough helicopters.'

Like most 'common knowledge', this was partially correct. Circumstance played just as much a part as availability. You could only ask a helicopter crew to put themselves, the onboard medical team and protection party in so much danger because you had a hole in you. If your position was still hairy with enemy contact you needed to move, or wait.

'What happened with you?' asked Fran.

'I was lucky.' If he'd had to wait he'd have died.

'Well, our suspect isn't going anywhere. The guv sent PC Barclay here to take over guard duty, plus this arrest sheet for you to fill in and a uniform car outside with orders to take us both home so we're fresh as daisies first thing in the morning. I'm sure he'll be ready to congratulate you by then.'

The guv'nor's congratulations consisted of an early start and a shitty assignment. Forensics had taken Maggs's outer garments but the ripe layers beneath had arrived from the hospital. He might not be in the cells but Maggs was in police custody and his belongings were in their trust. Stark was to help Mick catalogue it all. Another tick in Stark's Professional Development Portfolio. If Groombridge relished assigning him a thankless, smelly task, he knew even less about army life than Stark suspected. The trolley would be dropped back round to the supermarket; everything else had to be carefully described, bagged, labelled and stored. Stark was amused to find an army hexamine stove, the bane and blessing of many a bitter moorland exercise. He also found a battered Swiss Army penknife, the blades and tools showing signs of heavy use, plus a sharpening stone. There were signs of old blood on the blade. Stark labelled it for testing.

He was folding a foul-smelling pair of thermal leggings when he felt something. There was a crudely stitched U-shape, a secret pocket; once upon a time it had been a common way of concealing personal effects in case of capture. He reached in and pulled out a small bag made from the threadbare toes of a drab-olive sock, stitched closed.

'Found something?' asked Mick. Stark showed him. 'Open it up, then.'

Stark hesitated. It felt invasive. Mick passed him some scissors and Stark pulled himself together. He was police again: he'd pounded beats, stopped and searched, catalogued belongings many times. It was time to get his head back in the game. He carefully snipped open the stitches and tipped out a neatly folded waxed-paper parcel on to the plastic tray.

Inside were three medals.

Stark recognized two as campaign medals: the General Service Medal, with a Northern Ireland clasp on its purple and green ribbon, and the South Atlantic Medal, with its beautiful sea-green, white and empire blue ribbon embellished with a little silver rosette, indicating that Maggs had muddied his boots. Stark had two: the Iraq Medal and the Operational Services Medal (Afghanistan clasp), both ribbons bordered in sand brown. They were in their little boxes in a drawer at his mum's. She pretended she wanted never to see them again, part of his ongoing penance, but he knew she took them whenever she visited his dad's grave. He wished he didn't know that.

So Maggs had done his bit. Like most servicemen Stark was slightly in awe of Falklands veterans. They'd fought and won far from home in shitty conditions, outnumbered, under-resourced, ill-equipped and undermined by years of politically motivated cutbacks. Northern Ireland was no stroll in the park either.

The third medal sparked a memory. Stark's drill sergeant at Chilwell had worn one like it at Stark's passing out, he was sure, but the drill sergeant was not a man to invite enquiry. It had a red, white and blue striped ribbon and the Queen's profile, and the wording on the reverse side read 'FOR BRAVERY IN THE FIELD'. This was no campaign medal.

As soon as they'd finished he rushed upstairs and searched online. The answer came quickly. The Military Medal, awarded for 'acts of gallantry and devotion to duty under fire'. He'd not recognized it because it had been discontinued in 1993 when they finally stopped differentiating between bravery in officers and bravery in the ranks. Since that time all ranks had been eligible for the Military Cross, previously for officers only.

Stark stared at the screen for several seconds, picturing the Maggs he'd met. More research revealed only thirty-three awarded for the Falklands conflict, ten naval, twenty-three army. Oddly though, no H. Maggs was listed, only a Corporal A. Maggs, 2 Para. Either Harry wasn't his real name or the medal belonged to a relative. The former seemed more likely.

He tried to tell Fran when she bustled in but she cut him off. 'Where the hell have you been, the meeting starts in two minutes – and what's that *smell*?'

Stark explained.

'Who sent you down there?'

Stark opened his mouth to reply but stopped. DS Harper had sent him, relaying, he said, DCI Groombridge's orders. Sniggering broke out across the office and Stark closed his eyes. Cataloguing property was a legitimate task, for a *uniformed* constable; he simply hadn't questioned it.

Fran smirked. 'Did they tell you to drop by Supplies for some left-handed handcuffs too?'

'Bastards,' said Stark, firmly, smiling wryly.

Sniggering became outright laughter. Harper was doubled over, almost crying.

'Children.' Fran rolled her eyes and slapped a sheet of paper on Stark's desk. 'Preliminary pathologist's report. I persuaded my contact to email me an advance copy.'

Stark wondered if 'persuaded' was how Marcus would describe it.

'The autopsy leaves cause of death open to some interpretation. It says the knife in Kyle's back certainly contributed, but the blow to his windpipe might have killed him too. They won't know till they've completed all the tests.' She looked at Stark for some kind of reaction but he didn't know what she wanted him to say. 'Still looking like a murder charge, I reckon.'

'I suppose so.'

'You suppose nothing of the kind,' said Groombridge, entering the room. Stark was beginning to suspect the man of deliberately hovering in doorways. 'We've got some corners of the jigsaw, but we're a long way from a picture.'

'Guv.'

'Chin up, Trainee Investigator. You collared your first killer last night.' Harper smirked. 'We'll get the arrest sheet framed – you can give it to your mum.'

'Right.' Groombridge clapped his hands together. 'DS Millhaven's illicitly gained pathology update has narrowed the time of death to between one and four a.m. We've got nothing on the phone-location traces as per usual. The graveyard shift scanned through CCTV . . . We have the gang leaving the pub at eleven twenty and heading up towards the park. Parks CCTV shows figures climbing in via St Mary's Gate, just like before, and just like before we've nothing showing them leaving or travelling home. I've got . . .' he checked his watch '. . . six hours or so until I should start letting our guests go home. We'll take another crack at them, see if we can persuade one of the delightful little sods to turn on the others, but our main hope of shedding any light on Kyle Gibbs's unfortunate demise is Harry Maggs. Minor surgery to repair his insides, awake and unhappy with his care, apparently. Docs say he should be fit to interview today. What do we know about him?'

'Sweet FA, Guv,' replied Fran. 'I've checked. No Harry Maggs on the crime register, the MoD deny all knowledge and, according to Google, he's either an octogenarian silver surfer from California or a student in Bath.'

Stark smothered a laugh.

'Something amusing about that, Stark?' asked Groombridge.

'Harry probably isn't his real name, Guv. Army nickname more likely – Dirty Harry, Dirty Maggs as in porn magazines. It would be something around the word Grot now, but back in the eighties . . .' Conscious all eyes were on him, Stark explained about the medal and the initial A. 'Given his antipathy to the world around him, it's not that surprising he'd lie.'

'And when did you discover this?' asked Fran, tersely.

'This morning.' He wasn't in the right forum to add that he'd tried to tell her already: he was getting enough sideways looks without that. Harper muttered something about Miss Marple.

'Very amusing, DS Harper,' said Groombridge. 'Why don't you get on the radio to whoever is preventing our comedian doing a bunk and get me a real name? I'd like to know who I'm interviewing at the very least.'

Stark and others spent the morning on phones, trying to corroborate or undermine the string of alibis and denials that had emerged from the previous day's exchanges. They weren't getting far. The mothers, fathers, stepfathers or mothers' boyfriends were proving elusive and uncooperative. The ones Stark spoke to either didn't care or freely admitted giving up. Some became abusive. Stark quickly became despondent. Days of punishment had left his hip throbbing into the night. The morning dragged and he had to fight it off with coffee and a bacon roll.

'Do you ever stop eating?' demanded Fran.

'Have you ever considered decaf?'

'*Touché.*' She sipped from her steaming mug. 'Thought you'd like to know that your arrestee is ready for questioning. I'm heading up there with the guv'nor now.'

'Did uniform come back with a name?'

'Several. All of them derogatory.'

The bacon roll only got him so far. Lunch could not come quickly enough but, first, the unwelcome break. Another day, another hospital: the Queen Elizabeth, and the interminable Dr Hazel McDonald.

'You look tired,' she said.

'I may have mentioned that once or twice before myself,' replied Stark.

'More tired, then. Has something happened?'

'Nothing I can discuss in detail,' said Stark.

She raised an eyebrow, probably thinking her professional code should excuse some relaxation in his. It was a grey area. 'I heard something on the news. More killings?'

'Two.' He rubbed his eyes. 'You might have thought my past would've inured me to new horrors.'

'The first, the old vagrant, made you angry, you said. These new ones?'

Stark looked away. 'A teenage girl. Made me sick and guilty and . . .'

'And?'

Stark thought of telling her about the flashback and barely keeping a lid on his reaction in the mortuary, and about Stacey's mother, but she would seize on it, let it distract her. The thought of her jack-hammering was too awful to contemplate. Perhaps when he wasn't so tired.

'Why guilty, then?' she asked.

'I put the spotlight on her. She might've been killed for it.'

'Are you sure you're not inflating your responsibility?'

Again, she meant. She didn't understand guilt. She thought it was something to be negotiated, compartmentalized and moved beyond. She didn't understand its value. Remorse should be held close as both recompense and warning. 'Perhaps.'

'And the third?'

'Teenage boy. Some might say he had it coming.'

'What would you say?'

'He was a casualty of his own war.'

'You feel indifferent?'

'That's not what I said.'

'Then what did you mean?'

'Look, Doc, with all due respect, could we just focus on the actual problem?'

'Which is?'

Stark bit down on his retort. 'Sleep. I just want to sleep. If you can't help with that, then what are we doing here?'

Hazel tilted her head in her calculated manner, thoughtful, reassuring, depressing. 'You have a prescription for Zopiclone. Do you use it?'

'Dire need only, doctor's orders.' Headley Court cautioned against prolonged use. Among the potential side effects were dependency and depression, two dangers Headley patients faced already.

'Define dire need.'

Stark glanced at the clock but the ponderous second hand offered no quarter.

He had just got back and was heading to the canteen for a late lunch when Dixon intercepted him. 'Guv's on the line for you, not in a patient mood.'

Stark stared mournfully at him and took the phone.

'Stark, get your arse up here in the next twenty minutes or you'll be back in uniform till hell freezes over!'

'Of course, Guv. Is there a problem?'

'Yes, there *is* a chuffing problem! Not only will this bearded git still not tell me his real name but he also insists he will only speak to you. I'm choosing not to quote him verbatim for fear of offending your innocent sensibilities. I'm sure you have a rational explanation for this but I can't hear what you're saying because you're no longer on the phone to me. You're already on your way here at the closest thing to a dead run your dicky hip will allow.'

Stark felt as if he was trapped in some terrible game of hospital hokey-cokey. Maggie got him a lift to Lewisham, taking the opportunity to call him 'sweetie' again. He might have to address that before the rest of the station joined in. His tramp round the hospital in search of the police suite put a sufficient sheen of sweat on his brow to satisfy the DCI that he *had* run. He thought longingly of food, and the pills he'd not taken. Fran frowned at his appearance and stepped outside to watch proceedings on the monitor. Like most, Lewisham Hospital had a dedicated police room equipped with interview-recording equipment.

Stark settled into the chair next to Groombridge, who switched on the camera.

'Interview continued with suspect calling himself Harry Maggs, twelve twenty-five, Saturday, May the sixteenth, 2009, police interview room, Lewisham University Hospital. Present, Harry Maggs, DCI Groombridge, Dr Hassife Shamir and arresting officer Constable Joseph Stark. The suspect has been read his rights in full and confirmed his understanding of same. The suspect is detained pending charge relating to the death of Kyle Gibbs. The suspect has been offered legal counsel and refused. Mr Maggs, can you please confirm your full name?'

Maggs stirred but said nothing, glaring at Stark.

'You have been officially made aware of your rights, Mr

Maggs. Silence will not work in your favour. Is your name Harry Maggs, yes or no?'

'Get him to ask me.' The jerk of Maggs's head indicated Stark.

Groombridge made an after-you gesture at Stark, with a look of displeasure.

'Dirty Harry,' said Stark. 'Am I right?' Maggs stared, sizing him up. 'Dirty Maggs, army nickname?' Maggs's stare continued and Stark waited. Some people couldn't let a silence go unfilled, though he suspected Maggs probably wasn't among them. He was about to press on when Maggs appeared to make his mind up.

'Harry to my mates,' he said gruffly. 'Alan to the likes of you.'

'Alan Maggs. Any middle names?'

'Corporal. Five nine seven two six four five three.'

'Date of birth?'

'Find out for yerself, Blue Top.'

'We will,' said Groombridge. 'Interview suspended twelve twenty-nine.' He switched off the camera.

'Wait, I haven't said what happened yet. You got me wheeled all the way over here to listen to what I have t'say!'

'No. We got you wheeled all the way over here to find out who you are and what you did. And we'll get you wheeled all the way over here again once I'm satisfied with the first half of that question. And we'll keep getting you wheeled all the way over here till I'm satisfied you've answered all my questions in a truthful and co-operative manner.'

'That's enough, Inspector,' said Dr Shamir, seeing Maggs go red with anger, gripping his side in pain.

'Yes, it is,' agreed Groombridge. 'We'll pick this up again later today, Mr Maggs.' He stood and stalked out. Stark followed and outside found Groombridge casually watching the monitor with Fran. There was no sign of anger on his face.

Stark realized he'd just witnessed a piece of theatrical bullying, carefully applied just after the recording equipment was turned off.

'Are we not here for a statement, Guv?' asked Fran, warily.

'Change of tactic. He's not taking this seriously. We need to gain the higher ground. Isn't that right, Stark?'

'Guv.'

Groombridge gave him a long look.

'And the Ferrier Rats?' asked Fran, pointing to the clock.

'Spring them. Let them think they're in the clear, for now. I'm tired of being given the run-around. Let's get Maggs's history and come back armed. Come on then, Trainee Investigator, this is your area of expertise. Time to investigate.'

12

Theoretically the Ministry of Defence was as beholden as any other employer to provide the records of employees past and present. In reality their fastidious bureaucracy could drown any obligation. Knowing his two stripes wouldn't get him far, Stark started from the position that he was calling on direct behalf of Superintendent Cox. It was entirely possible this would land him in the shit, but he had inexperience and low rank to hide behind and, technically, it was true. Even so it was painful, bouncing from one low-ranking bureaucratic clone to the next, his misery compounded by hunger. But then a breakthrough: 'My superior will be back at fifteen hundred hours,' was the best and final offer from the last official, but the man made the error of giving Stark his name and direct number. This blunder revisited him at 15.01, then again at 15.15, 15.30 and 15.45. At 16.00 he lost his temper and hung up, at 16.15 he demanded Stark stop calling but Stark politely reiterated the vital urgency of the matter to his commanding officer, slipping in the fraternal underling card. At 16.29 the brother-underling phoned Stark. A copy of Maggs's service record had been emailed, now piss off, was the gist.

Stark took the printout to Groombridge, who was on the phone but waved him in. 'Yes, sir. In fact he's just appeared before me. I'll ask him now,' he said, hanging up. Stark's stomach growled in the ensuing silence. Groombridge raised an eyebrow. 'That was Superintendent Cox. He's curious to know why he received a call from a Ministry of Defence official complaining about harassment. Have you been claiming our leader's authority in your dealings, Constable?'

'Yes, Guv.' When the game's up, 'fess up.

'Did it work?'

'That, and making a nuisance of myself, Guv.' Stark handed over the printout.

Groombridge scanned the front page. 'Hmm, then the super can sleep at night, knowing he corroborated your base-less claims in a just cause.' He gestured Stark to sit while he read on. When he'd finished he pushed it to one side, leant back in his chair and considered Stark over steepled fingers. 'So, Trainee Investigator, are you going to tell me just what kind of shit you're in?'

Stark blinked. 'Guv?'

'Don't play dumb, Constable. The super received two calls of complaint this morning, both about you, both from the Ministry of Defence, yet apparently unrelated. The other call was, if anything, angrier and delivered from higher up. You stand accused of "failing to co-operate with a matter of the utmost seriousness".'

Had the caller said what it was? There was no subtle way to ask. Groombridge paused, which might mean he hoped Stark would explain. Stark said nothing.

'I can only imagine this relates to your avoidance of calls from one Captain Pierson, and subsequent public disagree-ment with her outside this very station.'

Stark was mortified: he had hoped the incident was forgot-ten. Was the whole bloody station discussing this? At least it seemed Groombridge didn't know more. Did Cox?

'You may be pleased to know that the super doesn't respond well to bullying. He told the caller to . . . Well, I'll leave that to your imagination, but the essential point was that this seemed a matter between the caller and you.'

Stark just managed not to sigh with relief.

'I, however, disagree,' added Groombridge, a menacing nuance in his tone. His eyes bored into Stark, unblinking. 'I need to know if this affects my case. So will the CPS. We need to know if you can be put on the stand or if you're . . . tainted.' A word with broad scope and nothing but the worst connotations.

'It's just a procedural matter, Guv. The army dotting *i*s and crossing *t*s.'

Groombridge's eyes narrowed. 'Constable Stark, if you think I can't spot a half-truth a half-mile off, think again.'

'It's complicated, Guv, but nothing to trouble you or the CPS.' What else could he say?

'I'm not big on secrets. I'll get to the truth.'

'It's just the usual military-level misunderstanding. It'll be sorted soon.'

'So you're not in trouble?'

'Only officers get into trouble. Enlisted men just do what they're told.'

Groombridge didn't smile at the joke. 'You'll have to do better than that.'

Stark cursed inwardly. Cornered, he made himself meet Groombridge's eyes. What he was about to say was not the kind of thing anyone should have to tell their boss, especially two weeks into a new job. 'I'm sorry, Guv, but I'm not at liberty to discuss it.'

Groombridge stared fiercely at him for several seconds. 'Then I suppose I cannot ask you to.' He was plainly vexed. Stark's profound relief proved short-lived. 'But,' added Groombridge, 'the CPS *will*, make no mistake. They'll want to interview you, in detail.' He paused, perhaps to see if Stark might spontaneously confess. 'Well, we'll put that aside for now.' He picked up the printout again.

That, it seemed, was that . . . for now. Stark's mouth was dry.

Groombridge tapped the page. 'This Military Medal. Big one, is it?'

'Big enough, Guv.'

'Hmm. Right. Let's go and see what he's got to say for himself. Maybe we can put your irreverent mood to good use.'

Groombridge made no allowance for Stark's limp, marching into the hospital at his usual brisk pace, which Fran matched with ease and Stark did not. On an average day Stark might applaud, but not today. When they arrived at the police rooms he felt sick. Fran took up station by the monitor, assessing him, catlike, coolly amused. Groombridge opened the door.

Maggs, still in dressing-gown and wheelchair, looked up as they entered. 'And I thought *I* was in bad shape.' He smirked at Stark.

Groombridge switched on the camera and ran through the spiel, then placed his plastic folder on the table, opened it and scanned it slowly. 'Alan Thomas Maggs, born June the thirteenth 1961,' he read aloud.

'Done your homework, then,' said Maggs, unimpressed.

'No fixed abode.'

'That what we're calling it, is it?'

'You prefer homeless?'

'What about street-person? Or down-and-out? Itinerant? Vagrant, vagabond, hobo, tramp, bum, dosser, drunk?'

'We'll put that down as a yes, then,' said Groombridge, evenly. 'You continue to decline legal counsel at this time?'

'What would be the point?'

'Another yes, then.' Groombridge smiled. Maggs affected not to care. 'Corporal, 2 Para. Wounded in the battle for Wireless Ridge, June the thirteenth 1982, not the happiest twenty-first birthday,' observed Groombridge, without irony.

'Made a man of me,' replied Maggs, coldly.

'Honourable discharge, September 1982.' Maggs said nothing. 'Fallen on hard times, Corporal?'

Maggs's stare darkened. 'Mister to you.'

'Mental scars, were there? To match the physical ones?'

'Ask the army docs.'

'We will.'

Maggs huffed. 'Good luck with that.'

Groombridge looked at Stark and gave a barely perceptible nod. Stark still wasn't too happy about this, but if the button had to be pressed, better it was by him. 'Worse day for some of your mates, was it?' he said, observing Maggs closely.

Maggs returned his stare and lifted his head a little. 'Know something about that, would you?'

Stark didn't deny it. Groombridge leant into the mike. 'For the record, Constable Stark is recently Corporal Stark of Her Majesty's Armed Forces.'

'Jack? Figured you for a Rupert,' said Maggs. 'Infantry?'

'Princess of Wales's Royals, 3rd Battalion.'

'Tigers, eh? 3rd Battalion?'

'Territorial.' Stark braced for the inevitable.

Maggs laughed sarcastically, 'Fucking STAB?' He shook his head. 'What's the matter, *Weekender*? Regular Crap Hats not good enough for you?'

STAB. Not exactly a term of endearment, it was an old name the regulars used to show how much they appreciated their part-time counterpart. It stood for Stupid TA Bastards. Weekender was another. Both were in less common use since the 1999 Strategic Defence Review ushered the TA into regular deployment, and into shape. Crap Hats was what elite units, like Maggs's Parachute Regiment, with their natty burgundy berets, called ordinary infantry with their standard khaki ones. Maggs was asking why he hadn't gone full time in the regulars. 'I considered it,' Stark replied.

'Before or after deployment?' scoffed Maggs.

'After.'

That shut him up. 'Iraq?' Maggs asked, after a pause. Stark nodded. 'Whining bitch. Least you had it warm!'

Stark smiled. 'You poor-me South Seas girls with your handbags. Try minus twenty at night, plus fifty in the day and then whinge about how much your Bergen weighs.'

For the first time a genuine smile touched Maggs's lips, wrinkling his eyes above his thick beard. 'That where you got the limp?'

He doesn't miss much, thought Stark. 'That was later. Afghanistan.' Stark held his stare.

'Bullet or bomb?'

'Bit of both.'

'Hurts, doesn't it?'

Stark didn't need to respond.

Groombridge obviously decided the ice was broken. 'What's a war hero like you doing like . . . this?' he asked.

Maggs stiffened, smile gone. He looked at Stark. 'What's a "war hero" like you doing with . . . *this*?' he sneered.

'Let's leave labels aside for now, shall we?' said Stark. 'I'll take a guess. Wounded in the line, shipped home, patched up, tossed out on your arse. No job, no useful qualifications, no support.'

Maggs pursed his lips. 'Tried security work. Didn't suit. You've done all right though. Flash tosser. Kept a boot in both camps, though, didn't you?'

'Let's talk about Kyle Gibbs,' said Groombridge, firmly.

'That his name, was it?'

'Whose name?'

'Well, Detective Chief Inspector, I assume you wanted to ask me about the lad you found dead, but if this is about your wife, then, yes, I confess, she was with me, all night . . . *long*.'

Stark managed not to guffaw. Maybe it was just his imagination but he might've sworn he heard Fran laugh outside.

Groombridge frowned. 'OK. Why don't you tell me what happened?'

'I was great, she was crap. Out of practice, apparently, said you couldn't get it up any more, but she promised she'd try harder next time. Gotta love fat ugly women – so eager to please.' This time Stark definitely heard a hoot outside.

'Prior to your arrest, you claimed to Constable Stark here that you wanted to turn yourself in for the killing of Kyle Gibbs,' said Groombridge, admirably unmoved. 'If you're willing to expand on that, I'd be delighted to hear it. Otherwise we can continue this tomorrow, or the day after, or the day after that. This isn't a missing-persons case. I've got all the time in the world.'

Maggs glared at them both for several seconds. 'I was drunk.'

'Yes, you were. Are you now denying the killing?'

'No.'

'Good, because we have your fingerprints on the weapon and the victim's blood on your hands and clothes.'

'I'll wager you found his prints on the weapon too, though, didn't you?'

They had, of course, but only Maggs's on the handle. Of course, his big hands would have obliterated earlier prints in the blood. He'd held the weapon last. 'Why don't you tell me what happened?'

'He attacked me. We fought. He died.'

'That's your statement?'

'You don't like it?'

'It's a little short on detail.'

'Perhaps you should write it,' replied Maggs. 'Isn't that what you people do?'

'How many people attacked you?'

Maggs's eyes narrowed slightly. 'What makes you think there was more than one?'

'Common sense, experience and forensic science,' said Groombridge, levelly. 'Care to try again?'

Maggs appeared to be considering options. 'Can't we keep this simple?'

133

'A futile wish in my line of work. Why?'

'Defence is a military strategy.'

'Meaning?'

'It's complex. What are you defending, why and from whom? Are you defending something worth dying for, killing for – people, collateral, arms, a position, time? Or are you merely defending your life? What are your resources, armaments, numbers and position relative to the opposing force? Can you hope to be reinforced or relieved? Do you have a path of retreat? All these factors must be assessed and decided upon, sometimes in seconds.'

'What's your point?' asked Groombridge.

'You're not qualified to assess my actions,' said Maggs. 'But he might be.' He jerked his head towards Stark.

'By all means let's see,' agreed Groombridge, conceding the floor to Stark.

'Go on, then,' said Stark, conscious of his governor's irritation.

'OK, Weekender. You're alone, behind enemy lines, surrounded, outnumbered eight to one, cold, hungry. The enemy has shown themselves merciless. Surrender will certainly be met without quarter. They attack. What do you do?'

'Counter-attack.'

'Give the man a medal. Sometimes offence is the best form of defence.'

'Are you claiming Kyle Gibbs attacked you?' asked Groombridge.

Maggs rolled his eyes but Stark interceded: 'It's tedious, I know, but we have to spell these things out for the record – for your good as well as ours. Please answer the questions as clearly as possible.'

Maggs leant in. 'For the record, Kyle Gibbs attacked me.'

'And you stabbed him in self-defence?'

'Defence. Yes.'

'How do you explain stabbing him in the back?' asked Groombridge.

'I couldn't reach his front at the time.'

'You think this is amusing?'

'Do I look like a cold-blooded killer, Detective Inspector?' retorted Maggs.

'It isn't my job to make that assessment.'

'Meaning you're not qualified again. How about you, Constable Weekender?'

'My opinion is irrelevant,' said Stark, warily.

'Is it? Then what are you doing here?'

'You asked for me. Now, are you going to tell us what happened or are we going to have to ask you again tomorrow? This is an interview, not an interrogation, and this isn't wartime. We're policemen, we can't *make* you say anything. You can make your report or shut up. It's your call.'

'For the record,' said Maggs, sarcasm tingeing his gruff voice.

'For the record,' agreed Stark.

Maggs's eyes flitted back and forth between Stark and Groombridge, distrustful. Eventually he leant in again. 'All right. It was a warmish night so I was sleeping. When it's cold it's better to move about at night, sleep in the daytime. But I was sleeping. I heard 'em coming, but yelling and shouting don't mean much to the likes of me, none of my business. Only they don't pass by, they stop. "Oi!" they shout. "Get up", "Lazy fucker" and the like. I ask for some change, or a drink, seems like they've had their share. They tell me to get up but I'm pissed and tired and I can't be arsed.'

'What time was this?'

'Don't know, late. After midnight, before dawn.'

'You can't narrow it down?'

'Well, forgive me, I know I was sleeping at the very home of global timekeeping but I couldn't see the observatory clock through the trees in the dark at three hundred yards.'

'You don't wear a watch?'

'What good is a watch to me? It's just booze you haven't cashed in yet.'

'What about clock bells?' asked Stark.

Maggs looked at him, then sat back thoughtfully, nodding. 'Yeah. Maybe. Next bell I heard might have been two. Couldn't swear to it.'

'OK. So then what?'

'One kicks me. Not hard, more scared, not like he means it. So I get up. They're young, teenagers, you know, dressed up in their stupid tracksuits and their stupid trainers and hats on under their hoods, lads and one girl.' Maggs shook his head. 'Wasn't even raining. Little fuckers wouldn't know about rain. Never sat out a night in their soft lives. Mummy keeps 'em full of fish fingers, wipes their arses and gives 'em video games instead of books. Could all do with a spell of freezing rain and sleet on a cold fucking mountain with the enemy on the high ground' – he looked at Stark – 'or a foot patrol through a desert town where the only difference between the civilians you're there to protect and the shits out to kill you is the blink of an eye. Let them watch their mates bleed out and see if they think their shoot-'em-up video games are so hilarious.'

Groombridge sat back and let him continue.

'Anyway, I try to pick up my stuff, to leave, turn the other cheek and walk away, but they shove me, call me lazy like they're something else, something better, and all the names they know. They should spend time on a navy transport, expand their vocabulary.

'I tell them what I am, what I was, I suppose, but they just laugh and take the piss. So I tell 'em they're a bunch of spineless little gobshites. I know what's coming, they don't need the excuse, so I give it anyway. So in they come. Shy at first, eggin' each other on, like bleating sheep. She's the worst, the girl. She's the one pulling their strings.

'Anyway, I'm not fighting back so they get braver. The main lad, not the biggest but the sharpest, he starts gettin' serious. She's shouting at him, telling him what to do, baying for blood. I'm only offering limbs and muscle, nothing soft. I've taken worse beatings in Basic. But she's screaming at him now and he's really goin' for it. Sooner or later he's gonna hurt me, so when a couple of the others try their luck I serve 'em out. Main lad keeps his distance after, sees things have changed, sharper than the average sheep. But she's still shrieking and he doesn't want to look scared so he pulls a knife. He shouldn't have done it but he doesn't know better. Doesn't know the rules.'

'Rules?' Groombridge frowned.

'The rules. As the man without the knife, you know you're gonna get cut, no question. As the man pulling the knife, you should know that you've just upped the ante, and if you lose, and you still might, *you* might now get cut.'

'Or dead?' suggested Groombridge.

'Or dead. That's the rules. Live by the sword, you gotta be prepared to die by it.'

Stark saw Groombridge roll his eyes. Maggs saw it too. 'You think I'm just some macho thin-dick sounding off.' He shook his head. 'Your STAB here knows better. The key to violence is the readiness to act without hesitation or restraint. A knife fight ain't Marquess of Queensberry Rules, it's war. The boy should've known that, but kids, these days, they think a shiny blade gives you balls when it's what's in here,' Maggs tapped the centre of his forehead, 'that counts.'

'You had a knife too, though, didn't you? We found blood on it,' said Groombridge. Maggs smiled, amused. 'Do you think this is funny?'

'Do you think I brought my own knife into a fight but stabbed him with his? Or did I stab myself afterwards with mine to make it look like he did it?'

'We'll see.'

'I suppose we will,' agreed Maggs. 'Until then, would you like to hear the rest of my current confession?'

Groombridge gestured invitation.

'OK, then. At first he comes at me half-hearted, like he doesn't really want to. I'm telling him what I am again, that this ain't a game any more, but she's still winding him up and he's getting more dangerous by the second. So he has a decent go and I break his nose as a warning. Now she goes mental. Starts into him, calling him all the things a girl can to rile a lad, and now he's coming at me proper. Maybe it was the video games, maybe he thought you get three lives, but he's too stupid, too scared, too weak to stop. And he's stronger than me, younger, quicker. I block some but he nicks my arm. I punch him in the throat but it's not good enough to stop him – he's too quick. I give him an opening to get him in close but I'm too slow and he gets me one in the guts before I get the knife off him. Like I said, you're gonna get cut.'

'So you get cut, but now you have the knife. How did he get dead?'

'There wasn't any time between the two. Most of me didn't want to hurt him, I'd given him enough chances, but part of me did. You know which part.' He nodded at Stark. 'The part that takes over, thinks quicker than the rest of you, does what needs doing.'

'What needs doing?' Groombridge's voice was cold.

'To survive. There wasn't time to stop and consider the niceties – I had the rest of 'em to worry about. He should've known that. I tried to warn him.'

'So the part of you that thinks quicker than the rest did what needed doing.'

'That's right. There's no sugar-coating fighting wars or sleeping rough.'

'Still, hardly the warmest words to put before the jury.'

'I'm not wagging my tail for a pat on the head.' Maggs's face said he meant it. The part of him that thought slower, the considered, non-instinctive part that held sway the rest of the time, was long past caring. Stark felt a rising sadness in that.

Groombridge pursed his lips. 'What happened next?'

'So there he is, face down with the handle sticking out. And for the first time the bitch doesn't have a word to say. It takes 'em all a few seconds to work out what's happened. Then she turns and runs and they all follow. I check to see if he's breathing but he's not, so I get my old field-kit out and stop myself following him. I think about trying to find someone, a blue top maybe, but I figure you lot are all tucked up nice and warm and I need some anaesthetic, so I have a medicinal and do likewise. I wake up, I go to the cop-shop, but your lot don't want to know, and you barely looked at me.' He pointed at them both with a thick finger, nail cracked, dirt ingrained despite a wash. 'Anyway, I figure you'll find me once you've worked it out. But you don't. So I decide it's my civic duty to try again and here I am, coddled in the warm embrace of your hospitality.'

Maggs was sweating now and pale. The doctor checked his pulse. Groombridge had to be quick. 'So, self-defence,' he said. 'Will our other witnesses tell a different tale?'

'Witnesses? Is that what you're calling them? So you haven't charged them yet? It's my word against theirs, is that it, Detective Chief Inspector Groombridge? The word of a drunk of "no fixed abode" against the fine upstanding youth of today?' The story had stoked Maggs's anger visibly.

'That remains to be seen. I have some mugshot folders here. Perhaps you can pick out the upstanding youths in question.'

'That will have to wait,' said the doctor. 'I'm sorry, but I can't allow this to continue. You'll have to come back tomorrow.'

Groombridge sighed but there was no point in arguing. 'OK. Thank you for your cooperation, Mr Maggs. This can't have been easy. Thank you, gentlemen.'

Maggs was wheeled away.

'Convincing.' There was a hint of query in Fran's tone.

'Perhaps,' said Groombridge, thoughtfully. 'It's the only statement on the table.'

'We haven't spoken to everyone yet,' said Stark, without really thinking. To their looks, he continued, 'Outnumbered eight to one, he said.'

'A figure of speech?' suggested Fran.

Stark shook his head. 'He counted.'

'What makes you so certain?' asked Groombridge. Not sarcastic, more intrigued.

'I counted them too, on the CCTV. It's automatic, training. If you know how many there are to start with, you know when you've accounted for them.'

'Accounted for them?' said Fran. 'Soldier-speak is worse than copper-speak.'

'And he said he'd "served them out", two of them. That doesn't mean politely asking them to go away. No one we interviewed seemed injured. But we haven't spoken to Naveen, Tyler or Colin yet.'

'No, but we checked A-and-E,' said Fran. 'You checked.'

'Yes. I even took copies of the mugshots.'

'Who went to the Queen Elizabeth?' asked Groombridge.

Fran pursed her lips. 'DS Harper said they got nothing.'

'And the QE is nearer to the Ferrier so they were more likely to go there. Maggs can't have hurt them that badly,' said Groombridge to Stark. 'I guess we'll have to ask him tomorrow. Anyway, until he's picked out photos I want to hold off questioning the others.'

'Just so you know, Guv . . . Forensics called while you were in there.' Fran smiled archly. 'The blood on Maggs's knife . . . duck, pigeon and squirrel.'

Stark couldn't prevent a laugh escaping. No wonder Maggs had been amused. Groombridge glowered at him. 'Sorry, Guv.'

*

'You can get the first round.'

'You said one drink.' Stark stifled a yawn.

'To start with. We're celebrating your first murder arrest.'

'Over *a* quiet drink. As in one.'

'Don't be a shandy, come on!'

Rosie's was midweek quiet, though coppers still outnumbered the civilians. 'Usual please, Harvey, and two packets of salt 'n' vinegar,' called Fran.

'Always a pleasure, Detective Sergeant. How about your friend?' asked the landlord.

'Double whisky no ice, thanks.' He could feel Fran's eyes trying to bore into him as he paid. He should've taken the pills in his pocket before they left; she'd notice now. They took the same tiny table by the door she habitually occupied with Groombridge.

'You're sweating,' she said casually, as he slipped off his jacket. 'And limping.' She took a long slug of her large dry white wine and pulled open a packet of crisps. Stark went to pick up the other and she slapped his wrist. 'This is my dinner, get your own.'

He sipped his whisky instead. It was better than the cheap crap he had at home – marginally.

'Neat spirits? Your usual?'

'It's quicker.'

'For what?'

'Dulling the pain.'

She met his eyes. 'That's either the first real thing you've told me or another fob-off.'

'Yes,' replied Stark. He still couldn't tell whether she liked him all that much but he was starting to enjoy her relentless directness. It was refreshing after months of medical platitude and familial sympathy. She had a touch of the army about her but without the restraint. She didn't seem to understand or care where the line lay between privacy and prying. He could live with that. It didn't matter so much in Civvy Street. Here you could choose your comrades, choose who to like, interact with little fear of watching them get blown to bits. No soldier expects to catch it, but the guy next to you? You kept something back, you all did, and stuck to the bullshit and banter.

'Are you going to tell me what happened in Afghanistan?' she asked suddenly.

I take it back, he thought. 'To me personally?'

'Yes.'

'No'

'Why not?'

'Because all the hero crap is bollocks. That's what you want to hear, isn't it?'

'Aha, touchy subject,' she crowed. 'Not to worry, I've got time on my side.' She necked her wine and rattled the empty glass on the table. 'Same again, thank you, Trainee Investigator Stark.'

Trainee Investigator. There were three steps to putting a D before your C. Phase one of the Initial Crime Investigators' Development Programme (ICIDP) was the eighty-question National Investigators' Examination, which Stark had aced. He considered he'd been at an unfair advantage, given the spare time he'd had to study, convalescing. Phase two was the six-week full-time course, which had been problematic for the same reason. Now embarked on phase three, he must build up his Professional Development Portfolio, an exercise in logging practical experience to demonstrate competency in core areas, ensuring he 'met a set of occupational standards within the workplace', in other words ticked a load of boxes and got it countersigned. This normally took up to or more than a year. Only upon completion would he join the illustrious ranks of the Criminal Investigations Department as Detective Constable Stark. His rehabilitation would inevitably handicap him but he was in no particular hurry. The last nine months of his life had been an impatient drive to recover, to get back his physical ability, to beat the odds. Now he was here and this was it. Either it would work out or it wouldn't.

He got stiffly to his feet, stifling a grimace. While he was at the bar he took two tablets and washed them down with the last of his whisky. Guessing she had a tab he put the round, including two packets of crisps for himself, on it without telling her and returned to his seat with an inward smile.

Sipping his whisky and looking around the pub, at Fran tucking into her crisps, at the knots of coppers at the bar, the dartboard, the pool table, Stark reflected on the strange dichotomy of human existence that allows us to subsume our pains, to ride on a wave of contentment in the moment, forgetting for a time the darker current beneath. He could feel it there, the chilling deep tugging at him, but it seemed powerless against the buoyancy of this room, these people, this moment. Perhaps he'd found his place, laid a new foundation. Perhaps this room of strangers would become family to him, this city home to him, this job purpose for him. He'd led a lackadaisical existence, following paths of least resistance, major decisions making themselves, life always working out for the best; an apathetic optimist, cheerfully coasting along. Iraq, Afghanistan and the months of recovery since had clouded that thoughtless, peaceful clarity in ways he perhaps hadn't fully acknowledged.

He smiled, tossed back his malt and slapped the empty glass on the table. 'Right, same again?'

PART TWO

13

'Christ, you look how I feel,' said Fran.

She looked OK. Stark felt dreadful. Another demonstration of his new infirmity. 'Rule number one, no effing sympathy,' replied Stark, artificially bright.

'Heartless bastard! What kind of stupid rule is that anyway?'

'Page one of the bloke handbook.'

'Bollocks, men don't read instruction manuals. The rest of the pages are probably blank.'

'We only need one page, not requiring hundreds more for sub-clauses, caveats and impenetrable small print.'

Fran made a face. 'Make sure you sit at the back in the team meeting so Groombridge doesn't see the state of you.'

'I never knew you cared, Sarge.'

'Piss off, lightweight. Go and get me a coffee.'

Ice was broken, it seemed. If this signalled the start of a beautiful friendship, Stark wondered whether to fear more for his privacy or his liver. He limped down the corridor and opened the door, hearing Groombridge's voice in the stairwell below.

'. . . simple enough question. Stark remembered to take photos with him, a trainee investigator. Why didn't Bryden? You're his supervisor, it's your job to check these things.'

Stark froze.

'It's not that simple, Guv.'

Harper's voice? They were between Stark and Fran's coffee but he didn't fancy walking in on a dressing-down.

'What's not simple? You send a man to check for fight injuries in A-and-E, he checks names and faces.'

'I didn't send him, Guv.'

'What?'

'We were busy organizing the round-up, Guv. I told Bryden to phone instead, save time.'

'He never went? For Christ's sake, Owen! Look, I know you're having a hard time at home –'

'That's not station business,' hissed Harper, urgently.

'No,' said Groombridge, despite being interrupted. 'And I've done what I can to respect that, but if your distractions begin to affect your judgement at work then it becomes my business . . .'

Neither man spoke for a moment. 'How is Jane?' asked Groombridge.

'She's fine.' Even muffled by the stairwell echo, Stark could hear the lie in Harper's words. 'We're fine.'

'*Stark!*' Fran's voice boomed down the corridor. '*Stop loitering and get my bloody coffee!*'

Stark winced, hesitated, then started down the stairs.

He was grateful to find Harper gone. Groombridge stopped him, checking to see if anyone else was lurking. 'You tread quietly, Trainee Investigator.'

'Force of habit, Guv.'

Groombridge nodded; they understood each other. 'A man's privacy may seem to him all he has left that is his. You know this, I believe.'

'Yes, Guv.'

'Good. Tell DS Millhaven she can get her own coffee, after she and you get back from the Queen Elizabeth. Don't forget the mugshots,' he added humourlessly.

Fran made light work of gaining access to patient information. She scanned down the list of admissions. 'The usual depressing list of drink-related injury and brawls . . . What's this? Arrived same time, one with broken arm, one with broken nose – Tyrone Smith and Callum Moss? Fast forward to three fifteen.'

The security man did as he was told. Stark leant in to watch the screen. His face betrayed nothing today, cracks sealed or plastered over, who could tell?

'Stop! Back up . . . There!' He pointed at two figures walking into shot, one holding a bloody T-shirt to his face, the other cradling an arm. Both had their caps on and hoods up and it took a moment to glimpse faces.

'That's Colin *Messenger*!' said Fran, peering at the youth with the bloodied face. 'His mother-of-the-year swore blind he was away at his gran's house *and* the old cow confirmed. And that's . . . *Tyler Wantage*! There's been no answer at his flat since yesterday. Damn it, we should've had these two in! Wait a minute.' She flipped back down the list. 'Broken arm . . . Tyler was admitted. The little shit's still here!'

Tyler was sitting up, watching his TV on its articulated arm, headphones on. His face when he saw Fran hold up her warrant card was a picture. She moved the TV away, dragging the headphones off his head with it.

'Oi!'

Fran smiled. 'Morning, Tyler, remember me?'

'Er . . .'

'Detective Sergeant Millhaven. I have some new questions for you.'

'You can't harass me here. You're duressin' me.'

'Thankfully, your doctor says you're well enough to leave.'

'I'm a minor, you can't take me nowhere.'

'You mean "juvenile". And your mother has agreed to meet us down the station.'

Now he looked really frightened. 'What did she say?'

'Only how eager she was to help us with our enquiries.'

Eager she may have been, but Tyler's mother proved far from

149

helpful. Naveen's mother was the very model of matriarchal restraint by comparison. She could not be deflected from haranguing her son, and Groombridge was forced to exclude her. The local-authority youth offending team had no appropriate adult available to stand in at short notice so Tyler was sent home under orders to reappear the next morning at nine prompt. His mother continued her verbal barrage all the way out of the building.

To make matters worse, Maggs had developed a minor infection and his doctors wouldn't allow him to be interviewed with the mugshots.

That afternoon Colin Messenger, his mother and grandmother were brought in. It wouldn't have been possible to decide which of them was more of a handful, according to Fran; they had to be interviewed separately. Colin was eighteen and free to answer questions. He wasn't a very good liar. Even after Groombridge had contradicted his alibi with the hospital admission sheet he continued to deny setting foot there. Even after Groombridge pointed out that hospital A&E departments have very good CCTV systems to protect their staff, he wouldn't admit it. So Groombridge showed him stills of himself and Tyler, plus footage of him climbing into the park where the arrested man was claiming self-defence from an identical number of attackers. Still Colin was too stubborn or too stupid to confess. He claimed the broken nose and black eyes came from a fall at his gran's house, that he'd been there for days. It was here that he came fully unstuck.

'"I don't know nuffin' about what 'appened to Kyle. I wasn't there. You should be stressin' the dosser, not me. I never done nuffin'!"' Fran quoted him afterwards. 'Not the sharpest pencil in the case. The guv picked him to bits. It was almost painful to witness.' Fran appeared anything but sympathetic. 'Left him in tears. My heart bleeds for the little prick.'

'With his granny alibi round his ankles, his arse is bare on all his other lies,' added Harper, darkly.

'Hmm.' Groombridge was visibly less triumphant. 'All right, what about Naveen Hussein?'

'No answer at the flat, Guv,' said Williams. 'I've asked uniform to keep an eye out.'

Groombridge nodded thoughtfully.

'You thinking he might've scarpered?' said Fran.

Groombridge looked uncertain. 'I didn't have him pegged. But I've been wrong on rare occasions.'

Stark returned to his desk, thinking about Maggs, 'the dosser', as Colin and his ilk saw him. A decorated veteran sleeping rough in a park. It shouldn't be possible, yet it was sadly all too common. On a whim he called the MoD underling. He was greeted warmly, though not in a good way. Nevertheless, the man knew better than to avoid Stark's questions again. Stark scribbled a name and number on his pad and thanked the man, who swore and hung up.

He dialled again, spoke to an adjutant and left a message with little hope of a speedy response. Five minutes later he answered the phone to one Brigadier Thomas Graveney, who was as cheerful, helpful and pleasant an officer as Stark had ever encountered. 'Bisto' to his men, he freely admitted. In 1982 Second Lieutenant Graveney, as he was then, of 2 Para had commanded Maggs and remembered him well. Maggs had been popular up to a point, but his comrades took the mickey out of his ill-concealed intellect: he had scored higher in IQ tests than his officer. Bisto laughed. Too high, really. Maggs saw through his officers too easily.

They talked for a good while. Stark thanked the brigadier profusely and relayed everything he'd learnt to Fran, who didn't bother concealing her lack of interest. 'Bollocks to all that. Come on, I'm gasping!'

'You've *got* to be joking.'

'I thought soldiers had stamina.'

'I'm just a poor weak civilian now.'

'Come on, hair of the dog.'

'Its bite was rabid. I'm going home to die,' said Stark, firmly.

She shook her head mournfully. 'Just as I was starting to dislike you less.'

'The perfect epitaph.'

'Last chance. I'm sure I must owe you a drink.'

Now she really was digging deep. Why? She was a strange one. 'In my next life.'

She huffed her disapproval and left. By the time Stark had hobbled into town, settled into a pizza-place corner seat, ordered the biggest, meatiest pizza on the menu and washed down two pills with a cold beer, his tiny twinge of guilt had faded. He hadn't the heart or the head for more of Fran's questions.

The other tables gradually filled with noisy families, noisier unsupervised teenagers and couples perhaps wishing they'd chosen somewhere more intimate. No doubt Stark looked out of place, a right Norman No Mates, but he liked the background din, the privacy it afforded, the vivid life surrounding his personal bubble. He demolished his pizza and sat nursing a third beer until the unsubtle hovering of the waitress told him they wanted their table back.

He hobbled home, where he stood contemplating the stairs with little enthusiasm. The physiotherapists said stairs were good for him but the lift tempted him daily. He took the stairs, cursing every step. His answerphone light was blinking but he ignored it; he'd sweated through his shirt, keeping a lid on the pain as it had steadily increased during the day, so he stripped, showered and fell into bed.

Half an hour later he sat up, swore and limped into the living room. The little red light mocked him. Stark sighed, sat down and hit play. Three salutations of joy: his mother worrying, his sister reminding him his mother was worrying and what she thought of his not calling back, and, of course, Captain Pierson. The world was not pleased with Joe Stark tonight. He considered going back to bed but it was still early enough to call and his conscience would only take so much ignoring, so he poured himself a double and dialled. An hour of familial torture later, all self-esteem buried beneath a steaming slagheap of guilt, he looked at the last scribbled number on his pad. Pierson. The clock said ten forty-five. His conscience would just have to live with one more night.

14

'Wanker!'

'Morning, Sarge,' replied Stark. Today obviously meant to start where yesterday had left off.

'Don't "Sarge" me. You put all those bloody drinks on my tab!' Fran looked suitably peeved.

'Only your rounds, to be fair,' said Stark, unable to prevent a smile getting through. He was sorry he'd missed seeing the look on her face, though her expression now was still priceless.

'I already told you no one likes a smartarse. I looked a right tit. You had to tell everyone first, did you?'

'I didn't tell a soul, I swear.' He tried to be sincere, but chuckling didn't help. 'Seriously.'

She appeared to accept this. 'Must've been Harvey. Ungrateful sod. The amount of drinks I've had in that dump.'

'How many have you paid for?' asked Stark, deadpan.

'Ha-bloody-ha!' She looked at him accusingly. 'I thought you were going home to die.'

'Medicinal euthanasia became necessary.' The pills and booze had done the trick, but there was sleep and there was sleep.

'From the look of you it almost worked.'

'It definitely worked. I just haven't stopped moving yet.'

'Like a chicken, you mean.'

He let her have the parting shot, hoping she'd tire of the topic. Sooner or later he had to run out of ways of pissing people off.

'Right,' said Groombridge, striding in. 'Tell me we've got an appropriate adult lined up and Tyler *sans* harridan.'

'Social worker plus legal already downstairs with him, Guv,' said Fran. 'And I've got the transcript of Colin Messenger's statement. We'll see if it doesn't jog Tyler's memory.'

'Give me five minutes.'

While Groombridge went to report to the super, Stark slipped into the quiet room where CCTV imagery was reviewed. He pulled out the crumpled paper, took a deep breath and dialled.

'Yes?' An instantly recognizable tone.

'Captain Pierson?' he asked anyway.

'Yes. Who is this?'

'Joseph Stark.'

'Ah . . . Corporal Stark,' she said, predictably lacking magnanimity in victory. 'Come to your senses at last.'

'If you say so.'

'About time. One more day and I'd have been back with those MPs.'

'What – no firing squad?'

'That, Corporal, remains a distinct possibility.'

Stark sighed inwardly. Today really was continuing yesterday's theme. He considered correcting 'Corporal' again. It would piss her off further but how much worse could he make it? Much, much worse, probably. He returned to his desk some time later, dejected.

'There you are, Tosspot!' Fran greeted him with little more civility than before. 'Come on, the guv thinks this will be good for your education.'

Stark watched through the glass as Groombridge began with Tyler Wantage. A tall, muscular kid with a stubble goatee and hair pleated in tight lines against his scalp, culminating in a rat-tail. He looked older than his sixteen years. Only the way he slouched, hunched in his hoodie, marked him out as the teenager he was.

'Why is you pest'in' me?' he complained. 'I ain't done nuffin' wrong.'

'Indeed.' Groombridge sighed, rubbing fingers and thumb over his temples as if soothing a headache. 'Few, if any, people have done *nothing* wrong. *You*, I would be willing to bet, have done *many* things wrong. Let's begin with the night of Sunday the tenth, around one in the morning.'

'That's Monday morning,' sneered Tyler.

'Well done. Where were you?' Tyler shrugged. 'If it helps jog your memory, that was the morning seventy-eight-year-old Alfred Ladd was fatally assaulted as he slept, minding his own business, in St Alfege Park.'

The teenager shrugged again. 'Home, in bed.'

Groombridge shook his head. 'Your mother says otherwise. So where were you?'

'Out.'

'Where?'

'Just out.'

'Where?'

'Greenwich.'

'With whom?'

'Mates.'

'Which mates?' Tyler didn't answer. 'The only bar open that late on a Sunday is Reds. Were you in there?' asked Groombridge.

The legal went to caution his charge against response but it was too late. 'That's right. It was mashin', a right laugh.'

'So when we review their door CCTV we'll see you and your mates, will we?' Tyler froze. 'Because they introduced a no-cap-or-hoodie policy last year, so we'll have no problem seeing your face.'

Silence. Groombridge let it drag out, allowing Tyler's uncertainty to fill it. Stark's respect for his boss was growing. He wasn't sure he'd have the patience to sit on his temper so carefully.

'Neat idea washing your clothes afterwards. Which of you came up with that one?'

There was no mistaking Tyler's faint smile.

Groombridge saw it too. 'Did you do it after every attack, or just the one on Alfred Ladd?' Nothing. 'Of course, it did help confirm exactly which articles you were keen for us not to inspect. Your mother was kind enough to confirm they were what you wore that night and who you were out with. And I have a building full of officers with nothing better to do than compare all your outfits to the hours of CCTV footage from the nights of the various attacks. I'm confident we'll soon spot you and your mates at various key locations and times, loitering with intent.'

'You've no grounds for "intent", Inspector,' the legal piped up.

'A helpless old man was killed. Kicked and beaten to death. And we can already identify you within yards of it, within minutes. And then there's the physical evidence –'

'That's circumstantial at best,' pointed out the legal. 'My client has explained that he was in that location the night before.'

Groombridge continued to direct his words at Tyler. 'Circumstantial evidence soon adds up. Who's a jury going to believe? A sullen little scrote like you?'

The legal gave him a warning look and the social worker stiffened on her seat. Groombridge switched tack. 'Where were you on Friday the fifteenth at around midnight? That's the night Stacey Appleton was pushed off a fifth-storey balcony,' he added helpfully.

'Playin' Xbox wiv Colin.'

The single mothers of both had confirmed this and, given Tyler's mother's propensity to forthrightness, Groombridge was inclined to believe her. 'Have you anything else to add?' Nothing. 'How well did you know Stacey? Were you close?'

This elicited a faint smirk. Groombridge waited. 'Please answer the question.'

'I knew her, ya get me. Proper.'

Groombridge frowned. 'You were sleeping with her?' A definite smirk now. 'I thought she was Naveen Hussein's girlfriend.'

'Paki wanker. Proper in love with little Stacey, must've been the only one who never 'ad a go. Virgin loser!'

'Stacey slept with more than one of you?'

Now Tyler laughed. 'I don't give a fuck where she *slept*, but she fucked us all. Except poor little Nav. I reckon he was the only one she actually liked. Pafettic saddos.'

'So why?'

'She was the Dutchie,' scoffed Tyler. Seeing their blank looks he added, 'Kouchie? Blunt? Pass 'pon the lef' hand side, ya get me? She weren't all that neither!'

Dutchie. A Caribbean cooking pot in the original song, a communal joint in the cover version and now gang slang for a sex slave – to be passed around, whether through initiation, subjugation or for mere entertainment. And Naveen loved her, the poor sod. Stark shook his head in dismay. Groombridge sat back in his chair and placed his hands palm down on the table. Stark recognized anger management when he saw it. 'All right,' he said eventually. 'Where were you on Monday night, between one and three?'

'Home, in bed.'

'Your mother says otherwise.'

'Lyin' bitch.'

'I have footage of you entering Accident and Emergency with Colin Messenger at three fifteen that morning.' Tyler rolled his eyes. 'Your poor mother was telling me how worried you make her. She's at her wit's end. Poor thing, she hasn't even had time to wash the clothes you were wearing that night.'

Tyler looked up sharply, then anxiously at his legal, who gave a minute shake of the head.

Groombridge raised his eyebrows. 'Still got nothing to say? No? How did you break your arm?'

'Fell.'

'Did you fall on Colin's nose?' Groombridge smiled. 'It's funny, this falling,' he continued evenly. 'Contagious, perhaps. Colin claimed he fell too.' He paused, letting Tyler try to guess what he might ask next. Stark observed intently. Groombridge silently placed the still of the pair at A&E together. 'Of course, that was before his confession to the assault that night on a vagrant that ended in the death of your ringleader Kyle Gibbs.'

Tyler jerked visibly. Groombridge held the transcript of Messenger's confession. The legal held out his hand for it and began to read, as Groombridge pressed on: 'That's what Kyle was, wasn't he, your leader, your superior? Bigger, better, faster, cleverer. Does that make you his bitch?'

Tyler looked angry now. His legal placed a cautionary hand on his shoulder but the teenager shrugged it off. 'Not while I was bangin' 'is bitch be'ind 'is back,' he snarled.

Groombridge raised an eyebrow. 'You and Nikki Cockcroft?' Tyler looked pleased with himself again. 'Was she a Dutchie too?'

The boy huffed. 'No way, man. Not Nikki.'

'Then I guess that makes you and Kyle *her* bitches,' concluded Groombridge.

'I ain't no bitch!'

Now it was the DCI's turn to scoff. 'She yanked his leash just like she yanked yours. Weak little bitches, the both of you, whining and yapping, doing what little Nikki tells you.'

'Fuck off, wanker! I ain't no bitch! I mess you up!'

'Just like you did those dossers?'

'Inspector, this transcript does not name my client in relation to that –'

'You're Nikki's little bitch! She kept her hands clean and told you to do it!'

'I ain't her bitch!'

'I think you are.'

'She's the one yappin'. I'm the one whackin'!'

'Oh, yeah, you're fine at "whacking" when it's some poor seventy-eight-year-old zipped in his sleeping-bag behind a public piss-house at night, but when you accidentally pick on an ex-soldier your bite isn't as big as your bark is it, little doggie.'

'Inspector –' the legal tried again.

'You got your arse kicked in that park on Monday night.'

'You is *jokin'*!' scoffed Tyler.

'Alan Maggs broke your arm and whipped your arse.'

'Detective Chief Inspector!' protested the legal.

'Sent you whimpering behind Kyle like a *little bitch*!'

Tyler shot angrily to his feet, clambering over the table to get at Groombridge, Fran restraining him as the legal backed away in the corner. 'I ain't no bitch! I'd have kicked his ass if Kyle hadn't fucked up! That old dosser was *nuffin'*!' Tyler yelled. 'I kicked his ass! Fuckin' dossers! I messed 'em up! I messed 'em *all* up! Fuckin' bitch! I ain't no one's *fuckin' bitch*!'

Stark was in the room by now but Fran didn't need his help. Tyler was face down on the floor with his arms restrained. Mick, the custody sergeant, and two PCs manhandled the struggling teenager back down into the cell block.

The legal packed up and left. The social worker gave Groombridge a severe look.

'Well, that was bracing,' said Groombridge, calmly.

Fran appeared equally unflustered. 'Two confessions, verbal at least. Three, if you count Maggs. Nice work, Guv. Time to get little Nikki back in?'

'Let's see if we can't shake a few more off the tree before we go for her. Get all the rest in. Let her stew a bit.' Groombridge frowned at Stark as they travelled up in the lift. 'You're quieter than average this morning, Stark.'

Stark hesitated a moment before replying. 'A wise person

once said, if you've nothing useful to say, say nothing, Guv.'

Groombridge shook his head. 'And my old granny told me that if someone has nothing to say, it's because they know you won't like what they're thinking. Spit it out, Trainee Investigator.'

Stark looked at Fran but found no help there. 'I just wonder if we should bring Nikki in now, Guv. We've seen what happens when she's left to roam.'

As an enlisted soldier, and a police constable, you raised doubts with your sergeant, never your officer. But no rebuke came. Groombridge merely shrugged. 'OK, she can stew in a cell. Next time speak up.'

Fran might not have agreed. She gave Stark a look, which he interpreted as, *I haven't forgotten about you, sunshine.* All he could do was shrug.

'Right,' Groombridge announced, as he strode into the office. 'What about Naveen?'

Williams didn't look happy. 'I just got back, Guv. Still no answer at their flat. And a neighbour thinks they left Monday, bags packed.'

'We got his mum's employment details from the Inland Revenue, Guv,' added Dixon. 'Tills at Tesco. But she phoned in Monday requesting compassionate leave for a death in the family.'

'The day after we found Stacey.' Fran's face said it all. 'Maybe he wasn't nearly as surprised or upset as he let on.'

'Five days.' Groombridge rubbed his eyes, the expanding implications visible in his pained expression. 'OK, put everything on hold. Look into familial connections, see where they might've gone. And alert the ports. Focus on flights to Pakistan. If they've left the country I want to know.'

If they had, the chances of getting Naveen back were iffy,

thought Stark. Pakistan had been quick enough coughing up the 7/7 bomber to their allies in the War on Terror, but their record on domestic crime was less encouraging. Had Naveen really killed Stacey? It hadn't appeared that way. It was harder to fit Naveen into the gang's activities than others like Colin Messenger. He wasn't made of the same stuff. He seemed ... softer. But appearances could be deceiving. Just look at Maggs.

The rest of the day was spent on the phones. The UK Border Agency confirmed that Naveen and his mother held both UK and Pakistani passports but that neither appeared to have fled the country by conventional means. There were no travel bookings under their names. Williams managed to extract a family contact from Social Services – Mrs Hussein's sister and her family in Birmingham – and asked local uniform to call round, but there was no answer. Stark listened with interest. He thought about talking to Fran but decided discretion was the better part of valour and approached Williams instead. 'This aunt of Naveen's, she has a seventeen-year-old son, right?'

Williams nodded. 'Yeah. So?'

So Stark's training had included not just anti-terrorism and counter-insurgency but also insurgency, escape and evasion, and the easiest way to obtain a false passport was to use that of someone who looked like you. And for a teenager whose passport photo might be years out of date ... 'Probably nothing.' He made a note of the names and a few quiet calls. You never knew.

'What was that?' asked Fran, as he hung up.

'Probably nothing, Sarge.'

She sized him up for a second but let it drop. She glanced at the clock. 'Right, come on, you horrible lot, I'm gasping!' She looked again at Stark. 'You too, chicken.'

'Thought I was *persona non grata*.'

'Time to re-ingratiate yourself,' she said, pulling on her jacket.

'I'll have to pass on that. I'm dead on my feet, if you recall?'

'Whose fault is that, Mr Medicinal?'

'Guilty as charged.'

'What are you gonna do? Sit home alone drinking whisky in front of the TV?'

'Nothing beats a good weepy chick-flick.'

'Stop pissing about. It's Friday, and I refuse to be blown out two nights running.'

There wasn't much Stark could say to that. He joined her and the rest at Rosie's with the intention of slipping away as he had before. Unfortunately it seemed Fran was wise to this now, and caught his departure with a disapproving look.

Her disapproving look was still there the next morning as the search for Naveen picked up where it had left off. More than one member of the team was wishing it wasn't Saturday morning and wondering why they hadn't opted for a regular job with regular hours and other perks, like weekends.

Later Groombridge came out of his office. 'Stark. The doctors say your pal Maggs has perked up. Get up there with the perp books.'

'On his own, Guv?' asked Fran, just shy of protest.

'You up to it, Constable?' asked Groombridge.

'Guv.' Stark knew a rock and a hard place when they loomed at either side of him.

Fran darted a glare his way. 'But, Guv –'

'I want every available body looking for Naveen Hussein, Detective Sergeant. Unless you feel you can't spare one trainee investigator?'

'No, Guv.' Fran smiled, teeth gritted.

15

'Please confirm your full name?'

'Not this again,' said Maggs, tersely.

'For the record, if you wouldn't mind.' Stark smiled.

Maggs shook his head, amused now. 'Alan Thomas Maggs, no fixed abode,' he said ironically.

'Thank you. I'm here to show you some mugshots to see if you recognize anyone from the group you claim attacked you. There's quite a few to go through, I'm afraid.'

'I'm not going anywhere.'

Stark got out the books, two thick ring-binders, one female, one male, known to the station as the Perp Books, or the Usual Suspects, or the Shitheads, depending on who was talking and who was listening.

'You still look like crap,' said Maggs, ignoring them.

'You look better,' replied Stark. 'I'm glad.'

'Civilized society.' Maggs waved a hand around. 'We like our murderers fit for the gallows.'

'We don't hang people any more.'

'No. Too squeamish.'

'That, plus it allows for the possibility of rehabilitation.'

'Or miscarriage of justice,' suggested Maggs.

Stark stared at him. 'Is that what's happening here?'

'No,' said Maggs, ruefully. He opened his hands to indicate himself. 'Only guilty man in Shawshank.'

'Good movie.' Stark couldn't help looking surprised.

'I haven't spent all of my years on the street, Constable Weekender.'

'How long *has* it been?'

'Let's just call it intermittent,' replied Maggs. 'Those rings under your eyes tell a tale,' he continued seamlessly. 'Still laying awake wondering what you might've done different?' Stark tried to keep reaction from his face but Maggs nodded anyway. 'Never stops, you know,' he said. 'Nearly thirty years on, round and round.' He considered Stark, his expression unreadable. 'Course you'll have worked out there was any number of ways you could've stopped 'em dying, any number of arbitrary decisions. And maybe you'll have realized it's futile wondering. Change one thing, affect another. Save that man, doom another. Reconciled yourself to the fact that none of it was your fault particularly. Still – round and round.'

Stark said nothing.

'I expect the shrinks told you not to blame yourself, how death in battle is random chance on both sides. Nothing personal. You did what you had to. Necessary force, necessary sacrifice. Survivor's guilt, perfectly natural, perfectly understandable. Your life a tribute to their sacrifice?'

'Something like that,' admitted Stark.

'Bit of pressure that, isn't it? Who we living for now then, eh, them or us?' A rhetorical question. Maggs's diamond stare gave no hint of sympathy, no condescending consolation. Rule number one in action. 'I didn't much like half the shifty fucks,' said Maggs. Some recognition in Stark's face elicited a sad smile and a nod. 'Have a beer, have a laugh, take a bullet for them till the day you die, but it's not like you chose 'em.'

'I was TA, just making up the numbers. They weren't even my regiment,' said Stark, not sure why.

'Christ, how the hell do you get a shrink's head round that?'

'Is that why you gave up on them?' asked Stark, keen to shift the focus from himself.

'Wasn't much to give up on. Didn't coddle their vets like

they do now. Made of sterner stuff back then, not like you soft toddlers playing in the sand.'

'Yeah, you coped just fine.'

Maggs laughed wryly. 'Still see their faces, the dusties you dropped?'

Dropped. Nowadays squaddies used *slotted*, like excited kids in some *Bravo Two Zero* video game, originating from the slot in the rear gunsight, or *brassing the enemy up*, from the brass shell casings. Such cosmetic euphemisms set Stark's teeth on edge. If you were willing to kill, you should own it. 'They were too far away,' he replied. 'Or I was too busy.'

Maggs shook his head. 'Most of mine were in the dark. No faces, just shapes on the ground as you pass. No real telling who dropped who. And then it's dawn and you pass one – glass eyes, shocked, lifeless.'

'That one gives them all a face.' Stark nodded.

Maggs raised his eyebrows. 'Most of the time it's blood from a stone and then, bang, the brutal truth. You sure you weren't a Rupert?' He stared hard at Stark. 'Never fancied a proper cap?'

Stark shrugged. That was too long a story, and too personal.

Maggs changed the subject. 'Got a smoke?'

Stark tilted his head at the No Smoking sign.

'Oh, yeah, filthy habit,' agreed Maggs.

'Want me to get you some?'

'I just gave up. Talk to Bisto, did you?' Maggs asked.

Stark was starting to expect the deliberate swerves. 'Said you were the most dangerous man in the army, the enlisted man with a Mensa card.'

'He never was the sharpest tool in the box,' said Maggs. 'Decent enough, though, for a silver-spoon. Not surprised they put you on to him. Can't be many still in but he was always gonna be one of 'em. What is he now, colonel?'

'Brigadier.'

Maggs snorted. 'God help us, he'll make fucking general. If you talk to him again, tell him we never did like him.'

'He also told me about your Military Medal,' said Stark, 'awarded for –'

'Failing to duck,' interrupted Maggs.

'"Conspicuous imbecility" were the words he used.' Stark considered pressing. He had questions but there was a line. Brigadier Graveney had told him Maggs earned the citation at Goose Green, dragging a wounded officer to cover under withering fire in broad daylight. Maggs would make light of it, no doubt, dismiss it as one of those momentary acts of poor judgement you later can't quite forgive yourself for. The then Second Lieutenant 'Bisto' Graveney had not – he'd been the wounded officer in question. Two weeks later an Argentine bullet had finished Maggs's war. 'Still have it?'

'Flogged it for booze years ago,' lied Maggs.

'Pity,' said Stark. 'Should've waited. Those discontinued baubles are getting quite valuable now, I heard.' He nearly added a quip about buying new socks but stopped himself.

Maggs met Stark's gaze coolly. 'Figured you for a bauble of your own. You seem imbecilic enough.'

'Campaign gongs are enough.'

'It's a good job we don't dish out Purple Hearts for splinters and blisters like the Yanks. You'd be littered with them.' He smiled. 'Show me your holiday snaps, then, Blue Top.'

It seemed the touchy-feely stuff was over for now, thank goodness. Stark opened the book of females and Maggs began skimming through, pausing occasionally. Suddenly he stopped and tapped an image. 'That's the shouty cow, the one egging them all on.'

Nikki Cockcroft. 'How certain are you?'

'Hundred per cent. Vicious little coward, that one. I'll never forget *her* face.'

Stark felt a grim elation as he leant into the microphone.

'For the record, Alan Maggs has positively identified photograph F/12/4211. Okay, keep going.'

In the book of males Maggs picked out Tim Bowes and Paul Thompson. He smiled when he found Colin Messenger. 'I expect this cocky shit's nose isn't so straight any more.' The smile returned with Tyler's picture. 'And this one. She had him wound up good 'n' proper too. Broken left forearm, cried like a girl.'

'He passed right over Harrison Collier and Martin Munroe,' Stark reported. 'Said he had to concentrate on the ones at the front. I think we might have more luck if we stood them up in front of him.'

'And you've got all this on tape?' said Fran, for confirmation.

'Sarge.' Stark thought about his preliminary conversation with Maggs and hoped Fran wouldn't double-check.

She looked at Groombridge. 'The word of a murder suspect against the fine upstanding youth of today.'

Groombridge nodded. 'It might not convince the CPS but it's another hook to trip up the Rats.'

'Usual suspects, Guv?' asked Fran.

'Not yet. When Maggs is well enough for an ID parade we'll get Collier and Munroe in front of him.'

'Guv?' Harper knocked on the open door. 'I've got him!'

'Naveen Hussein?'

Harper grinned. 'Birmingham airport. Tried to board a flight to Islamabad using his cousin's passport before I confirmed he was ours.'

'Good work, Owen!' Groombridge allowed himself a smile, though it made his next decision a little awkward. 'Fran, you and Stark get on up there, see what he's got to say for himself.'

Harper's indignation was immediate. 'But, Guv –'

'Sorry, Owen, I know this was your catch but these two

168

saw Naveen's reaction to Stacey's death. I want them to do this.'

'Guv,' replied Harper, but Groombridge thought he detected the briefest of glares at Stark's back. Something to watch for.

They took the train. Fran didn't like trains. Indeed, she loathed all forms of public transport and made this known at regular intervals all the way to Birmingham airport. Her complaints centred on reliability, inconvenience and the fact that she spent quite enough time with the public as it was. Stark was a little surprised at the especial venom she held for the Tube, but she claimed only Central Londoners loved it, and that although her home town of Croydon had been officially swallowed up into Greater London in 1965, Central Londoners still looked down their noses at it as Surrey. Her opinion of Stark seemed on a par with that of the Tube, and indeed Central Londoners, though she withheld specific accusations. Stark would dearly have loved to close his eyes but didn't trust her not to bellow in his ear, like a drill sergeant. He should probably be angry that Harper had claimed credit for Naveen's detainment, but he wasn't.

Naveen did not look happy to see them. He looked tired and scared, which was unsurprising: possession of a false identity document with improper intent usually meant time inside. His aunt might be charged too, for booking the flight. The locals had already brought in an appropriate adult and a legal.

'Well,' said Fran. She didn't smile. 'Naveen Hussein. I'm sorry for your loss.' Naveen looked confused. 'Death in the family? That was the excuse your mother gave to her employer for your sudden disappearance.'

Naveen gulped and tried to avoid their eyes. In the early interviews he had stonewalled with the best of them. Now he looked one nudge from rubble. 'I never killed Stacey, if that's what you think,' he blurted out defensively.

'You loved her.' He wasn't expecting that. He looked down, stone-faced, but didn't deny it. 'Love is a common motive for murder,' continued Fran. 'Jealousy too. It can't have been easy watching Stacey being passed around. What was it Tyler called her?' she asked Stark, though she remembered well enough.

'Dutchie, Sarge.'

'Oh, yes. Pass the Dutchie 'pon the lef' hand side. Only she was never passed to you, Naveen. Was that their choice or hers?'

Naveen looked down, anguished. 'I never killed her.'

'But here you are,' Fran indicated their surroundings, 'on the run. What are we supposed to think?'

'I ain't runnin' from you,' said Naveen, desperately.

'Then who?'

Naveen shook his head and looked down again.

'If you won't answer my questions here, you'll answer them back in Greenwich.'

His head jerked up. 'I ain't goin' back there.'

'The officers here will charge you. Your mother and aunt too, most likely. Then you'll be released on bail pending trial and told to return to your homes.'

The boy was shaking his head, eyes widening with every word. 'I ain't going back.'

'You have no choice. You have no other relatives we could trust you with. If you abscond you'll be remanded into custody.'

Naveen was beginning to panic. 'I can't go back! You don't understand! I can't go back!'

'Why?'

'They'll kill me, like they killed Stace!'

'Who?'

'They knew. Soon as I said I wouldn't go looking for that girl the next night, they knew. They'll think I was running, they'll think I was snitching, like Stace.'

'What girl?'

'Nikki said it was her, a girl sometimes hangs around the estate, with pink hair, dossin' in one of the empty flats, dunno which one. Nikki said she done it, killed Stace, but that was bullshit. They were going looking for her but I wouldn't go. I knew it was bullshit! I knew it was them done it!'

'Who?'

'Kyle and Nikki!' spat Naveen, then looked appalled that he'd said it aloud.

'They killed Stacey? Can you prove that?'

Naveen shook his head bitterly. 'They told us all to stay home that night, said something was up, needed sorting. But I knew, soon as I saw that text next day! That weren't from Stace!'

'How do you know?'

'She always signed off with "SXO", always, no matter what!'

'"SXO"?'

'Stacey, kiss, hug,' translated Stark.

Naveen nodded, tears welling. 'She never wanted to be in the Rats. Me neither. But you don't get a choice. They beat on you or worse . . .' Now the tears fell. 'Poor Stace,' he blubbed. 'Things they made her do! Poor Stace!'

Fran waited as Naveen got himself under control, angrily wiping away his tears. 'They can't hurt her any more,' she said, with surprising compassion. 'And Kyle can't hurt you either. He's dead – stabbed to death when he and your friends finally attacked someone who could fight back. It's safe for you to go home now.'

Naveen was shaking his head slowly. But when he looked up it wasn't in relief. 'You haven't got a clue. You think it's Kyle we're all afraid of.'

'He wouldn't say any more. And it might be days before he's bailed and delivered home,' Fran reported to Groombridge, when they finally got back. A two-hour delay had nicely made her point regarding all things public transport.

171

'You believe him?'

Fran shrugged. 'I think so. At least, it's easier to believe Kyle and Nikki shoved Stacey off a building. Though I'm not sure how much sympathy I have for Naveen, even if he was forced to join up – not after everything they've done.'

'But this girl with the pink hair again? A witness?'

'Explains a few things. The girl sees Kyle and Nikki off Stacey. They tell the others it was her and wind them up to go looking for her.'

'So why attack Maggs?'

'Pathology said Kyle's body contained high levels of cocaethylene, Guv,' said Stark, as if that explained everything. Fran's face suggested otherwise. 'It forms in the body from alcohol and cocaine,' he explained. 'One's a cultural disinhibitor, the other inflames self-confidence, both elevate dopamine and serotonin, reducing impulse control. Mixed in the bodies of a gang of thugs out looking for someone to hurt . . .'

Groombridge smiled in bewilderment. 'How do you know all this?'

Stark stared straight ahead, all but standing to attention. 'DS Millhaven says I read too much, sir.'

Groombridge masked his amusement for Fran's benefit. 'All right. So . . . wound up, boozed up, coked up and frustrated, they can't find who they're looking for so pick on who they can. That still leaves us with few hard facts. We need to find this pink-haired girl before they do.' He looked out into the late-evening dusk wearily. 'Speak with uniform first thing in the morning, see if she rings any bells. And ask around the estate – someone must've seen this girl. And get Harper to round up the usuals. I think it's time I shook the tree.'

Stark looked at his watch. 'Somewhere you'd rather be?' asked Fran.

*

Fran picked up a bottle of dubious Chardonnay and wrinkled her nose at the dust; a good sign in a wine cellar, not so good in a housing estate off-licence. Lager and spirits had the wine selection outnumbered and pinned down. Her expression again asked why they were there.

Her clout might help, but most of all Stark needed her distraction. 'Your bedroom faces into the courtyard, above the shop?' she asked the proprietor. 'Perhaps you could show me and describe what you heard.'

The big Sikh frowned unhappily. 'I've already told this officer,' he said, indicating Stark.

'Please.' Fran gestured through the back of the shop.

The man had little choice. They wouldn't be gone long. His wife busied herself with something behind the till and avoided Stark's eye.

'You saw something,' he said. She froze momentarily, then continued as if she hadn't heard. 'You looked out of your window while your husband was down here, checking the shop.'

She stopped what she was doing, but still would not meet his eyes. 'You must speak with my husband.'

'Your English is better than he let on.'

'Please.'

'He saw nothing. What did you see?'

'We do not wish to be involved.'

'Anything at all might be useful.'

'Please,' she said, glancing anxiously at the door behind her. 'He would be angry. If they see anyone looking out at them they throw stones at the windows.'

'Who? The gang kids? It was them you saw?'

She shook her head. '*Please*. We *cannot* speak with you.'

We cannot speak? Were they really so afraid? 'Just tell me what you saw, and I'll be gone,' he lied.

The poor woman looked trapped. Glancing again at the door, she spoke in hushed tones. 'The girl with pink hair. She comes in sometimes, only early in the morning when they are not about. Frightened of them. She must sleep somewhere but I don't know where, one of the empty flats – there are enough of them, more every year. Soon it will be us, but my husband won't listen. She never has enough money, poor thing, counting out her change coin by coin. Sometimes I let her off. You must not tell my husband. He blames the shoplifters. I saw her running past outside a minute after the scream. That's all. *Please*, don't tell my husband.'

Stark sighed inwardly. He would not tell her husband about the charitable stock losses but as for the rest . . . Fran would blow that open with a Photofit session.

A jarringly cheap electronic bell announced that a customer had entered the shop. Stark saw the wife's eyes widen in alarm and she turned away, pretending to be doing anything other than speaking with him. Looking round, he caught only a flash of a shiny black jacket over jeans as whoever it was spun on their heels and departed.

Hurrying out, Stark spotted a shadow figure disappearing around the nearest corner, but by the time he reached it no one was there.

The fine upstanding youth of today made their usual depressing spectacle, a tedious display of sullen silence interspersed with childish outbursts. Undismayed, Groombridge's performance was a master class, always the right side of the legals, nothing that could be used to argue duress, just clever, patient police work. Even the use of the word 'bitch', not technically a swear word but fantastically provocative. With alibis unravelling and each other's slips played against them, their stone wall finally showed itself a house of cards. By the end he'd tripped Bowes, Collier and Thompson into implicating themselves. Add them to Tyler Wantage and Colin Messenger and, with more work, one might be persuaded to name the others. So far none of the gang had done so, but it was a good day's work nonetheless.

The sour note was the absence of Nikki Cockcroft. Operation Poop-scoop, as Harper had dubbed the round-up, had arrived at her door to find her gone. Her mother had just said, 'Gone', nothing more, even after being escorted to the station. She was threatened with an obstruction charge, should she be proved to have lied, but uttered not a peep more. A search of usual haunts and hideaways failed to find the daughter. Several uniforms would miss their dinner going door to door. Stark thanked his stars he wasn't among them. The interviews had taken all day and, even as a humble spectator, he was hanging.

The other missing piece was Pinky, as the team had labelled the homeless girl.

Stark stared at her Photofit on the wall. White, mid to late teens, pretty, little more than five foot tall, a tattoo on the back of her right hand, studs through her eyebrows, nose and tongue, dyed hair in a shoulder-length bob. The composite was as alien and unreal as they always were. What had she seen, and where was she? It was out with the media now, and uniform were showing it locally. Fingers-crossed time.

'Earth calling Stark,' shouted Fran, pulling on her jacket. 'Come on, it's your round.'

'Not tonight, Sarge. I need an early night.'

She looked at him, perhaps wrong-footed by his honesty. 'You do look like shit. Get some beauty sleep, then, Princess. Tomorrow is another bright Monday morning in the force that never sleeps.'

16

Fran took one look at him and her face hardened. So much for beauty sleep. She probably thought he'd been on the whisky again. Fair enough. That he hadn't, that he'd resisted, was little compensation for the sleep delayed by soreness, then exploded by dreams.

'Look at the state of you!' she hissed. 'Don't let the DCI see you like that. Piss off home and sleep it off.'

'It's not a hangover.'

'Bullshit!'

For a second it was tempting to share: the shuddering awake and forcing your body to breathe, to remember that your lung wasn't shot through and filling with blood. Through the swirling stars he'd seen again the Taliban insurgent at the window. Had those bullets passed in mid-air? The 7.62mm calibre arching down to him, 5.56mm streaking up? Had he hit him too, killed him? With all his heart Stark hoped he had. There was a vicious, brutal truth for Doc Hazel to ruminate upon.

He recalled the line in one of Wilfred Owen's letters to his mother, not strictly standard army reading – 'I lost all my earthly faculties, and fought like an angel.' It spoke to Stark of crossing the line, the decision of a moment to become what you must, though it meant abandoning for ever the man you were, to take life. Some might call it the abandonment of humanity, but Stark still believed that depended on one's motivation. And one's recognition of the consequences.

He had killed. Not dropped, slotted or brassed-up: killed. With knowledge and forethought. And, reaching deep inside himself, feeling for regret, he found none. Not for the enemy, not even a little. What does that say about a man? Was there even a man left after that?

Then he'd thought of the woman and her boy, and there it was, the tight ball of heat twisting in the cold vacuum of his heart, proof of life, of a sort. Alone in the cool dark of his room, Stark had clung to it. Even as it burnt, he clung to it.

He could share, but how could Fran understand? She was staring at him, waiting for an apology, an excuse or quip, not the truth. She tsked and dumped an evidence box full of individually bagged mobile phones on the table. 'The gang's. Forensics are done with them. They've all changed SIMs since last time. We have to assume Nikki Cockcroft has too. See if there's a new number for her on one of those and cross-reference the rest. I assume they taught you that much in detective school. Consider it penance.'

Stark didn't get off to a great start. None of the phones had a listing for Nikki. In fact, apart from the ubiquitous Mum or Gran, half the contacts were acronyms or initials. Tags, thought Stark, recalling the graffiti plastered over the Ferrier Estate. Colin Messenger's number was saved on the others as MESS. Naveen Hussein was NAV or Nerdi. Kyle Gibbs was K-RAZY. Kyle's phone had a listing for N'Zone, which others had as G and Tyler had as N. The phone with that number wasn't present. Nikki? It seemed likely. If Tyler had been communicating with her behind Kyle's back it might make sense for him to have her saved as an initial. But why G? It wasn't unknown for kids to use the initial to indicate their dealer, as in someone who could sort them out with gear. Stark went in search of Ptolemy and was directed to the uniform locker rooms.

'You said Nikki was "the source of the vile". It's clear she's at the centre of the violence. What else might she be the centre of?'

Ptolemy look at him shrewdly. 'What makes you ask?'

Stark explained.

Ptolemy nodded. 'She's the go-to girl in the Ferrier Estate for anything in the personal-consumption range. We think she uses one or more of the empty flats as her stash-house but we've not the manpower for surveillance.'

'Who's supplying her?'

'That we don't know. My inspector is hoping to get on it next time Brass gets a bee in its bonnet. Let me know if you find out.'

'So this is Nikki Cockcroft's latest number?' asked Fran.

'Seems likely.' Stark nodded.

She huffed, unimpressed. 'All right, that's your Hail Marys. Here's your Lord's Prayer.' She handed him a disk. 'CCTV from Royal Parks. You should be nice and familiar. Maggs can't have climbed in with his trolley. I want his time and point of entry before the team meeting at midday. Stay out of sight till then.'

Hidden in the CCTV suite, Stark started with the main St Mary's Gate near town closing at 21.30, and wound backwards. It was a sound guess and he soon spotted the shambling shopper that was Maggs and his trolley: 20.07. He checked all the gates from that time to confirm that Maggs did not leave. Forbidden to show his face in the office he tried an experiment – whether it was possible to identify potential witnesses by tracking people who came in soon after Maggs to see whether they left by one of the gates that might have taken them past the bandstand. He started with an androgynous figure in one of those multi-coloured woollen earflap ski hats, with dangling chin-braids, thinking they would be easiest to track, but when he couldn't spot even this obvious target leaving he gave up. Their best hope was someone responding to the TV appeals and the fatal-incident signs set up in the park.

He started fast-forwarding to when Gibbs, Cockcroft and

the others would make their trespass but stopped as a figure in dark clothes appeared from the side-street and climbed the gate. It was over so quickly that Stark had to rewind to be sure. A man, fairly certain, face shrouded in shadow by a bloody hood, of course. Stark carefully scanned all the other gates to see if he could find the man leaving. Ten minutes later he climbed out over the main Blackheath Gate, adjacent to the Parks Police station. Talk about blatant. But that path did not take him past the bandstand. Not a likely witness, but someone who might have passed within two hundred yards of the scene. There was no chance of tracking the figure across the heath to his destination, so Stark began laboriously cross-referencing with footage from other cameras and traced the figure backwards into town. In the high street the figure suddenly detoured to one side for a few minutes, out of sight. Stark stared at the big wall map. Cash machine, he thought, his finger hovering on a bank. And cash machines often had cameras. By now he was sorely square-eyed. He took two tablets, not for hip or shoulder but his head.

It was nearly midday so he went to find Fran. She was busy on the phone, took his notes and waved him away. When the meeting formed she shooed him to the back and sat him down with a warning glare.

The meeting focused largely on Nikki Cockcroft, or lack thereof. There had been reports of a girl matching her description harassing homeless people in various locations, in broad daylight this time. There had even been a call-out to one violent altercation but by the time the uniforms had arrived it was over, and there was some doubt as to whether this had been Nikki: the perpetrator had arrived and fled in a BMW car and the description was vague. Dixon was following it up anyway. Since then, nothing. HQ had ratified Groombridge's request for a ping on the N-ZONE mobile but the phone company couldn't triangulate its location – switched off or in a black spot, they said. They'd let HQ know if and when it reappeared. Nikki's photo and name had been on the news all morning as a potential witness police would like to talk to in relation to, et cetera, and the team were to spend time talking to police in surrounding boroughs or places where she had past connections.

Various people chimed in, but when Fran started to move on, Stark raised his hand. She ignored it but he raised it higher. 'Sarge.'

'Not now, Trainee Investigator.'

'This might be important.'

'What is it, Stark?' Groombridge peered at him, a flicker of displeasure at what he saw.

Stark explained about the potential witness.

'When did you find this?' Groombridge looked between Stark and Fran. Her glare might have immolated Stark in his chair. She clearly hadn't read his notes past the time of Maggs's entry.

'I just finished, Guv. I should've told DS Millhaven.'

'Yes, you should.' Fran was still glaring.

Groombridge was unreadable. 'Okay. DC Dixon, go with Stark to the bank. I want a face and name on my desk. Right. What else is happening on my good streets?'

There was a brief round-up of other cases but Stark wasn't totally listening. Something had occurred to him. He considered raising his hand again but thought better of it. He waited till the meeting broke up, then spoke to Dixon. 'Does Nikki Cockcroft have form for car theft?'

'Don't know.'

'Did anyone get the BMW's plate?'

'Only a partial. You think it was her?'

'Who knows? I was just wondering if we might track it using the licence-plate recognition cameras. Did you run the partial?'

'Not yet. Want to try it now?'

Stark glanced at Fran. 'Better get to the bank first.'

'You all right?' asked Dixon, as they drove.

Stark stifled another yawn. 'Just tired. Sometimes I don't sleep well,' he said, in a tone he hoped would close the topic without offence.

'You know when I said not to worry about DS Millhaven?' said Dixon. 'I think maybe you took me too literally.'

Stark laughed. 'I'm sure she'll get used to me eventually.'

Stark and Dixon reappeared with a facial shot and a name. Fran thanked Dixon. Stark was below notice for now. His good call made up a little for appearing at work in such a state, but only a very little. Being smart wasn't enough. He seemed determined to infuriate her. Groombridge hadn't said a word about Stark's condition, even privately afterwards. More special bloody treatment! Fran was ready to raise it herself but Groombridge closeted himself with CPS lawyers to go over the evidence and interviews. With no witness ID or confessional slip, they'd have to let Martin Munroe walk for now. The rest would be charged. A decent barrister might argue away their interview slip-ups and the magistrate might grant bail, but for now the DCI emerged in a good mood and Fran was loath to spoil it. She'd gone off the boil anyway. She was just peeved that Stark had cried off drinking with her just to get pissed elsewhere again. She wasn't jealous: she wasn't interested in him that way – too cold for her liking, too young, too many things. But it was rude.

She looked up and found Dixon hovering.

Five minutes later she sat in Groombridge's office while he scanned the paper she'd passed him. Nikki Cockcroft had form in her juvenile record, two cases of taking without consent, driving without a licence or insurance, at least two more stolen and burnt-out cars attributed to her or those around her. Dixon had run the partial plate and got a hit, not against a stolen BMW but against plates stolen from a Ford in Rochester on Saturday night. But the BMW description matched one stolen nearby. Dixon had contacted HQ with the stolen plates and they'd been traced on the plate-recognition cameras as far as the A20 Sidcup Bypass. 'It's more her style to ditch and burn, but you never know.'

'Hmm,' Groombridge mused. 'Dixon came up with this?'

'Not entirely,' admitted Fran, reluctantly.

'Stark?'

'Guv.'

'Okay. Get on to the Highways Agency and see if we can get a face off any traffic cams.' He picked up the other printout. 'Our witness from the cashpoint?'

'David Phillips, Guv. I sent uniform round for him but his landlord said he'd skipped with the rent in arrears. Said Phillips worked as a security guard at Lidl so I guess that's my next stop.'

'Take Mr Initiative with you,' said Groombridge. 'Fresh air might perk him up a little.'

Fran silently cursed him. 'Guv.'

She collected Stark but said nothing until they were alone in the car. 'If you turn up for work in this condition again I'll have you breath-tested and disciplined.'

'I'm not hungover, Sarge.'

She had to admit there was no scent of booze sweating from him in the confines of the car. What, then? Drugs? No, it didn't seem like that . . . 'Whatever you are, you're fuck-all use to me and lucky guesses aren't going to wash away your sins. No one –'

'Likes a smartarse,' interrupted Stark. 'I'll take my chances.'

Fran nearly slammed on the brakes. 'Don't take a tone with me, Trainee Investigator. You're an infinite number of PDP sheets from CID rank.'

'Sarge.'

Just 'Sarge'. He had a way of packing the monosyllable with obstinate ambiguity. She let it drop. Either he'd toe the line or he wouldn't, and she was starting not to care which.

David Phillips's supervisor made a disgusted face and told them Phillips had been sacked for turning up 'unfit for work' once too often. Fran made sure to stare at Stark at this point. The store records showed Phillips's address as the one he'd skipped out on. Fran thanked the man politely, smiled, walked calmly back to the car, got in and slammed the door viciously. She took a call on the way back, casually driving one-handed with the phone pressed to her ear. God help the uniform who pulled her over.

'Yeah, he's sitting right next to me, Guv,' she said. 'He'll enjoy that, I'm sure. Will do.' She hung up and smiled. 'There's a CPS shark waiting to chew you up and spit you out. Time to polish up those closet skeletons, Trainee Investigator!'

Stark looked out of the window. Worried, perhaps. Who could tell?

The lawyer was waiting alone in one of the interview rooms. In his forties, impeccably dressed and sharp as a tack, he went through the Maggs case with a fine-tooth comb, nit-picking, adversarial, but there was nothing there to get his teeth into. Maybe it was just that the monotony hadn't overtaken the novelty but Stark quite enjoyed typing reports. They provided an outlet for his love of language, his delight in its exactitude, which, if he'd been more skilled, might have made him more concise. He wasn't particularly and it didn't, but he preferred long and unequivocal to short and ambiguous. Stark believed the lawyer was secretly pleased. If only it would end there. Ostensibly this was a standard interview to pick over his arrest report but it wouldn't stay that way. Fran sat in, of course, no doubt delighted at the prospect of peeping into his business.

Groombridge stayed out of it, no doubt confident of receiving a full report.

'This business with the Ministry of Defence?' asked the lawyer.

Bingo. Stark waited several seconds. 'Sorry, is that a question?'

'Don't play smart, Constable.'

'Okay.'

The clock ticked through several seconds. Fran rubbed her nose to mask a smile.

'Well?' The lawyer let his impatience show. Controlled. Calculated to intimidate. Laughable, really, thought Stark. Perhaps he should play nice, particularly as he was about to beg a colossal liberty, but sometimes you just had to choose funny. And you never knew with these *faux*-prickly types: sometimes they saw the funny side too.

'I'll tell you what,' Stark suggested, 'why don't you try asking me an actual question and we'll see where that takes us?'

Now Fran was definitely trying not to smile. The lawyer pursed his lips, hopefully hiding his own. 'All right, how about this one? What is the nature of your trouble with the Ministry of Defence?'

'Personal.' Stark kept any hint of cheek from the reply but Fran gave up any pretence and sat back, smirking.

The lawyer just stared at him. 'All right, what impact will this "personal" trouble have on my case?'

'None.'

'I don't believe you're qualified to make that assessment.'

'Then why ask me?'

'Constable Stark, are you going to tell me why the switchboard in this station was bombarded with increasingly impatient demands from MoD officials for you to contact them urgently? Why, indeed, an army officer in uniform turned up unannounced demanding to see you? Why Superintendent Cox

184

was called by a high-ranking army officer but refused to discuss the nature of that call with the CPS? Are you going to tell me what kind of shit you're in and whether it's going to balls-up my case?'

'If you insist,' said Stark. 'But only after you've given me your assurance that what I tell you will not leave this room and asked Detective Sergeant Millhaven to step outside.'

'What?' Fran exploded. 'Now hang on!'

'Constable, you're in no position to demand any such thing,' said the lawyer, sharply.

'And you're in no position to demand details of a matter personal to me following my insistence that it has no bearing. If you feel you must know more I'm willing to tell you. But *only* you.'

'*Stark!*' barked Fran. Stark winced, but ignored her.

The lawyer steepled his fingers and pursed his lips. Stark was torn between anxiety and amusement. He tried to remain poker-faced but the man opposite read faces for a living. That was the thing about lawyers, they knew faces – including when to change their own. The man smiled, then grinned broadly. 'Well played,' he conceded. 'Detective Sergeant, would you mind?'

'Yes, I bloody would!'

'Even so,' said the lawyer, pleasantly.

Fran glared at them both for several seconds, stood and left with an emphatically closed door.

'Now,' said the lawyer, a glint of shark grinning through, 'you have my assurance that, barring any disclosure of criminality, gross misconduct or bearing on my current case, your big secret stays with me. Just as you have my assurance that if you withhold something that later fucks up your credibility and damages my case I'll have you disembowelled and hanged from the city walls as a lesson to other would-be time-wasting ingrates. So,' he cocked his head, 'what the fuck did you do?'

*

'Right!' spat Fran. She marched Stark in silence to Rosie's, ordered, left him to pay and took her regular table.

She maintained her silence, like a smoking volcano, while she drank her wine, then pushed the empty glass towards Stark, who dutifully went to the bar for another. She was halfway through the second before she took a deep breath and finally spoke without looking at him.

'Funny, I'll admit. I'm not sure I've witnessed that level of cheek in my life. Kudos to you.' She took another breath. 'If you live out the day you may look back and smile. If I choke you with a bag of peanuts in the next few minutes you may even achieve cult following, like some rock star cut down in their prime.' She still didn't look at him. 'Which path Destiny has in mind for you will depend entirely on whether you tell me now, in a manner of contrite honesty, everything you told that lawyer.' Finally she turned to him, deadly serious. All he could do was look apologetic. 'Well?' she demanded.

'It's between me and the MoD.'

'Bollocks!' She glared at him. 'Tell me *now*!'

Stark rubbed his eyes and took a long, deep breath, wishing this were another dream from which he might wake. This, however, was a nightmare of his own making. He met her glare levelly. 'No.'

She raised her eyebrows. 'You'll have to do better than that.' A perfect imitation of Groombridge's best look.

'No, Sarge.' Stark could see he'd pushed her too far. 'I'm sorry, but it's MoD business and that's all I'm permitted to say. I told the guv'nor the same thing.'

'Bullshit!'

'Ask him.' What else could he say?

Some of the others came in but, perhaps seeing Fran's face, made for the bar without greeting. Fran finished her second drink, clearly livid, scowled at Stark and left without another word.

'Lovers' tiff?' called Harper. It was the first thing he'd said directly to Stark since the incident on the stairs and Stark wasn't sure how to take it. 'Don't worry, Lover-boy, moody as a sack of stolen cats, that one.'

Stark forced a smile in acknowledgement of the witticism, and reluctantly joined them. Hammed smiled and told him not to worry: DS Millhaven's moods blew over quickly.

Perhaps not this one, thought Stark, surreptitiously swallowing two more pills. Standing at the bar made his hip hurt but he stayed to finish his drink before making his excuses. Harper scoffed theatrically, but another sideways glance as Stark left suggested he was probably still wondering how much Stark had actually overheard.

Stark noticed little of the taxi journey. The perceptive cabbie did not attempt conversation. But by the time Stark had settled into one of the Carter's comfortable reception chairs the trials of the day had been replaced by a lighter problem. Other than Lucy's bombshell about his backside, he had little to go on as far as hopes were concerned. If hope he did. It had been a while since he'd allowed romantic, or even ignoble, thoughts much room in his head. His thoughts about Kelly definitely leant to the latter, but not exclusively. He wasn't at all sure he was ready for . . . something, but there was *something* about her that made him wish he was. Maybe it was her matter-of-factness. Certainly there were other noteworthy features. The fact remained, though: he was damaged goods and Kelly could do better.

'What's her name?' asked Kelly, startling him as she slid into the opposite seat.

'Whose?' he managed.

'With such a dreamy look on your face it had to be a girl you were thinking about.'

'Jealous?'

'Should I be?' she replied.

'No.' He wondered if she'd interpret that correctly, and wondered what had possessed him to ask.

She tilted her head, smile slipping. 'You look tired.'

'Work,' replied Stark.

She accepted this without comment. 'Been doing your exercises?'

'Religiously,' he lied.

'Hmm. Well, come on, then, let's see how you're getting on.'

At least this time she allowed him his own swimming shorts. In every other way the session was a disaster. The sight of Kelly in her swimsuit not only failed to help but actively exacerbated his discomfort: a worrying indicator.

If Kelly was equally disappointed or impatient she masked it perfectly, remaining positive and encouraging throughout. 'Moving up to two appointments. You can do Thursdays, same time?' she asked. Stark nodded. 'Give your regular exercises a rest till then. We don't want to overdo things.' She smiled reassuringly, but Stark knew medical code for 'You look like crap.' So much for hope.

He was ready to put the whole day behind him. He just wanted to eat and sleep. The stairs in his block looked like Everest and the lift finally won out. To his rising dismay, though, no amount of button-jabbing would summon it. He rested his head against the cold metal doors and swore quietly.

17

His sluggish re-entry into the waking world came naturally, woozily, what dreams there may have been dissipating like so much mist; none of the sharp focus of the ones that chased you awake and kept chasing. In comparison this felt like artificial sleep, time deleted. Perhaps it was – Scotch and painkillers were hardly Mother Nature's lullaby. At least he felt partially rested, particularly after a shower and a hearty breakfast. Better than yesterday at least.

He arrived at work with little hope of welcome from Fran. She wasn't at her desk. With little to do he stood staring at the big map, picking out the locations of the various happy-slappings, the deaths and the route of the foot search. A nebulous doubt nagged but he couldn't give it form.

'Good to see you fit to stand at least,' sneered Fran, as she swept in. 'And what gems of inspiration will you shower upon us today?'

Stark ignored her, deep in thought. 'There *is* something, Sarge, about the foot search, I think, but I can't pin it down.' Using the map he traced the route and timeline from the attack on Alfred Ladd to the Ferrier Estate. Then the search area and the reasons for its choice. Finally it clicked. They'd searched Kyle Gibbs's home, the route there and nearby likely spots. But he probably wouldn't have dumped his shoes on the way home or into town the next day. 'We searched the estate bins, right?'

'Yes, but if you want to go back and do them again, you're more than welcome.'

'The bins and the areas behind the shops too?'

'Oh, for Christ's sake, is this your glittering insight?'

'No, it's something Constable Ptolemy said. Uniform believe Nikki Cockcroft uses one of the empty flats as her stash-house, but they don't have the budget to search them. The whole estate is littered with derelict flats. What would stop Gibbs just dumping his shoes in one if he knew we'd search the bins?'

She looked dismissive. 'Budget isn't the only barrier. Christ knows how we'd establish ownership, let alone organize warrants.'

'What if we had probable cause?'

Fran stared at him. 'Forced entry?'

'Just start with any with damaged locks or windows. You never know, we might find Pinky's refuge while we're at it. Two birds with one stone.'

She said nothing for a moment and Stark couldn't tell if he was about to receive a dressing-down for being obvious. 'Hammed,' she said suddenly. 'Get Maggie to help you round up some bodies while I go and see the DCI. And you,' she said to Stark, 'get me some coffee.'

Two hours later they were in the estate, directing uniforms through any door or window with signs of forced entry. There were four in Gibbs's block alone but nothing was found in them other than the usual flotsam and jetsam of eviction, broken glass, drug paraphernalia and the ubiquitous stench of piss. They found no squatters. Perhaps Kyle and Nikki's reign of terror had scared them off, or perhaps they just had higher standards.

But then a local shown Pinky's Photofit directed them to a derelict flat in one of the towers. There was a broken pane in the front-door window. Inside, Stark crouched beside the puffy sleeping-bag, modern but grubby, lying on an even grubbier mattress. Beside it lay a rucksack. Stark pulled on a pair of gloves.

'Careful,' cautioned the PC behind him. 'Might be needles.'

Stark tipped out the contents. Clothing and the assorted belongings of a teenage girl sleeping rough. 'Nothing personal, nothing valuable,' said Stark. Escape and evasion, keep essentials about you in case you have to cut and run; a sensible strategy under the circumstances. A more sensible one might've been to find somewhere to sleep where you didn't have to sneak around in terror of Nikki and her pals.

He felt a lump in the sleeping-bag, reached inside and found a cuddly toy rabbit, its baby pink fur long hobbled by repeated wash cycles.

Fran peered over his shoulder. 'Right.' She turned to the PC. 'Round-the-clock watch, in case she comes back for this lot.'

The morning dragged on. If the embattled off-licence proprietor preferred to minimize police fraternization he would have to console himself with the bumper lunchtime rush on his limited supplies. Starting near suspect homes was a good idea but the estate was huge. And if they didn't find what they were looking for behind a broken lock they would have to start looking for incongruously shiny new locks, and that would require warrants.

They were halfway through Nikki's block when there was a shout. Ptolemy came out of a flat grinning like the cat that had got the cream.

'In a black sack stuffed in the kitchen service riser, Guv,' said Fran. 'Looks like he had a go at cleaning them but SOCO think there's easily enough sample.'

'Suede can be a bastard,' remarked Groombridge, admiring the photo of the blue-and-yellow Adidas Gazelles stained with what looked suspiciously like blood.

'Uniform are happy too. Pills, skunk, coke, crack, heroin – Nikki's stash, they believe. Quite a haul.'

'Mm,' Groombridge mused. Had Nikki been helping Kyle, hiding his evidence, or setting him up as a patsy should her stash-house ever be discovered? 'SOCO lift any prints?'

'Nothing on the drugs, dozens elsewhere. They'll let us know if anything triggers the register.'

'Good work, Detective Sergeant.'

'We've got Stark to thank mostly, Guv,' she admitted.

'Really? Growing on you, is he?'

'Like a fungus.'

'Yes. I heard about his little stunt yesterday.'

'Do *you* know what he's hiding?'

'No. But CPS appear content so it seems we must be too.'

Fran shook her head in disbelief. 'How can you accept that?'

'I've no doubt our young trainee is in serious shit. We may never know what shit, in which case we'll just have to console ourselves with the knowledge that he's in some.'

'Great!'

'Be like me, Detective Sergeant. Don't lose sleep over things you can't alter.'

'Guv.'

'And, you never know, he may improve on you on your way to Orpington.'

'Orpington?'

Groombridge laid a printout on the desk. It was a still from a traffic camera.

'The stolen Beamer?'

'Found in a pub car park.' He tapped the photo, indicating she should take a closer look.

The photo showed what looked like Nikki Cockcroft in the passenger seat, and a much bigger figure behind the wheel. A man, from the size, black baseball cap obscuring most of his face. 'Who's that, then?' she wondered aloud.

'Indeed. Take Boy Wonder, head over there and round up a posse for some door-to-door. Find out if anyone's seen our absconder and mystery accomplice. I'll lean on Forensics, make sure they get a shuffle on with those shoes.'

'Guv.'

The local force were expecting her but weren't enamoured about knocking on doors: they had their own stats to achieve. A call to Groombridge would get things moving but Fran was in a 'persuasive' mood and didn't resort to it. The problem with long shots like this was that nine times out of ten they wasted your time and effort. Much as that pained, you had no choice. Sometimes police work was a slog and that was that.

She and Stark did their bit, as was only right. Stark at least looked like he was taking it seriously today. He did seem fitter, more alert, but his limp was more pronounced, despite his stubborn effort to hide it. The sheen of sweat on his brow during the earlier search was back. He was in pain. She felt a twinge of guilt. She'd come in early to catch up on a few things, including watching Stark's mugshot interview with Maggs, partly to build her own picture but also to check if Stark had missed anything. He'd done a fair job. Perhaps she should've expected it. What she'd not expected was the opening conversation between the two men. She'd not made much of the military coincidence until now. Groombridge had both noted and used it. Perhaps it was a bloke thing. Nevertheless, it bothered her that she'd underestimated the significance.

But that wasn't the source of her guilt. Stark had trouble sleeping. Fran supposed that was understandable. A more palatable explanation than hangover or drug comedown, and she felt guilty about her accusations. But there was still an issue there. It might excuse blowing her out repeatedly but not repeatedly turning up unfit. Whether his problems were physical, mental or substance-related didn't matter: he should get it together or go away until he could. You had to hand it to him, though: he didn't complain. A man of few words. Stoic or just bloody-minded, she still wasn't sure. He'd said precious little on the drive over, nothing not directly related to the matter in hand. If he'd explained, would she have apologized? she wondered. Not likely, after yesterday's stunt.

SOCO arrived and began lifting prints and tape-dabbing for particle and hair evidence. In the photo the driver was wearing gloves, and a cap reduced the chance of finding his hair. There were no obvious CCTV cameras covering the pub. It was an idle chat with her opposite number that threw up the most interesting lead. There had been a few assaults on the homeless since the weekend. As a victim group, vagrants were little inclined to co-operate with the police, but rumour suggested a teenage girl as the attacker. Most had been minor assaults but one particular girl had taken quite a beating. Fran asked if she could speak with her and the DS called for the constable who'd tried to take the girl's statement. He led them to a few nearby haunts and eventually spotted the girl begging outside the shopping centre. She had pink hair! Stark pulled out the Photofit of Pinky, but close up there was little similarity. She also had a purple black eye, split lip and curved cuts that the constable suggested had come from the attacker's sovereign rings. But she was a local, known to share a squat nearby. This wasn't Pinky.

The girl wasn't much help. She didn't want to be seen talking to them, simply regurgitating her earlier statement – a girl had come up to her two evenings ago and started screaming abuse. The cause was never clear and the victim's confusion only worsened matters until she was laid into with fist and foot. A group of lads from a nearby pub heard the commotion and came out. The attacker screamed abuse at them too but was dragged away by a large man in black. None of the Samaritans had hung around after the police arrived.

Fran showed the girl Nikki's mugshot. 'Maybe, I dunno,' was all they got and nothing about the traffic photo of her accomplice or Pinky's Photofit. She couldn't get away from them fast enough.

Fran stared after her. 'Bit of a coincidence if it's not Nikki.'

'What's her beef with the homeless?' asked the constable.

'Over-developed sense of smell,' offered Fran, but then explained.

The constable looked at Pinky's Photofit. 'Oh, yeah, saw this one up in the station. You think she's here?'

'Nikki thinks so,' said Stark. 'We should check local hangouts and shelters,' he suggested, thinking about his search for Alfred Ladd's identity. Fran rolled her eyes.

It was getting dark by the time they bade farewell to the constable after an extensive and fruitless tour of Orpington's homeless nightspots. Stark did not look so perky. 'How would she know Pinky was in Orpington? Assuming she is,' he mused.

'Someone must've told her. One of Pinky's friends.'

'The last sighting of Nikki before she skipped town in the BMW. DC Dixon's report said her victim was a homeless girl, early twenties, new-age dress, piercings with dyed hair – orange and pink.'

'Fits the pattern, mistaken identity.'

'Or search by common trait. People who might know Pinky and where she went.'

Maybe. 'I'll get Dixon to talk to the victim again.'

If he'd been trying to get back on her good side he didn't try again, remaining silent all the way home. Where Fran's natural urge to pry had hitherto wilted, the taped conversation had sprinkled a little water. There were plenty enough cracks to pry, but she wasn't at all sure they'd open up or that she really wanted to see inside. There was a very blokeish mess in there.

Fran dropped him home. The only change in the lift's status was that it now wore an out-of-order sign. No apologies for the inconvenience, no suggestion that anything would be done, just – out of order. Yes, it bloody well is, thought Stark, limping slowly up the stairs.

Once inside the flat he stripped off his sweat-soaked shirt and rifled through his bathroom cabinet for OxyContin. He was out. *How could he be out?* Alarmed and incensed at the thought of having to go in search of a pharmacy he turned the flat upside-down, eventually finding some in his jeans pocket. He washed a couple down with whisky and waited until they started to work before forcing himself to shower, dress and order food. All in all, he hadn't enjoyed his day. This mood was still with him several hours later as the cocktail of pills and booze eased him into impenetrable sleep.

The next morning, as he stood outside waiting for his lift, Fran pulled up in her unmarked blue Ford. 'Get in.'

'What's up?'

'Nikki Cockcroft was arrested last night in Orpington. I'm going to ask politely if we can borrow her for questioning.' Her smile suggested the politeness would last only as long as it was met with total compliance.

18

'They're charging her with affray and resisting arrest. We let her stew overnight.'

'The accomplice?'

'No sign.' The way Fran cut through the traffic she should really have been under blues and twos, but beneath her evident impatience she seemed in finer spirits today, grimly pleased. 'How's your aqua yoga going?' she asked suddenly.

'Dandy.' Kelly's half-smile popped unbidden into Stark's mind.

'You're smiling,' said Fran, glancing at him. 'Why?'

'Watch the road, please, Sarge.'

Instead she pulled over and stopped, much to the consternation of the drivers left to manoeuvre past her, judging by the glances cast. Fran was too busy scrutinizing Stark's blank expression to notice. 'You met someone.' It was a fishing statement, but something in his face gave him away. 'You did! You met someone! Come on, let's hear it.'

'Back on inquisitorial terms, are we, Sarge?'

'Stop avoiding questions and we'll see about wiping away some of the black marks against your name.'

Stark didn't think that much of a bargain. 'Shouldn't we be doing some actual police work?' Denial was probably futile now, but the determined gossip deserves to be kept waiting.

'Bollocks. I'll get to the bottom of this, don't you fear. All I have to do is tell Maggie and she'll get the whole station picking away at you. Hot babe, was she? I assume it's a she?'

'Too hot for the likes of me. As far as gossip's concerned, this story isn't worth the bother.'

'I'll be the judge of that. Name?'

'Kelly.'

'Kelly can be a boy's name too.'

'Not in this case.'

That seemed to satisfy her for now and she pulled out into the traffic again with the minimum of warning, waving cheerfully at the driver furiously flashing his lights at her. 'So, tell me all about her.'

'There's nothing to tell. We met, she hurt me, I left. Same old, same old.'

'Wait . . . She's your aqua-yoga instructor!' Stark cursed himself, but couldn't deny it. 'How delicious! So, come on, on a scale of one to ten?'

Maybe Hammed had been correct, thought Stark. Either he'd served his penance or the emergence of some juicy gossip had eased the chill. 'You've spent far too much time in male company, Sarge.'

'I'm also a single thirty-six-year-old woman with no social life and a short temper. Salacious gossip is all that keeps me from the Chardonnay bottle of despair.'

'You should give Marcus Turner a call.' The car swerved momentarily. 'It's obvious you like each other.'

'What are you talking about?'

'I think you'd make a sweet couple.' It was a cheap diversion and probably wouldn't work, but he'd been saving it up and he was going to enjoy it.

Fran spluttered. 'He's *married*, you arse!'

'He's divorced.'

'How do you know that?' It was obvious she'd known too.

'The same way you do, quietly asking around.'

'Your head injuries are catching up with you!'

'I'm only saying –'

'And don't change the subject. *I'm* the inquisitor here. Come on, marks out of ten.'

Oh, well, it had been good while it lasted. 'A meaningless, subjective poll. Who's to say where a five in my eyes would score in your understanding?'

'She's a five? Bollocks, you're positively salivating. I'll factor in your obvious low frame of reference. How many?'

'Ten.'

'Shit, seriously?'

''Fraid so.'

'You're screwed.'

'Indeed. So can we drop it?'

'Absolutely not! A twinkle in your eye like that could keep the whole sorry station going for months. So, blonde?'

'Tell you what, get me to my Queen Elizabeth appointment by one and I'll give you a full suspect description.'

'Done.'

They checked it was Nikki first, peering in through her cell spy-hole, which seemingly offended her, if the barrage of abuse was anything to go by. The custody sergeant rolled his eyes. 'Charming piece of work, that one.'

'Shame you're besotted with Aqua-bunny, Stark.' Fran grinned. 'You and Nikki seem made for each other.'

'Maybe you can get me her number, Sarge,' he replied evenly.

Fran laughed. 'Better still, I could arrange you some time alone in our cells. Mick shares my romantic sentimentality.'

'Maybe not.'

'Probably right, I hate to think of the mess she'd make of your soft arse.' Fran mimed a nasty taste in her mouth. 'Honestly, I can't understand what boys see in the nasty little skank.'

The senior arresting officer was determined Nikki be charged locally but seemed happy enough to send her over to Greenwich the next day. Stark filled in the paperwork meticulously under the impatient eye of his DS. 'Wait,' he said suddenly. 'It says here she was arrested in White Hart Road. We were there yesterday, the homeless hostel . . .'

The officer nodded. 'She was trying to get in. Said she needed to see a friend but refused to say who and became violent. Took three officers to get her in the van.'

Fran smiled sweetly. 'Could we have directions?'

The hostel was a short drive and Fran made easy work of the traffic. It was indeed one they had visited the previous evening. They'd missed Nikki by just a few hours.

'I'm sorry,' insisted the manager. 'As I told you last night, it's against policy to divulge information on our guests. We require their trust if we're to do our work.'

'But unlike last night I now have reason to believe you're withholding information pertinent to my investigation.'

'I'm sorry, but I really must ask that you respect what we're trying to do here.'

'I do. And I hope you will respect my authority to arrest you for obstruction,' smiled Fran.

Stark wasn't sure on the law in this area but neither was the manager, who all of a sudden recognized the Photofit. The girl was new, he said. She'd first stayed there the night after the attack in Greenwich Park and only three nights, at random, since. He remembered her because she'd clearly taken a recent beating, not uncommon, of course, but noteworthy. Very few belongings, another common indicator. She'd signed in a few minutes before the trouble at the front desk, and left not long after.

Stark tapped Fran on the shoulder and pointed to the discreet CCTV camera above the desk.

'Bloody do-gooders!' cursed Fran, in the car. 'I've a good mind to charge the self-righteous tit. We could've had Pinky in an interview room by now.'

Stark stared at the CCTV printout still in his hand. Pinky. An androgynous waif in baggy new-age chic with very pink hair. She had given no name, but now they had her face. They travelled in silence for a while, Stark mulling over a thorny decision. Fran's sudden thaw had presented an opportunity. He'd anticipated needing to bypass her and ask Groombridge; it was still tempting. Of course, she might freeze again so he had to take advantage now. 'Any chance you could keep me off the roster for Saturday morning?' he asked cautiously, as they pulled into the hospital.

'Why?'

'It's personal.' A phrase she almost certainly didn't want to hear from him.

'Asking while you're in my good books, is it?'

Meaning he wasn't necessarily. Stark didn't bait her. 'It's important.' How important depended on one's point of view and he hoped she wouldn't delve.

She subjected him to a long, appraising stare. 'Tell me which department you're visiting today and you're on.'

Stark could have lied but this *was* important. Besides, she wasn't stupid: she clearly suspected and would find out eventually. 'Psychotherapy.'

To give Fran her due, she kept all but the faintest triumph from her face. 'And Aqua-babe?'

Stark described Kelly in dry police terminology, studiously avoiding undertone. Even so, Fran whistled. 'You're so screwed.' She grinned.

Stark could only shrug wryly.

'Okay, go on.' Fran jerked her head at the door. 'I'll see you back at the fort.'

There never seemed to be time to buy food before his allotted appointment, making it all the more irritating that Doc Hazel summoned him in fifty-four minutes late – a personal best, though Stark was sure she had the right stuff to break the hour barrier.

She began with the usual pleasantries, jotted a few notes and got started. 'When you wake up from these dreams, how do you feel?' She gave it that lilting tone, the artificial saccharine – there's no judgement here, honest. It was necessary to engage, he knew that, but he wasn't at all convinced she was worth the effort. At least she was hovering somewhere over the topic for once. He considered toying with her but decided it was easier just to throw her a bone. 'Are you asking if I feel remorse?'

'Is that what you feel?' She was probably congratulating herself.

'About some of it, yes,' he replied honestly.

'About the boy and his mother?'

Ouch. This was the first time she'd asked about it directly. 'Of course.'

'About the enemy soldiers?'

'No.'

'No?' She seemed curious, non-judgemental. Next she'd make a note.

'No.'

She scribbled a note on her pad. Would she ask the next question? Stark wondered.

'Why is that, do you think?' Bingo – the million-dollar question, a golden opportunity to flood her notepad with bullshit of the highest order. But that wouldn't be fair. He'd led her here, after all.

Piecing together the fragments, he reckoned he'd targeted and shot no fewer than nine Taliban in the last minutes of that firefight, probably more. Kinetic contact, they called it. Bloody shootout was nearer the mark. Most, if not all, would have died of their wounds. More would have died as a direct result of his actions. And they weren't the first. How many times had he returned fire, called in artillery or air support? It was a hard truth, not to know how many lives you'd taken. All were sons, brothers, fathers. Somewhere right now people still mourned them, and for that he felt remorse, genuine and painful. But for the men themselves?

Each had been actively trying to kill him, kill his comrades. That was enough for some. And this wasn't like traditional wars. Those men hadn't been luckless conscripts yanked from their lives by the idiocy of their leaders – you, but for the grace of God. They had been volunteers. Maybe most had been just the latest generation of ill-informed angry young men sick of poverty and too open to suggestion, defending their lands against a perceived aggressor. Maybe. But you are who you stand up with. Whatever the rights and wrongs of Western foreign policy, NATO was there to make things better and then go home. If you allied yourself with the fanatics, who wanted to kill the infidel and were willing to blow up civilians, behead charity workers live online, murder foreign doctors there to help, or execute teachers in front of their pupils simply for daring to educate girls, then you were stained by association.

And don't get him started on the sectarian madness, not after the Basra market bombing. There were so many ways to waste a life but to embrace bitterness, to choose corrupted theistic bigotry, to inflict that selfish hatred on others, was surely the very worst. He summarized the rest as best he could, badly probably, and with little hope of making himself understood. Hazel made notes and looked benignly interested as usual. 'Thank you,' she said finally.

He glanced at the clock. 'We've overrun,' he said, surprised. This was unprecedented.

'Yes.' She closed her pad and clicked her pen shut. 'See you next week.'

Stark closed the door behind him without the righteous anger he'd enjoyed after previous sessions and unsure how he felt about that. Drained, he drifted to the canteen, more to get his head straight than to feed the appetite long fled. More importantly, he was able to renew his OxyContin prescription at the hospital pharmacy.

Fran didn't question his late return. Much as he appreciated this, he hoped it didn't mark a switch to some excruciating tip-toeing around his mental health.

In a quiet moment he asked DC Williams whether he knew of a decent florist but, with unfortunate timing, Fran returned just as the question was put to the room. No doubt she'd assume the worst about his important personal need for time off. She did not look pleased, but maybe it wouldn't do any harm to let her imagination run away on this one.

The local hospitals had no records matching Pinky's description. Harper and Bryden were sent with a photo to double-check.

Dixon returned from tracking down the victim of the town altercation. 'Doesn't look like mistaken identity, Guv,' he reported. 'She said Nikki laid into her, screaming to know where the girl with pink hair was. Looks like Nikki struck gold. Rumour was already spreading about the latest attack. Apparently Pinky had texted someone that she was scared, that she was on the bus to Orpington where she knew someone. That's all.'

'And she told Nikki this?' asked Groombridge. 'She didn't mention it before?'

'I had to press her quite hard to admit it, Guv. I don't think she was proud of herself.'

'Thank you, DC Dixon.' Groombridge stared thoughtfully at the image of Pinky.

A little later Fran took a call from DC Hammed. 'Good. Politely insist he come down the station to help us with our enquiries.' She replaced the receiver. 'David Phillips,' she explained, to the faces turned her way. Given they already knew his name and that he was the kind of man prone to running away from his obligations, Groombridge had opted not to put Phillips's image on TV. Instead they'd simply contacted the dole office for his next appointment and sent Hammed down to wait.

Twenty minutes later Phillips was in interview room one, with Groombridge questioning him about the night of Kyle Gibbs's death. He was clearly aware that he'd walked through the park shortly before a serious crime was perpetrated and not come forward.

'So this was about what time?' asked Groombridge.

'Dunno, about quarter to eleven, I s'pose. I'd run out of cash, so I left before closing time.'

'You visited the cashpoint on the corner of Greenwich Church Street.'

'Right. How d'you know that?'

Groombridge smiled, ignoring the question. 'How much had you had to drink?'

'You can't arrest me for having a drink.'

'You're not under arrest, Mr Phillips. No one is accusing you of anything. We're asking for your help, that's all.'

Phillips shifted in his seat. He had a little form. Helping the police wasn't the usual relationship. 'Six, seven pints, so what?'

'Not all that much, then,' said Groombridge, offering a twisted olive branch.

'Right.'

'So, you can easily recall what you saw in the park.'

'Yeah, I suppose.'

'Did you happen to pass the bandstand?'

Suddenly Phillips looked cagey again. 'Yeah. Why?'

'You did? By my reckoning it was slightly out of your way.'

'I saw someone smoking, I needed a light.'

'You weren't worried it was Parks Police?'

'Been walking through there for years, never seen your lot after dark.' He looked worried again. 'You said I wasn't in trouble.'

'We're not interested in trespassing. We just want to know what you saw.'

'It was just a dosser. Who cares? I heard about that bloke getting killed. It wasn't me.'

'No one is saying it was. But the dosser, he might've seen something. Can you describe him?'

'You lot 'aven't got a clue, 'ave ya?' He chuckled.

'About what?' asked Groombridge, evenly.

'It wasn't a him,' scoffed Phillips.

'What?'

'The dosser wasn't a bloke. It was a bird.'

Hammed and Stark stood watching through the glass in shock. No expression passed over Groombridge's face. The only sign that he shared their surprise was that he took a few moments before he asked, 'At the bandstand? Are you sure?'

'You saying I can't tell the difference? Fucking waste, good lookin' once, makes me sick. If you can afford all that hair dye an' tattoos an' shiny studs through everyfin' then you don't need my spare fuckin' change. I hate those pretend dossers, new-age wasters. Probably lives in a better flat than me, claiming off the dole and sitting on her arse! Get a fucking job!' This glaring hypocrisy hung unchallenged in the air for several seconds.

'What colour dye?'

'Pink. Though she had one of those hats on too, you know, one of those new-age knitted things, with the flappy ear bits, all zigzags and colours.'

Neither Fran nor Groombridge made any outward acknowledgement of the coincidence. 'Age?'

Phillips shrugged. 'How can you tell these days? Fifteen, twenty, I don't know.'

'Think.'

'Look, you said I wasn't in trouble. I don't like being told what to do.'

'I appreciate that, but I also note you've been arrested twice for solicitation, both times with girls barely over the age of consent. Was that why you approached this girl?'

'No!' cried Phillips, defensively.

'I hope not.'

Fran had been rifling through the file and now slid the CCTV still of Pinky on to the desk. 'That's her!' Phillips was suddenly eager to appear helpful. 'Tattoo on her hand, all those piercings, not my type.'

After Phillips had been thanked and sent on his way, Groombridge frowned. 'Puts a curious spin on things.'

'I think I might've seen someone with a hat like that on the parks CCTV, Guv,' admitted Stark. 'Coming in St Mary's Gate not long after Maggs.'

'Maggs never mentioned the girl,' said Fran.

'Might not've seen her, Guv,' said Stark. 'She might've moved on after Phillips disturbed her.'

Groombridge looked thoughtful. 'Narrow escape or witness to a second killing in days? The sooner we talk to her the better. How long till Nikki Cockcroft gets here?'

Fran made a face. 'Not till tomorrow afternoon, Guv. She's up before Orpington magistrates first thing in the morning.'

'Right, then. Get on to Maggs's doctors and arrange an interview for tomorrow morning. I want to hear what *he* has to say about this.'

19

No longer in a gown, Maggs was wearing jeans and a mid-blue sweatshirt. Print on both marked them out as prison issue. Something about that struck Stark as wrong, but he supposed if Maggs wasn't here he'd be in Belmarsh. He looked less yellow, less slumped, fitter, and there was a sharper intelligence in his eyes. Fewer pain meds, thought Stark. He gazed at each of them in turn, perhaps longest at Stark. 'What do you want?'

Groombridge ran through the usual spiel, then invited Maggs to tell them again what had happened that night in the park, which he did, virtually verbatim with his previous statement. When he'd finished Fran silently slipped Pinky's photo on to the table. 'What can you tell me about this girl?' asked Groombridge.

Maggs pondered it, expressionless. 'Jailbait. Bit boyish too. More your type than mine, I'd say.'

Groombridge ignored the gibe. 'Look again.'

'Why?'

'We have a witness placing her at the bandstand shortly before midnight.' Groombridge tapped the photo again. 'She was there, Maggs.'

'If you say so.'

'You didn't see her?'

'It's a big park.'

Groombridge waited, but Maggs just shrugged.

'Do you know this girl?' asked Fran.

'It's not a community,' growled Maggs. 'Some of the young ones and part-timers mingle, but the old hands like me . . .

208

There ain't much mileage begging in the same spot as someone else now, is there?'

'What about sleeping?' said Groombridge. 'Safety in numbers, warmth, even?'

'Reckon I'm an attractive prospect for cosying up to, DCI Groombridge? Maybe I was right about you.' He looked at the photo again. 'Not sure she'd think so. Besides, you know I prefer fat, ugly women. How's the missus?'

Groombridge didn't rise to this any more than he had last time. Stark realized he had no idea if the guv was even married. He wore no ring. 'You've heard your rights. "It may harm your defence if you do not mention when questioned something which you later rely on in court." Last chance, Maggs.'

Maggs remained impassive. 'Are we done?'

Groombridge stared hard at him for several seconds. 'For now.'

'Think he's lying?' asked Fran, outside.

'I can't tell either,' admitted Groombridge.

'He was,' said Stark.

They both turned to him. 'Care to elaborate, Trainee Investigator?'

Stark hesitated, wondering if he could. It was the eyes, he thought. Combined with Maggs's shaggy, greying hair and beard, they'd lent him a wolf-like caginess. 'It's just a feeling, Guv.'

'Well,' said Groombridge. 'Let's see if little Nikki has any *feelings* on the matter.'

Nikki Cockcroft arrived that afternoon, having been remanded into custody by the magistrate in Orpington. She did not look happy.

'Affray and resisting arrest, Nikki,' tutted Groombridge. 'The latest in a long career of criminality.'

'Inspector.' The court-appointed legal counsel sounded a

warning tone. On a hiding to nothing he might be, but he would do his job diligently. Nikki just sat sideways in her chair, arms tightly folded, a deep scowl of phoney disinterest.

'Quite right. That's all on your juvenile record and can't be put before the jury.'

'Inspector, my client intends to plead guilty to the charges before her and as such will not face a jury.'

'The car, too?' asked Groombridge. 'I suppose we should all be happy she didn't burn it like the others.'

'*Inspector.*'

'You're still banned from driving, isn't that right, Nikki? Banned before you were even old enough to drive, in fact. Time was that might've been considered quite a feat. Not now.' He sighed. 'Now, I suppose, it's common.' This elicited a response, however fleeting. 'Not that I approve of the practice but it was rather stupid of you not to burn it, Nikki. We have your finger-prints inside. Still using it, I guess. I expect you thought swapping its plates would throw us poor dumb coppers off the scent, as far as you were thinking at all. But us poor dumb coppers have put rather a lot of work into alerting the public to the dangers of ID theft, including vehicle ID. People – that is, decent, law-abiding people, not stupid petty criminals – know to report stolen licence plates, these days. Of course, you're not a juvenile any more and the penalties for being that *common* are more serious. Stealing a car, driving without a licence and insurance while banned, not a slapped wrist now. No, that's time inside. Unless, of course, you weren't driving . . .' Still nothing from Nikki. He slid the traffic photo on to the desk. 'Who is this?' he asked, tapping the driver.

The legal interjected and the officers were made to turn off the tape and leave the room while he consulted with Nikki. After the brief hiatus, he spoke for her. 'My client was in the car. She accepted a lift from an acquaintance but did not know the car was stolen.'

Fran huffed derisively.

'Who?' demanded Groombridge.

'My client is not willing to divulge.'

'Then I'll be adding obstruction to the charge sheet.'

'Even so.'

'Then, of course, we have assault with intent. You can get at least five for that now.'

'My client has not been charged with assault, Inspector.'

'So far,' said Groombridge, pleasantly. 'But there's a rather battered young lady in Orpington who might be ready to identify your client. Nice sovereign rings you have there, Nikki. Then, of course, there's the assaults on the homeless persons here in Greenwich . . . James Wright, aged forty-eight; Thomas Stepney, fifty-nine; Margaret Tomlinson, forty-six; and Michael O'Leary, fifty-three. Enjoy soft targets, do you?'

'You have no evidence linking my client with those incidents.'

'So far.'

'Then there's the assault on Alfred Ladd . . . aged seventy-eight. *Seventy-eight*, Nikki.'

'You have no evidence linking my client with that either,' insisted the legal.

'Not incontrovertible perhaps. What happened to the old boy, Detective Sergeant?'

'Dead, Guv,' replied Fran. 'Kidney and brain damage resulting from severe beating.'

'That's the official assessment now, is it?'

'Yes, Guv.'

Groombridge shook his head, with a deep sigh. 'That poor defenceless old man, kicked to death by thugs. I'm sure they didn't mean to kill him, just having a laugh probably, but now they're in well over their heads. They must be soiling themselves. I reckon you'll get as much as twenty years for a murder like that.'

'Inspector . . .' The legal's sense of humour was failing.

'I wouldn't like to be in their shoes right now,' continued Groombridge. 'Talking of shoes, those blue trainers with the bloodstains on them, Detective Sergeant. Who did Forensics say they belong to again?'

'Kyle Gibbs, Guv,' replied Fran on cue.

'Oh, yes. Nice piece of work, that one. Whatever happened to him?'

'Dead, Guv,' answered Fran, deadpan.

'Oh, yes. Dead. But I'm forgetting. He was your boyfriend, wasn't he, Nikki? My condolences on your loss.'

Nikki said nothing. If anything, her tightly folded arms folded tighter.

'You don't seem that upset, if you don't mind my saying so?' continued Groombridge. 'Of course, you weren't the most loyal girlfriend, I suppose, giving it away to his mates behind his back. Bit cheap, that. Was it just Tyler or did they all get a go?'

Nikki glared at him, just for a second, then returned to glaring at the wall.

Groombridge shrugged. 'Tell me, Detective Sergeant, have the Forensic Science Service confirmed whose blood that was yet?'

'Just came in, Guv. DNA match for Alfred Ladd.'

'That implicates Kyle Gibbs, Inspector, not my client.'

'True,' agreed Groombridge, calmly. 'But we have CCTV footage showing your client in the vicinity minutes before the attack in the company of Gibbs and the rest of their shared associates.'

'Circumstantial at best. My client says she parted ways with Gibbs before the assault.'

Groombridge chuckled. 'Colin Messenger *says* you were never with them at all, poor lad. He has a hard time remembering how to speak, let alone what he's been told to say.'

'Inspector . . .' warned the counsel.

Groombridge kept his face blank. This was the bitter pill. None had fingered any other; none had fingered Nikki. He could lie and say they had: it always worked on TV. But lying in interview never played back well in real-life court. 'All of them have confessed in one way or another . . .'

For the first time Nikki looked at him, shocked, suspicious.

'Except Martin Munroe. I suppose this promotes him to ringleader now, last man standing, as it were. Leader of a gang of one. I shouldn't laugh but it's quite pitiful really. Don't worry, Nikki, I'm sure he'll remember you fondly.' She shot him a death glare. Perhaps she had slept with them all. 'Maybe he'll boast to his new gang about you in the long years ahead. Do you think he'll visit you in prison?'

'*Inspector* . . .' The legal sounded exasperated now.

'Here's the transcripts,' said Groombridge, slapping them down on the table. 'I'm sure your counsel here can read them for you – I know you missed a lot of school. Can you read, Nikki?'

She sneered in the affirmative.

'Good for you. I also have footage of you all together shortly afterwards –'

'From a distance, Inspector, at night.'

Groombridge ignored him, looking only at Nikki. 'Then I have a signed statement from an eyewitness placing Tyler, Colin, Tim, Paul and you, Nikki, at the scene of the next assault in the pattern.'

'And said "witness" is a drunk on a murder charge.'

Groombridge waved a hand. 'Even so, I rather think a jury will decide *circumstantial* is close enough. Do you understand the difference between concurrent and consecutive custodial sentences, Nikki?' he asked conversationally. 'No? Well, they're awfully long words – I'll try to dumb it down so you can get the gist. Concurrent means the judge feels there might be hope for you, so even though you get more than one conviction you serve all your sentences at the same time. But consecutive means the judge thinks you should rot for as long as possible and orders that you serve each sentence one after the other. It's entirely up to the judge. What will they think of you? Quite the recidivist you've proven.'

'Inspector!'

'Oh, yes. Sorry, Nikki. Recidivist means someone –'

'Inspector, I was objecting to your unsubstantiated accusation, not asking you to elucidate.'

'Oh dear.' Groombridge sighed. 'Now we have "unsubstantiated" and "elucidate". Perhaps I should get you a dictionary, Nikki.'

Nikki said nothing.

'It's a type of book,' explained Groombridge, kindly.

'Inspector! You go too far!' cried the lawyer, trying to mask a laugh.

'Really? I was just trying to be helpful. You have to admit the words "concurrent" and "consecutive" could come to matter to Nikki here rather a lot. I have to say, Nikki, it may not go well for you . . .'

'Really, Inspector –'

'I'm just hypothesizing, filling in the gaps in conversation while your client plays dumb. Are you dumb, Nikki?'

Ouch, thought Stark, watching through the one-way glass. Nikki shot Groombridge another death glare.

'Make a note of that, Detective Sergeant. "Nikki Cockcroft – dumb."'

'Piss off, wanker!'

'Ah, well, would you look at that? Make a note, Detective Sergeant. "Nikki Cockcroft – not dumb, just stupid, common and cheap."' Nikki kicked back her chair and reached across the desk with a pointing finger, but Fran was ready and restrained her as Stark rushed in to help. They couldn't restrain her mouth, though. It took quite a while and quite a tirade of repeated expletives before she was sitting back in her chair, steaming. 'You'd better watch your back . . .' she mumbled.

'Really?' Groombridge met her glare, unblinking. 'Only your brother's not eligible for parole for another twelve years, not that he'll get it, and once you join him inside, just who exactly should I watch my back against?'

From the way she'd behaved so far, Stark expected more teenage denial. Instead she fixed Groombridge with a chilling, malevolent smile. 'I'm afraid you can't frighten me with empty threats, like you did with Naveen, Colin and the others. It won't work for long on them either, you know. That's the problem with stupid people, common, cheap people. If they can be scared in one direction, they can just as easily be nudged back the other way.' Nikki's smile widened.

What did she know that they did not? wondered Stark.

Groombridge held his composure. 'By the time they get to court I'll have them all rolling over like little puppies, little girls, little girl puppies. What's a girl puppy called, Detective Sergeant?'

'Bitch, Guv.'

'Bitch. Rolling over like little bitches. Rolling over on you, Nikki.'

'Yeah, *right*!'

'You'd be surprised just how disloyal supposed friends can be, how eagerly they roll on their backs in betrayal, but then again, no, perhaps you wouldn't.' Nikki's smile slipped into another glare. 'Then there's the girl with dyed hair . . .' Groombridge let that hang.

Nikki looked positively shaken, if only momentarily. Her counsel seemed nonplussed. 'What girl?'

'Perhaps you can ask your client about her when we're finished. Not a drunk on a murder charge this time, Nikki. I can see how you might fancy a word with her. You have such eloquent fists.'

'Inspector, if you have another witness perhaps you should produce her.'

'I intend to.' Nikki's confidence had taken a visible jolt. Groombridge smiled. 'So, where did we get to? Oh, yes, the car and all that . . . say, six months to two years? The assaults, let's assume they don't just add them all up but, still, six counts . . . That'd be ten years at least, I reckon.'

'Inspector, so far you've presented no firm evidence linking my client with *any* of the recent attacks, let alone six.'

'So far,' echoed Groombridge. 'And then there's poor Stacey Appleton. Her murder will get you twenty-five years at least.'

'You have nothing linking my client with that either.'

'Add the old boy's killing on top, Nikki, and you're looking at life.'

'Inspector!' the lawyer protested.

'I didn't murder him!' spat Nikki. 'I never touched him!'

'No, you just stood at the back and pointed. You let Tyler and Colin and Kyle do your dirty work!' Groombridge's voice was raised. 'Like a little girl, like a little yapping puppy! Does that make them your bitch or you theirs?'

'I ain't no bitch!'

'They got stuck in while you cowered at the back, yapping like a little bitch!' scoffed Groombridge. 'Yapping away until you got Kyle killed.'

'*That was his fault, not mine!*' hissed Nikki. The lawyer placed a desperate hand on her shoulder but recoiled at her fury. '*Stupid wanker! That was his fault! HIM AND THAT PINK-HAIRED BITCH!*'

Bingo, thought Stark, racing in to help again. Groombridge hadn't mentioned the colour pink. Nikki had just implicated herself. She had to be restrained quite forcefully, so incandescent with rage that she could hardly speak, a blessing, given the words that did escape as she was dragged off, kicking and screaming, by Mick and two WPCs.

Her legal counsel sighed and packed his paperwork into his battered briefcase. 'Pleasure doing business as ever, Detective Chief Inspector.'

'Likewise, Martin. Give my best to Joan.'

'Will do. See you for round two.'

'You're an inspiration, Guv.' Fran grinned.

Groombridge cleared his throat. 'Know anything about Greek mythology, Stark?'

'A little, Guv.'

'They're like the Hydra, noisome little shits like that. Lop off one head and two grow back.'

'Not if you cauterize the stumps,' replied Stark, without thinking. 'And sooner or later you cut off the one head that kills it.' Groombridge stared at him. 'Heracles and his nephew Iolaus, Guv,' Stark explained lamely. Fran rolled her eyes.

'I was being rhetorical, lad,' said Groombridge.

Stark resisted pointing out the word had two modern interpretations, and Fran ushered him away. 'For a smartarse you don't learn all that quickly.'

'I'm learning all the time, Sarge.'

20

'Will you be gracing us with your presence down the pub this evening?' asked Fran, as they handed over to the night shift. 'Or is DS Harper right about you?'

'Harper?'

'He reckons you're frightened of me.'

'He also reckons we're having a lovers' tiff.' Stark chuckled.

'Perhaps he's jealous.' She laughed. 'So?'

'White flag.'

'Coward.'

Stark considered confessing to the doubling of his hydrotherapy sessions but decided her amusement would be too excruciating. As he waited out front for his cab, Peters and Ptolemy stopped to ask after Nikki. There was a buzz of contentment circulating on the lower floors that she might finally be due some comeuppance. Just as they were leaving, a question occurred to Stark. 'Who did you pull her claws out of?'

'Huh?' Ptolemy frowned.

'When she was thirteen? You said . . .'

'Some poor homeless sod who'd wandered into the estate. She gave him a right going over. Took two of us to get her off him.'

'It's not in her juvenile record.'

'He wouldn't press charges and no one would say how it started. Even at that age Nikki had the whole estate in fear of her.'

'I heard it was her dad,' said Peters.

'Her dad?' said Stark.

'Yeah, kicked out by the mum years earlier. Turned up one day looking for reconciliation or money. Or both. Nikki went ballistic.'

'Where'd you hear that?' asked Ptolemy.

'Sergeant Clark told me. Not sure who had it first. Nikki wouldn't have anyone talking about it, but the gossip got around eventually. All before my time.'

'I never heard it,' said Ptolemy. Peters shrugged.

The implications reverberated in Stark's ears as his taxi jinked through the rush-hour traffic. Could this whole thing, all the violence and death, be traced back to that one sorry homecoming? What a desperate, corrosive, futile motivation. How old had she been when he left? For a moment Stark felt sorry for Nikki. No, he *did* feel sorry for her, for the fatherless child – he knew something of that – but not for the vengeful teenager. He sighed and stared out at the busy world rushing past the window. All that life, all those stories, all that love and laughter, all that fear and loathing. He felt drained. The last week had really taken it out of him. It'd been exciting, excruciating, exhausting in every sense. He'd hoped to put on a better show this evening but the last two days had ground that hope into dust. Why did he care, though? The answer was as obvious as it was ridiculous.

Rather than a better show, the session was his worst in months. The ache in his hip allied itself with others to mount a revolution. Kelly could not fully mask her concern. Her frown said it all. 'Have you been on your feet a lot, with work?' she asked afterwards, without looking up from writing her notes.

'A bit.'

'Is there any way you might be able to take it easy for a few days?'

Stark didn't like where this was going. 'I'm not master of my time right now.'

'Because of the killings?' She looked up now and smiled at his surprise. 'Two and two.'

'Not just a pretty face.' The words were out of his mouth before his brain caught up again, an unfamiliar and unwelcome sensation. It seemed a different part of his anatomy altogether was staging its own coup.

There might have been a hint of a smile on that pretty face but it was gone in a moment. 'I'm serious. If work is undermining your health, that needs to be addressed. I can speak to your GP about signing you off.'

'No! Thank you, but no. I need to be doing this right now.' Because it's all there is, he didn't add. The last thing he wanted was another sodding sick-chit. Perhaps she'd understand if he told her but he wasn't about to make that leap.

'How long will "right now" go on? The news said arrests had been made.'

'I can't discuss it.'

'Fair enough. But, judging from your physical state, I'd say you were on the brink of exhaustion. If you don't start looking after yourself better we'll be wasting our time here.'

Stark was dismayed. There were quite enough women in his life queuing up to tick him off. 'I'm sorry.'

'Don't be. Just get some rest.'

'I'll try.'

'How do you get here?' she asked. She knew he didn't drive yet.

'Taxi.'

'Want a lift home? I'm just in Blackheath.'

'Actually, the taxi's picking me up,' he replied. He wondered what he'd have said if her question hadn't taken him so much by surprise. The thought of half an hour in a car with her was both appealing and unsettling.

'Oh,' she said, no sign of disappointment.

'Maybe on Monday?' he suggested.

'Okay. But only if you're a better boy this week.' The hint of a smile was back.

The search for Pinky continued the following day, but without development. The CPS lawyers were back. Fran pushed Stark to accompany Groombridge in her place, shamelessly quoting his need for experience and her own distaste for tedious meetings and lawyers, the last barb directed to the face of the one who'd enabled Stark's stunt the last time they'd met.

Stark observed Groombridge throughout. The DCI might've forged a fine career in the forces. The case wasn't airtight yet, but they were on track and a good mood pervaded the team. Even Fran was in better spirits as she demanded Stark attend Friday drinks, and for once he was happy to comply.

'Get them in, then,' she said, shrugging off her jacket and sliding into her usual chair.

'Fine,' replied Stark, cheerfully. He'd abstained the previous night, sticking with pills alone, and paid for it. He was hanging on his chinstrap, and he was going to sleep peacefully tonight, whatever it took. He had a busy Saturday ahead but it was Friday night now and that had to count for something. His hip hurt more than it had in a week, and other wounds throbbed too, not all physical. But another week was over. He was smack in the middle of a real investigation, too busy to brood and all the better for it. He plonked the large white wine on the table with the whisky and returned with four packets of crisps.

'Aye aye!' mocked Harper. His confidence had grown, it seemed, that Stark would not be spreading rumours behind his back. Stark ignored him. Fran told him to piss off.

'Thanks.' She held up her drink, chinked glasses and took a long pull.

'No worries. I put the first round on your tab.' He grinned as she spluttered and choked.

'Smartarse,' she managed eventually. 'Still buttoned up like a virgin bride, I see.'

It was an odd sideways dig. He habitually kept his tie done up, his shirt's top button fastened, his sleeves at the cuff. He didn't really think about it any more. Trust her to challenge it. 'The scars would draw more comment,' he said honestly, almost eliciting more spluttering.

Fran placed her glass down carefully. 'Do you always do that?'

'Do what?'

'Toss out a truth grenade when cornered.'

'Sometimes offence is the best form of defence,' Stark said, quoting Maggs.

Fran huffed. 'Show me.'

'I'm pretty sure stripping down to my undies would draw the most comment of all.'

Fran smirked. 'No scars under your pants, then?' He paused just too long. 'You have!' She laughed. 'Nothing . . . fundamental, I trust? Maggie would be devastated.'

'Perhaps it wouldn't hurt to let that myth spread.'

'Be nice, she's harmless. So, the hip, what happened?'

'Shrapnel. Nothing special.' He held up a hand before she could corner him with another question. 'That's enough truth grenades for now. How about you? What's your story?'

She shrugged. 'Barbadian dad came here as a boy. Mum from white middle-class Surrey family who, shall we say, took time to come around to the idea of a black son-in-law? Four elder brothers. Dad claims he was going for a five-a-side team. Guess who got stuck in goal. To be fair, he did teach me to cook. Been a detective sergeant six years now but only one here. Moved to shake off a few cobwebs, ex-fiancé, crappy boss, not the same person. Thirty-six, repeatedly single, like a drink, like a dance, dislike whisky and men who can't give as good as they get. Right, your turn again.' Stark let his pained expression show but Fran wouldn't be shaken. 'Tell you what,

I'll throw out a few guesses. Twenty-five years old – I know that from your file. Only child?'

'Younger sister, married with two in nappies.'

'Dad died young, making you the man of the house.'

Stark studied her. 'I was eleven.'

'Sorry,' said Fran. Perceptive guess, then, rather than inside information. 'So, why the police?'

'I thought it might be interesting.'

She raised her eyebrows and scoffed. 'So when it wasn't you signed your weekends away to the army?'

'Pretty much. I wasn't certain police life was for me.'

Fran looked shocked. 'And now?'

'We'll see.'

'Wow! Stick this man on a recruitment poster!'

'I could see the point, pounding the beat and all that, but, *Christ*, was it tedious. So I took up weekend soldiering for excitement and extra cash. Ironically a lot of my tour in Iraq was spent pounding beats.'

'Not all of it, though?'

'No.'

'What about Afghanistan?'

'It was different. In Basra we were mostly trying to stop them killing each other. In Helmand we were still trying to stop them killing us.'

'Yet you volunteered to go back,' she said, inviting him to explain.

Stark declined. 'And the rest is history.'

'Hardly. Tell me what happened out there.'

'No. And it's your turn to get the drinks. I want the change,' he said, passing her a twenty.

She snatched it, bought the drinks and slapped his change on the table but with more irony than rancour. 'So, how come you had so much free time at weekends? No wife, girlfriend?'

'Nothing serious.'

'How come so solitary?'

'I could ask you the same question.'

'I'm not solitary. I'm just frequently mistaken in my choice of company. What's your excuse?'

'I'm young.'

'Ouch! Rude sod.'

'Maybe I just haven't met the right girl.'

'Don't let Maggie hear you say that. So . . . uncomfortable in a relationship, uncomfortable with family and friends, uncomfortable in the police and not fit for the army. Pretty much good for nothing, then.'

'Ouch.'

'You're the original cat on a hot tin roof. Will you still be here in a year?'

'We'll see.'

Fran shook her head in disbelief. 'Seriously, what good are you? You can't live half a life. You can't be half a copper. Sooner or later you're gonna have to put up or shut up.'

'Maybe,' said Stark, keen to change the subject. Fran was career police; his doubts rang heresy in her pious ears. 'Dixon tells me we're all heading to a curry house later. Any good?'

'Connoisseur, are you? I should've known. Better get some more drinks down you to deaden the taste-buds. So, army nicknames. What was yours?'

Stark shrugged, smiling at her shifting angle of attack. 'I guess I wasn't a nickname kind of guy.' One particular officer had taken to calling him Private Sideways, in a Private Smart Alec tone, after a notable incident during a training manoeuvre, and various peers had experimented around the themes of stark raving mad and stark bollock naked. Thankfully nothing had stuck.

Fran harrumphed, unconvinced. 'I'm sure I can think of a few.' Indeed the theme proved depressingly popular when she introduced it in the curry house. The food was predictably mediocre but the *faux*-Indian beer masked that admirably and the crowd were soon in high spirits. It'd been a good week: a string of assaults and three killings all nicely solved with perpetrators in custody and in line to be banged up for sure. Stark, under numerous ad-libbed unflattering nicknames, was the toast of the evening; it seemed he was fitting in.

He kept his concern for Maggs to himself. That was out of his hands now. He was a copper and he'd done his job.

'Sarge?' Stark's voice sounded groggy down the line. Cross too, just a hint.

'Sorry to wake you, Princess. Heavy night?' asked Fran, knowing it had been.

'Not by your standards.'

'Lightweight.'

'Is there something I can do for you, Sarge?'

'You can get your arse in to work. The super is gracing us with his presence at this morning's meeting, so Groombridge would rather like the whole team present.'

'What time?'

'Nine.'

'It's six thirty, for God's sake!' Stark groaned.

'Well, I know how you girls need time to prettify.'

'And DCI Groombridge wants a pre-meeting meeting to make sure we look shiny for the super.'

'To make sure he looks shiny at any rate,' agreed Fran. 'So get your arse up and polish those shoes.'

'Can't do it, Sarge.'

Fran was momentarily stunned. 'This isn't a request, Trainee Investigator.'

'You agreed I could have this morning off.'

'You can't expect me to stand by what I may or may not have said three days ago!'

'I can be in at eleven.'

'You'll be in at eight or sooner!'

'No, Sarge, I won't.' His voice was alarmingly firm.

'Listen, soldier boy, when the super rings the DCI's bell he jumps. When the DCI rings mine I jump. When I ring yours you bloody well jump!'

'Absolutely. You'll have me at my jumpiest at eleven o'clock.'

Fran's hangover boiled over. 'Don't piss me about, Stark. You get cut far too much bloody slack already for my liking. We both know this mystery appointment of yours has nothing to do with your physical or mental well-being. Whatever it is can wait, so cut the crap and get in to work!'

'Sarge, with all due respect, I have somewhere I have to be. It's personal, it's important, it *can't* wait, and if it earns me fifty laps of the parade ground and a month of guard duty, then that's the way it has to be.'

'Tell me right now what's so important or I'll make your life a misery. Stark? *Stark?*'

He'd hung up. Insolent pissant gobshite! Just when she'd begun to like him! Trading on his supposed wartime heroism, swanning round like he was above it all. Freely admitting he didn't even want to be a copper, or wasn't sure at least. Well, the force was better off without prima-bloody-donnas like him! Steaming, she stomped into her kitchen for another coffee.

After the pre-meeting meeting she spoke to Groombridge, who appeared infuriatingly unfazed by Stark's mutiny – Stark had requested and been granted time off for important personal reasons, by her; he had every right to take it while Fran had no evidence to back up her suspicion – and, as it turned out, the super had postponed till midday.

Fran looked at her watch, a devious thought forming. She made up an excuse and slipped out, driving faster than she should to Stark's flat. He'd mentioned yesterday that his mystery appointment was at nine thirty. At eight thirty she sat watching his door through binoculars from her car. By eight fifty-five she was thinking she'd missed him and her anger was rising again. Then a florist's van pulled up outside. The driver climbed out, retrieved a white box and buzzed the intercom. Minutes later the door opened and Fran could just make out Stark's profile as he signed for the box and retreated back inside.

Intrigued, she weighed up the pros and cons of ringing his buzzer and demanding an explanation, but that would let the obstinate bastard know he was getting to her and, besides, it was always preferable to know the truth before the interrogation began.

A cab pulled up next. Stark stepped into the street in gleaming shoes, crisp grey trousers, black blazer with polished brass buttons, white shirt and a tie of blue-and-yellow diagonal stripes. He was carrying the white box of flowers. What the hell was he up to? If he'd pissed her about just to go courting, she'd have him suspended.

She had little option but to follow the cab. She even had to shave a red light to avoid losing them at one point. It'd been a while since she'd done anything so laughably clandestine but her anger took all the fun out of it. They headed west, then turned right at the old Shooters Hill nick, all boarded up. Rumour had it the pretty old Victorian building was being sold for conversion to trendy flats – another triumph for the forces of progress.

The cab turned right into what looked like a park, a promising destination for a romantic assignation. Perhaps the mysterious Kelly lived nearby. But then it passed through some gates. Fran pulled up and read the sign with a sinking heart.

She ditched the car out of sight and followed on foot. The cab driver sat with the door open, cigarette in mouth, reading a tabloid. He looked up as she passed, nodding as if she were to be commiserated. Beyond she could see Stark continuing uphill on foot, limping slightly as he did when he forgot not to or thought no one was looking.

Fran followed at a distance. On the far slope she saw a striking semi-circular war memorial set against a broad westward view of London, but Stark passed it with barely a glance. In the furthest, least fashionable corner of Greenwich Cemetery a simple casket sat on a trestle beside an open grave. The vicar and sexton stood by. Stark pulled a khaki beret from his pocket and set it on his head with practised precision. Its bronze badge had a square ribbon backing the same blue and yellow as his tie.

He stood to ramrod attention throughout the brief service. When it was over he removed a red wreath from the box and placed it on the coffin, stood back and saluted. Fran's anger had long dissipated. She watched from the shadow of distant trees, refusing to give in to an absurd prickling in the corners of her eyes.

Alfred Ladd. Seventy-eight years old, homeless, friendless, no living relatives to give a shit about him, kicked to death by a bunch of kids for a laugh. Teenagers. When he was a teenager he'd been called up to National Service and was fighting in the jungles in the 'Malayan Emergency', whatever bullshit war that was. Fran decided to look it up. Alf to his comrades, friends, family, probably. And here he was being lowered into the ground, watched over by a man he'd never met, an insolent tit with an over-developed sense of something. She should've guessed.

Stark shook hands with the vicar and sexton and walked slowly down the path. Fran didn't follow. She walked up and watched the sexton filling in the hole with an absurdly small digger. It was a double plot. The adjacent headstone read 'Nancy Beryl Ladd 1935–1972, Beloved Wife'. Had Stark found this? A fresh headstone leant against the trestle, ready to be put in place: 'Alfred William Ladd 1931–2009, Beloved Husband'.

The scarlet circle of fresh poppies sat on the trestle to one side. At its centre was a Union Flag, beneath it a small black card with words picked out in silver: 'Lest we forget'.

Fran turned and stalked away.

21

'See what you wanted to see?' asked Groombridge.

Fran considered denying it. 'He went to Alfred Ladd's funeral.'

He nodded. 'Figured as much.'

'How? How could you *possibly* know?' she demanded.

'Old-school instincts, Detective Sergeant.' Groombridge tapped the side of his nose, laying on the sage wisdom. 'Plus I overheard him on the phone to the funeral parlour.'

'What?'

'Never underestimate the value of pausing outside an open door, Detective Sergeant,' said Groombridge, pleasantly.

'But . . . why did you let me fly off the *sodding* handle?'

'I thought maybe you should see for yourself.'

Fran bit down a retort. 'Funeral parlour? He made the arrangements?'

'And paid for it all, I should imagine.'

Fran shook her head. 'He should've *told* me.'

'Why?' Groombridge tilted his head. 'What business was it of yours?' He waited while she searched for a good reason and found none. 'I can see how his preferential treatment might irk you, Fran, it would me. But the lad didn't get here on hand-outs.'

Fran was intrigued: Groombridge didn't say things he didn't mean. But she wasn't willing to abandon perfectly good indignation quite yet. 'Are you going to elaborate or be just as inscrutable as *him*?'

Groombridge leant back in his chair for several seconds, thoughtful, and then, seemingly coming to a decision, waved for her to sit. 'Has he ever explained to you how the Territorial Army actually works?'

Fran shook her head. That would require Stark *actually* talking.

'While regular soldiers are deployed with their units, a TA soldier must volunteer if they wish to serve overseas. And apart from medical units they typically serve as individuals, slotting into units of the regular army. They may have mates with them, they may not. Stark had actually finished his tour, could've been on the plane home, but volunteered to stay out for a few weeks to help another post. He was alone, replacing a dead man in an unfamiliar regiment, when he was hurt.'

Fran shrugged. 'He's never mentioned any of this.'

'No. It puts an interesting spin on it all, though, don't you agree?'

'I suppose.'

Groombridge frowned at her. 'It was his *third* tour, did you know?'

Now Fran frowned. 'I thought it was his second. He said he'd been in Iraq before.'

'True. He served as a lance corporal in Basra in 2006, then as full corporal in Helmand in 2007. Saw action in both tours. After that he undertook Special Forces Selection for the SAS . . . You're rolling your eyes.'

'Sorry.'

'He should've passed, I'm told. Made it all the way to the final phase, resistance to interrogation, but something happened.' Groombridge obviously saw the question in Fran's eyes and shook his head. 'I don't know. His CO stonewalled me, saying only that Stark was "returned to unit" and ordered to reapply.'

'Yet more fog,' complained Fran.

'Indeed.' The DCI disliked mystery as much as she did. 'According to his old super, Stark spent a brief spell in hospital afterwards before returning to work, but that's all he knew. In any case Stark did reapply, but he also volunteered again and a second Helmand posting came up first.'

'And the rest is history.' The guv'nor had a point to make but Fran was losing patience.

Her tone didn't go unmarked. 'But how much of that history do you actually *know*, Detective Sergeant?'

'Sod all. Not for the want of asking.'

'Well, then . . . They patched him up but told him he'd never pass fit for front-line service again. They offered him a choice between a staff job, a training post or medical discharge. He chose the last. Then the police told him he'd never pass fit for front-line there either. Picture it. Incapacitated in your prime, both your vocations in tatters. But then his old super visited him in hospital and they got talking about CID. The super thought it was a good idea and looked into it. Stark was told he could take his time, he'd remain on full pay, he could get himself fit, then come back to work and begin the Initial Crime Investigators Development Programme . . . I see you rolling your eyes again. You think he was handed it all on a plate. But he didn't wait. He enrolled from his hospital bed, unassisted, studied for the NIE, between hellish rehab and further surgeries, and passed with flying colours.'

'He really does have a talent for pissing people off,' Fran commented.

Groombridge didn't laugh. 'He pressed to get himself discharged early to attend the next available phase-two course, six weeks of which put him straight back in the hospital, which didn't stop him applying for any TI vacancy that came up. He could've waited, his old super wanted him back, but he didn't. He was passed over on medical grounds by *seven* stations before Cox gave him the nod.'

'Persistent is just another word for stubborn, Guv,' said Fran, but her heart wasn't in it any more.

'Maybe, but here he is, still not fully fit, perhaps, but through phases one and two and getting stuck into phase three.'

'Well, maybe he's worked at it,' conceded Fran, 'but if he thinks he's taking any shortcuts with his PDP he's got another think coming.' She was responsible for signing off his sheets, and her own mentor had been a stickler.

'Quite right, Detective Sergeant Millhaven.' Groombridge smiled ambiguously. 'Quite right.'

Stark was changed and in the office on the stroke of eleven. He was beginning to regret not telling Fran about the funeral, but the time and attitude of her call had crashed up against his hangover. He'd never responded well to threats. He'd let irritation and perversity get the better of him and there would be consequences. Fifty laps of the parade ground might be the least of it. Nevertheless, he was convinced she wouldn't have understood. It wasn't just his default privacy, or even stubbornness, not entirely anyway. His old life lay in ruins and he must deal with that, in physio, in psych and elsewhere. He'd been laid open, laid bare, prodded, poked and discussed, exposed to excruciating scrutiny, and it wasn't over. He needed control. He needed to crack on. This new life – career, location, people – it could be his. Alfred Ladd had earned the right to have his passing marked, to be buried alongside his wife instead of tipped out in some corner of a crematorium garden, the modern equivalent of a pauper's grave. But that was part of Stark's old life. As far as possible he needed to keep the two apart. As far as possible, for as long as possible.

Fran would hardly look at him.

'Stark.' DCI Groombridge summoned him into his office with a perfunctory jerk of the head. 'Close the door.'

Stark was not invited to sit. He stood braced for the inevitable dressing-down.

'Paid your respects, did you?'

Stark blinked. 'Yes, Guv. How did you . . .?'

'Old-school instincts, Constable Stark.' Groombridge tapped the side of his nose. 'You might pull the wool over Detective Sergeant Millhaven's eyes temporarily, but not mine.'

That or you're an even more accomplished eavesdropper than I suspected, thought Stark. 'I'm afraid I may be back in her bad books, Guv.'

'All too easily done, I fear. I'm sure you'll make it up to her. You could help yourself with a little less stubborn privacy.' There was a slight barb in that. 'Though I have to say your little stunt with CPS did make me chuckle.'

Stark hoped the lawyer had kept his word. This couldn't stay under wraps for ever, but the longer he kept it out of the station the better. He didn't wish to give them even more reason to restrict his involvement in the case.

'You get to keep your secrets for now.' Groombridge's gaze was penetrating. 'But don't expect DS Millhaven to accept that with my laudable magnanimity. I've seen her reduce hardened criminals to blabbing like teenage girls.'

'Hopefully I've sent her and the rest of the station sniffing down a different track.'

'Have you now.' Groombridge didn't need to put the question mark after these three words.

'Romance trumps intrigue, Guv.'

'Hmm. Don't underestimate Fran. The rest of the station may run on idle gossip but she needs the truth.'

Stark said nothing.

'But, of course, you're not at liberty to discuss it.'

'Guv.'

Groombridge looked at him thoughtfully. 'Why did you let DS Harper take the credit for Naveen Hussein's arrest?'

Blindsided, Stark said nothing.

Groombridge tapped a folder on his desk. 'The airport arrest sheet says his cousin's name was added to the list of flagged passports . . . by you.'

'It was just a hunch, Guv.'

'You're adept at avoiding questions, Constable Stark, but I've been asking them longer than you've been wiping your own arse.'

'I saw no need to correct the misunderstanding, Guv.' If you can't avoid answering, keep it short and ambiguous. There was a well-understood but hard-to-implement approach to surviving SAS selection: be the Grey Man; don't stand out, don't get noticed, don't come first, don't come last. Strength was picked on with as much venom as weakness. Roughly two hundred began, roughly twenty might pass. Drawing attention was a bad thing. It had suited Stark – until the end, of course. But he had no way to explain it to his DCI.

Groombridge wasn't fooled, but changed the subject. 'You look tired. Roster says your last day off was thirteen days ago. Take the rest of the weekend.'

'I was off this morning, Guv.'

'Hardly.'

'We all have to do overtime when there's a case on,' Stark protested.

'It wasn't a request.'

'The super said no special treatment.'

'Do you honestly think I'd have allowed any other person in this station to carry on so long in your condition?' For the first time Stark saw real anger in his boss's eyes. 'I think it rather depends on your interpretation of "cotton wool", Trainee Investigator Stark. Would you rather I'd sent you home days ago?'

'No, Guv.' Stark was mortified. The guv had been bending over backwards for him and he'd thrown the super's words in his face as thanks.

'Well, then. The super will be here soon. Let's get ready.'

The meeting was a good one. It had been a good week and Superintendent Cox was generous with his pleasure. The perpetrators had been charged, the CPS was looking pleased and the press were singing praises. Of course, none of this was news to the troops as several hung-over faces testified.

Stark observed Cox carefully. In appearance he was the very stereotype of the good-natured, over-promoted senior officer: bumbling, effusive, unsophisticated. Yet the way Groombridge said Cox had rebuffed both MoD complaints spoke of a different side: loyal, steely even.

It turned out that most of the team were to have the rest of the weekend off, including Fran and Stark. The search for Pinky was largely out of their hands for the moment, while Maggs was to be transferred from the hospital to the prison infirmary and Groombridge had decided to wait till Monday before confronting him again. Groombridge had known this, of course, had been testing him, and Stark had shown himself both stubborn and ungrateful. He determined never to underestimate Cox or Groombridge again. Fran wasn't speaking to him, of course, but that could wait.

That night, determined to make the best of his R&R he rooted around in a drawer and found the box of sleeping pills he'd been prescribed but never opened.

'Dire need only,' he said aloud. He read the box, ignored the advice, and washed two down with whisky, beer and a mammoth Chinese takeaway.

The Zopiclone delivered him dazed into a warm, late Sunday morning, nothing chasing him from bed but bladder and belly. It felt great just to shower, pull on jeans and T-shirt and do ordinary things, like laundry and throwing away everything that had spoilt in the fridge, then shopping online for more, which at this rate might also go off before consumption.

He limped into town and settled in the shade of a café parasol, reflecting on a mixed week. He'd pissed people off and his own stubbornness was mostly at fault, but they'd get over it. The greater concern was his physical and mental state. He'd underestimated how ground down he'd become and the effect it was having on his behaviour. He needed to do a better job of rationing his energy, perhaps even to stop being so bloody-minded. Perhaps.

The nightmares were the problem. And the 'medicinal' steps he'd begun using to avoid them couldn't continue indefinitely; he was under no illusion there. They hadn't been so bad since the early days. As far as she'd suggested *anything* particularly, Doc Hazel had linked the resurgence with his relocation and new job. She had a talent for the obvious. Nevertheless, he'd have to tackle it and she'd have to help. On a beautiful day like today, though, all that could wait.

He dipped in and out of the café's *Sunday Times* and local paper, smiling at the faint echoes of the former in the latter's parochial, nimbyish stance, but found himself as much engrossed in watching the world go by. The weather had brought out the town in fine mood. The covered market was buzzing, the tourists milling, the local young things heading for the park with cool-boxes, blankets and sun-cream. It soon occurred to him that he was looking out for Kelly, hoping to catch sight of her in jeans or a summer dress. The boy in him was excited to know she lived nearby. Perhaps normally he'd berate himself for such childishness but today, with warmth easing his pains, he seemed content to let it go.

He'd had his share of crushes and flings, the inevitable first-love broken heart. But he'd got all that out of the way early and moved on, settling into the comfortable rut of serial dalliance. Mixing police and army life had allowed time for little more over the last few years. Perhaps that was just an excuse, but it suited. Or had. What now?

Perhaps he should decide what he wanted, what he could offer, even, but not today. Today he could let a passing group of girls, giggling and gambolling on long slender limbs, bring a smile to his face, and imagine Kelly mocking his wandering eye with her wry smile.

Stark walked to work to begin his fifth week, feeling refreshed. His hip still hurt but the painkillers were knocking the top off that. It also had a penitent appeal, reminding him that however many times he told himself he didn't need fixing he still did.

Groombridge perched on a desk and spoke to the room. 'Maggs was transferred into the medical care of Her Majesty's Prison Service yesterday. He's up before the magistrate later today. There's just one piece of this puzzle missing. The homeless girl, Pinky. Orpington force have been looking out and her face has been on the news but we still don't have her. I don't like not knowing all I should know. Find me that girl.' He delegated various tasks and beckoned Stark and Fran into his office. He made no comment on Stark's improved appearance. 'Ever attended an arraignment, Trainee Investigator?'

'No, Guv.'

'Now's your chance, then.'

Fran drove in silence. He was getting sadly used to that. On consideration, he preferred her warm and nosy, though he'd probably regret that thought if and when she eventually came around.

Groombridge led the way into Woolwich Courts at his accustomed speed. Stark followed, taking in the unfamiliar surroundings, not sure what to expect. The guv obviously thought this would further his education, but the idea also occurred that Groombridge thought Stark's presence might make Maggs more predictable. Led in by a uniformed court official, Maggs spotted Stark almost straight away but made little acknowledgement of it.

Stark was shocked at the transformation. Maggs wore a suit, probably loaned by his legal counsel, cheap and baggy, but nevertheless . . . His hair had been cut, his beard trimmed. Both were greying in places, giving him an almost distinguished air. He looked taller, leaner, more potent than the shambling mess of hair, filth and layers Stark had first met, or the frail post-operative invalid. Despite recent abdominal surgery, he stood ramrod-straight throughout, and when called to speak, he did so concisely and respectfully. He might have been a different man.

His time before the magistrate was short. Charged with murder, he entered a plea of not guilty and was remanded into custody, in this case marched back along the tunnel linking the courts building with Belmarsh Prison.

'I thought they'd press for manslaughter, Guv,' said Stark, afterwards.

'CPS think they've got enough for murder.'

'But it was one against eight, self-defence?'

'Don't you start. DS Millhaven's banged that drum already. His military training and the fact that he stuck Gibbs in the back weaken self-defence. CPS think they can do better.'

'But –'

'Ours is not to reason why, Constable. Ours is to finger the collar of suspects. What the CPS do afterwards is their jurisdiction. We suspect, they accuse. Judge and jury do the rest.'

'Guv.'

'Right. Let's go and see if our suspect wants to change his story.'

So there *was* another reason for this trip. Stark was led for the first time into the embrace of Her Majesty's Pleasure. He looked about as they were led to the interview room. The prison was clean, austere, oppressive. In some distant fashion it reminded him of barracks, though only distant. He shivered. Life in a place like this would drive him mad. The men detained here must find some way to insulate themselves from that thought. As a policeman he supposed he should take some cold pleasure in knowing this fate awaited those whose misdeeds led them here, but he wasn't sure he could. An eye for an eye, society exacting restitution . . . Did Maggs deserve this? It wasn't as clear-cut as combat. Not for the first time Stark wondered if he was the right material for this job.

After a wait Maggs was led in wearing prison-issue clothing once more. Even without the court suit he still looked a world apart from the man Stark had arrested. The eyes still had that intelligent, lupine wariness. 'Thought we were done,' he said, sitting with a grunt.

'Your legal counsel knew I was coming,' replied Groombridge. 'Where is he?'

'I sent the poor sod away for a rest. I'm not sure his nerves are all they should be.'

'You'd be advised to reconsider.'

'Why? You about to get heavy? Perhaps you should ask the screw to step outside first.'

'Dial it down, Maggs,' warned the prison guard in the corner.

'You're on remand now, Maggs. Your lawyer should be here.'

Maggs chuckled. 'I think I'm more up to it than he is.'

'You've been watching too many crap movies.' Groombridge looked down at his paperwork. 'Miller. He's a decent enough man. You should take advantage. He might be the only thing between you and Life.'

'I've blood on these, Detective Chief Inspector.' He held up his large, thick-fingered hands, as if it were still clear to see. 'Kyle Gibbs was young and dangerous and stupid enough to come at a stranger with a knife. Maybe he was unlucky that stranger was me but it doesn't excuse him. I'm not sorry. I've no plan to throw myself on the mercy of the court, feign remorse, beg leniency, and I don't need a limp lawyer to spell that out.'

239

'Then why not plead guilty?'

'I'm no murderer,' said Maggs.

'You stand a better chance of proving that with legal counsel.'

'I'll take my chances with twelve good men and true,' replied Maggs. It was impossible to gauge if he was being sarcastic.

Groombridge gave up, turned on the tape, did the spiel and slid Pinky's picture across the table. 'What can you tell me about this girl?'

'Christ, you really have aching balls for this one. Does your wife know?'

'Cut the crap, Maggs. We know she was there, that she was directly involved.'

Maggs considered Groombridge for a moment. 'Tell you that, did she?'

'Yes.'

Maggs chuckled. 'Now it's your turn to cut the crap. It's nice of you to drop by, but next time leave the tripwire bullshit outside.'

Groombridge had misjudged but, as far as Stark could tell, it didn't seem to unsettle him. 'These are CCTV stills showing the girl entering the park. We have an eyewitness placing her at the bandstand just before midnight. Not elsewhere in the park, right where the attack took place.'

'The "attack took place" maybe two hours later, Inspector. I can't help noticing your little Lolita appears to be independently mobile.'

'Indeed,' said Groombridge, sliding another page across. 'I had Constable Stark here double-check. These are stills from the camera on Chesterfield Gate at one twenty-four. You can just see her climbing out and running away. We almost missed it – the street-light's out and we were concentrating on the gang – but there she is, Maggs, running away.'

Maggs didn't respond.

'And *this* is a transcript of our interview with one of your attackers in which she makes it clear that a "pink-haired bitch" was present.'

'And you believe that shouty cow over me? I'm hurt, deeply hurt.'

'It's in your interest to tell us about her, Maggs. If she witnessed what happened she can corroborate your self-defence claims. Withholding simply incriminates you further, makes it appear as though you believe your claims won't withstand scrutiny. Is that it?'

Maggs looked at Stark but said nothing.

Groombridge waited, and waited. 'Have you anything to add?' he asked finally. Maggs just stared, what was going on behind his eyes a mystery. 'This will only harm your case, Maggs.'

'I told you, I'm not making any case.'

'We *will* find her.'

'You don't need me, then,' growled Maggs.

'And when we do, she'll tell me everything,' said Groombridge. Maggs glowered but said nothing. 'So be it,' said Groombridge. 'Interview termina—'

'Leave her alone,' said Maggs. The remark was directed purely at Stark, with surprising ferocity. Groombridge's finger hovered halfway to the stop button.

'Why?' asked Stark. Fran kicked him under the table for speaking out of turn.

'Just leave her alone.'

'You'll have to do better than that, Alan,' said Groombridge.

Maggs ignored him, or appeared to, maintaining his fierce gaze on Stark. After what seemed an age he appeared to make up his mind. 'They raped her. Or tried to. The dead lad, Gibbs, right? Egged on by the others, by the shouty bitch most of all, if you can believe it. Head case, that one, baying for him to hurt the poor girl. I heard the shouting, tried to ignore it, but then there was screaming too . . . so I had to go and look.'

'Where were you?' asked Groombridge.

'Bandstand is a bit exposed for my liking. I'd bivvied up over in the Flower Garden. Plenty of cover. You should've guessed that much,' he said, mocking Stark. 'Anyway, I went over.' He picked up the photo now and stared at it. 'She was putting up a fight. She had guts. But she was getting a beating for it, so I stepped in.'

'Go on,' invited Groombridge.

'I waded in, barged one of them to the ground, shoved Gibbs off her, and everything stopped. Everyone was shocked, not moving. Then the shouting cow started up again, calling them all names for standing off, and they were going for me. The rest is like I said.'

'Why have you not mentioned this before?'

'What difference does it make?'

'It lends weight to your defence.'

'At what cost?'

Groombridge ignored that. 'What happened to the girl?'

'She ran off while they were busy with me.'

'Did you know her?'

'Like I said, it's not a community. But I'd seen her around. Just another frightened runaway.'

'Know her name or where she might have gone?' asked Fran.

'None of my business.'

'It's in your interest we find her,' insisted Groombridge.

Maggs shook his head. 'No. It's only in yours. Leave the poor girl alone.'

Something primal in Stark was deeply relieved to step out into the open air.

'So, is he still lying, Trainee Investigator Stark?'

'It wouldn't seem so, Guv.'

Fran rolled her eyes. 'Well, the sun continues to shine from your arse, New Boy. Another crime revealed and solved in a blink of your all-seeing eye.' Her voice was shot through with a thick vein of sarcasm. 'You're a walking stat-generator.'

'We don't have a crime until we have a victim, Detective Sergeant,' cautioned Groombridge. 'Until then we've only the word of a desperate man.'

Stark wanted to say that the only thing Maggs appeared desperate about was his desire to prevent the world shining its harsh spotlight on a frightened girl, but he was learning to keep his mouth shut.

Fran nodded. 'Want to talk to Nikki and the others about it?'

'I think tripwire bullshit has run its course with that lot too. With the magistrate looming, their legals will be keeping a tighter rein. No, the time for blundering about in the dark is over. I want to talk to this Pinky and get all the facts lined up. So let's direct Constable Stark's all-seeing eye to finding her.'

Stark's supernatural abilities did not manifest. Pinky's face was up in every station in Britain but so were a hundred others and, with the crime apparently solved, the TV companies weren't interested in finding an extra witness. The team were covering every base short of a directionless door-to-door. All Stark's all-seeing eye could do was stare at Pinky's face on the wall. Next to it was the traffic-camera shot of Nikki and the unknown BMW driver. Nikki's confident sneer came back to mock him. She believed her threats carried weight, and she'd had help. So who was the man in the black cap? Who would know?

'I'd better come in with you,' Ptolemy told Stark.

'I'm sure I'm safe from a teenage boy and his overbearing mum.'

Ptolemy and Peters chuckled at his naïvety. 'Maybe, but we don't want the little scrote making up stories about police brutality later.'

Naveen's mother answered the door, looked at the two officers, sighed and led them wordlessly into the flat. Naveen was no happier to see them. Around his ankle he sported an electronic monitor, condition of his bail. 'What d'you want?' he demanded.

'A bit less lip, for a start,' said Ptolemy.

Stark passed Naveen a picture of the faceless BMW driver. 'Any idea who this might be?'

The boy shrugged. His mother leant in. 'You know who that is, Naveen Hussein. Don't pretend you don't.'

'Mum!'

'Don't you "Mum" me! Not after the shame you've brought!'

'Who is it?' interceded Stark, before the familial spat escalated.

The mother tutted in displeasure at her son. 'Seen her with a big man like that,' she replied, shushing Naveen's frantic attempts to interrupt. 'Around the estate, that Cockcroft girl. Bad to the core, both of them. Big ugly brute. People are scared of him.'

Naveen clearly was too. 'Do you know his name?' asked Stark. Naveen shook his head. 'You told me it wasn't the police you were scared of. I thought you meant Kyle and Nikki. Did you mean this man?'

Naveen nodded. 'Him too. Nikki knows him. He sorts her stuff.'

'Drugs?'

Naveen glanced anxiously at his despairing mother. 'Don't know his name. I ain't even lyin'. Didn't wanna know. He's bad news, proper bad.'

'Is there anything else you can tell us?'

'He lends money, collects rent. He used to be mates with Nikki's brother. That's all I know.'

Ptolemy sat up. 'Tall bloke? Fat and muscle, shaved head and a goatee beard, always wears a black bomber jacket?'

*

Groombridge stared at the mugshot Stark handed him. 'You're kidding?'

'Sergeant Ptolemy recognized the description, Guv. And I remembered he was a suspect in your security-van heist.'

Groombridge stared at the photo, comparing it to that of the BMW driver. 'Liam Dawson?' He shook his head incredulously. 'I never even *thought* of him. He used to run with Gary Cockcroft . . . theft, drugs, intimidation, the usual spread, until they graduated to armed robbery and triple murder. But he moved away after the case against him collapsed. Last I heard he was working as a club bouncer in Dartford. Why would he be driving Nikki around?'

'I had Dixon email Dawson's mugshot to Ptolemy's phone, Guv. Naveen and his mum both ID'd him. And I've seen him before too. He was in the Meridian pub the night I saw Nikki, Kyle and the rest kicking off – I took him for a doorman. And remember I told you someone in a black jacket ran from the off-licence when they saw me last week? I showed the proprietors Dawson's mugshot. They all but soiled themselves – wouldn't say a word. Same story with the dentist and the doctor. The pharmacist begged me to leave. We should have someone look into their inventory, make sure they're not paying protection in pills.'

Groombridge nodded, like a weary adult indulging an over-eager child.

Stark glanced at Fran, who had not said a word so far. She had not reacted warmly to his initiative. He'd thought about waiting to tell her where he was going, but in all honesty it had been easier not to: he was still in her bad books for the funeral. If he'd thought it would lead to anything he'd have told her. Now he'd made things worse and she was leaving him to do the talking.

'There's more, Guv.' He slid a sheaf of paper in front of Groombridge. 'A list of known landlords – uniform have it to hand for disturbances and break-ins.' He'd underlined the same name several times in red. 'One company, Dawson Security Ltd, owns seventeen flats. We knocked on doors. The tenants all took one look at his photo and clammed up. I just called Companies House – Liam Dawson is listed as director.'

He slid a printout from the company website on to the desk. 'He offers agency door-staff, rent collection and bailiff service. Naveen Hussein suggested Dawson is also loan-sharking. We found one old couple who used to own their flat. Dawson lent them money to pay mortgage arrears at punitive interest rates. No matter how much they paid, the debt kept rising until they sold up to him, lock, stock and barrel. Now they pay rent to live in their own home.'

'They'll testify to this?'

Stark shook his head. 'Unlikely. It was all I could do to get them to speak to me.'

Groombridge sat back, disappointed. 'So he targets impoverished owners, traps them with loans and forces them to sell up. Meanwhile he targets tenants behind on rent, milks them with loans . . .'

'Maybe he even forces them out too. The more empty flats, the lower property values fall, the easier it is to buy. And in the meantime he's racketeering off what little life remains and peddling drugs to the rest.'

'With the likes of Nikki as his loyal foot-soldier, and the Rats helping him drive property prices down even more,' observed Groombridge.

'He's setting himself up as a slum landlord,' said Fran.

'It's more than that,' said Stark. 'He's playing the long game.'

Groombridge was already nodding. 'Property developers have been sniffing around the Ferrier for years now. The talk is that eventually one will buy the whole site, demolish and redevelop.'

'Offering owners a price they couldn't hope for at current market values,' added Stark.

Granite to begin with, Fran's expression had been hardening throughout. 'How do we not know about this?'

Groombridge shook his head unhappily. 'He's kept things under the radar. It's only seventeen flats out of hundreds, too small for Specialist Crime Directorate. And uniform don't have the budget to target the estate. I think, knowing it might not be there five years from now, we might all be guilty of giving the place up as a lost cause.' He puffed out his cheeks. 'So, you and Ptolemy unearthed all this by yourselves?'

'And Constable Peters, Guv.'

'How did you drag them into it?'

'I needed a lift up to the estate, Guv. Everyone here was busy.' Another glance at Fran showed what she thought of this explanation. 'They were very interested to establish a link between Nikki and Dawson. They've been wanting to shine some light on the drugs problem up there.'

Groombridge turned a wry gaze on Fran. 'And you sanctioned all this?'

Fran smiled thinly. 'TI Stark was thoughtful enough to leave me a note.'

Groombridge winced slightly. 'Right. Well, let's see what else the pair of you can find out collaboratively.'

Stark hesitated. 'The van heist, Guv?' he asked, cautiously 'Why did Dawson walk?'

Groombridge's eyes bored into the mugshot. 'He was one of the crew. I know he was. I just couldn't prove it.' He was clearly still angry about that. 'Same with the getaway driver. They terrorized an office worker, threatened to hurt her family unless she supplied information on van routes and manifests. They hit a van when it was nice and full, shotgunned the tyres, then stuck a fake bomb to the windscreen – batteries, curly wire and grey Plasticine for Semtex. Threatened to blow up the cab if the drivers didn't get out, then put guns to their heads till the guy in the back opened up. Bound them with cable ties while they cleared it out. Shot all three dead before they left.' His jaw clenched.

'We tied one of them, Ben Travers, to the purchase of two sawn-off shotguns. We never really had him for the robbery but he was scared enough to think we did. CPS offered leniency in return for the location of their lock-up. The cash was gone but we found enough evidence to nail Gary.'

'Don't suppose he liked that very much,' said Fran.

'No. There were threats. Travers had to be moved to HMP Maidstone.'

'But the money, Guv?' asked Stark. 'Who got the money?'

'No sign of it. Gary squirrelled it away somewhere, we guessed, but it never surfaced.'

'And Gary was definitely the ringleader?' Stark persisted.

Groombridge seemed unsure. 'We thought so. He was the real deal, nasty piece of work. I had Dawson down as muscle to begin with but the longer it went on . . . And after what you've just told me . . . I don't know. One thing's for sure.' He placed the mugshot on his in-tray and stared at Stark and Fran. 'I'd very much like another crack at locking him up.'

Fran said nothing to him for the rest of the day that wasn't an order or a rebuke. Stark weathered the storm: a warmer sunset beckoned.

Hours later, Kelly slipped into the opposite seat with a smile. Stark felt certain this couldn't be standard procedure. He glanced at the receptionist and caught her looking away with a barely suppressed grin.

'You're less limp today,' said Kelly. 'Can I expect improved performance?'

Stark couldn't pass that up. 'I'm sorry about last week.' He grimaced. 'That's never happened to me before.'

'I'll try not to think less of you,' she teased. 'After all, you were quite satisfactory first time round.'

'Ah, well, there's nothing to lose on the first date, is there? It's after that the nerves kick in.'

'If that's your idea of a first date it's no wonder your nerves aren't up to much. Come on, let's see how well you stand up tonight.'

Stark felt better rested, fresher. Nevertheless he wasn't far into the routine before his hip began to impede him, even with the water taking most of his weight. The painkillers he'd swallowed saw him through without it showing too much, but it was gruelling. He finished rather deflated.

'So much for improved performance.' Kelly's smile held a question. 'If you don't mind me saying so, you seem to be going backwards.'

So much for not showing, thought Stark, not sure what to say.

'Is it still work? I thought the killers had been caught.'

'It doesn't stop there.'

'Perhaps you should reconsider letting me talk to your GP.'

'Thank you, really, but I've just come back from nine months off. The last thing I need is more.'

'It doesn't have to be one or the other. Perhaps you could scale down your hours.'

'I'm a trainee. I'm already taking all the liberties I can comfortably ask for.'

'Are you comfortable right now?' Kelly asked.

'I'm sure this is just temporary.'

'We'll see,' she said. 'But if you keep getting worse, we'll soon reach a point where hydrotherapy won't be any use.'

Stark felt like a schoolboy. The oft-repeated 'It's your own time you're wasting' floated up from memory, though he also remembered feeling that it was more often his time *they* were wasting.

'Cheer up,' said Kelly, smiling brightly. 'I had no idea you'd miss me that much! Still need a lift home?'

'More than ever,' replied Stark.

'Okay, then. Wait in the lobby and I'll be out in five.'

Ten minutes later she appeared, denim jacket over the top half of her uniform. 'Come on, then.' She grinned.

A parting glance at the receptionist showed she was grinning too.

Kelly drove a small blue VW Polo. Stark noticed quite a bit of clutter stuffed behind the seats as if the front had been rudimentarily tidied at the expense of the back. She drove confidently, chatting away, telling him about growing up in Bromley, escaping to Edinburgh University, her three younger sisters. She asked him about his family, skilfully avoiding his father, whose premature death would have been noted in Stark's medical history. She asked about the army, whether he'd liked it, but not about his experiences abroad. She asked about the police, whether people treated him awkwardly when they heard what he'd done, whether he liked it, but not about the details. It was a master class in small-talk with only a hint of checking out. She was easy company. She asked what he thought of Greenwich. She liked the town, its pocket-size cosmopolitan scale set against the endless sprawl of Greater London or the hemmed-in stonework of Edinburgh. She liked the gentler pace, the freedom and views of the park, the liberal friends she'd made. Stark asked about the borough; she was indifferent – London boroughs were too big for individual identity, their borders too arbitrary, she said. London worked street by street.

When they finally pulled up outside his flat Stark was amazed that time and distance had passed so fast. For a second or two an awkward silence crept in.

'Which one is you?' she asked, peering up at his building.

If that was a prompt to invite her in, Stark couldn't tell. It seemed a bit premature to pop the coffee question. 'Top floor.'

'Nice views?'

'Defunct lift.'

'Bugger. Take your time on the stairs, then.'

A prompt to go. 'Will do. Thanks for the lift. See you Thursday.' He opened the door.

'Aren't you going to ask me out, then?'

Stark froze, gob-smacked. 'Aren't there rules against going out with patients?' he asked, playing for time.

'Bollocks to the rules. Anyway, I'm not licensed to prescribe to you. Lucy is very disappointed that her unsubtle hint hasn't galvanized you into action. She has half the hospital debating when you're finally going to pull your finger out.'

Stark was part amused, part horrified. 'And what is the consensus?'

'Tonight.' She grinned. In the half-light it seemed to Stark she was perhaps masking shyness with bravado. 'But if you make me work any harder they'll accuse me of cheating!'

'Would you like to go out with me some time?' he asked, echoes of schooldays ringing in his ears again.

'No,' she said firmly. 'I'd like to go out with you on Friday night. I'll book a table at my favourite Thai place for nine and you can meet me in the Princess of Wales for drinks and lively chat at eight.'

'That's what I like, spontaneity. No prior planning, just go with the flow.'

'Careful – I've still got Thursday to punish you before then.' She leant over and kissed his cheek, a gentle brush of warmth and perfume.

'I can live with *that* kind of punishment.' He touched the spot. 'Goodnight.'

'Aren't you forgetting something?' she asked, as he turned away. He turned back, confused. 'God, you're rubbish at this. You're supposed to get my number! Here.' She handed him a slip of paper from her pocket; she'd come with a plan. 'Okay, you can go now.'

'Don't you want mine?'
'Don't be silly. Girls don't chase boys!'
'You could've fooled me,' joked Stark.
'Get out!' she cried, laughing.

23

The search for Pinky had produced no substantial leads and the morning meeting was short. Stark was glad to retreat to his desk and take more pills. His dreams the night before had begun pleasantly with Kelly, but then taken a more disturbing turn. Kelly became the woman cradling the child, but still with Kelly's face. And the boy had her face too. Then Collins, shouting in warning. And then that desperate run across open ground and the RPG knocking him sideways, like a charging bull out of nowhere, and the bullet spinning into him, twisting in slowly, like a corkscrew, and the medics in the field hospital all talking in a language he couldn't fathom while he pleaded for news of Collins in a voice he didn't recognize, Margaret Collins crying with Kelly's face and finally Collins, life leaching out of him into the dirt.

He'd woken with a shudder, rushed to the toilet and thrown up violently, retching and dry-retching until the images were driven from his mind by spinning stars. He'd lain on the bathroom floor in the dark for an age, letting the night seep in bone-deep, and woken stiff and aching in cold dawn light.

'Ready?' Fran stood over him impatiently.

They drove to Eltham to speak with the owner of a nightclub who employed Dawson Security Staff to run his door. Silent admonition continued to roll off her, like fog from a glacier.

The nightclub door absorbed some of her ire as she banged on it with her palm. A man peered out questioningly. Fran slapped her warrant card against the glass. 'James Yates? Open up.'

Yates reluctantly led them through the club. With the lights up, the place looked sadly absurd, dated and shabby, all the wear and tear, cigarette burns and drink stains, normally hidden in darkness, cruelly evident. A couple of cleaners glanced at them as they passed. Yates made sure his office door was fully closed before he uttered one syllable. 'Look, I know why you're here and I can't help you,' he said. 'As I said on the phone, Dawson Security provide a reliable service. I have nothing else to add. I'm sorry you've had a wasted trip.'

They'd had a similar reaction from the other clubs they'd phoned but Fran had thought this guy sounded the least intransigent. Talking with uniform in Eltham, as well as in Kidbrooke, Charlton, Woolwich and others, had revealed a common thread: rumours that Dawson Security provided more than door staff.

It was a neat little racket. Bouncers can make or break a club, add glamour, evoke fear. Control the door and you controlled the club – protection money neatly invoiced for services rendered. Muscle your way into several and you can play them off for price too. Not forgetting the potential perks – kickbacks from suppliers and cabbies and the three pillars of the underworld, illegal drugs, illicit booze and prostitution, with Dawson sitting atop his little pyramid of people either incentivized or terrorized into silence, or both. And that was the problem, finding the loose stone.

Fran slid Dawson's mugshot on to the desk. 'Look. We understand your hesitation. But Dawson has form. We're looking at him now, for this and other crimes. We're going to nail him. All it takes is for one person to speak out and more will follow. You'll be free of him.'

Yates considered this, his face giving little away. 'Four years. That's how long he's been ... providing his services. Where have you lot been?'

'Not looking where we should,' admitted Fran, frankly. 'Help us change that.'

'I can't promise anything. If you arrest him, charge him, if I know he's going down, I'll testify to help you bury him. Others would too. A few of us have talked, compared notes. I could sound them out, see who'd stand up with me. But you won't get anyone to go first. Not until they believe he's history.'

Yates was right. They spoke to two others, the only two who would even let them through the door, and got a similar answer. No one would go first.

'Classic protection psychology,' said Groombridge, when they met up. He looked across the road at the offices of Dawson Security Ltd. A small rented unit with a yard containing three liveried vans and a gleaming black Mercedes, de-badged with a private plate – Delta Four Whisky Sierra Zero November: D4WSoN. Money doesn't buy taste, thought Stark.

There was no reception, no secretary, just a pair of burly guys in shiny black bomber jackets unloading boxes from the back of a tatty old Transit. They gave the three coppers their blankest stares as they passed. More boxes were stacked inside, a few open. One contained black boots, another bomber jackets.

'Detective Inspector Groombridge?' drawled a voice. Dawson stood in the door to the only office, bigger than his photo suggested, overweight but gym-bunny hard. 'To what do I owe the displeasure?'

'Detective Chief Inspector,' said Groombridge.

Dawson chuckled. 'Good old Met, still promoting failure. Who're your pets?'

'This is DS Millhaven and Constable Stark,' said Groombridge.

'Constable?' Dawson smiled unpleasantly at Stark. 'A wannabe detective? Drew the short straw – your mentor here couldn't catch a cold. Where's Darlington? Pushing up daisies?'

'Enjoying retirement.'

'Put out to pasture,' said Dawson. 'Not before time. I must send him a card. Better still, I'll drop round with some flowers for his wife, poor woman. Must be a burden having the shuffling old flat-foot under hers. How she must long for the day he shuffles off for good. They still live in that poky mid-terrace in Lime Road?'

Stark's fists clenched involuntarily. Dawson caught the movement and grinned. 'Oh . . . the pup has teeth? Down, Sparky, you're not ready to play with the big dogs.' Stark's failure to be intimidated drew a second glance from Dawson. The big man sized up threat for a living. He stared at the scars, perhaps reassessing. 'Won't you come in and take a seat, Officers? I'd offer you a cuppa but I don't like you.'

There were only two visitor chairs, the cheap plastic stacking variety. Stark remained standing.

'So, how can I be of assistance?' asked Dawson.

'Where were you on Monday, May the twenty-fifth, at six twenty p.m.?'

Dawson's big black leather office chair creaked as he leant his considerable frame back. 'You tell me, *Chief* Inspector.'

'You were driving Nikki Cockcroft to Orpington in a stolen BMW.'

Dawson was amused. 'If you could prove that we'd be having this conversation in Royal Hill.'

'Why were you helping her?' Dawson didn't answer. 'You've been seen together on the Ferrier.'

'She's a mate's little sister. I promised I'd keep an eye on her.'

'You and Gary still close, then? Prison records show you've never visited.'

'We're not the Christmas-card type, Inspector. I'll be there when he gets out.'

'Long time to wait for your cut.'

'Why, Inspector,' Dawson drawled, with exaggerated coyness, 'whatever can you mean?'

'Eight million and change, stolen at gunpoint and never recovered.'

'Now now, Inspector. Surely you're not still barking up that tree.'

Groombridge smiled. 'Oh, you know us police hounds. We never lose the scent.'

'Do I look like a man with that kind of cash?'

'No. There really is no honour among thieves, even *mates*.'

Now Dawson's smile looked painted on. 'If you're done yapping, Inspector, I have a business to run.'

'I've been hearing a lot of things about your business recently. You've moved up in the world too.'

Dawson spread his arms expansively. 'My little contribution to the taxman's purse, Inspector. It's all above board here.'

'Like an iceberg is all above water. I have a witness says you supply the drugs Nikki peddles around the Ferrier.'

Dawson's eyes narrowed fractionally. 'You should know better than to listen to Rat tales, Inspector.'

'People are starting to talk. Your iceberg is floating south. It's just a matter of time now, Liam. I'm going to feel your collar.'

The polite dance was over. 'Darlington thought that too – and all it got him was a gold watch. What is it they say about old dogs?' He looked up at Stark and the two locked eyes. Dawson smiled malevolently. 'Careful, Sparky. Some dogs don't just bark.'

'Well, you didn't think he'd just cave in and confess, did you?' said Fran, outside.

'No, no. He's not some snot-nosed kid. He's a proper villain. I just wanted to get reacquainted.'

'If Nikki was his loyal foot-soldier on the Ferrier we might use charges against her to flip her into disloyalty,' said Stark.

'Yes, I had thought of that, TI Stark,' replied Groombridge, tartly. Stark wasn't the only one to have let Dawson get under his skin.

The next day's morning meeting was lively. News of Dawson's fledgling empire had given the team new impetus. 'We don't have enough for a warrant,' explained Groombridge, 'but I don't think he'd be stupid enough to keep anything on the premises anyway. See what else you can find out. Who does his books? Does the business rent other property? Is Dawson listed as director of any other firms? I've asked Serious Crime Directorates six and seven to take a look, see where Dawson fits into the food chain and whether they can give us any kind of steer. I want something on this bastard.

'And keep banging the drum for Pinky. If she can finger Nikki Cockcroft we can really turn the heat up.'

'There,' said Fran, thrusting a box and clipboard at Stark after the meeting. 'Your phone. Sign here in blood.' Stark settled for ink. 'Don't break it, don't lose it, don't abuse the taxpayers' grudging generosity, and don't use it to beat suspects – the paperwork is a bitch.'

Some saintly techie had already endured the pain of setting the damn thing up, probably some necessary security protocol. Stark spent the next hour adding numbers, business and personal. Tapping in Kelly's resurrected a brief smile. It was a simple phone, robust over cutting-edge. Stark preferred that, though he supposed the camera might be useful in his new line of work. For some reason that stirred a memory of his first day, of Kyle Gibbs sneering and swaggering, alive and full of malice, and of Fran's words: 'The spiteful little shits like filming their exploits on their phones.' They'd abused the technology at their fingertips to immortalize their hateful exploits. He was angered once again. Then a thought occurred to him. 'Sarge?'

'What?'

'Their phones were checked? The gang? They were checked

for pictures, film?' He'd held those phones and never thought to look.

'We do think of some things, Constable. There was nothing incriminating.'

'Did FSS check for deleted files?'

Fran rolled her eyes. 'If you're going to waste my time with ideas, can they at least be about how we can nail Liam Dawson for something?'

'I read somewhere that sometimes computer files can be found even after they've been deleted. Ghost files. They're still there unless their space in the memory has been reallocated.'

Fran stared at him. 'You *do* read too much.'

'Is that a no?'

'Nikki's was a new one, though,' said Dixon.

'What?' barked Fran.

Dixon looked up warily. 'The one she had on her when she was arrested. It was new. Well, the SIM was. Pay-as-you-go. Registered the day after the Maggs attack. Nikki stole the handset from that girl she jumped.'

'The day she skipped town?' asked Fran.

'So it wouldn't have anything pertinent on it,' confirmed Dixon.

'Why didn't I know this?'

'It's in the report, Sarge. The theft was added to her charge sheet.'

'All right, all right!' Fran made a face. 'So where the bloody hell is her *original* phone?'

'Good question, Detective Sergeant,' agreed Groombridge, sipping a steaming coffee in the doorway to his office. 'We heard nothing on the network ping. Did she dump it? Lose it? Was it damaged somehow in the attack and discarded? Stark, go and ask your pal Maggs if he saw one. Fran, you ask Nikki. I'll await news of their eager co-operation.'

*

259

Fran drove with her habitual fatalistic abandon. Stark held on without comment. She still wasn't ready to pass the time of day with him. At the prison she was led away to the female wings while Stark was taken back to the same dismal room as before.

'On your own again?' remarked Maggs, as he was ushered in. 'I told you, I won't help you find her.'

'That's not why I'm here.' Stark did the formal business for the tape.

'All right, Constable Weekender, how can I help the cutting edge of the thin blue line today?'

'I have a question for you. Did you see any of your attackers filming the attack on their phones?'

'No.'

Stark was certain there'd been a hesitation, and a flicker in the eyes. 'Your assailants have filmed their attacks before.'

'So ask them.'

'We will. I'm particularly interested in Nikki Cockcroft . . .'

'Rather you than me. There was me thinking your inspector was the only one with poor taste.'

'In whether you saw her with a phone.'

'I was fighting for my life.'

'You picked her out of a book of mugshots, said you'd never forget her. If she was holding up a phone, filming, I can't believe you wouldn't have noticed.'

'Believe what you like, Blue Top. Why are you so keen to know?'

'If we find footage of the attack on their phones, it strengthens our case against them.'

'Maybe, but that's not the reason.'

'If we find footage of the attack on Pinky it might help corroborate your claims.'

'I told you, I'm not interested in strengthening my case. Try again.'

Stark met Maggs's gaze. 'All right, we could also charge your attackers with sexual assault or worse, make sure they stayed behind bars as long as they actually deserve.'

'Nice try. But just supposing you're right, do you think she'd want to see footage of herself being pinned down and stripped splashed all over the news? Do you think she'd want to see it herself? What makes you think I'd help you do that?' The anger was back in Maggs's voice.

Stark actually sympathized. 'I have a job to do. I'm duty-bound to find the truth.'

'*Duty?* Truth isn't necessarily justice, Stark! Look at yourself in the mirror some time and tell me I'm wrong!'

'Maybe not, but the first answer you gave me today was a bare-faced lie, justified or otherwise. Someone *was* filming. My guess would be Cockcroft herself. And if that footage exists I will find it, with or without your help.'

'Go on, then,' sneered Maggs. 'But don't talk about duty to *me*.'

Fran's conversation with Nikki was even shorter in both time and pleasantries. 'No luck either, then. We're wasting our time with this. We should be kicking in doors after Dawson.'

Stark disagreed, but suspected Groombridge had an ulterior motive. 'A suspicious mind might think the guv'nor sent us out on a wild-goose chase to give us a chance to kiss and make up.'

'If you try to kiss me I'll break your nose,' said Fran.

'Just a little one, Sarge, I won't tell.'

'Piss off.'

'Don't fight it, Sarge. I know you feel it too,' replied Stark, deadpan.

'In your dreams, smartarse.' There was no mistaking the suppressed smile. 'You're still on probation after that funeral stunt.'

Groombridge had told her. Why? To get her off his back a little? Stark wished he hadn't.

Fran looked him in the eye. 'You should've told me your-self.'

'I'm sorry.'

'An *apology*!' she exclaimed. 'This is a new and welcome addition to your so-called personality.'

'It was a personal matter, Sarge. I needed to pay my respects.'

'Because he was a military man.'

'Because there was no one else.'

She seemed to consider this. 'Fair enough.' Another pause. 'Next time don't piss me about, just tell me. There's a limit to my forgiveness.'

'I hope I never find it.'

'Don't push your luck. I haven't forgotten about your little impromptu jaunt to the Ferrier, or your stunt with the CPS lawyer – don't think I won't get to the bottom of *that*.'

'You sound like my shrink, Sarge.' Stark smiled. 'Talking of which . . . any chance you could drop me off?'

Suddenly she laughed. 'You really are a cocky, ungrateful, secretive git!'

Fran decided to wait for Stark. Now she knew for sure what these Wednesday sessions were, she didn't have to tiptoe. She called to update Groombridge from the hospital car park.

'Can't say I'm surprised,' he replied. 'I suppose I'll have to take a crack at the rest of them, but they'll be wise to my tricks now.'

'Guv.'

'Is there something else?'

'Constable Toerag's idea about the phones – ghost memories? He may have a point.'

'We have the culprits, Detective Sergeant. Why would I go cap-in-hand to Cox for funding just on the off-chance of a little more evidence?'

'The CPS might like more. All we have so far is agitated

confessions and some blood on Kyle's shoes. We could add sexual assault. If we could, it might help shake Pinky out from whatever bush she's hiding under.'

'I agree, so I called the FSS while you were out.'

'Did you?' Fran managed not to sound annoyed.

'I did.' Groombridge managed not to sound smug. 'Apparently Constable Toerag did have a point. Not a new one, sadly. The case officer told me they'd already checked, as a matter of course. He was kind enough not to make me feel a twit. He did, however, draw my attention to the subject of "transfer activity logs". He emailed me some.' Fran could hear paper being waved. 'It seems that, among all the other traffic, every one of the gang's phones reports receiving video files via Bluetooth from the number saved in their phones as N-Zone or G. Nikki's missing phone. They were all deleted, of course, and the clever little shits had filled their memories with new footage, garbage, all recorded in the hours after Kyle Gibbs died, all ensuring there was no chance of finding any of Stark's "ghost files".'

'Someone in that gang was smarter than they looked.'

'Yes. My money would be on Naveen Hussein, under duress or otherwise. He seems to have been the most computer literate. He was the only one who had a laptop. Stolen, of course.'

'But let me guess, the laptop was wiped too.'

'Yes and no. Naveen slipped up. There was a Trojan hiding on it, which they tell me was designed to generate . . .' Groombridge consulted his notes '. . . pop-ups. Specifically, links to a series of unpleasant websites, porn mostly, but a couple were dedicated to the nefarious business of happy-slapping. The same Trojan was apparently also sending keystroke records back to its masters, password fishing apparently, looking for banking access. The forensics techie said he'd be happy to look into it.'

'If only their reports weren't so dull, people might read them instead of leaving it to the CPS to pick over. So?'

'So it's all being referred to the National Internet Crime Unit as we speak.'

'Bloody hell.' Fran shook her head. 'Just when I thought Stark had run out of cages to rattle.'

'Indeed. Though Cox is pleased with his small investment and I look rather shiny. So how are you two getting along now?'

'Meaning, has your scheme to sit him in my car for the last two days worked?'

'Did it?'

'If he crosses the line one more time I may kill him.'

'He will and you know it, and not just once. He's one of those rare individuals you meet in life who know exactly where the line is but have no qualms about stepping right over it whenever they see fit.'

'Yes, Guv.' Fran sighed.

'I quite like that he rubs you up the wrong way.'

'You would.'

'I think you do too.'

Fran could all but hear him grinning. 'With all due respect, Guv . . . piss off!'

After the usual wait, Stark settled into Dr Hazel's couch with an odd determination to engage. When prompted, he spouted every remembered detail of his recent most disturbing dreams, if not the ill-advised method he used too frequently now to avoid having them, then segued into Kelly. Poor Hazel had probably never taken so many notes in one session. She made little or no comment, either too stunned by his unfettered sincerity or simply unable to get a word in. Whatever. His time was up and Stark left, feeling unburdened and rather virtuous.

Fran had waited, saving him the cab fare but killing any chance of lunch. She'd had calls to make, she claimed, but it was more likely that she hadn't finished prying. Her news was startling. The investigation now had national implications and she teased him that he'd started a wildfire. Stark sighed inwardly. So much for the Grey Man.

Fran pulled in at a petrol station. 'Lunch.'

Stark made them both large instant coffees at the franchised machine. Fran added a Danish and went to wait in the car, leaving Stark with the bill. He picked up a Red Bull and a triple all-day-breakfast sandwich, paid, glugged down the can in the shop and gathered up the rest, burning his hands as he carried it all to the car.

'Jesus,' said Fran, as he tore open the sandwich packet. 'What is it with you and food?'

'Old habits, Sarge. An army runs on its stomach.'

'I thought you all crawled on your bellies,' joked Fran. 'Give that here.' She held out her hand for the receipt.

'You paying?' It seemed highly unlikely.

'Don't be daft. Lunch on the road is on the Great British Taxpayer. Though they might wonder why you necked that energy drink hoping your sergeant wouldn't see you.' Stark handed her the receipt. 'Needed a pick-me-up, did we?'

'Asked the lady on her *n*th coffee of the day.' He laughed.

'Fair enough. Buckle up.'

'Don't you want to finish your Danish before driving?' Stark asked innocently.

'Bollocks.' She shot the car out into the traffic one-handed, munching and ignoring the flashing of lights behind her.

The journey back couldn't have been more different. Once he'd fobbed off her questions about his shrink, they got talking about work. Fran was still firmly of the opinion that chasing Nikki's missing phone was a waste of time.

'It could be vital in cementing the case,' argued Stark.

'Granted, but even if we find it, she's probably wiped it like the others.'

'Then why doesn't she have it? Why would she toss it?'

'Maybe she panicked, maybe she just lost it. Either way it

265

could be anywhere. We found a handful of phones just on our little foot search – people lose them all the time. If someone hands it in, fine. In the meantime we've got proper villains to chase.'

If someone hands it in. 'There is another possibility,' said Stark, slowly. It wasn't like a light-bulb going ping above his head, more like a dimmer, slowly brightening. 'What if Maggs took it?'

'Oh, for God's sake!'

'No, seriously. What if he did?'

Fran glanced at him, frustrated. 'Why would he? To sell?'

'I was thinking more that he doesn't want anyone else to have it. What if the person he barged to the ground wasn't one of the lads but Nikki *because* she was filming? Think how angry you'd be if you saw what was being done, with Nikki egging it on and filming the whole vicious business for kicks.'

Fran rolled her eyes. 'So he's furious and intervenes. Maybe he even barges Nikki aside and the phone goes flying, Pinky runs off, then the fight, the killing, the gang flee . . . leaving Maggs *stabbed* and *bleeding*,' she said.

'Right. But what does he do? He doesn't stagger about looking for help. He sits down, gets out his thirty-year-old field kit and patches himself up as best he can. Considered actions. What if he saw the phone, knowing what was on it, looked at Kyle's body, realized there was no way out for him but made up his mind there and then to try to shield Pinky from further trauma?'

Fran considered this, drumming the wheel with her fingers. 'Utter bollocks!'

'He decided to at some point, why not then?'

'He was drunk. And stabbed, in case I haven't already mentioned it.'

'He was drunk by the following morning, but that was analgesic after being stabbed. We've only his word that he was drunk before. He had time to decide what to do, time for his training to kick in.'

'Thirty-year-old training?'

'They ram it home pretty hard, especially when you're in elite forces like Maggs was,' replied Stark. 'You're hard-wired to assess, plan and act under pressure.'

Fran was shaking her head. 'This is meaningless. It's nothing but what-ifs.'

'Will you at least take it to the guv'nor?'

'What for?' cried Fran. 'Even if by some weird quirk of the universe you're right, Nikki doesn't have the phone, Maggs doesn't have the phone and we don't have the phone!'

'We've searched in the direction Nikki and the others ran off. But Maggs couldn't get out of the park with his precious trolley till the gates opened in the morning. Either he dumped it somewhere in the park or on his way to the station to turn himself in.'

'*If* he had it,' insisted Fran. 'And if you're proposing another foot search, you can tell the DCI yourself.'

24

'Do you derive twisted pleasure out of making work for us?' enquired Groombridge. He looked at Fran whose shrug reiterated that she was mere spectator, not participant.

'I've checked the cameras, Guv. Maggs didn't leave before morning. The gates were unlocked at oh six hundred. Maggs is seen trundling his trolley down the hill through St Mary's Gate shortly before eight and weaving off down Nevada Street on his way here. The next camera to pick him up was the one out front. The time differential suggests no deviation. He said he'd bivvied up in the Flower Garden.'

Fran made a face. 'Bivvied?'

'Bivouacked. Camped. His belongings included an old army bivvy bag and a small camouflage tarp.'

'More Boy Scout bullshit.'

'All right, all right,' Groombridge intervened. 'Take Stark and Dixon and walk the route.'

Fran looked horrified. 'Oh, come on, Guv, this has gone far enough. We know who killed Alfred Ladd, we know who killed Stacey Appleton and we know who killed Kyle Gibbs. Surely we *must* focus on Liam Dawson now.'

Knowing who did something was not the same as proving it, thought Stark. Of course the bigger fish wanted catching, but he intended to see that Alf, Stacey and her mother, Maggs and even Kyle got justice too. Otherwise what was the point?

'Surely you're not suggesting we leave stones unturned?' Groombridge chided.

'Send the Boy Scout and some uniforms,' protested Fran.

'He can turn over stones, leaves, squirrel shit and stinking bins to his heart's content.'

'I agree TI Stark is uniquely qualified for the task,' replied Groombridge, 'and as his PDP mentor you will be uniquely placed to ensure he doesn't take any shortcuts.'

'Should we ask Marcus Turner along?' asked Stark, innocently.

Fran's expression darkened. If Groombridge noticed, he played along seamlessly. 'Capital idea.'

Fran looked back and forth between them, daring either to smirk, then stalked away in frustration.

Marcus met them at the bandstand, greeting them cheerfully. He walked them to the Flower Garden duck pond. 'You've no wish to know the foetid jetsam we dredged out of there,' he said.

'You already searched it?' asked Stark, failing to check his surprise. Of course they had.

'I apologize for Trainee Investigator Stark, Marcus,' said Fran. 'He thinks he's the only one around with a brain.'

Marcus smiled. 'Seemed a likely spot to ditch a weapon if you scarpered this way. Or other evidence. I have a notion I can show you where your man Maggs camped, though.' He led them to a secluded dell and pointed out linear marks around forks in branches about a metre off the ground. 'I wasn't sure what to make of these. They've been deepened by repeat use as you can see. Something tied here regularly. Tarpaulin perhaps? And here.' He pointed out faint wheel marks. 'The trolley, I'd say. There's little other evidence that anyone camped here but . . .' He was looking at Stark.

'He'd clear up behind him, especially if he was coming back regularly,' confirmed Stark. He glanced up and spotted what he was looking for. High up in the twisted fork of a branch was a dark green bag. He shimmied up awkwardly and retrieved it. It contained some energy bars, some tinned rations, a silver space blanket, some matches and a small penknife wrapped in waxed cloth.

'Boy Scouts,' muttered Fran.

There seemed little more to be gleaned from the area so they followed the various routes Maggs might have taken back to the main paths, finding nothing. Marcus was meticulous, and Fran made a faint show of impatience, though only faint and only a show, Stark noted.

The main diagonal path down towards St Mary's Gate had no steps to impede a trolley and was the most direct route. There were few opportunities for concealing anything along the way, apart from the hollow remains of the fallen twelfth-century Queen Elizabeth Oak. Fran was not shy with her impatience as Stark rummaged inside. Nor when he paused to take in the view north over the stately Queen's House and Old Royal Naval College to the upstart monoliths of Canary Wharf just across the winding river Thames. To the north-west the Gherkin and Tower 42 marked the City, London's financial district, and to the north-east the defiant brick chimneys of an old power station juxtaposed before the extra-terrestrial Millennium Dome on the Greenwich Peninsula. The elevation and green generosity of the park highlighted just how surrounded it was, how besieged, as if it must inevitably fall to the rampaging urban sprawl stretching away to every horizon. London was as oppressive as it was impressive.

Marcus joined him in silent contemplation.

'Daydream in your own time,' barked Fran.

At the gate there were bins and countless other places to ditch something but the CCTV footage had shown Maggs taking no such action. The camera on a pole also covered the length of Nevada Street all the way to where it crossed into Burney Street, which culminated at the station. On one corner of that crossroads there was a tiny square park with shrubs and benches shaded by the fat leaves of a broad London plane.

'Sorry to drag you out, Marcus,' said Fran. 'For the record it was Stark's idea.'

'Was it? Oh, well, never mind,' replied Marcus, rather enigmatically. Fran caught Stark suppressing a smile and scowled at him. Dixon studiously ignored eye contact.

Seemingly unaware, Marcus was peering at a nearby parking meter. He pulled on a surgical glove and wiped his finger across its domed top, inspecting the dust on his fingertip in the sunlight. 'Glass powder.' He glanced at the ground and crouched to collect a tiny piece of glass. Stark spotted another. Marcus rummaged around in the shrub behind the courtyard's low wall and pulled out a piece of plastic casing and then a larger piece of glass. It was thin and faintly curved, not a bottle or sheet glass but, unmistakably, a piece of mobile phone screen. He mimicked the action of smashing an object on the top of the parking meter.

They looked around but found no phone. Then Dixon called out. By a drain gully in the road lay another fragment of glass, very like the others. Dixon prostrated himself to peer down the gully, shielding his eyes from the sun. 'All I can see is reflection on the water,' he said. 'Can you find me a stick or something?'

'Here.' Marcus produced a crowbar from his small bag as if it were a perfectly ordinary item to carry about. 'You can try this, but we'll probably need the jack SOCO use.'

Dixon tried to prise the grate up but it was cemented in place with decades of gunk. Stark crouched to help, gripping the iron grate, but the second he tried to lift, his hip sang out in agony and he let go with a choice curse, hobbled to the low wall and sat flexing his leg gingerly.

'Okay,' said Fran, ignoring Stark's discomfort. 'Where youth and brute ignorance fail, wiser heads prevail.'

An hour later SOCO pulled the smashed remains of a broken mobile phone from the drain.

'Did you have any luck with that photograph?' asked Marcus, as they looked on.

Fran frowned. 'What photograph?'

'The faded portrait among Alfred Ladd's effects – came to me with the body. Constable Stark asked for it.' Marcus immediately saw he'd spilt a secret but it was too late.

Stark shrugged. 'His wife, Nancy, most probably.' Social Services had drawn a blank but his friendly MoD underling had come through again. Alf's military records listed his wife's name. The General Register Office had had their marriage and her death certificates. From parish records Stark had tracked down her grave. 'Died in 'seventy-two, no children or living relatives. That's all I could find.'

'The age of the photo and clothing fashion support your theory,' said Marcus.

'And where is it now?' asked Fran, though she surely suspected.

'Alfred Ladd's breast pocket would be my guess,' said Marcus. 'Next to his heart?'

Stark nodded, avoiding Fran's eyes.

'The world loves a romantic.' Marcus grinned. 'Wouldn't you agree, Detective Sergeant?'

Fran didn't comment.

An FSS boffin called later to say the phone's SIM card registration matched that of the N-Zone number but it would take longer to discover if anything could be salvaged from the phone's memory. No fingerprints or DNA evidence had survived immersion in the sludgy water.

Fran hung up and relayed the news. 'Well, Trainee Investigator, if FSS find anything useful the great British taxpayer will know they got their money's worth out of that energy drink. Come on, you owe me a proper drink.'

Stark was heartily glad to knock off early. Fatigue and the pain in his hip were crushing him.

'You okay?' Fran asked, as he flinched sitting down in the pub.

'Bit sore,' he admitted, taking a grateful swig of whisky, feeling its burning warmth rush to his aid.

'You've looked like shit for days. Having trouble sleeping?' She'd watched his conversation about it with Maggs. 'Global warming, Sarge. I just can't sleep for the worry.'

She looked at him. 'You're an artful dodger. I hope your shrink sees through your crap.'

'She's yet to convince me she can see far past her own pre-assumptions.'

'It's a she? Have you got a crush on her too?'

'No, she's nosy enough but, until she has your passion for roughshod inquisition, she'll never hold a candle to you in my eyes.'

'And your other therapist, Tantric Aqua-babe?'

'I told you, she's out of my league.'

'And yet you aspire to me?' Fran chortled.

'Not me. I know when I'm outclassed.'

'Good.'

'Yep, that Marcus is a helluva guy!'

It was worth it. Besides, a punch in the arm was nothing to the fire in his hip. He'd definitely pulled something trying to lift that sodding drain gully. Pills hadn't helped much, and while whisky on top did, it also reinforced the fatigue. After a while Fran sent him home. There was a message from Captain Pierson on his phone, demanding to see him in her brusque manner. One by one, thought Stark. But winning round the icy captain was beyond him for now.

'Ah, there you are, Stark! Guess what I have here.' Groombridge waved a memory stick.

Stark was in no mood for guessing games. He'd woken before dawn, not from dreams for once but pain. Despite more OxyContin he'd struggled to get comfortable and had hardly fallen asleep again before the radio woke him. 'Footage off Nikki Cockcroft's phone, Guv?'

'You could at least pretend sometimes not to be a smart-arse,' said Fran.

Groombridge just laughed. 'FSS just emailed it over. They could hardly believe it'd survived. Let's see where your luck and intuition have led us. If you would, Trainee Investigator . . .'

Bodies jostled for space around Stark's computer. The file took a few seconds to open and several long minutes to run. The image was small, packaged for a mobile screen. Once enlarged to fill his screen it was pixellated but clear enough to identify faces and actions. Everyone watched to the end in silence.

'Still think we should have every officer in the station rub Stark for luck, Guv?' said Fran, humourlessly. No one was in the mood for jokes with those images fresh in their minds.

'At least it seems Maggs intervened in time.' Groombridge's tone was grim.

The film had shown familiar youths surrounding Pinky by the phone's dim video-spotlight, taunting her. Nikki Cockcroft's voice could be heard jeering. Jeering became baying for violence, then worse. The rest of the gang stepped back, perhaps shocked, as Kyle used his knife both to threaten and cut at clothing. One voice even called for him to stop, but Cockcroft spat invective at whoever it was and urged Kyle on with more.

Pinky's pleading became screaming as Kyle fumbled down his trousers. Just as it seemed too late for hope a bellowing roar erupted. There was the briefest flash of olive drab clothing and a thump, the image became a blur, a crash of the phone tumbling across the ground and then nothing. That was it. It was enough.

'CPS are going to crucify them with this,' said Fran. There was a chorus of satisfaction from the team. Someone even patted Stark on the shoulder as if this were all his handiwork, but he was still too sickened to be embarrassed.

'Everyone except Nikki Cockcroft,' said Groombridge. '*We* all know it's her phone and her voice but you never see her face and there's a lot of background noise.'

Fran frowned. 'And no one has that number saved in her actual name.'

'It's enough, though, Guv, right?' asked Hammed.

'Maybe. And we've got her interview slip-up. Depends what the jury call reasonable doubt. What we really need is for one of the others to turn on her, place her at the scene, or we find that girl and get a positive ID. Otherwise the only ID we have is from Maggs, a homeless drunk charged with murder. I think it's about time I leant on Naveen Hussein. In the meantime get Munroe back in a cell and find me that girl!'

Sobered, the team dispersed.

The first frame of footage sat on Stark's screen with an invitation to replay: a girl with pink hair looking up in confusion and alarm, unaware of the horror about to be inflicted on her. Stark was transfixed. 'Who are you?'

'Good question.' Stark jumped. Groombridge stood right behind him. 'At least she escaped the worst, lad. We've Maggs to thank for that.'

'Still think murder is the just charge, Guv?'

'Don't you?' Groombridge perched on the desk and looked down at him seriously. 'Are you saying Kyle Gibbs deserved to bleed to death in that park?' Stark didn't answer. 'Who would we be to say that? We don't even hang people when we're as sure as we can be of the worst possible guilt.'

'Surely the CPS will see that Maggs intervened with good intent.'

'All we have is his confession and fingerprints on the bloody knife. Everyone else present is shut up tighter than a drum for fear of making matters worse for themselves. And we have the body of a boy with a knife in his back, his *back*. We work with hunches, suspicions and bloody-minded legwork, but the CPS can only work with what we present to them.'

'You're forgetting someone, Guv,' said Stark, indicating his screen.

'No, I'm not.' He looked deep into Stark's eyes, perhaps sensing the fury. 'You must stop looking at this through a soldier's eyes. Outside combat, moral absolutism is a dangerous precept.'

It felt as if Groombridge was seeing into the very heart of him and Stark had to look away. The moral certainty that let you pull the trigger was a vital but perilous thing; from good versus evil and all the way down to kill or be killed. It could lead to triumphs or tragic mistakes and, like most certainties, might crumble with time or the effort of holding it together. He wondered sometimes whether his own lack of remorse for most of what he'd done was real, merely a legacy of training or, worse, a psychotic construct of his own that might fall to dust once probed.

'Look at me.' Groombridge's voice was soft now, but Stark looked up into a gaze still alight with unnerving penetration. 'You're a copper now, Joseph; there's no going back. Whatever demons and furies pursue us cannot be vented. They must be seized upon and channelled to drive us forward as *we* choose. The other path leads to bent coppers, or ex-servicemen with blood on their hands.'

'Point taken, Guv.'

'Good. So let's find her, shall we?'

Naveen didn't crack. Regardless of what Groombridge had suggested, it seemed he remained too scared of Nikki to be nudged back the other way. Munroe was arrested and charged but kept up his silence throughout.

The forensic investigation into the phone found little else.

The full report told them that no other videos or images of interest were present, though the log files showed many more had been made. Correlating the dates and times, it appeared that footage had been shot around the time of every one of the assaults on the homeless, but all had been downloaded and deleted and subsequent files had wiped further trace.

Later in the day Groombridge was summoned to Superintendent Cox's office. He returned with a broad smile. 'Gather round, everyone. Earlier today, using what they'd gleaned from the Trojan on Naveen Hussein's laptop, the National Internet Crime Unit raided offices in Manchester. They made several arrests and seized numerous computer servers. In total over thirty illegal websites were shut down. As it was we who first drew their attention to some of these websites, they had a root around and found, on a site called SlappinUK.net, five files uploaded from Naveen Hussein's IP address. Each file was uploaded within twenty-four hours of one of our assaults. All the victims and perpetrators' faces were blurred out before upload but not uniformly well. NICU say that . . .' he consulted his notepad '. . . the high amount of individual movement means that faces frequently appear momentarily from behind the block of blur layer placed to hide them. They suggest that at least three individual assailants can be clearly identified, possibly more, and two victims. Copies are being emailed to me now. I want you in twos ready to scan through each video with a fine-tooth comb. Have the relevant photos in front of you. This is our big break, people!'

Within minutes the videos were arriving.

Because they'd been to the scene soon after, Fran and Stark took the one dated just after the attack on Alfred Ladd. The location was instantly recognizable, the attack almost unwatchable. Poor Alf's face was always blurred but his anguished cries were not.

'There!' said Fran, pointing to part of the screen. 'Rewind!'

Stark backed it up and paused the image. Poking out from the side of a rectangle of blur was half a face. Tyler Wantage.

Elsewhere around the office cries of excitement and anger mingled. Within half an hour they had clear identification of three perps: Tyler Wantage, Colin Messenger and Stacey Appleton, plus glimpses of Tim Bowes and Harrison Collier that ought to be enough. Only two victims had been identified but all of the locations could be matched to crime-scene photos.

'Naveen was careful enough to cover his own face consistently,' commented someone.

'But not his clothes,' said Fran. 'We could get them all from the clothes alone.'

'Add the locations, the upload timings and the interview slips and we've got them bang to rights,' said Groombridge. 'The magistrate will remand them all for sure now.'

'Still not Nikki Cockcroft, though, Guv,' Fran pointed out. 'It's her phone. It's always her filming.'

Groombridge didn't seem about to let that spoil his evident satisfaction. He returned from relaying the good news to the super with a spring in his step and clapped his hands together for attention. 'Despite my best efforts to take all the credit, the super seems determined to reward you lot as well. Tonight the drinks are on him.' He raised his voice over the ensuing hub-bub. 'Attendance is mandatory, no excuses accepted! Anyone not hung-over in the morning will be back in uniform by ten.' The cheering redoubled.

Stark allowed himself to be caught up in the prevailing good mood. It was only a while later that he remembered his hydro appointment. There was no way he'd be allowed to duck the party. With regret he called the Carter and made his apologies.

The evening was in full swing when two uniform officers entered Rosie's. Their serious manner said they weren't here to take advantage of the super's generosity. Stark watched them

accost the nearest copper, who turned and pointed. They jostled their way through the crowded pub to Fran and
Groombridge. Stark was already making his way over as both
stood, faces grave, drinks forgotten. 'What is it?' he asked, over
the noise.

Fran sighed. 'Naveen Hussein.'

25

Crossing the police tape was rapidly losing its thrill. Bloody dressings showed where the paramedics had worked on the boy before rushing him to A&E. He wasn't out of the woods yet, apparently.

'A taste of his own medicine,' suggested one constable, earning a quiet rebuke from his sergeant.

A trail of blood led back along the landing to the door of the flat. Not dragged, thought Stark, crouching to inspect the markings. 'He crawled out, Guv.'

Fran rolled her eyes. 'Here we go . . . Are you going to tell us what he ate for supper next?'

'Lamb curry, if the ready-meal packaging in the kitchen is anything to go by,' announced Marcus Turner, from the hallway.

'Marcus,' Groombridge greeted him.

'Detectives.'

'Nothing better to do with yourself of an evening?' asked Fran.

'Ah, well, sometimes the little orphans' clinic has to take a back seat to serious police matters,' he said, unruffled. He, at least, hadn't come from the pub. 'SOCO asked me to assist.'

'All right,' said Groombridge, pointedly. 'Let's take a look, then.'

Marcus led them through his initial thoughts. Blood splatter in the hallway suggested the initial attack had taken place right by the front door. A deep mark in the wall from the door handle was either long-term carelessness or a sign that the attacker had forced their way in once the door was open. Door

280

spy-holes had had no place in sixties urban Utopian idealism and the Husseins had not followed the trend for putting one in. Someone had fitted a chain. Naveen had used it. It hung now, screws torn from the doorframe.

The rest of the beating had taken place in the boy's bedroom. Probably he'd fled there, hoping to lock himself in. Stark pointed to the smashed mobile phone and computer modem. Marcus nodded. 'Found and smashed all the landlines too. Shows a rather considered ruthlessness, don't you think?'

'He underestimated his victim, though,' said Stark. 'The boy crawled outside to set off the ankle bracelet.'

'Yes. He even knew to keep going along the landing as far as he could to make sure it had triggered before he passed out.'

'Smarter than the average Rat,' observed Groombridge.

'Bet he's glad he got slapped with it, after all,' commented Fran.

'I doubt he's glad of anything much right now,' said Marcus.

Fran picked Stark up early. Naveen was alive and awake. The hospital had reluctantly agreed to let them see him.

The teenager was barely recognizable. Stark recalled an Afghan man, beaten by the people of his neighbouring village who believed him guilty of raping a young girl. He had looked this bad – and he had died, his guilt or otherwise untried. The doctors assured them Naveen would live. His lucky day. A nurse was helping him drink his breakfast through a straw tucked into one cheek. They'd wired his broken jaw shut. His face was one huge bruise, nose badly broken, right eye closed, with stitches above and below. His wrist had been broken too, along with four ribs and the bones in one hand. When he saw them he flinched.

His mother sat up, bristling. 'And where were you when that thug did this to my boy? Where were you? You were supposed to be keeping watch!'

The woman's understanding of police bail and ankle bracelets was faulty, but Fran granted her some licence under the circumstances. 'Do you know who did this?'

'That monster Dawson!' she spat. Behind her Naveen groaned and squirmed. 'He won't tell me but I know it's true.' The mother ignored his pleading. 'Who else would do such a thing?'

Who else indeed? thought Fran, with all the other Rats on remand. This was their fault, hers and the guv'nor's. They had tipped Dawson off that tongues were wagging. He'd put two and two together. 'Is it true?' she asked Naveen. The boy shook his head, his open eye panicked. 'We can protect you –'

Naveen's despairing laughter cut her off, but quickly became strangled sobs. The nurse and his mother tried to calm him, lest he choke.

'If you tell us it was him . . .' tried Fran, but Naveen shook his head again, eye closed.

'Go away!' said his mother. 'Leave him alone!'

They did just that. He wasn't going anywhere, but she called for uniform to send a babysitter all the same. You never knew, Dawson might not be finished.

'Where were you last night at nine?' asked Groombridge.

Dawson's lawyer answered for him: 'My client was at work. We can provide you with corroborating statements.'

'And these statements would all come from employees of Mister Dawson?'

The lawyer smiled. 'Indeed.'

Groombridge leant back, staring at Dawson, who returned his gaze dispassionately. 'May I see your hands?'

'Is that necessary?' demanded the lawyer.

'Unless your client has something to hide.'

The lawyer nodded to Dawson, who placed his huge calloused hands on the desk. The knuckles on both were bruised,

the left worst. Naveen's nose and eye suggested that the blow
had come from a left-handed assailant, most of the rest from
the boot. 'My client sustained that bruising from training with
the heavy bag, a boxing –'

'I know what a heavy bag is,' interrupted Groombridge.
Dawson allowed himself a thin smile.

'You would also know that my client has one in his garage
along with his other fitness equipment – if you had grounds
for a warrant.' The lawyer was not court-appointed. Dawson
had brought his own.

The man might just be doing his job, but Stark watched
through the mirror with growing dislike as he diligently shot
down one question after another. Dawson said not one word.
Stark could almost hear Fran's teeth grinding. As the big man
was led out by his lawyer he saw Stark and smirked.

The previous day's euphoria had been premature, they had all
known that, but the super didn't put his plastic behind the bar
often. At Groombridge's insistence the rest of the team had
stayed in Rosie's to make sure the credit card took a respectable
hammering. The best you could say of them that day was that
their hangover was uniform. Stark felt little better. The pills
had not settled his hip as they should. But there was work to be
done.

Dawson's alibi, four identical signed statements, had arrived
by courier from his lawyer. Williams was ordered to check
them out, but the four men would have been rehearsed already.
A statement from Naveen was the only thing that could contradict them and that didn't seem to be on the cards. Unless
something else came up Dawson was untouchable for the
assault. A canny lawyer didn't bode well for the investigation
into his business illegalities either.

The other fly in the ointment remained Nikki Cockcroft.
All the video evidence put the other Ferrier Rats in the frame,

but unless one of them flipped on Nikki she might still slide on the assaults. They still needed Pinky. Her picture on the wall served as a solemn reminder that they had yet to uncover her name, let alone her whereabouts. By late afternoon the camaraderie of the shared hangover was fraying at the edges and the CID floor was looking thin on warm bodies.

'Man, is this party over!' said Fran, in the doorway.

'Looks like Friday-night drinks didn't survive Thursday night,' agreed Stark.

'Come on, lightweight, I'll drop you home.'

Stark accepted gratefully. At home he fixed himself a snack and then tried to steal a nap before his date, but even with painkillers his damn hip wouldn't let him settle.

On the dot of eight he entered the Princess of Wales, Blackheath. It had been Kelly's recommendation, though nothing in her voice suggested she realized the significance to him as a soldier of the Princess of Wales's Royal Regiment. A pretty, gentrified town pub with a proud rugby history. Its website and memorabilia testified to its continuing association with Blackheath Rugby Club, the world's oldest, and its service as the changing room for the first ever international between England and Wales, played on the heath in 1881.

He fully expected to wait, yet Kelly was perched on a bar stool like she owned it. She waved him to another, which she appeared to have protected from the other denizens on a busy Friday evening with little more than her denim jacket. Then again, there couldn't be many blokes present who'd argue the point with her. Free of its usual ponytail, her dark brown hair hung loose over her shoulders in glossy waves. She wore faded jeans and a bright red T-shirt with 'Love-Life' in white, parodying the Coca-Cola logo; impossible to read without enjoying the shape it fitted so snugly. He'd seen her in a swimsuit and a clinical uniform, but this simple outfit made Stark swallow.

'Ready with your lively chat?' She grinned.

He would've been happy to sit and stare. No, that wasn't true, to be blunt. But very little of what he'd be happiest doing right now required lively chat. And in the long tradition of men before the object of their basest desire he was in sorry danger of getting tongue-tied or blurting out some mind-numbing inanity. Time to concentrate. 'I was hoping you'd be providing that.'

'Oh, no. You got my potted history in the car. I let you off once but now I intend to get to the bottom of you.'

'On the first date? What kind of boy do you take me for?'

'Well, maybe you can hold back some hidden depths for next time.'

'I'm afraid all you might find are hidden shallows.'

'Jagged rocks below the surface, perilous to shipping!' Kelly shivered theatrically.

'Perhaps just one large, dull sandbank. Been here long?' he asked, nodding to her half-consumed pint of Guinness.

'This is my local. My flat's just round the corner.'

Stark raised his eyebrows and smiled. 'I told you, I'm not that kind of boy.'

'Don't flatter yourself. What'll you have?'

'Double whisky, no ice.'

'Interesting. I took you for a beer man.'

'I have my moments.'

'I'll bet. Katy,' she called, over the hubbub. The nearest barmaid looked over and smiled. Then she noticed Stark and smile became grin. 'Double whisky, no ice, when you get a second, the best you have, my tab.' Stark thanked her. 'You can get the next one. I intend to loosen your tongue.'

'Many have tried.'

'Have they now?'

'I'm trained in counter-interrogation.'

Kelly beckoned him closer and leant in. Her hair ran across his neck like silk, her warm breath tingled and her perfume was intoxicating. He thought she wanted to whisper something but she just paused for several seconds, every exhalation building the electric charge. 'We'll see about that,' she breathed finally, in his ear, sending a jolt right through him. He shivered. Kelly sat back and gave him probably the most dangerous smile he'd ever seen. The worst thing about it was that it gave every impression of being a purely genuine smile; it simply achieved nine-point-nine on the sultry scale as an after-shock. Stark shivered again and rubbed his neck. 'That is cheating.'

'All's fair.'

'Is this love or war?'

'Too early to tell.' She smiled.

Stark tried to gauge whether her boldness was as much a front as his, but couldn't. It was a sad fact of life that the more you liked a girl the less you could be sure whether she liked you. That was why the bastards got the girls; if you could put feelings aside, you had all the power and it became just a numbers game. Fortune favoured the brazen. Hit shamelessly on ten girls in a club and one would take you home. You didn't have to be a soldier on twenty-four-hour liberty to see it – just look in any nightclub. Girls liked confidence. He'd played the odds in his time, too often in truth. Chalk it up to callow youth, but that didn't make it right. At least those morning walks of shame usually carried just enough actual shame to persuade him he wasn't quite an all-out bastard. It would be nice to think that was why he'd sent Julie packing but of course it wasn't. Doc Hazel was right in that respect. But the walls he'd built after his injury weren't new: they'd merely risen. Julie was just a fling, last in a long line. He couldn't shoulder all the blame, though: he'd neither begun nor finished them all.

And here he was, back in the game, tentative, rusty, more entrenched. A fling was probably just what he needed. A practice swing. A loosener. But this didn't feel like that and Kelly seemed far too smart for it even to be an option. He liked that.

It was terrifying, but he liked it a lot. And it was pointless worrying whether or not he was good enough for her, whether or not he deserved her: that was for her to judge and for time to tell.

His drink arrived and they chinked glasses. He took half in one go and savoured it all the way down. She watched him with evident pleasure. 'Wow,' he said finally. 'I must drink the good stuff more often.'

'Careful,' cautioned Kelly. 'Too much of a good thing can be bad for the soul.'

Stark studied her face for a long moment. 'Some good things,' he said, 'are worth the risk.'

She fanned her face theatrically with her hand. 'Well, *now* look who's cheating.' Either she was covering a genuine blush or she was mocking him. Stark rather suspected the latter. Pity – he'd not meant it as a line. Well, not entirely.

'Nice place,' he said, looking around for a change of subject.

She smiled appreciatively. 'I thought you'd like the name.'

'I'll take all the good omens I can get.' He didn't mention the foot search that had passed within a few hundred metres of the door, or the vicious killers who hailed from the Ferrier Estate barely a mile away. London, as she'd said, worked street by street.

As he ruminated on this his phone rang in his pocket. He fished it out, read Fran's name and put it away again. Kelly looked enquiringly at him.

'They'll leave a message,' he said simply. Instead it rang again. Still Fran.

'That had better not be another woman,' warned Kelly, playfully.

'Not in that way. It's my sergeant.'

'Shouldn't you answer it?'

'It's Friday night, I'm in a pub with a beautiful girl and I'm off duty . . .' It stopped.

Kelly blinked and glanced down into her drink. It took a second for Stark to realize that she really was blushing now, and a moment longer to understand why. So much for concentrating. Damn Fran. The ringing returned. 'Why can't you just leave a message?' Stark wished aloud, before answering. 'Sarge?' He could make out Fran's voice but her words were lost. 'Sorry, Sarge, I can't hear you . . .'

'Where the bloody hell are you?' came the shouted reply.

'Off duty,' replied Stark.

'Not any more. We've got a shout on Pinky.'

'Great. Good luck with that.'

'Shut up and tell me where you are.'

'Those are contradictory instructions.'

'Don't piss me about. Tell me where you are and I'll pick you up.'

'You can't be serious.'

'I'm always serious. What's the matter? You on a hot date with Hydro-babe?'

Stark slapped his hand over the speaker though he didn't think Kelly had overheard. 'Excuse me.' He smiled, turned away and spoke as calmly as he could. 'You know how unlikely *that* would be, Sarge.'

'Okay, so where are you?'

'Surely you don't need me for this.'

'I can't think of anyone more deserving. Come on, this could be a defining moment.'

I hope not, thought Stark. 'Don't make me beg, Sarge.'

'Don't make me pull rank, Constable. Besides, I already told Groombridge you volunteered. Now, *where are you?*'

Stark closed his eyes and swore inwardly. 'Blackheath. Princess of Wales pub.'

'Drink up. I'll be outside in three minutes.'

Stark turned to Kelly. 'I'm sorry,' he said. 'I . . .'

'Duty calls?' The pained look on his face probably said it all.

She tilted her head to one side and smiled. 'Is it important?'

'It could be.'

'I quite like that you're needed at a moment's notice to dash off and fight crime.'

'Now all I need is my Spandex, cape and a phone box to change in.'

'Now *that* I'd like to see.' She giggled.

'There can't be much left to your imagination after you and Lucy made me parade around in those skimpy shorts.'

Kelly threw her head back and gave a deep-throated belly laugh.

Half the occupants of the pub must be looking her way with desire and the other half with jealous hatred, thought Stark, admiringly.

'Lucy bet me ten quid I wouldn't get you to wear them,' she said.

Stark closed his eyes. 'I *knew* something was up.'

Through the window he saw Fran's car approaching. 'That's my sergeant. I'm sorry, I'll make this up to you.'

Kelly took his drink, knocked it back in one gulp, with a flourish, and tossed her hair with a flick of her head. 'Yes, you will.' She grinned wickedly.

Fran skidded to a halt outside and tooted the horn. Stark peered out and saw her beckoning impatiently. The horn tooted again.

As he climbed into the car Fran craned her neck. 'If that's her, you're in much bigger trouble than I thought.'

Stark kicked himself for not getting outside before she arrived. 'You have no idea, Sarge.'

26

The shout was a flat in Bromley. An anonymous caller had sworn blind Pinky was inside. He'd seen her face on the news; it was definitely her. The local force had sent three uniforms led by a grizzled sergeant, who greeted them with a warm handshake and a dubious look. 'Your missing girl on the game, then?'

Fran frowned. 'Not that we know of. Why?'

The sergeant jerked his thumb up the road. 'Looks more like a home than a squat, that's all. Leastways, no one's complained about one on this street. Still, I suppose we'd better have a look.'

It was a first-floor flat, accessed from the back, and there was only one way in. Nevertheless two constables took up rabbit position on the street out front in case anyone thought a fifteen-foot drop from window to paving slabs was more appealing than a talk with the police.

Fran banged on the door. 'Police, open up!'

'No one home?' suggested the sergeant.

Fran peered in through the letterbox. 'I saw someone move. POLICE, OPEN UP!'

The sergeant's radio crackled into life: 'Step away, Sarge. Bloke just took a look out the front window with a pistol in one hand.'

The sergeant hastily ushered them all to a safe distance. 'You sure, Tom?'

'Positive. Tried to hide it when he saw us but I got a good look. Silver automatic.'

The sergeant radioed for armed response. There was no further sign of movement from inside.

When CO19 arrived they made no attempt at stealth, busily ensuring surrounding buildings were empty or evacuated, cordoning off the streets front and back.

'Why didn't you try out for this lot instead of joining the weekend army?' asked Fran, sipping on the coffee she'd sent one of the local constables to fetch for her.

'I wanted to broaden my world, not narrow it further,' replied Stark.

'Say that louder, I dare you.'

It became a tedious evening. A standoff, with the CO19 negotiator on the phone every now and then to the man in the flat, who wouldn't say if he was alone and refused to come out. To pass the time Stark formulated strategies, with and without luxuries like C4, flash-bangs and CS grenades, to breach the perimeter and eliminate the threat, indulging in idle euphemism. Of course, his training for this stuff had been less squeamish about lethal force. These specialist firearms officers had to walk a more delicate line. Even so, Stark couldn't believe the man wouldn't surrender while he had the chance. Unless he was prepared to shoot it out, what was the point? It escalated achingly slowly until eventually the decision was made to go in.

Stark observed with interest as officers armed with Heckler & Koch MP5s and all the gear sidled up to the door behind the lead man holding a large bullet shield. The second man swung a heavy ram and the door burst in, followed by the rest of the team. There was a volley of shouting but no shots. Then silence.

The radio announced the all-clear, weapon confiscated and made safe. A man was led out, his hands bound with a long white cable-tie. A tall, skinny white streak of a bloke with his jeans yanked down round his ankles, making him waddle. He was freely insulting his captors now any chance of an actual fight was over.

'Anyone else in there?' Fran asked the officer. He wandered over to ask his senior, who looked their way and shook his head.

'Bugger!' said Fran.

The grizzled sergeant came over to them. 'Sorry you've had a wasted evening. Looks like someone with an axe to grind used you. This bloke's known as a bit of a wannabe in the dealing world round here. Either he stepped on someone's toes or he was getting too big for his boots. Nice result for my lot, though, thanks.'

'Anytime,' replied Fran.

To Stark's mild surprise, she sounded like she meant it. He supposed it had been a result for the good guys. Even so, he'd been standing in increasing pain for nearly four hours, having missed out on a Thai meal and his first proper date in what felt like a lifetime.

'Don't sulk,' said Fran, to his silence. 'She was light years out of your league anyway.'

It got worse, of course. A report had to be written. Fran broke the news over a bag of chips as they leant against her car back in Greenwich. A perfect opportunity for anyone trying to build up their PDP experience. So Stark spent his Saturday morning conferring with officers in Bromley to make sure he did his bit well enough to withstand any criticism Fran might later cook up.

'What are you doing here?' asked Groombridge, looking in. Stark explained. 'But you were off duty.' His boss frowned.

'I thought you knew about all this, Guv.'

'She used my name to get you on board, didn't she?'

Stark closed his eyes.

Groombridge chuckled. 'Pulled the old "volunteer" ruse, did she?'

'It's not important, Guv.' Stark wasn't about to turn informant.

'Fair enough. You've got to admit, she's got you back. Finish up that report, then clear off, I don't want to see you till Monday.' He was still chuckling as he left.

Stark swore quietly, finished the report, left a copy on Fran's desk and limped outside, wincing at the midday sun. He'd taken painkillers and whisky for a decent night's sleep but while the dreams had kept their distance his hip had woken him early again. Knackered now, he considered going back inside and trying to round up a ride but he'd already hobbled all the way here so he might as well hobble into town and make something of the day, starting with a decent lunch.

He chose a little Italian place, with tables and chairs spilling out on to the street, and called Kelly.

'Did you catch your wrongdoers?' she asked, by way of greeting.

'How did you know it was me?' he asked.

'You tell me, super-detective.'

Stark's eyes narrowed. 'I gave your receptionist my new number.'

'Elementary!'

'Why do I feel like a hunted man?'

'Because your lack of chivalry forces a lady to take matters into her own hands. So how did it go last night?' Stark told her. 'Hope your Spandex didn't chafe.'

'The armed-response unit insisted their Kevlar was more stain-resistant.'

'Ah, so you let them have a play instead, sweet of you.'

'They enjoyed themselves, that's the important thing,' agreed Stark. 'So, in the spirit of chivalry, when can I make up for last night's calamity?'

'Monday, after your session.'

'No sooner?' he asked, disappointed.

'I have plans.'

'Plans can be rearranged.'

'Why should I change them? You're the one who still owes me a first date.'

'Last night didn't count, then?'

'You must be joking, especially if you're thinking your nice-boy first-date rule is out of the way. Besides, I don't need to hunt you any more.'

'Why's that?'

'Well, last night may not count as a date, but it was enough to get you well and truly hooked. See you Monday!' And with that she hung up.

Stark laughed. Monday night now seemed a long way off.

That night he was sorely tempted to repeat his success with the sleeping-pill/whisky combination. Unfortunately he was expecting a visit from Captain Pierson in the morning. She was still army and Sunday morning didn't mean around lunchtime with bed-hair and pillow creases on your face. He tried the painkillers alone but, as with previous nights, he woke in the small hours and couldn't settle again even after the new pills went to work.

When his intercom buzzed at eight sharp, he was showered, shaved, fed, dressed and half dead.

He buzzed her up and opened the front door with trepidation.

'What the hell?' She grimaced. 'You look like you've come off a five-nighter on Brecon.' She was referring to training exercises on the Brecon Beacons in Wales. 'Out of the way, then.' She marched past him into the flat.

'Make yourself at home,' muttered Stark.

'Well, then,' she said, sitting down on his sofa and pulling out reams of paperwork from her tan leather satchel, 'we've a mountain to climb and not long to do it. Put a brew on, Corporal, no sugar.'

Stark made two mugs and set one before her. She gave no thanks but picked up the nearest of the piles she had laid out on his table in neat regiments. 'I haven't time to repeat myself so listen carefully, don't interrupt, and I'll try to use small words.'

It was a long and tedious morning. She went through his actions on that day in minute detail, bombarded him with things to remember, quizzed him relentlessly and rehearsed him mercilessly. 'Well, you'd better make a better fist of it on the day or we're sunk,' she said, packing away her papers. 'This is my reputation on the line now, not just yours.' She closed her satchel with a snap. 'Right, let's see your uniform.'

Stark brought it out to show her.

'*On*, you twit, let's see it *on*!'

Stark went away and changed, pausing to study his reflection. He'd spent all Saturday afternoon preparing. His No. 2 dress uniform was immaculate, crisp khaki, buttons burnished, brilliant white belt with regimental belt plate gleaming, boots polished to mirror shine. His peaked cap was a thing of beauty, but the face peering out beneath it was all wrong. He couldn't put face and uniform together: they wanted to jump apart like negative magnets, just as they had when he'd put on his police uniform for his first day back.

'Jump to it, Corporal, I don't have all day!'

Stark muttered under his breath and stepped back into the living room.

Pierson stood and inspected him coolly. 'Corporal Stark, if you think you're wearing *that* to court you've another think coming!'

Stark was dismayed. He glanced at the tall mirror by the front door. Maybe the tunic and trousers were a bit loose in places now but –

'You're a disgrace!'

'It's not that bad.' He knew the cause was already lost. She had that parade-ground company-sergeant-major look in her eye.

'*Not that bad?* I can't help thinking you've not grasped the gravity of your situation, soldier. There'll be no second chances here. If this goes badly for you, it goes badly for the army. Is that what you want?'

'No.'

'No *what?*' she bristled.

This was going too far. She could call him 'Corporal' and 'soldier' till she was blue in the face but . . . 'If you're waiting for a "sir" and a salute you'd better not hold your breath.' He held up a hand before she boiled over. 'I fully understand the seriousness. Colonel Mattherson made it painfully clear. But I no longer take the Queen's shilling. Her Majesty's Armed Forces have listed me "medically unfit" and my formal discharge is due any day. If some adjutant had done their bloody job on time I'd have it already and I'd be standing here in a blue uniform, not green. I'm playing along, *Captain*, but don't push your luck.'

She looked fit to explode. So much for winning her round, he thought dismally. The pity of it was that he was starting to like her. She fitted the pattern: forthright, clever, a little spiky, pretty in an understated way. In another universe entirely, one without uniforms, he might have gone for a woman like her. Unfortunately, the flip-side of the pattern was that attractive, forthright, clever, spiky women brought out his stubborn streak. 'I'm sorry, Captain,' he said, softening. 'I don't mean to be rude. We both want the same thing here, for me to acquit myself well. I'm just as anxious as you are, believe me.'

This appeared to mollify her a little. 'Quite! Well, if I can't hope for you to *behave* like a soldier I can at least make you look like one. I'll have my regimental tailor sent round so we can at least stand you to attention in something presentable and dispose of this disreputable sack. A pity we can't do the same for your disreputable character,' she added. If they'd been six, she'd probably have kicked him in the shins.

Stark let that go. The futility of lamenting hours of meticulous preparation tossed aside on the capricious whim of one's betters was a lesson every soldier learnt quickly in the first weeks of intensive training. During one inspection his CSM had chucked all his beautified kit out of a window into the rain and mud because Stark had failed sufficiently to tighten the lid of his boot polish. The next day he'd done the same because the lid was too tight. It was all a game, right or wrong. He thought of Maggs, scrubbed, shaved and pressed into a suit for his ten minutes in court. There had been something of the same humiliation, which he hadn't considered until now. Perhaps in another universe entirely, one without uniforms, a man might be judged for himself, impressions be damned.

27

Stark woke in discomfort around four, again. As with previous nights he topped up on painkillers and made a futile attempt at more sleep. He was deep in the cycle now, where the very urgency for sleep drives all hope away and the mind churns ceaselessly.

'Fuck!' Frustrated, he swung his legs out of bed – and gasped as a sharp stab of pain shot through his hip. There was no getting away from it: he'd have to talk to someone about this. He'd see how he got on that night in the pool and discuss it with Kelly.

He tried his exercises, gave up in frustration and made himself a snack instead. The omelette stared back at him from the plate. He'd not felt like this in a while. Upping his OxyContin was beginning to dull his appetite, a reprise of those post-op morphine days: a depressing leap backwards. Still, food was fuel: he'd soldiered through then, so he'd soldier through now and eat every joyless scrap.

The image of Maggs in court drifted up, his performance in front of the magistrate – unexpectedly cool and controlled, no fireworks. Given what he'd witnessed and the simmering anger that had emerged in interview, it seemed remarkable. Then again, even that anger had an aspect of control. Maggs was careful. But *why* was he being careful? What was his goal? He seemed determined to go to prison: why? To get it over and done with before Pinky was found and put under the spotlight? Surely he couldn't expect that.

There was mixed incentive on the CPS side: Pinky's

testimony might strengthen the sexual-assault charges against the gang but weaken the murder charge against Maggs – his defence counsel would wave Pinky like a flag. After which the prosecution would cross-examine her rigorously – Stark felt a pang of guilt at the prospect. It would certainly shore up the case against Nikki if Pinky could ID her, but maybe there was enough evidence already. Did they need another witness, another victim? Perhaps it wasn't necessary to find her. Maybe she could stay hidden and get on with her life without being traumatized all over again.

'Jesus!' exclaimed Fran, the second she saw him. 'What the hell happened to you? There's no way you got *that* lucky!'

'After your timely interruption on Friday?'

'You should be thanking me. I saved you from dismal humiliation.'

'Thank you, from the very heart of my bottom.'

'So why do you look like Doctor Frankenstein couldn't jump you a pulse?'

'A pure soul never rests easy in a wicked world, Sarge.'

'In *this* wicked world there's no such thing. Come on, intravenous caffeine might at least get you through the meeting.'

It was blessedly short. A fresh TV appeal had generated hundreds of calls, ranging from mistaken to misleading to wildly fanciful, but nothing solid. The news companies wouldn't run it again. They were on their own now, and there was little more they could do. DI Graham's territorial CID team, who'd been shouldering the rest of the workload since Alfred Ladd's death, were instructed to divvy it out as appropriate. Fran accepted a burglary case with poor grace and generously shared her irritation during lunch.

'So, one usual suspect with a whiffy alibi, nearby at the time but denying involvement, closely associated with a second in possession of items stolen claiming to have bought them from a stranger in, of all places, a pub. And they'll both get off because we can't disprove their bullshit. How many times have we seen this? No wonder the little sods turn recidivist.'

'What about SOCO?' asked Dixon, humouring her.

'Fingerprints all proved to be family, and a boot-print cast from the flowerbed was traced to the window cleaner.'

'Has anyone looked at the window cleaner?' asked Stark, forcing down another mouthful.

Fran gasped. 'You mean we're supposed to consider *all* the options, not just the first, most obvious one? *Shit.* I must've missed that lesson in police school. Does everyone know this? We should make an announcement! Think of all the blindingly obvious clues we might've missed over the years,' she wailed. 'God, this is *awful*!'

'That'd be a yes, then?' smiled Stark.

'Clean as a whistle apparently.' Fran pushed the file away from her. 'Bloody lame pony.' A case not worth a punt, fit only for the knacker's yard.

'Can't win 'em all,' sneered Harper.

Looking around to gauge what others made of the remark, Stark accidentally met Harper's eyes and was shocked by a flash of malevolence. The man had missed his weekend shift with an unspecified 'illness' and returned today in caustic mood, bearing fresh physical evidence of his troubled home life. This had reignited the whisperings about his wife's mental health and drinking. To make matters worse, Stark had noticed one idiot sympathize, quietly but in plain view. It was clear Harper had convinced himself Stark was to blame. Stark tried wearily to put that thought from his mind.

After lunch Fran delighted in relaying Stark's revolutionary new theory on investigative procedure to the whole office. It was only on the third retelling that it hit him.

'Shit!' he said aloud.

'Don't be a poor sport, Stark,' said Groombridge.

'No. I didn't mean . . .' Stark was still trying to grasp the squirming thought. 'What I meant was, have we made that exact mistake?'

'What mistake?' asked Fran, still amused by her own joke.

'Overlooked a possibility because we were handed a better one on a plate. What if Maggs didn't stab Kyle Gibbs in the back?'

'Of course he bloody did!' scoffed Harper. 'Want me to show you the photos?'

More laughter, but Groombridge saw Stark was in earnest. 'What do you mean?'

'What if Maggs isn't trying to shield Pinky from exposure but trying to shield her from a murder charge?'

Harper gave a mocking laugh, but finding himself alone fell silent, embarrassed and displeased.

Fran hardly looked happier. 'Give it a rest, Stark. You just don't want to think he did it.'

'You think I've lost objectivity?' he asked, keeping his voice measured.

'You arrested him! We have his confession! Why would he lie?'

'Because he's a broken-down old soldier with an over-developed sense of nobility,' Groombridge intervened. 'I have to say, I don't buy it. It's plausible, I'll give you that. I can even see it in my head. Maggs doesn't get the knife off Gibbs but he does knock it flying. He catches Gibbs in the throat but while everyone's watching the two of them a poor girl, traumatized half out of her wits, picks it up and does the unthinkable. But I don't buy it. Maybe some people out there would take a murder rap for a complete stranger, but would Maggs?'

It was a serious question. 'I don't know, Guv,' answered Stark, honestly.

*

'CPS aren't going to thank us for this, Guv,' said Fran, still unhappy, as they waited for Maggs to be shown into the gloomy prison interview room.

'Her Majesty's Crown Prosecution Service are never ungrateful when justice is served, DS Millhaven. Especially when it's served before they are publicly shown to have wrongly convicted someone – again.' Groombridge smiled at her, then frowned at Stark. 'You up to this, Stark? You look all in.'

'Guv.' Stark wasn't at all sure he was.

The door opened and Maggs took his seat opposite them.

'Well,' he said gruffly, 'Inspector Questionable Orientation, Sergeant Hardarse and Constable Weekender, to what do I owe the pleasure?'

Stark ignored him and conducted the preliminaries for the tape.

Maggs chuckled. 'They letting you make the running today? Is this like a practical exam, interrogation for beginners? D'you get a little sew-on badge?'

Stark waited in silence.

'What do you want?' asked Maggs, eventually, irritably.

'Still wishing we weren't too squeamish for the noose?' asked Stark.

Maggs indicated his surroundings. 'What's the difference?'

'Scope for redressing miscarriage of justice,' replied Stark. He watched Maggs for some reaction but saw little.

'I'm getting a strange *déjà vu*,' said Maggs, looking at the others for some clue.

'And I'm starting to wonder if you're the only *innocent* man in Shawshank.'

Maggs stared at him. 'You calling me a liar, Constable Stark?'

'I think you'd have to have had good reason. I'm wondering what reason would be good enough.'

'What are you on about?'

'It would have to be a point of honour,' mused Stark, aloud.

'Where's this bollocks coming from?'

'The more I see of you, the less I can reconcile myself with the idea of you stabbing an unarmed teenager in the back.'

'He wasn't unarmed –'

'He was, once you had his knife.'

'The little shit stabbed me, twice.'

'And attack is the best form of defence?'

'Right.'

'Bollocks. You know as well as I do that once you had the best of Gibbs the rest would fade away. And if Gibbs was still coming at you his wound would be in front.'

'Not if I grabbed him and turned him in a neck-lock. Hand over the mouth, knife up under the ribs through a kidney into the diaphragm, nice and quiet. You remember, I'm sure, *Corporal* Stark.'

'I remember. But that wasn't the pattern of the wound. Besides, this wasn't national defence. I think if you'd got him in a neck-hold, simple threats would have been enough. And you know it too.'

'I was drunk.'

'So you claim, but adrenalin can have a very sobering effect.'

'Your sleep deprivation is dulling your wits!'

Stark shook his head, impressed. 'And you're defending by attacking again. Tell me about the girl with pink hair.'

Maggs was riled now. 'I've told you everything!'

'I don't think you *have*.'

'Then ask her yourself, *if* you ever find her.'

'We already did.' Stark paused just long enough to see alarm in Maggs's eyes. 'In a manner of speaking. We found the phone, Maggs. Robust little thing. Smashed against a parking meter, immersed in drain water for days, but still holding on to its precious recollections.'

Fran slipped a series of stills from the attempted rape on to the table one by one, culminating in a blur of olive drab.

'Not just stills, Maggs. Video and audio too. Nice war cry, by the way.'

'*You heartless shits!*' hissed Maggs. He picked up the image of Pinky, half naked, pinned beneath Gibbs and waved it at Groombridge. 'Is this what you wanted, you *sick fuck*? I bet you can't wait to see it on the front page!'

'This isn't just about that, though, is it, Maggs?' said Stark, as evenly as he could.

Maggs glared at Stark. Then, just for a second, there was pleading in his eyes. Stark groaned inside. He was right, and Maggs saw it. 'Don't,' said Maggs, quietly. 'Please.'

Stark sighed. 'He didn't do it, Guv. He didn't stab Kyle Gibbs. It was Pinky.'

Maggs shook his head sadly. 'Which of us is doing the right thing, Weekender?' he asked. 'What will *your* reflection tell *you*?'

'Maybe we both are, Maggs,' replied Stark.

'Ow!' Stark rubbed his arm where Fran had punched him. A passer-by looked disapproving.

'*That*'s for showing me up in front of the whole of bloody CID!'

'I must remember it's not nice to ridicule people before their peers,' replied Stark, pointedly.

'Now, now, children.' Groombridge played father. 'Play nicely or I won't let you listen in when I call CPS and tell them their killer is still at large. Don't look like that, lad. If she comes clean she might even walk. This has diminished responsibility, or at least provocation, written all over it.' He must've seen Stark's thoughts in his face, something Stark was determined to learn to prevent.

'We have to find her first,' said Fran. She punched Stark again. 'That's for bollocksing our stats.'

'At least you can hand that lame pony straight back,' said Groombridge. 'Come on. We're about to get busy again.'

CPS took the news without much rancour, candidly admitting the murder charge was always a long shot, brought to help secure a lesser conviction. And even if the new theory could be corroborated, there was still the blow to the windpipe. The coroner's report was inconclusive on whether it might've proved fatal, had Gibbs not then been stabbed. Maggs wasn't going anywhere.

According to Groombridge, Superintendent Cox took the news stoically enough too. Those who didn't were DI Graham and his team, as Groombridge's gleefully handed back all the lame ponies they'd accepted just hours earlier. A new TV appeal, slanted towards Pinky as a victim of violent assault rather than possible witness, or indeed suspect, was organized, and the process of keeping her uppermost in the minds of the regional police forces redoubled.

All Stark cared about was making it through the day. He even considered ducking out of his evening with Kelly, but couldn't face the defeat. He doggedly hit the phones and at the end of the day went to freshen up. He sensed someone follow him into the changing-room and turned just as Harper grabbed him by the lapels and shoved him against the lockers. Stark could have freed himself without difficulty but not without violence, so he let himself be lifted on to tiptoe by the heavier, taller man. 'I don't like gossips and backstabbers!' hissed Harper, leaning in, eye to eye.

The natural reaction in this predicament was to pull your head away from your assailant's face, grasping at the hands gripping your lapels. Throw in a fearful expression and you have the perfect disguise for a retaliatory head-butt. Few things said fuck-you quite so eloquently as a Glasgow Kiss. Harper's nose had been broken before and would break very nicely again. If Harper had pulled this kind of amateur theatrics away from the station Stark might not have let him get away with it. 'And I don't like bullies,' he replied. 'You've got ten seconds to come to your senses.'

'You've been talking behind my back, spreading lies about me and my wife.'

'I have not.'

'*Don't lie to me!*' growled Harper. 'You were eavesdropping on the stairs – that was a private conversation and whatever you think you heard –'

'I wasn't eavesdropping,' interrupted Stark, 'and what little I heard I've kept to myself. I'm no gossip. And you have five seconds left.'

'*You're a lying snake!*'

'*Four* seconds,' said Stark, levelly. Doubt finally flickered in Harper's eyes. 'Three. Two. One.'

Harper pulled Stark forward, slammed him back and let go in one motion. He stepped back a pace, breathing heavily, thwarted and, if anything, angrier. He glanced around, for the first time checking they were alone. 'You don't want me as your enemy, boy!'

Stark shook his head. 'No, I don't, and I've done nothing to make you mine. But I've faced enemies deadlier than you, and if you think you can intimidate me, you're mistaken, again.'

Harper sneered. 'Got an answer for everything, haven't you? Don't think I don't know what you're doing – inveigling yourself into the guv'nor's good books, sucking up to Mill-haven and trying to make me look a bloody fool!'

'You're wrong.'

'*This was my case!*' barked Harper. 'Everyone else may think the sun shines out of your arse but I'm not falling for your golden-boy act. I know what you are.'

Stark's eyes narrowed and cold fury crept into his voice. 'You're right about one thing, *Detective Sergeant*. I'm not what people think. Nurse your paranoid delusions if you must, but if you ever lay hands on me again you'll get a glimpse of what I really am.'

For the briefest moment Harper's uncertainty flickered into

fear, but then he huffed derisively, yanked open the door and left.

Stark stared after him, still fuming, but also wondering if he might have done more to avoid it. He'd sensed resentment brewing, but this escalation . . . If there had been opportunities to nip this in the bud he had missed them. He let out his breath with a resigned sigh. Occasionally in life you ran up against someone with real or imagined cause to dislike you. Just knowing they thought ill of you was sickening enough but direct confrontation was worse – always unpleasant, always pointless and always sad, leaving you replaying the scene over and over, wishing you had thought quickly enough to explain the misunderstanding or defuse the situation.

After their father's death had rendered Stark and his little sister targets for playground bullying, he had learnt quickly to meet threats head on, but success in addressing the causes was never as simple. He could have told Harper that what he'd heard on those damn stairs was nothing to the whispers already circulating in the station, but that would only have made matters worse. The unfortunate sod had had every reason to suspect he was being talked about and every need to blame someone other than himself or his poor wife. He'd chosen the stranger in town, and nothing Stark could say would alter that for now.

Crappy traffic delivered Stark to the Carter with barely a minute to spare, tired, despondent and sore.

'No book today?' asked Kelly, from the doorway.

Stark forced a smile. 'I just got here.'

'Come on, you've got work to do to get back on my good side.' Stark followed, trying not to limp. He got changed, met her by the pool and slipped off his gown.

She looked him up and down, frowning. 'You're losing weight.'

'Am I?' He stared at his reflection in the floor-to-ceiling mirror. She was right. He hadn't really looked at himself in a while. There'd been little fat on him a few weeks before. Now there was none.

'And you look like you haven't slept in a week,' she added.

'I've been pining since Friday night.'

'Glad to hear it.' She didn't seem glad. 'Ready?'

Never less so, thought Stark, wearily, but he set about the routine with all the gusto he could summon, determined to make a good showing. The harder he tried the worse it got. His hip felt like it was full of sand.

'Stop,' said Kelly. 'Stop!'

Stark obeyed, shocked and frustrated in the extreme. She took hold of his left leg in the water and lifted his knee. At a certain point he winced. She moved it to one side and a sudden, sharp stab shot up through the whole left side of his body. He clenched his jaw to prevent the yelp escaping but she was watching him too carefully to miss it. 'Okay, that's enough pool work for tonight. Get yourself dried off.'

As he was changing she called over the cubicle, 'Just a towel round your lower half, please.'

'*Just* a towel?'

'Don't be shy. I want you on the couch and I need to get at you unhindered.'

Stark might have burst out laughing but for the lack of humour in her voice. A beautiful double-entendre gone begging.

'On your back, please.' She laid a second towel over his groin and peeled his away, preserving his modesty while leaving him naked down one side from torso to toe. 'This was the shrapnel?' she asked, feeling the largest scar.

It was disconcerting having her touch him intimately in so matter-of-fact a manner. He definitely no longer thought of her as just his clinician. 'Yes.'

'Fractured and punched a hole through your pelvis just

above the hip joint. They considered a metal plate but needed to close the gap so they went for a bone graft from your heel and sat you still for eight weeks instead. I bet you were a model patient. Bone fragments were found in the hip joint itself, causing some cartilage damage, which had to be repaired here.' She touched the lower keyhole scar. 'That damage causes inflammation and discomfort if you overexert yourself, making your limp more pronounced. This hurt?' She articulated his leg as she'd done in the pool and the jolt of pain strangled his answer. 'On a scale of one to ten?'

Stark recalled Fran asking him that very question about Kelly but his chuckle died as Kelly repeated the move. 'Six or seven,' he hissed.

'This is new, I take it? It hasn't been like this since your surgeries?' Stark shook his head. 'So when did it start?'

'Recently, I suppose.'

'You said you'd been on your feet a lot at work. Has there been a gradual worsening in line with that?'

'Yes.'

'Which you put down to what? Wear and tear?'

'I guess. I've tried walking it off, walking to work, but it hasn't helped.'

'Hmm.' She tilted his leg the other way but Stark was ready and swallowed the yelp.

'You're not fooling anyone, you know,' she said. 'It's possible the cartilage has deteriorated, or even that there are still tiny bone fragments rattling about. Unless you've fallen or twisted it sharply recently?'

'I tried lifting a drain gully last week. I don't think that helped.'

'No, I don't suppose it did.' She articulated it one more time. Stark wished she wouldn't. 'Hmm,' she mused. 'This may be more tear than wear. We'll need to monitor it. If it gets worse I'll refer you for an X-ray.'

'Okay.'

'Can I trust you to tell me if it gets worse?' It was a serious question.

'Yes.'

'Okay, then.' Her finger traced the big scar for a second more, then she covered him up. 'Get yourself dressed. We're done for now. Are you still up for tonight?'

'More then ever,' replied Stark.

'Good. You could use a decent meal.' He must've looked a little crestfallen. 'Chin up, I've finished being severe with you.' She smiled. 'Wait for me in the lobby – I'll be ten minutes writing this up.'

It was twenty minutes before she emerged but Stark didn't begrudge her one second. She'd changed into jeans and a scarlet top with sequins around the neckline. Hair still up, drop earrings and matching pendant on a slim silver chain, she looked elegant and relaxed at the same time. Fran had been right: this girl was light years out of his class.

They set off, Kelly talking about Thai food. Stark almost felt hungry. The next thing he knew she was gently shaking him awake.

'What? Whe– Shit, did I nod off?'

'In the middle of my wittiest anecdote. You sure know how to flatter a girl.'

'Sorry. God, I'm really sorry.' He looked about and realized they were parked outside his flat. 'Ah, this doesn't look like the restaurant.'

'Sizzling Crying Tiger will have to wait again.'

'Really? 'Cos I'm starving . . .' he lied.

'If I thought you'd make it through the starters without going face down in your plate I'd consider it.'

'I'll be fine, honestly. I'll start with a coffee –'

'If you think I'd settle for a first date where my opposite

310

number needs a double espresso just to listen to a word I say without falling asleep, you've got the wrong girl.' She laughed. 'You're not fit for company.'

Stark could see he was losing and fell back to a secondary position. 'Why don't you come up instead? I'll make us *both* coffee and a bite to eat.'

'I've heard some come-up-for-coffee lines before but never from anyone less able to deliver.' She shook her head. 'Get yourself upstairs, make *yourself* something decent to eat and get to bed. Do not pass Go and do not drink any coffee.'

'Doctor's orders?'

'Something like that. Now go.' She looked a little less playful now.

'Can I get a rain-check at least?'

'Thursday. If you turn up in better shape.'

'How about a kiss goodnight?'

'Don't push your luck.'

'But I might not make it to Thursday. I'm deteriorating fast. This could be our last chance.'

She laughed again, that full throaty laugh, head thrown back, elegant, kissable neck exposed. Stark cursed himself.

'I've gotta give you credit for thinking on your feet,' she continued. 'I'm surprised you didn't use the broken-lift excuse to get me to help you up the stairs.'

'That was my next line.' He smiled.

'Come here,' she said softly. She placed a warm hand on his cheek, leant in, and slapped him playfully. 'You'll have to do better than that if you're gonna make up for *two* failed first dates.'

Stark sighed. 'Third time lucky. Thursday, then?'

'Uh-uh. It'll still be the first date, remember. Now, good-night.'

Stark got out and closed the door. The window slid down.

'Eat, then sleep!' she called.

'Goodnight.' He waved good-natured defiance, closed the door, grinning a lot less than the week before, and did exactly as he'd been told.

Stripped of distractions, though, his mind accelerated into spin cycle once more. His thoughts ranged from Harper to Maggs to Kelly's neck to telling his mother the truth. When the phone rang at eleven it actually came as a relief. 'Sarge?'

'Did I wake you?' asked Fran.

'No.'

'Good. I thought you might already be flat out. You looked like death warmed up all day.'

'Your concern is always welcome, Sarge. Was that why you called?'

'You wish. We've had a decent shout on Pinky.'

'Great. Good luck with that.'

'Ha-ha. Get downstairs. I'm two minutes away.'

'You've *got* to be kidding.'

'Don't be like that. This is the real deal. The manager of that Orpington hostel called. He's heard Pinky's linked with a local squat.'

'Have I done something to make you hate me, Sarge?'

'Put it this way, I can't think of anyone more deserving.'

28

As soon as she saw Stark limp to the car and climb awkwardly in, Fran wished she hadn't called him. He'd looked like death warmed up earlier but now he seemed corpse-cold. His eyes were sunken and his drawn face was taut, rigid. 'Get out. I'll call Dixon.'

'I'm okay, Sarge. Let's go.'

'Bollocks. You're no good to me like this. Go to bed, for God's sake.'

'I've tried that. This is better,' replied Stark.

Fran bit off her frustration. Why did he always hit you with honesty just when you were ready to accuse him of lying? She really didn't want to lose time calling Dixon, but she had a feeling she'd regret this. 'Jesus, you take all the fun out of torturing you.'

She flicked on the car's concealed police lights and siren and passed him the hastily scribbled postcode, which he dutifully typed into the sat-nav. She kept her foot to the floor all the way there. Stark held on tight without comment. As they neared their destination she killed the lights and noise.

They pulled up next to a uniform van. A sergeant and five constables stood ready to assist. This squat, they explained, was notorious for drug use and dealing, but recent rumour suggested prostitution and possibly even trafficking. The sergeant eyed up his guests and clearly found both wanting, politely suggesting they take the rabbit hole with one of the constables. Fran gave him the benefit of the doubt and put this down to Stark's appearance rather than hers. They were stationed by the moonlit plywood back door when they heard the loud banging from round the front and the sergeant calling, '*Police, open up!*'

There was a few moments' silence, and then the back door burst open as two men rushed out. The constable was ready and wrestled the first, struggling viciously, to the ground. The second shouldered Fran flying. As she went down she saw the man bounce off Stark with a curse. Light glinted off a blade. The man bellowed and charged again.

The next moments were a blur as Fran lay winded on the ground, watching helplessly. Only later, replaying it in her mind as she'd been trained, was she able partially to separate out what had happened. One thing was for sure: it was nothing like unarmed combat training; no telegraphed single thrust to block and disarm, more a series of vicious little stabs, snake-strike fast, barely blocked or dodged, Stark giving ground, twice having to arch his back to keep his guts from the blade, landing counter-attacking blows to little effect. Then, suddenly, he stepped towards one thrust and drove his fist sickeningly hard into his opponent's face. The man staggered back, blood gushing from a twisted nose, screamed and charged again. This time Stark sidestepped, blocking, then used his shoulder and the attacker's own momentum to slam him against the adjacent brick wall. In one movement Stark grasped the wrist of the knife hand with both of his own, turned so the whole arm was tucked under his armpit and sat down with his whole weight, slamming the man face first into the ground, breaking his jaw and dislocating his shoulder. In a flash Stark was kneeling with one leg over the dislocated arm and the other knee pressing down between the man's shoulder blades on the back of his neck, holding the long double-edged knife dagger-like, raised ready to stab.

Fran looked into Stark's face and recoiled. It was a terrifying mask of focused, burning hatred. For a horrible moment she thought he meant to kill the prostrate man, but instead he pressed even more weight on to the man's neck, eliciting a scream of submission. The hatred in Stark's face tightened into anger, contained, quivering, utterly immovable.

The sergeant and another constable appeared and stepped in to take over, and suddenly the tension was gone. Stark crouched quickly beside Fran, placing the knife on the ground and checking her over with eyes and hands. 'Are you cut?' he demanded.

'Get off!' She slapped away his hands, touched by his concern but alarmed by the impertinent thoroughness of his search, and not a little humiliated at being so easily brushed aside.

'*Are you cut?*' he demanded again.

'No! Now get your bloody hands off me before I slap your ugly face!'

He complied, still checking her out visually to be sure. Then he stood and pulled her up, as if she weighed no more than a feather. He was barely short of breath.

'Thanks!'

'You're welcome,' he replied, either missing the sarcasm or ignoring it. His voice now sounded mechanical, distant. He glanced at his left hand, tugged off his tie and wound it round his palm, like a bandage.

'You okay?' she asked.

He nodded.

An ambulance was summoned. Stark received several sideways looks from the uniforms as they tended the injured suspect. Whatever had happened there, it hadn't been standard police self-defence technique. Questions were bound to arise about reasonable force. They were probably thanking their lucky stars they could honestly say they'd seen nothing. Fran looked for the constable who *had* been there but couldn't pick him out. Stark watched impassively as his groaning assailant awaited medical attention.

She pulled out an evidence bag and carefully bagged the knife. Blinking, as if he'd never seen it before, Stark watched her zip the bag and hand it to the nearest officer.

'You'd better take a look.' The sergeant led the way inside, shining his torch ahead of their feet as they stepped over the rubbish, and worse, littering the filthy old carpet. Half of the doors in the rambling old house were padlocked. A constable stood ready at one with a crowbar. Fran nodded. Some were empty but in one room they found a girl sitting on a grubby mattress, terrified, and in another room a second woman, who was drugged out of her wits. The sergeant called for reinforcements.

Two more doors were forced. One stood empty. In the other they found a girl with pink hair.

Fran waved everyone back as she and Stark entered. The girl was cowering in a corner, curled up in a foetal position, cradling her knees, one wide eye visible. Beside her Fran heard Stark gasp. His face was pale, shocked, almost frightened. Looking quickly around she saw no cause so waved at him to stay where he was and approached the girl cautiously. As she reached out a hand the girl snarled at her, sending her reeling backwards.

'Get a blanket, Sarge,' said Stark, suddenly, and before she could stop him he was sliding his back down the wall to sit a foot away from the girl. Her hand shot out in a claw. He caught it but not before it had raked his face. The other shot out but he caught that in time with his other hand. She struggled futilely against his grip. Stark was murmuring to her, reassurances, calm, firm. Fran snatched up a thin quilt from the mattress, cautiously placed it around the girl's shoulders and backed away again. The struggle gradually ceased. Stark kept up the reassurances and slowly shifted from gripping her wrists to holding both hands. He was still like that when a WPC and some paramedics arrived and slowly coaxed the poor girl away.

It was Pinky, no mistake. Her face was marked with yellowed bruises and healed abrasions; her lip had a tight scab where it had been split. Most of the marks looked old, but not all.

'Which hospital will they go to?' asked Stark.

Fran looked for some recognition of events but he seemed strangely calm. 'Princess Royal mostly, but I asked that Pinky go to the QE. Is your face okay?' It was bleeding from four diagonal scrapes. Stark felt them and looked at the blood as if he had no idea where it had come from. 'Let's have someone clean that up.'

He let her lead him out. It wasn't that he was elsewhere: he seemed right there in the present, but he let himself be led, like a child unthinkingly holding an adult hand.

The scrapes weren't deep. A paramedic cleaned them and taped a small dressing over Stark's cheek. He didn't flinch. He'd have to be tested for HIV and hepatitis now, of course, a matter of routine, but the paramedic was reassuring him that the risk was negligible. Everyday infection was far more likely. He asked Stark if his anti-tetanus protection was up to date. Stark gave the barest of laughs and nodded.

The bloody tie was unwound to reveal a cut down the fleshy muscle of his palm beneath the little finger. Stark looked at it. 'You're gonna get cut,' he muttered, under his breath.

'Quoting Maggs again?' asked Fran.

Stark shook his head. 'Training. So was he. Barehanded against a knife you're gonna get cut. It's just a question of how badly.'

'They teach us to run away.'

He nodded. 'And when you can't, you're –'

'Gonna get cut.' She shook her head. Who'd join the army?

'Take your jacket off and roll up your sleeve,' the paramedic ordered.

Stark had completed only the first half of the order when Fran gasped.

'Don't move,' commanded the paramedic.

Stark's white shirt, from a little under his left armpit to his waist, was sodden with blood. He stared at it dumbly, barely registering surprise, then held up his jacket to the light. In the front left panel there was a small slash. He tutted and let it drop.

'Keep *still*,' hissed the paramedic. Using the larger slash in the shirt, he tore it open to reveal a two-inch horizontal cut, bleeding steadily, halfway up Stark's left ribs.

Stark stared down at it. 'Just a question of how badly,' he said.

'Looks superficial,' said the paramedic. 'Rib stopped it. You were lucky. Hold still while I clean it. This'll need a stitch or three.'

It needed nineteen. The hand needed four. They were straight cuts, the paramedic commented, as he worked: the knife had been sharp. They'd heal quickly, neat as you like. Soon to be lost among all the others, he didn't add.

Stark never winced. Fran was growing more certain by the minute that this wasn't bravado. Adrenalin could leave you unaware of injury, but so could shock. It seemed obvious now to her that Stark was barely present, after all. She called to a nearby uniform, who scuttled off and returned with two large evidence bags. 'I'll need that jacket and shirt.'

With a soft sigh Stark stood and removed the ruined shirt.

'Jesus!' The paramedic's eyes widened.

In all her curiosity Fran had never imagined such scarring. Almost as shocking, though, was how painfully lean he was. She'd noticed he was a little gaunt in the face, but his torso was all muscle and sinew ... She realized her mouth was ajar and pulled herself together. 'That's the end of your demob suit then.' She forced a smile, holding open the bags for him, but it was a crap joke and didn't even register with him. Atop his left arm she noticed a tiger tattoo, monochrome and stylized, really quite beautiful once, now marred by a diagonal scar. The irony was not lost. She would never have taken him for the tattoo type. Then again most people wouldn't have guessed at hers.

She relieved the uniform of his over-jacket and handed it to Stark to put on as the paramedic finished checking him out. They left him perched in the rear door of the ambulance as the paramedic led her aside to talk quietly. 'He's still in shock. We *could* take him in, but he should be fine in an hour or less.'

'I'll drive him home.'

'Keep him warm. If he feels faint, get his feet higher than his head – you know the drill.'

'Will do.'

'There's more going on there . . .' The paramedic didn't quite pose it as a question but it was.

'Maybe,' said Fran.

The man waited but she said no more. 'All right. Well, see he's tucked up in bed as soon as possible.'

She put Stark into the car and drove him home in silence. By the time they arrived he did seem more aware, alert, certainly more himself as he firmly resisted her offer to see him in. She waited outside instead, and was starting to worry when his light eventually came on. Then she took out her phone. It was nearly two in the morning but Groombridge would be expecting an update.

29

You slam against the wall, gasping for breath. Check the safety is off for the tenth time. A nod. Collins kicks the door and you pile in, weapon raised, Collins behind you. Movement in the corner. Collins shouts! Swing the gun! The girl with pink hair, cradling her knees in the corner, looks up at you, terrified, defiant, angry as a snarling cat. He comes at you, knife flashing. You feel it drive into your back, a wild pain, a numbing wrongness. You twist and block and slip his arm out of its socket, mercilessly efficient. You have his weapon now and your knee on his neck; he squeals, pleads. One stab down and it's over. You want to do it. You want to do it. But you're dying, you can feel life leaching out of you, trousers slick with blood as you kneel in the dust, rifle aimed; relax, breathe, aim, hold, fire. Relax, breathe, aim, hold . . . Feel it draining from you. Must stay conscious as long as possible. Sleep is death. Relax, breathe, aim, hold . . .

'*Still see their faces?*'

Stark blinked awake, Maggs's voice so present in his ears that he looked round for him in the dark. His hand drifted to his back for a wound that had never existed. He groaned. Three pills, with three full fingers of whisky, and still this. Even his improper regimes were unravelling.

He'd neglected to close the curtains and the sky, from where he lay, hovered between blues. Somewhere below the horizon the sun lurked, bugle ready.

Stark let out his breath with a shuddering sigh, levered himself out of bed, limped awkwardly into the kitchenette and, after a minute's fruitless rummaging, cursed his empty fridge and cupboards. If Kelly had accepted his invitation they'd have been looking at takeaway menus. He slammed the cupboard door so hard it hung off one hinge.

Leaving it, he went and showered, ignoring any thought of exercise. Afterwards, dripping, he wiped his hand across the steamy mirror. A stranger stared back at him. Grim, gaunt, rings beneath sunken eyes. He peeled the damp dressing off his face and looked at the scratches. They were tender to the touch. There was no point in trying to shave round them so he left them to the air. Steam gradually re-obscured the stranger's face. A great urge to smash his fist into it nearly overwhelmed him. Instead he dried, dutifully changed the dressings on his hand and ribs, dressed and limped out into the morning sun.

The bakery owner unlocked the door from inside, eyeing Stark warily. Stark waited in silence as the man put out the first of his stock. Armed with a cinnamon whirl and a double espresso, he took a stool by one of the tall tables wedged into the tiny space and ate. The owner continued to watch him, too unsure to make conversation.

Stark left a pocketful of small change as tip and departed with a nod. The pain felt distant as he walked, the painkillers doing their work. It was only when he neared the station that he remembered he hadn't taken any.

The few uniforms he saw as he entered the station via the tradesmen's door gave him odd looks. The office was all but empty. The clock read 07:31.

'Wake up.' Someone was shaking Stark's shoulder gently. 'Wake up! The sarge'll be here any minute!' Dixon's voice.

Stark looked up. There was a crick in his neck: he'd been asleep with his head on the desk. Pain flared in his hip and he groaned.

Dixon recoiled. 'Christ, are you okay?'

'Hanging on my chinstrap,' admitted Stark.

'I looked that up,' Dixon told him.

Stark checked the clock. 'Just enough time for coffee.' He stood but his hip sang out and he nearly sat again. Kelly had been right: this might be more tear than wear.

'Jesus, what happened? Should you be here? Sit down, for God's sake, before you fall. Wait here, I'll get you coffee.'

The office was busier. Stark couldn't help notice people craning their necks over desk partitions to peer at him. Dixon reappeared and brought water, too, which Stark gratefully used to swallow three pills.

'What happened? I heard you found her. It's all over the station.'

Before Stark could explain Fran walked in and did a double-take. 'What the ... Have you not *one* ounce of sense in you? What the hell are you doing here? Jesus, you look even worse than when I left you!'

'I'm all right, Sarge,' lied Stark. At least, I will be once these pills and the coffee get to me, he thought, taking a scalding swig.

'Dixon, get this idiot out of here before the guv'nor sees him.'

'Before the guv'nor sees who?' said Groombridge, from the doorway.

Fran made a face at Stark and turned. 'I was just suggesting to Constable Stark that he appears unwell and should go home to bed, Guv, and he agreed that would be best.'

Groombridge looked past her. 'That right, Stark?'

'Only the first part, Guv,' replied Stark. Fran glared at him.

'You look like crap. Maybe DS Millhaven has a point.'

'I'll be all right, Guv.'

'Constable, you have two knife wounds and a face out of a werewolf film.'

Stark was in no mood to remind them he'd had worse. 'If you're interviewing Pinky today I'd like to be there.'

Groombridge considered him for a moment. 'That'll depend on her doctors. If she's not ready, you go home.' There was no invitation to argument in his tone.

'Guv.'

For a while it looked as if that might be how it would go. The doctors were hesitant. But it gave Social Services time to come up with an appropriate adult. Until otherwise proved, anyone who looked like they could be under seventeen was assumed to be. You had to be eighteen to get a tattoo legally, of course, but they'd be foolish to rely on that as an indicator. Stark felt oddly isolated while they waited, as if people were moving around him, consciously avoiding him. Fran was in Groombridge's office and he thought he heard them arguing, though they might just have been talking. When the door opened neither appeared ruffled.

'It's on. You sure you're fit, Stark?'

'If you'll have me, Guv.'

'I suppose you'll have to do. Come on, let's see if we can finish this.'

For the first time Groombridge slowed his walk right down. Stark railed inside but there was no point in denying the necessity.

A doctor was waiting for them. 'She's traumatized, Chief Inspector, and was clearly beaten badly a while back. There's no sign of recent sexual activity, which, given where she was found, is a blessing, but judging from the cuts and scrapes we found below, she was either raped, or very nearly so, a while back.'

'When?' asked Fran.

'Two or three weeks? But so far she's only spoken to the psychotherapist.'

'Do you have a name?' asked Groombridge.

'Paula Stevens. Nineteen. That's all.'

'No fixed abode,' said Groombridge, softly.

'As you say. She'll be here in a minute. The psychotherapist will sit in and it's over the second she says so. Understood?'

'Understood. Thank you, Doctor.'

The social worker was dismissed. Stark saw who the shrink was and shook his head. Of course, he thought, chalking it up to karma, or a universe with a spiteful sense of humour.

'This is Dr Hazel McDonald,' said the doctor. 'She's in charge here.'

Seeing Stark, Hazel checked her nod of recognition, but Stark would have bet a million that Fran and Groombridge had noted it.

'DCI Groombridge.' He shook her hand. 'Dr McDonald.'

'Hazel, please.'

'Hazel, we must know Paula's version of events. Is she up to it?'

'You'll need to tread carefully, Chief Inspector. Her memory of the attack on her remains sketchy. I don't believe we're looking at retrograde amnesia but she is disassociating.'

'But she remembers the attack?'

'In part. I'd need more time to be sure. Are you certain this can't wait?'

'In my experience it's better to harvest partial memories early before the brain sows weeds in the gaps.'

Hazel smiled politely. 'Perhaps.'

Paula was wheeled past them into the interview room. She was capable of walking but hospital policy spoke loudest. She looked alert, wary, fragile. She caught Stark's eye fleetingly, but with no flicker of recognition that he could discern.

They waited outside while Hazel and the lawyer went in to speak with her. The sound was off, for privacy, but Stark watched Paula nod wordlessly from time to time, occasionally glancing at the mirror-glass as if she could see him.

When they were called in he took a seat in the corner out of the way. Groombridge introduced everyone, explained the presence of the tape and cameras and thanked everyone for being there. Paula looked ready to bolt.

'For the record,' said Hazel, 'Paula has been told what to expect and has agreed to take part. In some instances I will answer for her. She has asked me to do so. If I cannot, Paula will answer if she feels able to. If not, I will not allow you to press her. Is that clear?'

'Perfectly,' said Groombridge. 'Thank you, Paula. We're here in the hope that you might shed light on two fatal incidents. On the night of Friday, May the fifteenth, around midnight a scream was heard on the Ferrier Estate. A girl, nearly your age, member of the local youth gang known as the Ferrier Rats, was found dead at the foot of a building – we believe pushed off it. Immediately after, you were seen running from the area. Can you tell us what happened?' Paula shook her head. Groombridge smiled warmly but she wouldn't look at him. 'Perhaps I should tell you what I think happened. The girl, Stacey Appleton, was accosted in one of the derelict properties, hit on the head and tipped over the balcony to her death. And you saw this happen. Just nod if I'm right.'

A shake, hesitant, uncertain. Hazel pitched in. 'I'm sorry, Paula and I have not had much time together and I wasn't aware of her link to this event. Might we be allowed a few minutes to talk?'

Groombridge nodded, cut the tapes and the police withdrew. After a brief discussion inside the lawyer was ejected too, his body language faintly betraying frustration. Stark sympathized, but he had to give credit to Hazel for her quiet command of the proceedings. And she, at least, was able to get Paula to speak. It tested his patience to watch the facts they needed being discussed beyond their hearing. Stark found himself wondering whether any copper had ever secretly learnt to lip-read.

Talking she might be, but Paula glanced anxiously at the

mirrored glass throughout. This was going to be difficult. Groombridge would have to bring all his experience to bear. Fran seemed surprisingly relaxed. Stark would have expected her to be the very model of impatience.

Eventually Hazel came out to them.

'Are we ready?' asked Groombridge.

'Yes and no. She's frightened, obviously, but particularly of you, Chief Inspector. There may be past traumas to explain that. But I'm not sure it's wise for you to question her further.'

Groombridge didn't take offence. 'Fair enough. I'll wait out here and let Detective Sergeant Millhaven take over.'

'Actually,' said Hazel, 'she says she'll only speak with you, Constable Stark.'

'*Me?*' exclaimed Stark.

Fran was already shaking her head. 'No. He's just a trainee.'

'How much specific experience do you have with trauma victims, Detective Sergeant?' asked Hazel.

'More than my constable,' said Fran.

'Perhaps.' Hazel looked at Stark, ignoring Fran's obvious annoyance. Surely she wasn't thinking his experiences were more applicable here than Fran's. 'She told me earlier about a man who'd held her hands last night. She thinks it was you, Constable. Was it?'

'Yes.'

'Well, then. I understand your hesitation but if you want answers now, Chief Inspector, my advice would be to let Paula be the judge of whom she feels comfortable with.'

'Guv, he's in no shape for this,' insisted Fran. 'Look at him! He shouldn't even be here!'

'I agree completely, Detective Sergeant. Yet Fate seems determined to spite us. Let's just see if we can wrap this up, shall we?'

30

Stark took the seat opposite Paula, Hazel the one beside her, the lawyer the other. Stark re-started the equipment, spoke the required words and paused, perhaps ordering his thoughts.

'Do you remember me, Paula?' he asked. She nodded, meeting his eyes for a moment. 'You've been through a lot. I'm sorry we have to ask you these questions. Dr McDonald here might say talking about things helps. I don't know how true that is. I would say talking about things makes them more real, more frightening, but perhaps we're both right.' He sighed, rubbing his eyes.

Watching from outside, Fran still thought this was lunacy. 'He's coming apart at the seams, Guv,' she complained. 'What if he fucks this up?'

'What if he doesn't?' replied Groombridge, without looking away from the glass. 'He can be irritatingly likeable.'

Stark seemed to pull himself together a little. 'Paula, did you actually see what happened to Stacey Appleton?'

A shake of the head. She exchanged a look with the shrink, who seemed to be waiting, encouraging Paula to speak up. 'It's okay, Paula. Are you happy for me to tell Constable Stark what you just told me?' The lawyer did not look happy, but Paula nodded.

'Paula just told me all she knows or is sure of,' began Hazel. 'She was round the corner, two floors down, on a balcony-corridor of the perpendicular block, returning to her ... lodgings. She heard raised voices, a cry perhaps of pain, then a scream. She saw something fall, peered over to look, then saw the body. Hearing voices across and up, she turned and saw faces looking down, two, though it was dark on the balcony.'

'Did they see you?' asked Stark. 'Is that why you ran?' Paula nodded, her hands were trembling. 'Do you know the names of the people you saw?' Paula shook her head. 'But did you recognize them?' A faint nod.

'Could you pick them out from these photographs?' Stark slid prepared female and male perp-sheets on to the table, the known gang mixed in with mugshots of similar-aged offenders.

Paula closed her eyes, steeling herself. 'It's okay, Paula,' Hazel reassured her. Paula leant in. Her finger crept forward and pointed to Nikki Cockcroft. She closed her eyes again before looking at the male sheet. Gulping, she picked out Kyle Gibbs.

Craning her neck to see, Fran barely contained a whoop of triumph. Nikki had motive, means and now opportunity. It wasn't watertight: her barrister would call it circumstantial and no doubt pin it on Kyle, with Nikki as unwitting bystander. And Paula would not have an easy time of it if she took the stand, particularly after what was coming next.

Stark read out the photo numbers for the record. 'Thank you, Paula. That took guts. You should know the girl in this picture, Nikki Cockcroft, is already in custody. The boy, Kyle Gibbs, is dead – but I believe you already know that.'

Paula immediately became more withdrawn. Stark looked at Hazel, but she indicated he should try again.

'He died on the night of Monday, May the seventeenth, by the bandstand in Greenwich Park. He and his friends had been looking for you, we think. Was the girl, Nikki, there also?'

Paula lifted her eyes slowly to his, searching for something, it seemed to Fran, judgement, perhaps, or reassurance that Nikki could not hurt her. Either way she nodded. Stark verbally noted each nod for the tape. It was an odd process, but

Fran watched with grudging respect. The doctor was calm, authoritative and thorough, and you had to hand it to Stark, he was doing okay. Beside her in the dimmed room Groombridge stared through the glass, still as stone.

'Can you tell us what happened that night?' asked Stark.

It was too clumsy. Paula shrank in on herself, a cornered animal, frozen between fight and flight. Hazel stepped up. 'Would you like me to answer for you again?' Paula gave the barest nod. Hazel referred to her notes. 'After witnessing the death on the night of May the fifteenth Paula fled, hoping she'd not been recognized. Afraid, she stayed away from the usual haunts, sleeping in Greenwich Park each night. But they found her there, the boy and girl already identified. There were others, perhaps five or more, but the attack on her was so sudden she doesn't remember any other faces. I'm afraid this is where it gets sketchy. The boy punched and kicked and attempted to force himself on her at knifepoint but someone intervened. She doesn't know who or indeed remember much beyond that point, only fleeing across the park.'

Stark indicated the perp-sheets again. 'Would you take another look, in case they jog your memory of the others?' Paula looked reluctantly, but shook her head. She was trying very hard not to cry.

'After that, time becomes a little elastic,' continued the shrink. 'She went to Lewisham station and in the morning caught the train to Orpington, hoping to find friends in a squat she knew, but it had been boarded up. She heard about a hostel and stayed there on and off until someone tried to get in to see her. Was it this girl, Paula?' She pointed to the picture of Nikki and received a nod. 'After that she planned to get on a bus or train, but she was out of money. A man she'd met suggested she stay the night at a local squat – he knew the headman. Once there, she was locked into a room and forcibly injected with something – the rest is a blur.'

Stark produced pictures of the men arrested at the house. Paula recoiled but made herself look, nodding to both. 'They were dealing drugs and using girls as favours, keeping them doped up,' said Stark. 'Do you remember anything else?'

Paula leant to whisper to the shrink, who spoke for her again. 'She remembers the headman being very angry with her suddenly, shouting at her and the other man.'

'Perhaps he'd discovered his latest victim was the centre of a police hunt,' said Stark.

His face as Paula looked up sharply showed he knew he'd blundered. Fran tutted. 'Patience,' rumbled Groombridge. She couldn't tell if it was for her or Stark.

Stark took a deep breath and let it out slowly. 'If so, it probably spared you exposure of a worse kind. He dared not show you to anyone.'

And didn't have the courage to sneak her out and dump her somewhere in case she remembered too much, thought Fran. It was lucky he hadn't killed her. Maybe he wasn't the cold-blooded type. Stark's hand and ribcage showed what the bastard would do in hot blood.

Stark peered at Paula thoughtfully. 'Is everything Dr McDonald told us accurate?' A nod. 'Is it everything that you remember?' He placed a faint emphasis on everything, just enough. Paula glanced up at him again, searching, anxious. She did not nod.

'There is a gap, Paula,' said Stark, softly. 'Between the attack on you and your escape. A man came to your aid, fought to protect you, told you to run. A good man, whose pride and honour would see him take the blame for what happened next.' He waited but she said nothing. 'I can't imagine how scared you were, how powerless you felt, how angry.'

She shook her head. A tear fell into her lap but she said nothing. Fran found herself holding her breath. They waited.

'Actually, Constable Stark,' the psychologist broke the

silence, 'I think maybe you can.' Fran saw momentary shock in Stark's expression, anger, even. It was obvious now that she was his shrink: surely she wasn't about to betray professional confidence. The woman continued calmly, 'I read in the newspaper that you used to be a soldier, that you were involved in heavy fighting and badly wounded. Maybe you know more about fear, powerlessness and anger than you think.'

'Maybe we should stick to the matter in hand,' said Stark, curtly. Fran watched, fascinated. Jesus, he looked terrible. This was madness. 'What Dr McDonald says is true, but deeply personal. There are things I don't like to talk about. Perhaps we *are* alike there, as she suggests. I've . . . done things . . .' Stark's face remained fixed, even, but the words faltered. 'Perhaps we all have,' he said quietly.

Paula watched him but said nothing. Then her hand inched across the table and into his. Fran stared, spellbound. 'Yes,' said Paula, so quietly it almost passed unheard.

Stark closed his hand on hers. 'I know why you did it,' he said quietly.

Her lip quivered. 'Will I go to prison?' she asked, looking into his eyes.

'I don't know. But whatever happens, few people will blame you for what you did.'

Paula's other hand reached out over Stark's, grasping it so tightly her knuckles whitened. Tears began to streak down her face, unheeded. 'Do you?'

'No.'

She broke down and wept, clasping his hand as she sobbed uncontrollably. Fran expected the shrink to close the proceedings but she just let the sobbing go on and on. Stark held Paula's hands but obviously could think of nothing more to say. Eventually, the weeping subsided and Paula let go to wipe her face. The shrink produced a packet of tissues from somewhere, which Paula accepted, with murmured thanks, blowing her nose apologetically and wiping her eyes.

Stark waited until she had regained some composure. 'Paula,' he said gently. 'I'm sorry, but I have to hear it from you.'

'Careful,' murmured Groombridge.

Paula looked up at Stark, biting her lip. A strange look came into her eyes, almost like defiance. Fran couldn't believe Stark would ask. She didn't think he had it in him to press the point.

'I have to ask,' he said softly. 'Did you stab Kyle Gibbs?'

She took a deep breath and let it out in a shuddering sigh. 'Yes.'

'What happened, exactly?'

'They were fighting. The knife landed near me. I picked it up and . . . and . . .'

'You did what you had to do.'

'Yes.' She looked up, eyes red.

Yes, thought Fran, what she had to do. In that moment. You could see in her eyes that it made little sense to her too, now, with the heavy consequence of the law bearing down on her. But in that moment it had made absolute sense. And who could argue with that, sitting here now, a world of understanding away? Not for the first time Fran wished herself judge and jury, though this might be the first time she'd wished for acquittal.

Paula was wheeled away by her doctor.

'Well done, lad,' said Groombridge.

'Yes, well done,' said Hazel.

Stark rounded on her sharply. '*Walk . . . away*,' he growled.

Alarmed, Fran grabbed his arm and pulled him away. Groombridge apologized smoothly, though the shrink seemed unfazed. She accepted his thanks and left.

'Constable Stark,' said Groombridge, like a displeased

master calling his dog to heel. They left the hospital without another word, Fran shaking her head most of the way.

Stark simmered, almost hoping Groombridge would demand an explanation, but nothing further was said.

'Get some lunch,' said Groombridge, when they got back to the station. 'When you're done you're coming to Belmarsh to talk to Maggs and then you can clear off home. Understood?'

'Guv.'

Stark found it hard to eat. Either the pills or the fact that he was still boiling with anger that his own shrink would use him like that. He gave up after a few bites and took more painkillers instead. He nearly added coffee but he was already fidgety. He'd have to stay awake on his own. He was just getting up to find Groombridge when his phone rang. 'What now?'

'Don't take that tone with me,' barked Pierson. 'Sit down and don't interrupt!'

'I'm in no mood to take orders from a stuck-up –'

'Rupert?' she interrupted. 'You can only call me that if you're still a corporal. And if you still are, you'll think better of it.'

Stark took a deep breath, wishing he'd just rejected the call. 'Okay, Captain. How can I improve your world today?'

'Short of getting off it, you could shut up and listen. It'll be in this Friday's *Gazette*.'

Stark felt sick and his legs went weak. He sat in the nearest chair, unable to speak. This day was always going to come but it was still a kick in the guts.

'The tabloids will have it too, I expect,' she added.

Of course they would. The *London Gazette* was the state's premier journal-of-record – probably the only people who read it were other journalists.

'I deduce from your stunned silence that I have your full attention at last,' continued Pierson. 'If you're capable of heeding advice, request some leave.'

'I've got work to do.'

'And criminal investigation will grind to a shuddering halt without its latest trainee?' she scoffed. 'This isn't a drill, Corporal – the press will be all over it. Are your family prepared?'

'The letter said *confidential*.'

Pierson was momentarily silenced. 'Surely you understood that you could tell immediate family.'

'I was following orders, remember?'

'Bullshit! Just how long did you expect burying your head in the sand to work?'

'As long as possible.'

'Well, that point is now. Is there anyone else, a significant other?'

'Captain Pierson, are you making a pass at me?'

'*Yes or no?*'

'No.' Stark thought of Kelly but the longer he kept her away from this mess the better.

'Can't say I'm remotely surprised. Is there somewhere you could stay for a while – family, friends?'

'Not local to work, no.'

'A colleague, then?'

'Definitely not.'

She tutted her frustration. 'Then repeat after me . . . "No comment".'

'What?'

'Practise those words. There'll be hacks banging on your door. If you say anything other than "no comment" I'll hunt you down like a dog. Understood? "No comment", full stop. And, if you come to your senses, take time off and hide.'

'Till this all blows over,' Stark said sarcastically.

'Or Hell freezes over you. If you need help you know my number. Less than four weeks now. Make damned sure you're ready!' She hung up.

Several minutes later Stark was still staring at the phone

when Fran appeared next to him. 'On your feet, soldier boy,' she said harshly. 'You're off to prison.'

Maggs was led in and took his seat. He looked resigned. Perhaps he knew what was coming. Nothing came. Stark turned to Groombridge.

'Don't look at me. Today seems to be the Constable Stark show.'

Stark groaned inside, concentrating just to get through the preliminaries.

Maggs watched him impassively. 'You look fit for triage, Weekender.'

'No-duff,' replied Stark, meaning genuine casualty, not an exercise.

'They use those posh tags now. What colour would they hang on you?' Triage tags used a traffic-light system. Red for life-threatening injury, yellow for non-life-threatening, green for minor. There was also black – pain treatment only, until death.

'We found her, Maggs,' said Stark, bluntly. 'And she's confessed to stabbing Kyle Gibbs.'

Maggs closed his eyes for a moment, then stared at him, like he was dirt. 'Well, bully for you, Blue Top.'

'I think, in time, she'll be ready to testify on your behalf.'

'No.'

'What?'

Maggs stared impassively. 'It's a simple enough word.'

'We have her confession, Maggs. Her testimony in court would help you.'

'You just don't get it, do you?' said Maggs.

'Of course I bloody do,' said Stark, suddenly angry.

'Constable,' warned Groombridge.

Stark bit down on his anger, turning it in on himself, furious at his own lack of control. 'She can't be shielded from what's already happened,' he continued, outwardly calm. 'She's been through what she's been through and she's done what she's done. She'll come to terms with that or she won't.'

'She's got a better chance left be,' growled Maggs.

'That's not for you to decide.'

'Why not?' demanded Maggs. 'Justice must be done? Where's the justice in standing her in the dock, making her relive it, then letting some shyster say she asked for it, call her a delinquent, a drug-addled slut. How's that gonna help her? And what good would it do? It's not like she can help lock him up.'

'She'd help make sure you're not. The CPS still have a coroner's report saying your punch to Gibbs's throat might have killed him, even if he hadn't been stabbed. You need the jury on your side.'

'No jury's gonna give a shit about me and I don't give a shit what they think. But what's gonna happen to her, eh? I'll bet your precious Crown Prosecution Service will have a shot at her too, don't deny it.'

'I won't. But both of you have mitigating factors.'

Maggs sneered. 'Will a conviction help her "get over it"?'

'It might. You know about atonement, "don't deny it".'

'Fuck you. You should lose her confession and let her go.'

'Why? So you can atone for her too?' Stark felt his anger rising again. 'The knife was in his back, Maggs. A judge will look kinder on a sexual-assault victim for that than they will a soldier. They'll look at your training and punish you.'

'What they gonna do? Hang me?' Maggs met Stark's eyes with a twisted smile. 'Fuck it, I'm fucked already.'

'Poor you.'

Maggs waved his hand around the room. 'Twenty to life, three meals a day with hot and cold running water, a bed and a roof? You know I'm better for this than her.'

'You'd sell your freedom that cheap?'

'Do you know how much this country spends per prisoner? Look it up some time. Then look up MoD pensions or veteran welfare.'

'What – so this would be your way of getting your dues?'

Maggs ignored the question. 'Did you know that, on average, a male veteran suffering PTSD symptoms will not seek help for *fourteen years*? So instead of appearing on military statistics they get chalked up later as mental-health issues, domestic violence, alcohol and drug abuse, unemployment, homelessness, suicide. Two hundred and fifty-six British soldiers died in the Falklands conflict, but more than that have committed suicide since. Gulf War One we lost twenty-four. Since then nearly *two hundred* have opted out. It's different in America. They look after their veterans. We treat ours like shit on our shoes and the public look the other way because, after all, war's just a video game now – "Hardly anyone gets hurt any more, do they?" It's just a segment on the news between political sleaze and celebrity divorce.'

Stark was in no mood for setting the world to wrongs. 'People still care,' he insisted.

'When they stop to think about it,' said Maggs, bitterly. 'That uncomfortable twinge of guilt. Take two mock talent shows washed down with a celebrity humiliation show and get a blame-free night's sleep. You'll feel better in the morning.'

Stark rubbed his eyes wearily, suddenly exhausted again. There was altogether too much suddenly this and suddenly that going on in him. Not a good symptom. He tried to cling to the anger but it slipped away, unstoppable as an ebbing tide. 'For a tramp you know a lot about pop culture.'

'Newspapers ain't just for sleepin' in.'

'So this is your fifteen minutes of fame, is it?' asked Stark. 'It's not about shielding the girl, it's about getting a bigger soapbox.'

Maggs ignored the accusation. 'Someone has to keep shouting. When the last voice falls silent, life has fled.'

'All in the hope of change?'

'*Hope?*' Maggs was incredulous. 'Wake the fuck up, Dorothy. There's no such place! Hope is for sheep, opiate of the masses, the pill they pop to help them sleepwalk through life. The definition of stupidity is repeating the same mistake *hoping* for a different result. What good is hope when the bullet comes your way? What good did it do our mates or the fellas we killed, gasping their pitiful last? What good is hope when you're betrayed by your state, cast aside, left to rot? *What fucking good is hope to me?*'

Stark sat silent, too tired to argue and not sure what he'd say if he could.

'No,' said Maggs, calming down without an adversary. 'She's got more use for hope than me.'

'Very noble.'

'*Kiss my arse.*'

'We won't let you take the blame for the stabbing. You're innocent.'

'Am I?' Maggs's piercing blue eyes bored into him. 'Are you?'

Stark closed his eyes for a second. 'We did what we had to, because someone had to.' The stock answer: truthful, awful, incomplete.

Maggs chuckled darkly. 'Doesn't help you sleep at night, though, does it?'

Stark sighed. 'You can't tell me you've no hope. Otherwise why bother banging the drum?'

Anger flared in Maggs's eyes. 'Duty, you feeble-minded tit!' he spat, his voice rising. 'You remember – to the *truth*! Lest we forget! *Lest we fucking forget!*'

'*Fuck you, Maggs!*' Stark's anger flooded back. How *dare* Maggs fling those words at him? Groombridge had hold of his arm but Stark wrenched it free. 'I'm not here to help you flush yourself, you self-righteous shit!'

'Constable Stark, sit down now!' bellowed Groombridge, his voice booming around the small, hard room.

Stark looked around. The prison guard was hovering by his side. Fran had hold of his arm. He was standing, fists planted on the table; his chair lay on its side by the far wall. Fran tugged him towards it, stood it up and sat him firmly down.

'I apologize for my subordinate, Mr Maggs,' said Groombridge. He cast a warning glance at Stark to stay sitting and silent, or else. 'But Constable Stark is quite right. We won't aid you in some personal crusade. Justice isn't what *we* say it is, any more than it's what *you* say it is. You can instruct your barrister not to call the girl, if you wish, but you won't take the blame for the stabbing. You saved that girl from a terrible fate. Whether you like it or not, the rest is up to her.'

31

Fran sat Stark in his chair and followed Groombridge into his office. She made herself close the door quietly instead of slamming it, but then could contain herself no longer. 'I told you not to take him! What did *any of that* achieve?'

'I am not beholden to explain myself to *you*, Detective Sergeant!' Groombridge rarely let his anger show and it was plain she'd overstepped the mark. 'I've had enough of this from DS Harper. Now sit down and keep that sharp tongue behind your teeth.'

Shocked, Fran took a seat, angry with herself, Stark and now Harper too. Harper's ridiculous resentment of Stark was thinly veiled at best but surely he wasn't rash enough to repeat his petty mutterings to Groombridge. It was a slip made in anger and Groombridge clearly wished he'd not said it, so Fran had to swallow the question for now, but Stark was *her* trainee – if anyone was going to give him hell it was her, not bloody Harper! She took several deep breaths and tried to simmer down.

'Right,' said her boss, his glare softening, if only slightly. 'Now, listen and learn. You'll wear pips on your shoulders one day, but only if you shake that chip off first. *Two* things were achieved. First, Maggs was brought to see the futility of further lies. If he can shake the chip off *his* shoulder in time, he may get justice, not just punishment. Second, and you might like this one better, Constable Stark was brought to see that he is wholly unfit for duty. If *he* can shake the chip off his shoulder, he might now engage the help he really needs in time to prevent us losing a promising copper. Now, have I satisfied you that I'm not a complete bloody fool?'

'Yes, Guv.' Fran felt about as small as she'd ever felt. She wanted to blame Stark for bringing her to this but saw herself for a second as Groombridge must now and kept the blame to herself.

'Good! Now, the man Stark hospitalized last night is making noises about police brutality *and* saying the knife was planted. You're a witness. Tell me again that we're squeaky on this. It would be a shame if we had to toss Stark to the wolves just when we're all so enamoured of him.'

Fran was relieved at the change of subject. 'We're squeaky, Guv. As well as my statement, Forensics confirmed this morning that Stark's prints are on the knife but so are the perp's. They can demonstrate Stark held the weapon second. As for brutality, the paramedic will attest that Stark was lucky the perp didn't gut him. He incapacitated and disarmed a man who attacked and wounded him with a knife. The force used seemed reasonable to me.'

'Incapacitated.' Groombridge ruminated on the word, the very word she'd used in her written statement. 'Broken nose and jaw, dislocated shoulder?' Groombridge subjected her to his most penetrating gaze.

'Even so.'

'The IPCC might not like us using the he-got-what-he-deserved defence, especially when the officer involved is ex-military, trained to respond instinctively with anything up to and including lethal force.'

Fran made a face. She was just about angry enough with Stark right now to regret this, but the truth was the truth. 'With all due respect, Guv, the Independent Police Complaints Commission can kiss my beautiful behind. I've signed my statement.'

Groombridge pursed his lips, then nodded. 'Okay. The other witness, Constable Davis, corroborates. So we stand by

Stark. Now take the arrogant, insolent, ungrateful gobshite home and put him to bed. Hit him over the head if you have to. I don't want to see him for a full week! Understood?'

'Yes, Guv.'

She let herself out. Stark looked up at her. She hoped he hadn't been listening at the door, as she would have done, but the glassiness of his eyes suggested not. 'On your feet, Constable Weekender, you're done. You're not to set foot near this station for a week.'

Stark stood but said nothing.

'Oh dear, Golden-boy, losing your shine?' chuckled Harper, over his partition. 'The missus has you right under her thumb.'

'That's rich coming from you,' said Fran. The look on Harper's face was almost worth it.

She took Stark by the arm and hustled him into the lift as fast as his dicky hip would allow, before too many people saw the state of him. He let himself be handled, childlike, as he had the previous night. Maybe it was a military thing: once injured, you let the medic take over completely, or maybe it was still shock.

As they emerged from the lift Fran stopped to answer her phone. 'Hello?' She listened, frowning, visibly irritated. 'What, *now*? He only just sent me . . . Yeah, okay, I'm on my way.' She hung up, rolling her eyes. 'Bryden says the guv'nor wants another word. Wait here and don't speak to anyone.'

Stark did as he was told. A minute later when he heard someone coming down the stairs he turned away, waiting for whoever it was to pass.

Instead a hand grabbed his shoulder and spun him around. Harper had his right fist drawn back ready, his left gripping Stark's right shoulder. Stark grasped the nearest hand with his left and rolled it inwards, pressing the elbow over and down with his right. Instead of launching the intended punch, Harper found himself on one knee, pinned in a classic submission hold, his war cry dying in a strangled gasp. In *jujutsu* this wrist control would have begun with a counter-strike to the face or throat but Stark used the simpler *aikido* version, though not out of mercy – he was simply too tired right now for the repercussions of breaking a superior's nose.

In too much pain to cry out or plead, let alone attempt escape, Harper groaned. Stark stared down pitilessly. 'I told you what would happen,' he said coldly. 'This is still me being nice. I won't warn you again.' He gradually let the pressure build until he saw panic and tears well in Harper's eyes, then let go.

The big DS collapsed on to both knees, gasping for breath. After a minute he climbed awkwardly to his feet, cradling his arm and avoiding eye contact.

'You should put ice on that,' said Stark.

Slowly the big man straightened and met his eyes, face pale and unreadable. If his intention was to make it clear that he blamed Stark for Fran's comment he had succeeded, but in that alone.

Before either could speak Fran stepped from the lift. 'Harper? What are you doing down here? Bryden said you told him –'

Harper barged wordlessly past her into the lift and jabbed the buttons furiously. Fran watched the doors close, then turned to Stark with a suspicious look. 'Should I ask?'

'Probably not.'

Fran hustled him into the car and away before anything else could go wrong. There was little doubt about what had just occurred. If Harper's foolishness overcame his wounded pride, he might press a complaint.

'Am I suspended?' asked Stark, as if the thought had just occurred to him, but with no discernible concern.

'Be thankful you're not,' replied Fran. 'We'll chalk it up as time-in-lieu of overtime, save you having a sick note on file.'

'Okay.'

Not 'Thank you, Detective Sergeant Millhaven', just 'Okay'. He stared out of the window the rest of the way. Part of her wished to know what he was thinking; the rest of her definitely did not. She took his keys from his jacket and let him in. He was limping slowly now. She stood before the lift doors and read the sign. How long had it been like that?

'Come on, stairs it is.' She took his arm to help and he didn't object. He grunted quietly with each step but Fran was aware that he wasn't letting her take much weight. The stubborn streak inside him hadn't let go yet.

They reached the first-floor landing and paused for a moment to rest. Only three more to go, thought Fran, wondering whether Stark would make it. The lift doors mocked them with another sign – OUT OF ORDER.

Stark pulled his arm free of her and punched the notice with all his might, leaving a deep dent in the metal doors, the deafening bang echoing dully in the shaft behind. He stepped back and slid down the opposite wall to sit, cradling his fist, head bowed, eyes closed tight.

Fran overcame her shock, crouched down and prised his hand out. The knuckles were split and bleeding. He didn't wince as she felt for breaks but, the state he was in, that might not mean much. It was the first time she'd looked closely at where his little finger finished at the first knuckle. She'd got used to it, she supposed. She touched the smooth skin there. Stark silently pulled his hand back and tucked it away.

'I think you're done, soldier,' said Fran, quietly, took out her phone and called for an ambulance.

PART THREE

32

When Stark awoke he was told it was Thursday morning.

A sedative, then. He remembered the ambulance and waiting in A&E. He remembered an X-ray and being told two bones in his right hand were broken. He remembered a doctor making sure the bones were aligned properly, strapping a plastic splint to the back of his hand, wrapping it up in a blue glass-fibre cast and the heat of the resin going off. And he remembered Dr Hazel bloody McDonald appearing at his side, talking over his head and prescribing something he didn't recognize, a drip; he'd assumed it was a painkiller.

He tried to be angry but couldn't, even when Hazel blithely confessed to stealing two days of his life. She'd see him soon, she said. Stark didn't look forward to it.

The aroma of missed breakfast hung over the ward, taunting him. Then an orderly appeared with a covered plate on a tray. Stark could've kissed her. He ate every scrap and drank about a gallon of water. Then he realized he was catheterized and wished he hadn't. He hated catheters. He'd sworn never to piss in a bag again. He called the nurse to remove it but she wouldn't without a doctor's say-so. Stark begged her to find one and held his fire grimly. The doctor eventually turned up, argued with him for several minutes, conceded and left. Stark suffered the indignity of de-catheterization with little grace, waited till the nurse stepped outside the curtain, seized the bedpan and relieved himself, blissfully. One small victory. One small step. Here we go again.

The only good news was a negative on his HIV and

hepatitis tests. Otherwise he sat up in bed, bored and fighting the inclination to feel sorry for himself. Hospitalized, bedridden, again. He looked around the ward without really taking anything in, lost in dour thought. Then another part of his brain alerted him to a new and attractive shape in the corner of his vision. He looked round and did a double-take. Kelly?

A nurse pointed his way and Kelly wandered over, glossy hair swaying in time with slim, denim-clad hips. 'Hello, stranger,' she said. She picked up his notes from the end of his bed, sat in the adjacent chair and began reading.

'Are you allowed to do that?' he asked.

'I explained my professional interest to the ward nurse,' she answered, without looking up. 'They called the Carter after you were admitted.'

'So this is a professional visit?'

She still didn't look at him. She pulled out a pair of X-ray films and held them up to the light. The first was his hand. She put it aside without comment and looked at the second.

'You have a hairline fracture of the pelvis above the hip joint.' The consultant had shown Stark but he couldn't see much. 'Bit hard to spot among the old damage but the leading culprit for your recent discomfort. The key feature . . . Here,' she pointed, 'it skirts this thickening where the bone healed over the graft. The consultant suggests it can only be the result of a fresh impact. Any ideas?'

Stark shook his head. 'I thought it might be more tear than wear, like you said, but I've been on my feet so much recently.'

Kelly tilted her head. 'He called to ask my opinion. I told him how careful we were to avoid impact, how careful we'd told *you* to be.' There was a slight barb. She was calm but cool. Stark realized, with dismay, that she was angry. 'Think. A fall? Car accident? I know you wouldn't risk my wrath tackling any assault courses and I'll assume a prisoner hasn't thrown you down the cellblock stairs. You must remember something. You told me your symptoms were recent.' Her gaze took on an alarming similarity to Groombridge's inquisitorial technique.

'Ah . . .'

'Define recent,' she said.

'Well, I suppose . . . a few weeks,' he admitted.

'Weeks!'

'I suppose. I think it began not long after I started work. That's why I thought wear and t–' He stopped. 'Ah.'

'What?'

'Well, there was one time . . .' Stark sighed, the truth finally crystallizing in his mind when it should've been obvious all along. The day he'd arrested Maggs. 'In my second week, I vaulted some railings. It jarred but there wasn't time to pay it much attention.'

Kelly remained expressionless. 'Not enough to notice you'd just broken your pelvis?'

'A man had been stabbed.'

'And afterwards?'

'There was a lot going on. That hip's always stiff and sore.'

'This stiff and sore?'

'Well, no, but I had to spend so much time on foot –'

'Wear and tear,' she interrupted, with a strong waft of sarcasm. 'And now I find you admitted to hospital, mentally and physically exhausted. Why didn't you say something?' she demanded. 'I could see you were struggling but . . .'

'I was trying to impress you,' he admitted, hoping wry honesty might defuse the tension.

'Think it worked?' she asked, indicating their surroundings. She had a point. She stared at the X-ray again, shaking her head. 'Six or seven. On a scale of one to ten you think walking around on a broken pelvis is a six or seven? Or was that supposed to impress me too?'

Stark puffed out his cheeks, trying to think how to explain. On a scale of one to ten, kneeling in the firing position, with shrapnel through your pelvis, leg, neck, face, head and half a dozen other places, with burnt hands and a missing finger isn't a ten. It doesn't even become a ten when a bullet punches through you. Chemicals in your brain quash the pain and then, if you're lucky, the medics quash it with more. The nearest Stark thought he'd ever come to ten was in the days following surgeries when his brain had sometimes seen through the morphine's smoke and mirrors.

'I thought seven was pretty bad,' he offered lamely.

Kelly jabbed at the X-ray. 'You've been walking around on this, letting me put you through entirely inappropriate treatment for weeks, to impress me?'

'My judgement may have been clouded.'

'Is that supposed to be a compliment?'

'Yes.'

'Well, perhaps if I could discount the levels of opioid found in your blood toxicology screen I might take it as one.' She was visibly angry now. 'Tell me that was about pain control and not putting on a face for me.'

For a split second Stark considered explaining about the nightmares, but their mutual opinion of him had sunk too low already for him to bear it. No doubt Hazel would be asking him the same question soon enough.

'How could you be so bloody stupid?' Faces throughout the ward turned at her raised voice.

Inside, a piece of Stark died. He'd thought he'd reached a new low in pissing off Groombridge, but this . . .

Kelly's expression softened. 'Don't look like that.' She laid the notes carefully on the bed. 'Now I feel like I've kicked a puppy.'

'A puppy isn't quite the impression I hoped to make.'

'No,' she agreed sadly. Why sadly? Stark wondered. 'You look better at least.'

'Better than when?'

'I stopped by on Tuesday evening but they'd already sedated you.'

Had she? So he hadn't burnt all his bridges. 'I'm trained to respond quickly to food and rest. It's a Pavlovian military thing.' Perhaps a bad analogy, given Pavlov's famous experiment centred on training puppies.

She rubbed her eyes. 'Look, you've obviously got a lot going on in your life and, I think, in your head, and you're hiding it all behind glib hand-offs. That's fine, I've no right to expect anything more and I won't ask. I'm not interested in a project.' There was something rehearsed in her delivery. If she'd arrived undecided she had still come with this option prepared. He'd never know now if she'd had another.

'I'm not interested in being one,' he agreed evenly. A small part of him shouted at him not to be so bloody stubborn, just this once, but he clenched his jaw against futile words. She was right and they both knew it. She'd seen through his bullshit from the start; now she saw through him completely, clear through the hole in him.

She nodded. Stark thought he saw tears well up but she blinked and stood to go. 'I'm glad you're feeling better. You're going to need an operation and recuperative treatment afterwards. I'll see you're referred back to the Carter once the physios here are done with you. I'll ask Lucy to take over.'

'Whatever you think best.'

She hesitated, then leant in and kissed him on the cheek, a warm, soft, brief kiss and a lingering hint of perfume. 'Please take better care of yourself,' she said, then left without another word or backward glance.

Stark stared at the point where she'd disappeared and felt numbness inside, nothing more.

Fran came to see him too. She didn't say much. Maybe she was still angry with him as well, he couldn't tell. What would she think tomorrow morning? He thought about saying something but didn't. He wouldn't know where to begin. Having apparently satisfied herself he was alive, she left.

When lights-out came Stark struggled to settle. It wasn't that he wasn't tired – he was depressed to discover that even after two days out he still was – but a hospital ward is never a silent place. Nurses come and go, huddle around the nurses' station and gossip or bid on eBay, while the other patients shift or moan. One night after he had been moved to the NHS ward in Selly Oak, Stark had heard a demented old man with terminal cancer groan incoherently for hours, repeatedly trying to get out of bed, unwittingly pulling out his catheter. Every time he began to do it again Stark pressed his call button. Every time a nurse arrived too late and the poor old sod had to be held down and re-catheterized. In the end Stark levered himself off his bed and, using his visitor chair as a zimmer, hopped across himself. The old guy calmed down the second Stark took his hand and slipped away before dawn. It was that night that Stark's opinion of nurse empathy hit bottom. Perhaps that was unfair: there was little they could do for the old man – was it their fault they were too busy to sit with him? And perhaps it was guilt that had made them react so angrily, calling Stark a fool and worse as they shooed him back to bed. Perhaps they didn't like being reminded that no one should die alone if they didn't have to.

This ward had no such distractions, but with his mind reeling over the next morning's *Gazette*, it was enough. He wistfully thought about discharging himself, but in his condition there was no way they'd accede. It would be futile anyway: there could be no hiding. One of the more attentive nurses asked him if he'd like something to help and he reluctantly agreed.

He was woken by an explosion. He sat up in shock as several more blinding flashes rocked the darkness. There was a shout, then furious shouting, and the silhouette of a man with a large camera chased from the ward by a bewildered nurse. It took several seconds for Stark to realize what had happened, and when he did, anger and despair fought for space in him.

It was just before three in the morning. The ward was in turmoil. Security guards appeared and disappeared. Nurses tried to quieten the other patients. The ward sister demanded to know why a photographer had snuck into her domain to photograph Stark in his sleep. He didn't know how to explain and resented the implication that it was his fault, even if it was. Gradually everything settled down but, groggy as he was, Stark slept no more.

It had begun.

Even before the rounds began to wake the patients, Stark saw orderlies and nurses, even doctors, saunter through the ward to peer at him. He didn't wait for a nurse, but levered himself off the bed on to one leg and yanked the curtain round the track to shut out their stares.

Of all angels, it was Doc Hazel who appeared to save him. She had him moved into one of the side rooms normally used to isolate infectious patients. Apt, thought Stark.

When they were alone she laid several newspapers on the bed. Stark could hardly bring himself to look. Most made do with his army service photo, a serious young man in uniform, but the most loathsome tabloid splashed the hours-old picture of him laid out in this hospital bed, looking half dead; a fine scoop. The huge strap-line read, 'FROM HERO TO THIS!'

He should've expected it, he supposed, but he'd naïvely thought the mainstream papers would take a day to catch up with the *Gazette*.

'You and I are going to talk about this,' said Hazel. 'I knew you were holding back but . . .'

Another person angered, thought Stark. Another tick. Sooner or later he'd piss off the entire world. The hum of his phone crabbing across his side table on vibrate prevented her saying more. Stark looked at the screen and made a pained expression. 'Later,' said Hazel, and left.

Stark closed his eyes and answered the phone. 'Hi, Mum.'

33

There was a reporter on the front steps of the station with a camera crew. News about Pinky was out then, thought Fran, as she drove past, parked and used the side entrance.

In the office DC Dixon and the others were huddled around a copy of the *Sun*.

'Don't you boys ever tire of page three?' she asked wearily.

'Haven't you seen this?' asked Dixon, with incredulity.

'Seen what? You know I don't read the comics.'

'Stark, splashed across the front page of every newspaper in Britain!'

'What?'

Dixon held up the crumpled red-top. Fran's eyes widened. She snatched it and read furiously, muttering frequent expletives. Eventually she looked up at the others' mixed expressions. 'Stupid, *stupid* bastard!'

'I know,' agreed Dixon.

'Christ!' Fran thought of the reporters downstairs. 'Get me two uniforms now – no, get a van together. The hospital must be crawling with sodding press. See if Dearing's free. No one gets near Stark without a hospital ID. Is the guv in?'

Dixon shook his head. 'He's with the CPS this morning.'

Fran thought back to the day the CPS lawyer had pressed Stark to confess. The guy must have choked on his latte! Had Groombridge known about this? She thought not. But Cox? Well, she couldn't go demanding answers from the super.

She beat the van to the hospital where she had to barge through a crowd of reporters and cameras. She made the

355

mistake of flashing her warrant card and was bombarded with questions as microphones and cameras were thrust in her face. She pushed all aside and stormed into the hospital. Security men tried to stop her getting on to the ward but she brushed them aside too.

Stark was standing on one leg by the window, looking down at the reporters. 'Morning, Sarge,' he said, without turning.

'Get back in bed before they see you, for God's sake!' she said.

'They've already got their picture,' he said, indicating the top tabloid on the bed.

Fran picked it up. 'When was *this* taken?'

'Three o'clock this morning.'

'Jesus! Well, I'll have a uniform on your door soon. Don't argue – you know you've left us no choice. There'll be a van here any minute now.'

'It's just pulling up.'

She joined him by the window. Sergeant Dearing and a dozen other coppers climbed out. Dearing was six foot eight and broad to match. The swarm gave way before him like waves before a super-tanker. Stark sighed quietly. Fran stared disconsolately down at the reporters. 'What the hell were you thinking?'

'I wasn't. Not in any considered sense. There wasn't time.'

'Like outside that squat?' Fran shuddered, remembering the murderous look on his face.

'Something like that.'

She considered this for a moment, but none of it made much sense. 'I don't understand these wars.'

'These wars, or any wars?' he asked. There was a tiny defensive slant there.

'These more than most,' she admitted.

'You're not alone.'

'So why do *you* think you were over there?' asked Fran.

'What does it matter?' replied Stark.

356

'What? No "We're there to make life better for the people, to help build a stable democracy and improve UK security"? Isn't that the soldier line?'

'I was only a part-time soldier.'

'You're being evasive.'

'You're being *in*vasive.'

'I'm just making conversation but it's like getting blood from a stone, as ever.'

Stark rested his forehead against the glass. 'I don't mean to be impenetrable,' he said, after a moment. 'I've just never been comfortable discussing these things.'

'Must make your shrink sessions a barrel of laughs.'

'Indeed.' He sighed. 'Look, I have an opinion on Iraq, Afghanistan, of course I do, but as a soldier I recognized that my opinion didn't matter. You don't sign up for specifics. You don't get to opt in or out. You sign up to serve. The nature of that service is up to your elders and betters. You put your faith in the command structure and if that lands you in harm's way there's probably good cause.'

'That's ducking responsibility,' protested Fran.

'Is it?' Anger fizzed in the question. 'War is the least democratic thing a democracy can do. It isn't one soldier one vote! That would give a new meaning to death by committee. Indecision costs lives. So soldiers do what they're bloody well told and keep ethical or moral concerns to themselves.'

'No wonder you all go doolally afterwards.'

'Or end up drunk in a park or kicked to death for being homeless and old,' agreed Stark. 'How else would you have it? What better method would you propose?'

'I'd propose not fighting at all.'

'As would I, as would any soldier, but this isn't a Miss World speech. Armies cross borders, corrupt despots starve their populations and fanatics carry out genocidal insanities, and until they stop, someone must be prepared to stand up and say no. If that means some politician bullshitting his apathetic armchair demographic to get it done, then that armchair demographic only have themselves to blame.'

'How can you say that? They lied to us! How can you, of all people, not care?'

He looked at her now, intently. 'Because in the end someone has to make the difficult decisions. We elect people to do it for us. Whether they're right or wrong becomes a matter for debate, and the methods they use to sell us the hard decisions will be endlessly picked over, but we ask them to decide for us and they do their best. If they get it wrong they're out, fair enough, but anyone thinking they can do better should get out of their armchair.'

'You think I'm some apathetic, armchair whinger?'

'Of course not! You serve! You put yourself in harm's way so other people don't have to. You know all this crap already –' Stark stopped. The look dawning on his face showed he'd finally realized he was being baited.

'Not bad for an impenetrable sod who doesn't value his own opinion.' She laughed openly.

Finally he smiled. 'Piss off.' He hopped to the bed and sat down with a grunt. 'What did the guv'nor say?'

'He wasn't in. He's with the CPS. He didn't know, then? What about Cox?'

'It's possible.'

'He's a wily one, the super.'

'So I've heard.'

There was still something distant, disconnected, in his voice. Not as bad as before she'd brought him here, but an echo. He looked bone weary. 'The shrink spoke with me after I brought you in. How's that going?'

'Who can tell? She's not best pleased with me.'

'I'll bet.' She stared hard at him but that was all she was going to get, it seemed. 'What about your hip?'

'Nothing a metal plate and some nuts and bolts can't fix. This afternoon. They've been starving me since yesterday.'

'Don't they know you bite if you're not fed?' She thought for a moment. 'I'll send someone round to pick you up some things. Uniform saw reporters outside your flat this morning. You'll need somewhere to lie low when they kick you out of here.'

'Is that an offer, Sarge?'

'I suppose.'

'Thanks, but forget the press. If I did a bunk we'd have my mum hunting us down.'

'Fair enough. Christ knows how we'll get you out. We'll have to use a riot wagon.'

'Maybe the crowd will have lost interest by then.' He sounded unconvinced. Fran wouldn't have banked on it either. 'How's things in the office?' he asked.

Not 'How's the case going?' Fran almost smiled at the subtlety. 'Oh, you know – same shit different day. DS Harper's been in the wars again,' she mentioned casually. 'Poor thing has one arm in a sling. Nothing broken, thankfully. Took a tumble on the station stairs apparently.'

Stark gave the barest laugh. 'Will he sue, do you think?'

Now Fran did smile. 'No, I don't think so.' She was pleased to note a flicker of relief on Stark's face. She asked what he needed from his flat and left him sitting forlornly on the bed.

At the nearby nurses' station a storm was brewing. Dearing was politely out-looming two Military Policemen while their female officer demanded access with increasing irritation. A senior nurse and a hospital security guard hovered uncomfortably while a girl with dark hair tried to be heard.

Fran recognized her at once, and the officer. A copper never forgot a face, and both were blessed with faces to remember. The army officer who'd door-stepped Stark in the station reception and the girl . . . She'd been hanging around the nurses' station on Tuesday evening when Stark was out for the count, she'd been in the Princess of Wales pub and she fitted Stark's description to a T.

'I'm his clinician,' she managed to get in. 'I have every right –'

'Hospital staff only, miss,' Dearing interrupted politely. 'No excep–'

'Never mind that,' interrupted the officer brusquely. 'This is a military matter, Sergeant. Now stand aside.'

Dearing had stood in uniform too many years to be daunted by her ilk. 'You're welcome to take up the matter with my superiors,' he replied calmly. The MPs stiffened ominously.

'Perhaps I can help.' Fran stepped in, smiling.

The officer looked her up and down coolly. 'And you are?'

Fran flashed her warrant card. 'Detective Sergeant Millhaven. Captain Pierson, I presume. This is a civilian hospital, Captain, and the sergeant here will stand aside when ordered to and not before. Rest assured, no one is getting in or out of Constable Stark's room without a hospital badge. You will be allowed to see him during visitors' hours *if* the nursing staff allow it.' She turned away from the woman before she could voice the protest evident in her face. 'And now Kelly, I presume?'

The girl nodded in surprise. 'I'm sorry, do I know you?'

'I'm afraid the same applies to you, unless your urgency is indeed clinical, in which case you must take it up with the nurse here.' To her credit she looked fit to object vehemently but the captain got in first.

'Now look here –'

'I have looked,' Fran interrupted firmly. 'I have seen, and I have spoken. And if you don't like it you are both welcome to have your superiors speak to mine.' Neither woman looked ready to back down one inch. 'Or,' Fran smiled, 'we can sort this out pleasantly over a coffee, like the capable women we are.'

34

Various people came to see Stark. The consultant, the anaes-
thetist, a physiotherapist, then an orderly with a wheelchair to
collect him for his appointment. It took him a moment to
grasp that Doc Hazel meant to make good on her threat.
Stark was wheeled into her office in his tatty hospital
dressing-gown with only his hospital gown beneath. He felt
exposed and embarrassed and hungry. Always hungry with
Hazel. Two of his least favourite things. At least his appetite
was resurfacing.

'You have secrets,' said Hazel, without preamble.

'Not any more,' he replied.

'I find that doubtful. I take it you kept this one from your
employer.'

'I kept it from everyone.'

'Do you wonder about your motive there?' she asked.

'I was under orders.'

'Most people would confide in someone, friends, loved
ones . . .'

'Military orders don't leave wriggle room.' A convenient lie.

'Even so.'

'You think everyone had a right to know?' Of course she did
but she wouldn't say so. She'd couch it in another question.

'Don't you?'

Stark made a pained expression. 'Right doesn't come into it.'

'It's bound to impact on –'

'Of course it will,' Stark interrupted impatiently. 'But telling
people sooner wouldn't mitigate that. Nothing will. The only

thing I could control was how soon I had to deal with the consequences.'

'What consequences?'

'The inevitable fall-out, the bullshit, the misinterpretation –'

'Misinterpretation?'

'Yes . . .' Stark rolled his eyes. 'How did I just know you were going to write that down?'

Hazel laid her pen flat on her notes. 'Because it's an interesting choice of word, and you know it. One I find curious, as you probably knew I would. Do you mind if I ask you again about that day?'

'I mind. I minded the first time I was asked and every time since.'

'I wonder if you actually enjoy it.'

Stark was stunned. How dare she?

'Feel compelled to, is perhaps closer to the mark,' she allowed.

'I'm compelled by you, by this process!'

'Consciously, perhaps, but there's no disputing that unconsciously your brain takes you back there almost every night, when you're not confounding it with medically unwise cocktails, that is.'

So she knew, or had guessed. No doubt she couldn't wait to start tugging at *that* thread. But that wasn't where she was going for now. 'We're back to survivor's guilt, are we?' he said.

'Were we ever away from it?'

'You tell me,' said Stark.

'Okay.' Hazel counted points on her fingers as she spoke. 'The nightmares; your visiting the dead men's families; your fixation on the mother and boy; your unrelenting drive to recover faster than medically cautioned; your decision to move away from family, friends, colleagues, to start again alone against the advice of both your physio and psychotherapist; your refusal to face up to your spiralling debilitation since that point; and, my personal favourite, walking around on a broken pelvis.'

'I didn't know it was broken.'

'You knew it hurt and that it was getting worse. Did you think you deserved it?'

'Can't you do any better than that?' asked Stark, exasperated. Christ, he was weary of her fat-fingered fumbling!

'We've talked about why you might be putting yourself through all this. We've talked about guilt. You've acknowledged it. But you haven't accepted it,' said Hazel, bluntly.

'Of course I have,' replied Stark, in surprise.

'Intellectually perhaps.'

'You think I haven't, what, taken it to heart?'

'Have you?'

'Are you deliberately trying to provoke me?'

'Perhaps it isn't guilt,' suggested Hazel. 'After all, you've said yourself they weren't friends of yours.'

Stark's rage exploded. 'Sweet Jesus, woman!' Tears were welling. 'Can't you understand? What fucking difference does it make whether they're friends or you fucking hate them? You fight alongside them! You'd die for them! They're not friends, they're family, from the second they take the coin to their blood-choked last breath, you *witless fucking cow!*' He was on his feet, spittle on his lips, fighting the urge to lash out, to kick the table over, pull down the shelves of unthumbed reference books on her stupid fucking head, to smash, to beat some sense into her.

He stood there quivering, his fractured pelvis adding its top-note to the chorus of pain.

Hazel's eyes were wide with fear and incomprehension, her face flushed, her hand on the panic-alarm button that hung around her neck.

'*Don't,*' he managed to say, holding a hand up, palm outwards, the other clasping his hip. Slowly, jaw clenched, fists curled, chest heaving, he dialled it down. 'Don't,' he said eventually, as calmly as he could manage. 'I'm done. We're done.'

Her eyes were still wide; her hand still hovered near the button.

As the fury ebbed away, the thought of having scared her left him sick and ashamed. Loss of temper was weakness, the selfish act of the child. This poor woman was probably one step closer to signing off long-term sick for stress because of him. Clueless, incompetent to the point of harm, she didn't deserve that and, God knew, the public sector had too many already.

'I'm sorry. I was out of order. Please don't be scared.' He took another deep breath, leaning on his good leg, teeth gritted, unwilling to move. 'Look, this is getting us nowhere. I'm sorry to be blunt, but you don't have a clue. You've never dealt with PTSD before, have you?' She wasn't about to admit it but she admirably managed not to avoid his eyes. 'Look, why don't you see if there's someone you could refer me to?' Dump me on, he thought privately. Had she the nous to seize the chance?

'Yes,' she agreed, scribbling on her notepad to hide her relief. 'Yes, perhaps that would help. A colleague . . . I could confer with my peers and find the best person . . . soon have you ship-shape, send you a new appointment . . . *blah, blah, blah,*' she finished sarcastically.

Stark was shocked. She wasn't smiling, but she was holding his gaze and . . . there was something in her eyes. Triumph, almost.

'Feel better?' she asked. 'I know I do,' she continued, before he could think. 'Though for a moment there I thought I might be looking for a decorator or even a dentist.' Now she smiled. 'Why don't you sit down before you fall?' Unbalanced, he complied. 'I wonder if you realize that's the first emotion you've ever displayed in this room?'

'I –'

'I also think it might be the first time you've told me the truth.'

'Wh–? I've never lied to you! I've always answered your questions. Last week I sat here and unburdened my bloody soul!'

'You sat and talked for a solid hour without telling me a single thing I didn't already know.'

Stark was gobsmacked. 'How can you say that? I told you everything!'

'You told me everything you thought I wanted to hear.'

'And you sat and wrote it all down.'

'I wasn't writing what you *said*, Joseph, I was writing what it told me.'

'And what was that?'

'That you think I'm an idiot.'

Stark blinked.

She cocked her head at his surprise. 'That even after all this time you're not ready to engage. That inheriting the role of man-of-the-house at a tender age fostered an imbalance in you, setting duty before desire as if that might forestall further tragedy. That to manage this you instinctively limit the number of people you allow close. But that in "taking the shilling" you unwittingly adopted new family, breaching your own barriers and exposing you once more to bereavement beyond your control. That the horrors you experienced, including the marketplace bombing you never mention, played a significant role in your SAS application and repeat volunteering. That physical incapacity has further undermined your sense of potency, forcing long-suppressed emotion to surface as simmering anger you would rather lose another finger than express.

'That all this has left you resenting any help offered you, that you now link remedy with cause as if by holding the former at bay you can exert some control over events past and present. And that you're in serious danger of sliding further into self-destructive behaviour simply to feel as if your life belongs to you and not the memory of those you think you failed.'

'How dare y–'

'You're a bright man, Joseph, but a little too capable of knowing it. I may be an idiot in some ways but not in this.' And suddenly she didn't look it. 'Your therapist at Headley Court warned me you were a tough nut to crack. He thought my experience with trauma victims would be useful.'

Stark blinked again. 'Your –'

'PTSD isn't always combat-related.'

They locked eyes, appraising each other. For his part Stark saw for the first time that she had the upper hand completely. 'You've been playing dumb, all this time. This has all been a wind-up.'

'He also mentioned you had a discernible superiority complex that might prove useful.'

'Christ! Whatever happened to doctor–patient confidentiality?'

'I am your doctor. *We* are your doctors. What exactly did you think was in this file?' she said, tapping the thick folder.

Stark was still reeling. 'Aren't you supposed to be like the Magic Circle or something? You're not supposed to show dupes how you dupe them.'

'There's little we won't stoop to, Joseph, if it's called for. And I think it's time you and I showed each other what's up our sleeves, don't you?'

35

The post-operative nursing care was spookily attentive. Stark was a curiosity. He coasted through the first week in a depressingly familiar stand-by mental state: meds, meals, blood pressure, wound inspection, pay TV, books, naps, maternal visits. To avoid the misery of a full pelvic cast he was confined to his bed. Groombridge popped in with Fran on day two, talking about the case to avoid predictable awkwardness.

Naveen had been granted bail with electronic monitoring, the rest remanded into custody. CPS were pressing them all to plead guilty. Nikki Cockcroft's barrister had pressed hard for bail, claiming Nikki's 'pink-haired bitch' comment was based on rumour circulating after the event, a thin lie but a canny one, and that everything else was circumstantial or the result of Kyle Gibbs's action alone.

'A dead accomplice is even better than a stranger in a pub.' Fran laughed. 'I honestly thought the judge might let her out. You should've seen her face when he refused!'

Stark wished he'd been there but was too uncomfortable to share Fran's mirth. 'Still, a thin case. What will happen?'

Groombridge shrugged. 'It depends on whether Paula Stevens is perceived as a credible witness. CPS think they have it. I guess we'll just have to wait and see.'

'And what about Paula?'

'Murder looks flimsy, so CPS added manslaughter due to provocation to cover all the bases until the outcome of the sexual-assault case is known. In the meantime she was bailed into the custody of the local battered women's refuge.'

And in the meantime she faced the prospect of giving evidence against her attackers and the subsequent cross-examination. The cold eye of justice Maggs had tried to divert. 'And Maggs?'

'That's up to him, I reckon. Anyone else and I'd say fifty-fifty.'

'Liam Dawson?'

Groombridge pursed his lips in displeasure. 'Naveen Hussein still won't press charges — soils himself at the mere mention. SCD7's racketeering project team have been talking to Dawson, putting pressure on, but last I heard they weren't getting any-where.' Groombridge wouldn't be feeling Dawson's collar any time soon. Sometimes the big fish got away, but the pain in his eyes said those were the ones you never forgot.

The following week Stark pleaded with his doctors to be allowed to attend the first of the hearings. They laughed at the notion, of course, and he had to wait for Fran to fill him in.

On the first four assaults Harrison Collier, Martin Mun-roe, Paul Thompson and Tim Bowes had pleaded guilty to grievous bodily harm, Section 20, and assault without intent, and received sentences from six months to three years for each. The judge ordered that their sentences be served con-secutively. Colin Messenger and Tyler Wantage had pleaded guilty to GBH Section 18, assault *with* intent, and got sixteen years apiece. Naveen Hussein pleaded guilty to Section 20 as an accomplice, claiming duress, and as a juvenile received only six months in total, with a concurrent six months for trying to board a plane with his cousin's passport, for which his mother got three months suspended. He still faced charges relating to Internet crime when the much larger case came to trial, but he insisted Kyle and Nikki had forced him to upload the videos.

All had pleaded not guilty to the murder of Alfred Ladd and sexual assault on Paula as joint principals. They would await that trial in their prison cells. Nikki pleaded not guilty on all charges and would await trial on remand.

Other than that, the second and third weeks were a return to the bad old days of mind-numbing tedium and discomfort, plus awkward conversations with Doc Hazel.

On the Friday of week three the cast on his hand was replaced with a removable splint and, after demonstrating he was an old hand on crutches, he was discharged. Late that evening Fran smuggled him out of the hospital via a secondary delivery bay hidden in the back of an unmarked van. The press had slithered away but there had been two further attempts to sneak past security. A nurse had been suspended for taking a picture of him on her phone and selling it to a tabloid.

Streets away they switched into Fran's car and headed for Hampshire and the dubious sanctuary of his mother's house.

It didn't take long for news of his escape to leak. The following morning a reporter door-stepped his mother and received short shrift. A pair of photographers hung around all day and the curtains had to remain drawn. Despite the crutches, he might've paced like a caged animal were his mother not there to insist he rest.

His sister, Louise, visited with the kids but friends and old comrades were politely told that he needed peace, quiet and rest. There was no turning away Colonel Mattherson or Captain Pierson, of course, or the CPS.

On the day of Maggs's trial the press were back on the lawn. A dozen local uniforms held them at bay as Stark was whisked away in a van. Paparazzi on a motorbike tried to snap his picture as they raced along the motorway but were pulled over by the unmarked car trailing them.

As a material witness, Stark was forbidden to contact Maggs. To his dismay the murder charge hadn't been dropped. A secondary charge of manslaughter due to provocation was entered, though Maggs had maintained his not-guilty plea to both.

As Stark took his seat in the witness stand Maggs nodded to him but nothing else. The questions were simple, the cross-examination painless. He had worried that everything would be dragged up, from the media storm to the painkillers and whisky, but the truth was he was insignificant to the case.

That night he stayed in Fran's spare room. The press were watching his flat. His neighbour had confirmed that the lift was still broken. He expected to find Fran's flat devoid of life, a barren monument to her skewed work–life balance, empty fridge, pristine flat-pack furniture. Within seconds he realized he'd completely misjudged her. Almost every wall was lined with family photos, Fran posing with parents, brothers and their wives, endless beaming nieces and nephews and Caribbean relatives of every shape and size. Many had been taken in Barbados. Her fridge was full to bursting with fresh ingredients, many of which Stark didn't recognize, and the tiny kitchen was a-clutter with the kind of robust cooking paraphernalia that spoke of practicality and heavy use. He was hard pressed to remember her consuming anything other than coffee and a Danish in his company.

She settled him with a beer and the TV remote and set about the noisy preparation of flying-fish with cou-cou and plantain to a secret family recipe. When it was done she plonked the tray of stunning food on his lap. 'There you go, Constable Sideways.' She smirked.

Stark grimaced. She'd been digging. She'd done well to get this gem, given the lockdown there had to be around his records right now. She was a formidable terrier.

'Funny, most of your old comrades agreed that you weren't really a nickname kind of bloke. They didn't make that sound flattering. But most agreed that if you had to have one it would be Sideways. I found the story behind it quite revealing.'

Private Sideways. Of course she'd winkled out the full story. Captain Delaney had not meant it as a term of endearment. The exercise was a standard one: defend a poor position for as long as possible against overwhelming odds. Perhaps suspecting NCO material, they had handed newly recruited Stark a corporal's stripe for the night and command of the defenders. Delaney had led the attackers. But when his superior force had assaulted the indefensible position they had found it abandoned. Under cover of darkness Stark had moved his force sideways up a nearby hill behind a highly defensible ridge. Infuriated, Delaney had demanded they return and begin again. Stark had asked if he was therefore surrendering. When the captain had said he most definitely was *not*, Stark had sent a skirmishing force to break the stand-off with a sudden burst of fire. Under the wry eye of his major, Captain Delaney had had little option but to lead his assault uphill.

Stark and his force were, of course, annihilated to a man, but only after several hours and after inflicting humiliating losses on the attacking side, including the captain himself. Despite eventually seeing the funny side Delaney had pegged Stark for a smart Alec and never let him forget it. His peers had never let him forget it either and on subsequent night-time exercises someone would often cry out, 'Where's Stark gone?' to which others would answer, 'Sideways again!' Half of the officers and NCOs he'd had since then seemed to have heard the story. Infamy is not a trait desirable to the enlisted man. All you could do was keep your head down.

'Wow, this is fantastic,' he said, after one mouthful. Without the OxyContin, his appetite had returned with a vengeance and big, complementary flavours like this were just his kind of food.

Fran raised an eyebrow at the obvious change of subject. 'Not too much chilli for you?'

'No, it's perfect,' he replied, tucking in.

'I put in what I'd give my three-year-old niece.'

Stark ate another forkful, murmuring appreciation. 'You're a *magician*! The world should know.' His flattery coaxed the beginnings of a smile from her. 'I bet Marcus likes Caribbean food,' he added sweetly.

'Shut up and eat!'

Maggs took the stand and stood to attention as he was questioned. He admitted punching Gibbs in the throat, adding only that he had a right to defend himself. He was invited by the defence barrister to say he was defending the girl too, but replied that he'd already told her to run and believed she had. He was accused by the prosecution barrister of a calculated act. Maggs agreed. The punch, he said, had come after Gibbs had stabbed him but he made no attempt to link the two. He had been entirely focused on disarming the boy and, yes, he had known the blow had the capacity, at least, to kill. Stark couldn't tell what the jury thought.

'Where do you live?' asked the wigged accuser, conversationally.

'Somewhere dry, quiet and, if possible, warm,' replied Maggs. 'Preferably with decent passing trade and pleasing views of the nearest off-licence.' There were chuckles around the court.

The barrister smiled too. 'How long have you lived in this way?'

'Twenty years or so, on and off.'

'Why?' asked the barrister.

'Because the world has little use for me any more, and I little use for it.' Again there were chuckles, but Stark began to worry.

'You had heard about the recent attacks on your brethren. Had you discussed or considered what you might do if confronted yourself?'

'Discussed, no, considered, yes.'

'Had you resolved to defend yourself?'

'I'm not the kind who needs to resolve on that.'

'No. Had you then considered the lengths you'd go to, if required?'

'You either defend yourself or you don't. The lengths depend on your enemy.'

'Your enemy? You considered Kyle Gibbs your enemy?'

'I did.'

'What about the rest of your attackers?'

'Them too.'

'You broke one boy's arm, another's nose?'

'Yes.'

'You didn't kill them. Why not? Weren't they your enemy too?'

'I've said they were.'

'So you disable some and kill others?'

'M'lord!' The defence barrister shot to his feet. 'The coroner's report does *not* conclude that the blow was fatal. Kyle Gibbs was stabbed to death by Paula Stevens.'

The prosecution was ready for this. 'M'lord, as has already been discussed at great length, the report equally does not show that the blow would *not* have proved fatal and the accused has admitted to knowing it might.'

Both barristers had made their point; the judge instructed Maggs to respond.

'They weren't the real threat. I served them out as a deterrent.'

'Why did you not "serve out" Kyle as a deterrent?'

'The other two were his deterrent. He didn't listen.'

'He didn't listen. You also claim that you verbally warned the group of your training. What did you say exactly?'

'I said to walk on. I wasn't a tourist, I was a paratrooper.'

'None of your alleged attackers have confirmed your warning.'

'Have they confirmed standing by while their mate tried to rape a defenceless slip of a girl?' retorted Maggs.

The barrister ignored the question. 'What do you claim was their response to your warning?'

'They laughed.'

'And that made you angry?'

'I was angry the second I saw that little shite pinning a girl to the ground, fumbling for his dick!'

'The accused will moderate his language,' warned the judge.

'So you were angry, furious perhaps, demented with rage.'

'M'lord!' protested the defence.

'Withdrawn, m'lord,' conceded the prosecution, smoothly. 'So angry your one thought was to "serve them out". For insulting you, for what you thought they'd done to other homeless people and what you thought they were trying to do to Paula Stevens.'

'*Trying to do?*' spluttered Maggs. 'They'd done enough –'

'"They'd done enough!"' interrupted the barrister. 'They had to be stopped – by any means.'

'Yes.'

The barrister let this sink in before asking his next question. 'You display no remorse for the killing?'

'*M'lord!*' protested the defence.

'I'll rephrase the question, m'lord,' said the prosecution. 'Mr Maggs, do you regret the death of Kyle Gibbs?'

'No.'

'He deserved it, you think?'

'That's not what I said,' said Maggs, impatiently.

'Yet it might explain why you made no effort to seek help for the wounded teenager.'

'He was beyond help,' said Maggs.

'Who are you to make that judgement? Are you a medical professional?'

'I'm a soldier.'

'And once a soldier always a soldier. You can judge when a life has expired, you can "serve out" justice, you decide which youth lives and which dies.'

'Who are you to do better?' demanded Maggs.

'I wouldn't presume. I wasn't there. But you were and you did what you had to do. They had to be stopped by any means necessary, they had to be served out for what they'd done and you were there to do it, to pay them back, to pay everyone back – society, the world, the Argentine junta, the British Army.'

'M'lord . . .' tried the defence, desperately.

'I've no grudge against the army,' growled Maggs, visibly angry now. The barrister was winding him up. Stark silently pleaded for Maggs not to bite.

'Your whole life is a grudge! You hate the world, you hate the army!'

'No!'

'They used you up and when you were broken they threw you away like a soiled rag.'

'*That was the bloody MoD!*'

'Language, sir!' growled the judge again.

The prosecution hardly drew breath. 'Yes, the Ministry of Defence. You hate them too! Your whole life has been about nothing but hate, for thirty years! Why, sir?'

No, screamed Stark silently, as Maggs leant forward and planted his big fists on the dock.

'Because they fucking lied to us,' spat Maggs.

'*Language, sir!*' barked the judge.

'They wave their precious Military Covenant but it's just *bullshit.*'

'Restrain yourself, sir,' warned the judge.

Maggs paid no heed. 'Every year the same news stories of woeful equipment, appalling family accommodation and shameful veteran support – every time met with MoD denials. Then nothing happens till the same story pops up again and everyone acts like it's some shocking scandal, like it's news. Where's the moral fucking outrage?'

'One more profane outburst and I will hold you in contempt!' shouted the judge.

'You already do!' yelled Maggs, with a wild look in his eyes. 'You, the MoD, the sleepwalking public, you "good people of the jury"! You already do! Whining about legality and lack of exit strategy while poor fucks like him are getting blown to hell.' Maggs jabbed a finger towards Stark.

'Sit down now, sir!' shouted the judge.

'Bleeding into the sand and mud, watching their mates die begging for help, and for what? For you, you thankless fucks!'

'SIT DOWN NOW!' bellowed the judge, beet-faced, slamming his leather-bound notes on the desk, gunshot loud. If this were an American courtroom drama he'd be banging his gavel like a man possessed, thought Stark, but contrary to popular belief, British judges didn't use them. 'Sit down! This instant! Confine your answers to the questions and not one stray word, do you understand?'

Maggs glared venomously round the silent, shocked room. 'Ask yourself, all of you, would you fight for you?'

'You are in *contempt*, sir!' ordered the judge.

Maggs sat down, fuming.

'No further questions, m'lord,' said the prosecution barrister, smugly, casting a knowing look at the jury.

Stark's head dropped into his hands.

36

The jury retired to deliberate. Fran spirited Stark through a side door into the judge's antechamber where Groombridge had arranged to keep him away from the press.

'That didn't go well,' said Groombridge, joining them.

Stark was still shaken. 'Christ, Guv, I knew he wanted his say but I thought he might've been dissuaded since then. I could've dissuaded him –'

'He had been, lad. I spoke to his barrister at great length. But the prosecution knew what buttons to press and that's that.'

'What'll happen?'

'Not guilty of murder. Guilty of manslaughter with provocation.'

'Really?'

Groombridge nodded. 'The CPS knew what they were doing. That's what they wanted and they'll get it. The rest is down to the judge.'

'He hasn't made much of a friend there, Guv,' commented Fran.

'No.'

'What will he get?' asked Stark.

'Strictly speaking, with the high degree of provocation including violent assault, he should get no more than three years.'

'But?'

'But with military training, lack of remorse, his evident fury . . .'

'Not to mention contempt of court,' added Fran.

'Indeed.'

'Was he right?' asked Fran. 'Is all that stuff true?'

Stark sighed. 'Up to a point.'

It was too big a conversation for now. The bottom line was that in peacetime people resented paying taxes for defence and, as Maggs himself had said, to the majority of voters modern wars felt no different from peace. The MoD had to prioritize spending, like any other ministry. That didn't make it any more excusable, just perennial, and Maggs knew the futility of railing against it. Despite thirty years of bitterness, his answer to his own question would always be the same as Stark's and most other serviceperson's. Would you fight for you? Perhaps not, but I will.

Two days later Fran drove out of the back gate of the court-house, tooting her horn angrily at the photographers who tried to get in the way. 'Five years, minimum three? For manslaughter with provocation?' She shook her head for the umpteenth time. 'While proper villains like Liam Dawson walk scot-free.'

'As you said, Maggs did little to befriend the judge,' said Groombridge, sadly.

Through his own dismay Stark was surprised by their sympathy for Maggs's plight.

'Grounds for appeal, Guv?' asked Fran.

'I think so, but will Maggs pursue one? What do you think, Stark?'

'I don't know, Guv. Not for his own sake, it seems. I suppose it depends on whether he's done making his point.'

'When's *your* fifteen minutes?' asked Groombridge, though surely he knew well enough.

'Wednesday.'

'You ready?'

'No.' As Pierson seemed to take morbid delight in telling him.

'Scared?'

'He's immune to pain and fear, Guv, you know that,' said Fran, sarcastically.

If only, sighed Stark silently.

On Wednesday Captain Pierson arrived at Stark's mother's with two burly Red Caps, Royal Military Police, who made short work of keeping the photographers at bay. Monkey Hangers, regular soldiers called them, shortened to Monkeys, a reference to an infamous incident in Napoleonic Hartlepool; the town's residents had also suffered and embraced the term. As a policeman Stark shouldn't have disliked them, but as a soldier it had been the standard sentiment. That little irony did not lift his spirits.

They drove sedately up the M3 and into Wellington Barracks on Birdcage Walk, where Stark was led into a small, plain room to change into his brand new No. 2 dress uniform. It fitted perfectly even though several weeks of voracious eating had begun to fill him out to something of his former self, but one glaring error sang out.

Pierson knocked and came in. 'There,' she said. 'I suppose that's at least made you look halfway a soldier.'

'But this tunic has three stripes,' pointed out Stark, anxiously.

'You were wearing three on the day so you'll damn well stand up in three for this.'

'But that isn't right,' he insisted.

'That is not for you to say, *Acting Sergeant* Stark,' she replied firmly. Stark recognized the tone: pushing his protest would not go well.

He had to admit Pierson's tailor had done a grand job, but the crutches spoilt the effect. 'How about that walking stick?' he asked, giving ground to attempt a flanking manoeuvre – Acting Sergeant Sideways. Thus far Pierson had taken the same line as his doctors on this topic. Strictly speaking, the rules said no weight-bearing for another week.

'I shan't ignore common sense and medical advice to soothe your vanity.'

'This isn't about vanity and you know it.'

'Don't presume to tell me what I know.'

'If you want me to stand up like a soldier you should let me face this on my own two feet,' he insisted.

'You're as stubborn as you're stupid.'

Stark wasn't ready to concede the point but she was too intent on tutting and adjusting his uniform to listen. When her disdainful expression had eased into a mere frown, she led him to the waiting car, ridiculous for a journey of less than a minute. Stark had hoped to walk it but the crutches and press hawks made that impossible.

They were shown in through an informal side door and led through a maze of intricate corridors and rooms to a large antechamber where Stark was separated into a small side room and left alone to stew. His mouth was dry. He stood there on crutches and one leg, feeling sick.

Pierson reappeared and wordlessly held out a handsome walking cane. The tip was silver, the tapering shaft fashioned from a rich brown wood with a natural amber variegation, like tiger's eye stone but wavier, warmer. There was a triple band of silver near the top and the curved silver handle, which seemed moulded to his hand, was fashioned in the shape of a leaping tiger.

'Snakewood,' said Pierson. 'Gets its name from the grain but I think the stripes are more tiger-like. All rather apt.' Stark's regiment was known as the Tigers, due to its gold-on-blue Royal Tiger arm badge, a two-hundred-year-old honour for service in India by its Royal Hampshire Regiment forebear.

'Where?'

'Don't ask,' she said firmly. 'And for God's sake have a quick practice. If you fall on your scrawny arse I'll have you shot. I can't believe I've let you talk me into this.'

Stark was amazed, too, and grateful: this wasn't about vanity, it was about pride. He tentatively placed his left foot down. The muscles were atrophied, but the physios had been manipulating his joints to keep the tendons limber and he'd been trying it out on the quiet. It felt like jelly and he had to take most of the weight on the cane, but he stood. He took a faltering turn around the room.

'Jesus!' hissed Pierson, as he half stumbled.

'I'm all right. It's not as bad as I thought.' He took a few more turns and grew in confidence. 'Will I do?'

She didn't look happy. 'Stand straight,' she ordered, fussing over the uniform again. 'You'll have to, I suppose.'

A knock came at the door and an officer told them it was time. Stark was ushered past the milling faces to stand in front of a closed double door.

'Thank you,' he said quietly to Pierson.

'Stand like a soldier,' she whispered. 'And don't fuck up!'

The door opened, silent as a fanfare of doom. Then a voice boomed in the vacuum, 'Sergeant Joseph Stark, Third Battalion, Princess of Wales's Royal Regiment!'

Pierson pressed the small of his back and he took five steps forward to stand beside a senior naval officer in full dress uniform.

To his right, in the huge, sparkling Buckingham Palace ballroom, hundreds of people watched in absolute silence. Somewhere back there his mother and sister were probably crying under their new hats. To his left, behind a lectern, stood the Lord Chamberlain in full regalia. Ahead and to the left the Queen waited, flanked by two Gurkha orderly officers and five Yeomen of the Guard.

In a clear, powerful voice the Lord Chamberlain read aloud.

'For services in Afghanistan: the Victoria Cross.'

37

Pain flared in Stark's hip, leg and shoulder as those surreal syllables pierced his bubble of self-consciousness. There seemed to be no way to pin the flat, colourless words to those distant moments of frantic desperation, fear, pain and death, nothing to link them with the terrified mother and her child and how close he'd come to shooting them. How he'd stopped his trigger finger he'd never know; in his dreams he failed to again and again. He'd intended to fire, had begun to, all his fear and training screamed at him to do so, but in that last desperate millisecond another part of his brain had intervened. The thought made him shudder. Everything about that day made him shudder.

The IED had shunted the Snatch Land Rover six feet sideways, knocking him flat and very nearly tipped it over on him. Staggering up, he had shaken his head at the ringing in his left ear. His right was blown, adding to his disorientation. He felt something trickling down his face and neck, put up a hand and stared at blood on his fingers, confused, confused also to see half of his little finger gone where he still held the neck of the plastic water bottle, just the neck. There was no pain. He was told later that a piece of the shrapnel had pinned his Kevlar helmet to his skull but he'd felt nothing at the time.

He yanked open the door of the badly damaged vehicle. The IED had ripped into the far side of the cab. Walker must've died instantly. Smith lay sprawled across the bench seat, hardly less bloody. A quick check found a weak pulse. He groaned but didn't stir.

Something made Stark look up, a noise above the ringing. Then another. Bullet, he thought absently. A bullet just hit the cab. Looking out through the blackened, crazed windscreen and wisps of black smoke leaking from the engine compartment, Stark noted his comrades ducking for cover. The sound of AK47 fire and yelling finally pierced his dulled wits.

Ambush!

He grabbed the radio handset to call in the contact but it hadn't survived the explosion. Cursing, he backed out of the cab and looked around for Collins. He was kneeling in a closed doorway across the street. Seeing Stark move towards him, Collins yelled and pointed wildly. On a rooftop fifty yards away three figures were firing into the street around him. Bullets rang into the panels of the Snatch and the ground just metres from him. The unmistakable shape of a rocket-propelled grenade peeped over the parapet of another house. Stark instinctively knelt and shot the man aiming it. Two other figures appeared, trying to wrestle the launcher from the dead man, but bullets knocked them both back. Stark couldn't tell if he'd shot them or someone else had.

He backed hastily into the partial cover of the Snatch and bellowed '*Man down!*' at the top of his lungs. '*Two men down! Medic!*'

The call was repeated down the line.

'Walking?' Collins demanded, meaning walking wounded.

They locked eyes and Stark shook his head. 'Alpha!' The highest priority category for the Nine-Liner radio medevac request. 'Comms down, boss!' He pointed at the vehicle.

Collins nodded and screamed across the street at whoever had the hand-held radio.

Suddenly bullets hit Stark's side of the vehicle. They were now taking fire from two directions, while at the far end of the street he saw a beaten-up white pickup truck being pushed into place as a roadblock-cum-barricade. Their position was untenable. Collins was shouting something but Stark couldn't make it out. Others too. The gist had to be 'Let's get the fuck out of here!'

Hunkered against the vehicle, Stark could feel the engine still running. He tried what was left of the driver's door but it wouldn't budge. Running round to the other side again, he dragged Smith and Walker towards him and clambered over both into the driving seat, fought the stick into gear, stamped on the accelerator and let out the clutch. The heroic vehicle responded. He braked central to the positions the others had taken up each side of the street and yelled out of the imploded window at Collins. They didn't need telling twice. Bodies were suddenly clambering into the rear, shouting, swearing. Collins appeared at the side door and froze, staring at Walker and Smith. Shoving them both towards the middle he just about got in and slammed the door, shouting back for a head count. Eight: everyone, no more hit. Bullets were impacting like hailstones on a tin roof but the Snatch's armour was enough for small-arms fire. It didn't cover every inch of the cab, though, and the door beside Stark wasn't up to much any more. He fought to find reverse but it was either damaged or he was trying too hard.

'RPG!' shouted Collins, pointing. On the roof another Taliban had picked up the fallen weapon. Stark fought it into first and did his best to stamp the accelerator through the floor. They lurched forward just as the RPG struck where they'd stood, the explosion rocking the whole vehicle forward on its suspension. Still taking fire, rattling and squeaking, as if half of the bolts were missing, the battered Snatch accelerated towards the roadblock, weaving despite Stark's efforts to keep it straight. God help them if there were more buried IEDs ahead. Bullets impacted on the remains of the windscreen now, one right in front of Stark's face, further restricting his view.

A pothole made the twisted vehicle judder with the grinding shriek of metal against metal. Smith groaned again as Collins called to him. Tyler was shouting into the radio over general yelling and the sharp retort of bullet strikes rattling through the din, all remote behind the monotone whine in Stark's left ear.

Flames appeared around the buckled bonnet and then the dashboard. They licked across Stark's hands but he gripped the wheel for grim death. Collins grabbed a hand-held extinguisher and put out the fire, filling the cab with white gas. Half-blind, Stark watched another RPG race across their path and explode against a building just ahead of them, showering the Snatch with rubble.

He gunned the accelerator, shifted gear, aiming for the little gap between the back of the pickup and the wall.

'*Brace!*' he yelled.

The Taliban beside the pickup dived aside as the Snatch crashed through into open ground.

'*That way!*' bellowed Collins, pointing diagonally across the wide square of wasteland.

But the Snatch was mortally hurt now, its steering clunky and unresponsive. It died less than two hundred metres further on, in the centre of the open stretch of ground with buildings dotted around the perimeter. Stark tried frantically to restart the engine but the dashboard was on fire again and Collins was shouting '*Out! Out! Out!*'

Collins was already out, dragging Smith with him. Stark climbed over Walker, then dragged him out too.

Bullets were whipping past, the crack-thump of aimed fire passing close by. Collins ordered them to make a run for it in the direction of the combat outpost and away from fire. Stark bent to lift Walker but Gaskin shoved him aside and threw Walker over one shoulder.

And so they ran for it, jumping down a low wall, racing towards the nearest building, a house. Stark and Collins were there first – Collins kicked the door in and Stark came within a heartbeat of killing an innocent woman and her small boy.

Instead, Collins hurried them out through a side door and away just as the others staggered in. Stark would always wonder what happened to the mother and child, but would never know. All he could do was try to picture them sitting beside the Helmand river enjoying a quiet moment, laughing together, fear forgotten. All he could do was hope.

Then came the hammer blow. They were a man short. Tyler. They could see him on the ground beside the smoking Snatch. He was moving.

Collins asked for volunteers and Gaskin and Stark stepped forward. Collins bluntly told Stark to piss off, but Stark pleaded that his injuries were superficial, hiding his hands from view. The two privates – only later did Stark learn their names, Lovelace and Khan – were frantically working on Smith so Collins reluctantly nodded. They ditched their superfluous kit and ran for it as the bullets whipped past. Terry Taliban probably couldn't believe his luck.

Sustained fire and an incoming RPG forced them to dive the last metres to the low wall, roughly halfway. The RPG detonated to the right and Collins cursed in pain. Shrapnel had clipped his thigh, not bad, but enough that he had to stay put. Under his covering fire Stark and Gaskin counted three, clambered up and ran.

Tyler was no longer moving as they reached the relative cover of the Snatch. The cab was ablaze now, and somewhere in the back there was an unexploded IED. Stark began firing on the Taliban while Gaskin dragged the limp Tyler behind the vehicle, hoisted him over one shoulder and set off. He'd gone no more than ten paces before he went down with a bullet through his right leg.

Stark turned to help. Gaskin shouted at him to take Tyler but a quick glance confirmed the sergeant was already dead, so Stark hoisted the protesting Gaskin on to one shoulder instead and set off. Gaskin was a big, heavy man and Stark fell as he tried to jump down the wall by Collins, earning a flurry of vitriol from Gaskin. Ignoring his redoubled protests, Stark hoisted him up again and yomped back to the house where he dumped him unceremoniously, turned and set off back, passing Collins to get Tyler.

He wasn't really thinking, just doing. Maybe it was shock of some kind but there was a strange, detached belief that he was invulnerable. And there was anger too. They were just trying to take their wounded and run away but the spiteful pricks were still shooting. It's ridiculous to think of war in terms of fair play, but a line was being crossed and Stark was infuriated.

He grabbed Tyler by the body armour and dragged him back towards cover. He was about to lift him when he saw it. The Bowman radio, their only lifeline, on the ground where Tyler had first fallen. He ran towards it but bullets drove him back. He ran out again, snatched it up and dived back into cover, heart racing.

Kneeling in the cover of the burning Snatch, he called in a revised Nine-Liner and air-support request in case he didn't get the radio to the others. Tyler was smaller than Gaskin but Stark struggled to lift him, fatigue setting in. Cursing it he set off, noticeably slower. Behind them the IED finally tore the Snatch apart, the explosion nearly knocking Stark down. At least the surprise stopped Terry firing for a moment. The wall drop caught him out again and he only just avoided falling. It seemed as if, with each trip, distance and height doubled. Collins shouted, 'Get a *fucking* move on!'

He dumped Tyler beside Gaskin, who was shouting angrily in pain as Khan worked on him. Stark thrust the radio at Lovelace and turned to go back for Collins, only to find the major manfully hopping towards them, dragging his wounded leg.

By now fire was coming not just from behind but also from a building off to one side. Collins tripped and fell. Someone tried to grab Stark's arm but he was already on his way. Collins was up in a kneeling stance returning fire calmly and efficiently as Stark reached him. He threw his arm around Stark's shoulder and they set off together, Collins hobbling and singing a ribald song between laboured breaths. Bullets whizzed by but they were half way – they were going to make it.

Then a warning yell, and the RPG exploded right beside them.

Stark tried to stand but his left side, thigh and hip had been peppered. One look at Collins and it was obvious he wasn't going anywhere either. Stark managed to kneel and shuffle over to shield Collins from the increasingly accurate fire. Bullets were striking all around and another RPG whooshed overhead, exploding against an innocent house.

Unable to do anything more practical, Stark resolved simply to return fire.

Simple, but not easy. The Terry in the upper window seemed happy to just point his AK47 roughly in the right direction but the fruit of his minimal efforts spat dust not twenty feet from Stark. Stark literally had to force himself not to do the same. His body cried out at him to flinch, to fire madly and duck. At least these cries out-shouted the numerous screaming pains.

Relax, breathe, aim, hold half a breath, fire, he repeated to himself, just like back on the range. The figure with the AK collapsed from sight.

In another window an RPG launcher appeared. Relax, breathe, aim, hold, fire. The black turban snapped back and the RPG whooshed up at a steep angle into the sky as its erstwhile owner fell backwards into darkness. Stark watched it climb, trying to gauge where it would land. Off to the right, he guessed, and put it from his mind.

He felt a growing nausea. Firing in the kneeling position, his blood was soaking the left leg and hip of his combats, plus a dozen other places. Blood loss was beginning to dull his mind and he raged against it. He started mumbling obscenities, venting his fury in a tight, high-pressure stream.

The RPG landed far enough away but close enough for him to feel the hot, dusty shockwave.

As he paused to reload he was aware that Lovelace and Khan had broken cover and were dragging Collins away, shouting at Stark to follow. They had no idea he couldn't stand. So he resumed firing, hoping to draw fire till they were clear, shooting at any Taliban who presented a target.

They were popping up in windows, doorways and behind walls now, 7.62mm calibre flying everywhere, dust popping up all around. From behind him the lads were sending 5.56mm calibre back the other way. Stark picked out targets one by one. Sometimes he missed, sometimes not; whichever, he remained finely balanced between hot anger and cold determination. His vision was beginning to tunnel, time stretching.

Then the line started towards him. In that split second he saw the Taliban off to one side in a first-floor window. This one was calm. This one was using his iron sights. If they'd been adjusted properly, Stark would have been on his back by now but the first rounds fell short.

Peck – the next one was closer. Peck, peck, each jet of dust closing in regular steps. Ignoring them Stark swung his sights, picked out the muzzle flash, picked out the man. Peck. Relax, breathe – peck: it made a particular sound, a bullet striking the earth inches from you. It had a synaesthetic quality, the feel of it through your boot, the jet of dust, the smell of your sweat, the metallic tang of fear in your throat all merging into one surreal, sensual stab. And even though you saw it coming, watched its predecessors erupt in a regular line towards you, there was no time to absorb the inevitable, inconceivable truth that the next one, already on its way, would fail to strike the earth behind you because you were in its path – aim, hold, fire.

The next bullet struck him in the chest. All these months

later he could still feel its path front to back, piercing him through, long healed yet fresh in the mind. Phantom-wound syndrome they said, like the sensations in his missing half-finger, like all those poor sods aching to scratch itches on lost limbs; at least his lived only in the dreams and confused awakenings.

At the time he'd just landed on his back where the bullet had carried him, knowing something was very, very wrong; he felt sick, and woozy, finding it harder to breathe, harder to concentrate. The fighting carried on around him as he lay staring up at cloudless blue. Gunfire and shouting. His heartbeats felt wrong. He was thirsty and oddly cold. And tired.

He closed his eyes and let go.

They say you don't feel fear as the darkness closes over you, that your brain is too pumped with adrenalin and denial. Stark couldn't say. He remembered only the sound of rapid heavy-calibre shaking him awake. The Taliban positions were being raked mercilessly. Turning his head, he picked out the spitting insect silhouette of an Apache attack helicopter. The cavalry. Good. He closed his eyes again.

Then there were boots beside him, soldiers dragging him, faces crowding round, shouting and swearing at him, slapping his face, hands and bloody field dressings, a tourniquet tightening on his left thigh. He remembered being told repeatedly that he was going to be okay. He remembered asking about Collins and Gaskin, not recognizing his own voice and getting no answers. He remembered opening his eyes in the medevac helicopter, the lips of the medic moving as she spoke, the grave look on her face and the hot draught through the window as they lifted into the sky and raced to Camp Bastion. And after that, nothing.

The full citation, published in supplement to the *London Gazette*, had stated:

Acting Sergeant Stark's quick thinking in extracting the vehicle from the killing zone saved the lives of all who survived, while his courage was demonstrated further in volunteering to return for the fallen casualty, belittling his injuries to do so, in carrying Corporal Gaskin to safety, returning for the body of Sergeant Tyler and recovering the vital radio, all under withering fire, in returning for Major Collins and finally in shielding him while badly wounded and calmly laying down lethal fire against a determined enemy. It is also adjudged that the ambush was prelude to an assault on Combat Outpost McKay itself, timed for maximum effect before the scheduled relief-in-place, and that by effectively halting it Acting Sergeant Stark helped prevent greater losses.

For all this, they said, he had earned a VC: for 'valour in the face of the enemy'. Stark could only wonder why he'd been singled out, for surely anger and bloody-mindedness had played more part than valour. He had done what he could, what he should, what any soldier would, and that would remain his opinion till his dying day.

38

As the Lord Chamberlain's words echoed round the ballroom, subtle classical music came to life, the naval officer tapped the small of Stark's back and he took five steps forward, turned left, bowed his head and stepped forward to stand before the Queen. A step higher than him, she took the bronze medal with its crimson ribbon from the plush cushion held out by a brigadier and, smiling warmly, hooked it on to the small brass hook secreted in the ribbon line above Stark's left breast pocket.

She spoke a few quiet words to him, then held out a hand. He shook it gently, stepped back, turned to his right and limped out of the door opposite to where he'd come in as the next recipient's name was called out.

Pierson must've darted through some back rooms to meet him. 'This way,' she whispered, leading him into another grand room.

'How did I do?' he whispered.

'Bloody shambles. I'll most likely face a court-martial.' She held out his crutches.

'Could I hang on to this a while longer?' he asked, indicating the cane.

'Don't get too attached, and for God's sake don't break it. The Duke's valet made me sign in blood.'

'The Duke?'

'Of Edinburgh.'

Stark froze. 'You're not serious?'

'Where the hell else was I supposed to rustle up a respectable cane at such short notice?' she replied, deadpan, but she was enjoying this. Stark swallowed hard. 'Here . . .' She handed him a letter stamped with his regimental badge.

'What's this?'

'Your promotion.' She adjusted his tie, brushed imaginary dust from his lapel, stepped smartly back, stood to ramrod attention and snapped off a salute. 'Sergeant Stark, VC.'

Stark had expected the salute but it was disconcerting nonetheless – salutes were for officers, not enlisted men. But a salute was for the rank not the man and the VC was a rank of its own. He had *not* expected the stripe, and maybe it was weeks of tension finally letting up but he was deeply moved. He pulled himself together and returned the salute. 'Sir!'

'Ha, I knew I'd get you to show me the proper respect eventually!' She laughed quietly. It was the first smile he'd ever seen on her and she was suddenly disconcertingly pretty.

A staff sergeant came next, wearing a George Cross. A bomb-disposal specialist, Pierson had told him, like Tyler. Now, that took balls. No reckless anger or stubborn stupidity to account for it. Just cool, methodical action under pressure, a trembling finger from death, again and again. After several soldiers had been badly injured by an IED he had, without waiting for protective clothing, disarmed three more IEDs so the injured men could be extracted in time to be saved. Stark wanted to say something, but what could you say?

Other recipients arrived one by one . . . Grand Crosses, Orders of this and that, knighthoods and gongs, all after Stark and the staff sergeant. Some nodded to him, none approached.

'What did she say to you?' asked Pierson. 'Her Majesty?'

Stark hesitated. 'She thought my name rather apposite.'

'Stark?'

'She commented on the Anglo-Saxon derivation.'

Pierson chuckled. 'Simple, downright, inflexible?'

'Something like that.' The words the Queen had actually used were 'strong, resolute and brave'. Stark knew this definition but was more comfortable with Pierson's. He'd just nodded and smiled, like a simpleton; this whole thing still felt like a daydream.

Pierson pointed out Margaret Collins being escorted in through a small side door. In her hand she held a slim case containing her husband's Distinguished Service Order, posthumous, received from the Queen in a private ceremony earlier. Head held high, every inch elegance and grace in a pale yellow dress, not a note of mourning black, she accepted a glass but didn't drink. Champagne was hardly appropriate. Stark heard Pierson tut. No one approached Margaret, leaving her to her feelings, no doubt. Stark thought she looked lost, so excused himself from Pierson and went to join her.

'Joe.' She smiled, taking in his stripes. 'Promotion?'

Stark waved the envelope. 'Ink's still wet.'

'Then congratulations, *Sergeant*.'

'Thanks. How are you holding up?'

Her smile tightened. 'What was it you boys say, "rule one"?'

'Always ditch your mates for a shag?' suggested Stark, jokingly. That was rule one when you were out on the pull – if successful you went 'missing in action' without a word, no questions asked till you'd made your escape and reported back to camp.

'Perhaps the other rule one.'

'Quite right, ma'am.'

'Sergeant Stark, with all due respect, if you call me ma'am again I'll shove that medal up your arse.'

'Please don't. The insurance company would send in a retrieval team.' He wasn't kidding: Pierson had told him to insure it for a million, minimum. Indeed, he was to be given a replica of regular, non-Sebastopol bronze to wear so the other might be locked away.

She chuckled. 'I understand that servicemen of any rank must now salute you.'

'That's tradition, not requirement, and to be honest, I'm not sure it applies now I've left the service.'

394

'You're still a reservist, still in uniform.'

'Pending medical discharge.'

'They're fools to let you go.'

'It was my decision.'

'Yes,' she said seriously. 'Time to move on, eh?'

'I'm sorry.'

'Say that one more time and I shall slap you. My husband died doing what he loved and believed in. So, on his behalf . . .' She snapped off a smart salute, her serious expression betraying nothing of what it cost her.

It was perhaps the bravest act Stark had ever witnessed. In that moment the weight of the small bronze cross on his breast took on its rightful significance and the last of his self-concerned reluctance evaporated. A medal was to be worn with pride, not just for those who stood and those who fell, but also those who loved them. He returned the salute, sharp, brief, but something of his deep sadness must have shown through.

'Now now, none of that.' Margaret blinked brightly. 'You'll set me off too.'

Pierson materialized at their side. 'Forgive my intrusion. I wondered if perhaps you might both prefer to wait somewhere quieter.' She had a prescient knack for timing. Stark's hip ached and his leg was beginning to tremble.

Pierson led them to a quiet room with comfortable chairs. On a silver tray stood two crystal tumblers. She relieved Margaret of her untried champagne. 'Gordon's and tonic for Mrs Collins, ice and lime. Two fingers of Royal Lochnagar for you, Sergeant, no ice.' Stark smiled at her unfailing attention to detail. When he tasted the whisky, doubly so.

She left them to their thoughts. They didn't chink glasses. Margaret sipped hers with an appreciative sigh. They asked who each had brought as guests but were mostly happy to sit in silence until Pierson returned to usher them out for the photographs.

The huge courtyard was bathed in sunshine. The palace photographer and a phalanx of assistants were already busy marshalling recipients. One guided Margaret smoothly away.

'Do try to stand up straight for the cameras, lest my court-martial end in a firing squad,' said Pierson, taking one last chance to readjust his faultless uniform. 'Talking of which . . .' She pointed.

There were his mum and Louise in their new hats and dresses. They hadn't seen him yet.

Stark's smile froze and faded into shock.

Kelly wore a broad-brimmed cream hat and a stunning sky-blue dress that fitted like a glove. Elegant and poised, she glowed.

Stark opened and closed his mouth several times.

'You're welcome,' said Pierson, her starchy façade barely concealing her amusement.

'How . . .?'

'Detective Sergeant Millhaven. A romantic soul and a force to be reckoned with, much like myself. Miss Jones's exasperation with you had commendable momentum, but after the depth of your endearing stubbornness was made clear to her she went away and had a good long think. Of course, your mother and sister colluded most willingly.'

Stark was speechless. 'Thank you,' he managed eventually. 'I think.'

Pierson nodded. Enough said.

Stark shook his head. Awkward conversations loomed. Talking of which . . . 'There is something else you might do for me,' he said. She waited for him to elaborate. 'Alan Maggs. Formerly Corporal Maggs, Two Para. You know who I mean?'

'I don't spend my waking hours with my head up my arse, Sergeant.'

'He'll need a helping hand.'

Her expression did not exhibit enthusiasm. Maggs's widely reported courtroom outburst had burnt every bridge, except perhaps one. 'He once stood where I just stood, with the Queen hanging the Military Medal on his chest.'

Pierson looked unhappy. 'I'll do what I can,' she said finally. Knowing what he did of her tenacity Stark suspected that that was far more than Maggs had any right to expect. 'Can you manage on that?' she asked, indicating the cane.

'God, I completely forgot. You need to give it back.'

'Actually the Duke just bent my ear. He says it's yours.'

'What? No, I couldn't . . .'

'Perhaps we should go and find him so you can refuse him in person. As well as being the second highest royal in the land he is also a colonel-in-chief a dozen times over.'

'Perhaps not,' conceded Stark.

'Perhaps not. I've tucked your crutches away until you need them. You will tell me when you need them. You will suppress your mulish streak in this regard. Understood?'

'Why, Captain, I never knew you cared so passionately.'

She harrumphed. 'I'm under strict orders to prevent you over-exerting yourself.'

'My mother.'

'Miss Jones. She was quite firm on the matter.'

'I'm fine, honestly.'

'She said you would say that. She also said that if I didn't get you to pace yourself she'd hunt me down and kill me. Why she's so keen for you to save your strength is a question I'll leave you to broach. Perhaps she's looking forward to torturing you to death herself. She remains quite exceptionally peeved with you.'

'Comforting,' replied Stark.

Kelly turned and smiled her knowing smile.

His mum was already bustling over. 'There he is, my boy!' She kissed his cheek, then busily rubbed away the lipstick with her hanky.

'Does this mean I'm forgiven?'

397

'Promise you'll never do anything so bloody stupid ever again and then ask me. You must've got it from your father. And where are your crutches? Now, come on, it's time you formally introduced me to that lovely girl of yours.'

'She's hardly my girl – the last time I saw her she dumped me.'

'A lot's happened since then. Now come on!'

What had happened? She hadn't visited or called. Maybe she'd been prevented, or maybe it was part of the Machiavellian conspiracy she'd joined against him. Before he could find out, however, one of the photographer's assistants diverted him to pose with Gaskin. Stark hadn't seen the corporal since Selly Oak when he'd still been on crutches. His limp was all but gone. Grinning in crisp number-twos and glittering Military Cross, he looked a million miles from the gruff, weather-beaten veteran who'd set off from COP McKay with Stark all those months ago.

Then, to Stark's immense pride, Margaret appeared and posed with him, holding open the DSO medal case for the camera. She kissed his cheek before going to pose with her husband's CO. For the rest of the day Stark never once saw her left unattended.

Finally the assistant set about arranging him into various familial configurations. Kelly stood to one side, but his mother had other ideas. 'Oh no you don't. In you go!' she said, bustling Kelly into the frame beside him.

Kelly took his arm and they posed together. Alone at last. Stark couldn't think what to say. Kelly just smiled for the camera.

'Come on, Louise,' said his mother, brightly. 'Time to touch up our mascara. I want to see what the loos are like in the Queen's house!' Taking Louise's arm she steered her away from Stark and Kelly, adopting the unashamed unsubtlety of mothers the world over whose sons have *finally* brought home a nice, normal girl.

'I like your mum,' said Kelly, watching them go. 'Very outgoing. Pity you don't take after her more.'

Stark sighed. 'So she keeps telling me.' Was this the lowest point, he wondered, or did the universe have anything more excruciating to offer?

'Still,' Kelly added, her gaze wandering around the architectural finery. 'Not bad, I suppose, as first dates go.'

And there, glowing before him, the door to redemption. 'This wasn't quite what I had in mind.'

'Why was that?'

'I suppose I wanted you to like me for myself.'

'You don't think that cross is part of who you are?'

Stark looked for his usual self-rationalization, all those words and excuses, but Margaret's salute had exposed them as chaff. And, besides, looking into Kelly's crystal-blue gaze he knew for a fact that she would see straight through the lot. Her eyes were the exact shade of her dress. 'You are quite the most beautiful woman I have ever seen.'

She blinked, blushed, smiled broadly but shook her head. 'Nice try.'

'A friend of mine once said that when cornered I use truth like a grenade.'

'To cover your escape.'

'This time I think I'll fight it out.'

'Hmm.'

'Why didn't you call?'

'I did have quite an eloquent bollocking planned, but I was persuaded to pause for thought.'

'For weeks?'

'You're a conundrum.' She looked serious. 'I had no idea whether you even wanted to see me. Eventually I decided you were probably just being stubbornly male again.'

'*You* dumped *me*, I thought?'

'Typical boy . . . You never know when to read between the lines.'

No, thought Stark, we *could* use a little help there. 'And after that?'

'I figured you had enough to contend with. And Fran and Wendy thought you'd see the funny side.'

'Wendy?'

'Captain Pierson.'

'*Wendy!*'

'She told me to tell you to stop being a tit. Sound advice, I thought.'

'Indeed.' Stark wasn't sure he'd ever squeeze the word 'Wendy' into his Captain Pierson paradigm. 'Well, I'm glad you're here,' he said.

'Good.' She smiled – but then frowned, her expression turning to concern. 'You look pale. You're in pain.'

'I'm fine.'

She saw through the lie. 'I told Wendy to look after you.'

'She mentioned that. She worried about your motive.'

'Are you well enough for this? Perhaps you should bow out now.' Photos were to be followed by 'tea' in the palace gardens, then dinner at the Haberdashers' Hall. It was going to be a long first date.

'I'm hungry enough.'

'You'll certainly need to build up your strength if you hope to put up a fight.'

'Doctor's orders?'

'Something like that. Which hotel are you staying at tonight?'

'They've booked me a room at Park Lane.'

'Me, too. What a waste,' she said.

Stark blinked. A devilish twinkle of laughter creased Kelly's eyes. He thought of mentioning that this was still, technically, their first date, but decided on balance to shut the hell up.

PART FOUR

39

Fran waited till the door closed behind the two SCD7 detectives, slowly counting to ten. 'Arseholes!'

'Now, now.' Groombridge closed the report and placed it atop his creaking in-tray. 'You can't say they haven't looked into it.'

'And now they've stopped!' cried Fran.

'"Deprioritized pending new information",' Groombridge corrected.

'They've bloody parked it!'

'They can't access Dawson's accounts or raid his offices without probable cause, which they can't establish unless someone goes on the record.'

'Stop arguing their *side*!'

'What would you have me do instead?' demanded Groombridge, losing his cool. 'Kick down doors, knock heads together, is that it? What those "arseholes" were too polite to say was that the reason witnesses are too frightened to talk is because I let my ego get the better of me and tipped Dawson off that he was under suspicion. He'll have covered his tracks by now anyway. All they can do is keep tabs on him in the hope that he eventually slips up. So until then I'd say our indignation was worse than useless, *wouldn't you?*'

Fran kept her big mouth shut, wondering when she would ever learn that railing against his mild manner was as unwise as it was cheap. All the more foolish, given that she wanted Dawson so badly because she could *see* it eating at Groombridge. Dawson had walked on the van heist killings, and nothing *burnt* like a cold case. Now the bastard was getting away with half-killing Naveen, helping Nikki, supplying drugs, loan-sharking, racketeering and God knew what else. And he was laughing at them. She'd diverted all the resources she could in the last few weeks to uncovering something, anything, but Cox was starting to sniff around the timesheets and Groombridge couldn't turn a blind eye much longer.

The DCI sighed. He looked tired. Fran ground her teeth.

There was a knock at the door and Dixon peered in cautiously. 'Sorry, Guv. Just got a call from Belmarsh prison. You're not going to like this.'

Stark read the last page of his book, closed it and tossed it on to the coffee-table. He stood with a grunt and limped to the window, considering another turn around the block. The rain was getting heavier.

He slid open the door to the balcony, letting the humid air and summer-rain-hiss roll in over him. Lightning strobed to the west, silhouetting the jagged skyline on his retinas. He counted seconds: one, two, three, four . . . The crack-rumble accompaniment shook the air.

He breathed in a long draught of ionized air, savouring the storm's wild freedom. He ached to be out in it, drenched and laughing, running till his lungs burst.

It was two weeks since he'd escaped his mother's claustrophobic care, but the walls of his flat offered scant liberty. Being cooped up felt like purgatory, a limbo life relieved only by Kelly's heavenly visitations. Alone in the day, he was still on another sick-chit with only the discomforts of exercise, physio and psych appointments to break the monotony of books, straight-to-TV movies and rolling news. Little reinforced a sense of isolation and boredom more than daily makeshift bloke-lunches eaten before the unblinking flat-screen accusation of daytime television.

Behind him the landline rang but he let it go to the machine. It would only be another round of motherly clucking or, worse, another interview request or offer to publish his ghost-written autobiography. The caller rang off without leaving a message.

Then his mobile phone began its own song and dance, crabbing angrily across the coffee-table. He let that go too. But a few seconds later it rang again. Muttering, he turned and scooped it up, frowning at the caller ID. 'Sarge?'

'Where are you?' demanded Fran.

'Guess.'

'Moping about in your flat.'

'Bingo.'

'Then get off your bony arse and meet me downstairs in ten. I'm off to ask your pal Maggs why he keeps getting stabbed.'

Maggs was sitting up in his hospital bed, a prison officer outside his door. 'Is it just me or have we been here before?' he asked wryly.

'I wonder if it's something about you personally that incites people to stab you,' mused Fran.

Maggs shrugged 'You gonna charge me with attempted murder this time, Sergeant Hardarse, or will you settle for assault?'

'That depends,' said Fran. It didn't seem likely, from what she'd told Stark on the way. As different categories of prisoner, Maggs and Gary Cockcroft should never have met, but Maggs had been attending the prison dentist in weekly penance for years of underwhelming oral hygiene and Gary had feigned toothache to engineer a coincidental visit, attacking Maggs with a plastic shiv fashioned from a broken chair. 'We're assuming his motive was revenge for implicating his little sister Nikki, and to prevent you testifying against her in court.'

'He could've just asked nicely,' joked Maggs.

'Would you have listened?'

'No.' Maggs grinned. 'But I'd have enjoyed saying so a lot more if he hadn't stuck me first. How's he doing anyway?'

'You broke his cheekbone, nose, wrist, two ribs and – I know I shouldn't laugh – several teeth.'

Maggs smiled at the irony, but when he looked at Stark his expression hardened. 'You've less to say for yourself than last time we met.'

Stark shrugged. 'Officially I'm still on the sick 'n' lame.'

Maggs didn't look at Stark again. He was still angry. Stark had expected as much. When Fran had what she needed, she announced she'd wait in the car and left them alone, probably her plan all along.

Stark and Maggs watched each other, like cats strayed into uncomfortable proximity.

'Fancy cane,' said Maggs, eventually.

Stark offered it for a closer look. 'A gift.'

'Friends in high places.'

Stark let that go. News of the gift had made it into the tabloids. It apparently dated back to the 1890s Buddhist revival in India. It was valuable. He ought to get something more everyday but it fitted his hand and height so well he was loath to seek another and he had been given it to use, not admire.

'So what *are* you doing here? Guilty conscience?'

'How about *esprit de corps*?' suggested Stark.

'Thought you'd been discharged.'

'Officially I'm still waiting on that.'

Maggs nodded. 'You're too useful to them. They'll lose your paperwork if you let them.'

'There's not much I can do about it for now.'

'So much for friends, eh?' agreed Maggs. 'Talking of which, I had a visitor.'

'Yes?'

'Tasty captain. Two words I'm not used to putting together,' said Maggs.

Pierson. That was quick. 'Times change.'

'So it seems.' Maggs was watching him carefully. 'She told me when I get out I'll be entitled to thirty years of uncollected pension.'

'You never collected?'

'Wasn't worth the bother. Only now I'm told there was a clerical error. I should've been in a higher category. Backdated, it adds up to a pretty penny.'

'The off-licences of Greenwich can lay in extra champagne.' Maggs ignored the gibe. 'Interesting timing, I thought.'

'Well, you did make the papers.'

'I'm not the only one, though, am I? This was your doing.' Despite the firm assertion, it was still a question. 'Partly.'

'When are you going to learn to mind your own damn business?'

'When are you going to learn to accept help when it's offered?'

'When you show me a world where help comes without strings,' riposted Maggs.

'Wake up, Dorothy, there's no such place.' Stark flung Maggs's own line back at him. Maggs looked away. Stark could have sworn he was masking a smile. 'How's the food?'

'I'm on liquid bloody food till my guts heal up.'

'Nothing new there.'

'Ha-ha.'

'I'll bring you some soup.'

'Piss off.'

Clearly Maggs wasn't in the mood for jokes; understandable, thought Stark. 'How's prison?'

'It only hurts if I laugh.'

'Will you appeal? You should never have got more than three. With good behaviour you'd be out in eighteen months. You've made your point.'

'We'll see,' said Maggs gruffly.

407

'We'll see' if he'd made his point yet, or if he'd reconsider appealing – Stark couldn't tell which. He'd leave that for next time. 'I brought these for you.' He held out the bag.

'That's not grapes.' Maggs eyed the bag warily, perhaps guessing the contents. He pulled out three slim leather cases, nodding. 'Where d'you get the boxes?'

'The tasty captain.' Pierson had come up with originals, of course.

'Should've guessed.' Maggs opened all three and stared at his medals, lost in thought. 'Haven't looked at these in years. You've polished them. Still can't walk past a button without shining it?'

'Said the man who carried his field first-aid kit around for thirty years,' responded Stark.

'They never gave me a third stripe, though, *Sergeant* Weekender.' Maggs snapped the boxes shut. 'These are no good to me inside. Some scrote would thieve them if a screw didn't first. Put them back where you found them.'

'Languishing in some personal-effects locker?'

'Better than an old sock.'

'It's not right.'

'If you're that soft-hearted why don't *you* hang on to them till I get out? They'd be in good company. I'd salute but the MoD didn't procrastinate with *my* discharge.'

'I've had enough salutes,' said Stark, thinking of Margaret Collins.

Perhaps something of that showed in his face. Maggs nodded gravely. 'Medals glitter, but also cast their shadows.'

'Quoting Churchill now?'

'I've heard it said yours casts the longest,' added Maggs. 'Personally, I don't think it's the medals that cast the shadow at all.'

'No,' agreed Stark. There was plenty of shadow without glitter.

They both sat staring out of the window for a while. A grey-studded sky rolled slowly past, carrying the rain away with it.

'Still,' said Maggs, 'you get a little pension with it too. We're both quids in.' He was right: the VC came with a £1,500 annuity. 'And how much compensation did you get for getting blown up and shot?'

'Enough,' admitted Stark, conscious that Maggs had received little or nothing back in 1982.

'What will we do with our new-found riches, eh?' mused Maggs, mocking them both.

Stark had already donated his compensation payment equally between Help for Heroes and the Soldiers, Sailors, Airmen and Families Association. The annuity would go to the British Legion. He hoped Maggs wouldn't do something similar: he needed it. 'Soup and champagne?'

This time Maggs couldn't help chuckling. 'Don't make me laugh, you sod.' He winced, holding his bandaged stomach.

A beginning, thought Stark. Rapprochement, if it were possible, would take longer, and depend in no small part on what happened with Pinky. But laughter, however painful, was a good start.

'Kiss and make up?' asked Fran innocently, sipping takeaway coffee as Stark slid into the passenger seat with a grunt. 'That's two you owe me.'

'I've been meaning to talk to you about your sentimental streak,' replied Stark. They hadn't spoken since the Kelly conspiracy was revealed..

'You're very welcome.' Fran grinned. 'Talking of which, I thought you were supposed to be a corporal?'

'Sorry?'

'They kept calling you Sergeant Stark, on TV.'

'I was acting sergeant when our patrol was attacked. The powers-that-be decided to make it official.' Stark still wasn't sure whether this was because they felt it only right or that they thought it good PR. Perhaps it was both.

'Well, don't get any funny ideas about equal rank. You're still Trainee Investigator Stark around here.'

'Sarge.' He saluted sloppily.

'Don't push your luck.' She checked her watch. 'Right, I'm done for the week and you owe me a drink.' She held up a palm before he could respond. 'And don't say you're under doctor's orders not to imbibe because the important part of my previous statement is that *you* owe *me* a drink.'

'Actually I was about to say I'm gasping.' Friday drinks in Rosie's sounded like a splendid notion.

'So long as you're buying . . .'

On the way back she grilled him about his visit to the Palace but didn't ask about the citation, which he'd thought she would. Was she starting to respect his boundaries? Surely not.

They were into their second round before the pub began to fill with coppers. People covered their surprise at seeing him with varying levels of over-enthusiastic welcome and hesitant congratulations. Groombridge, however, frowned at finding them sitting together. 'Good to see you, Constable Stark, though I must say, I'm a little surprised.' He looked pointedly at Fran. 'Coincidence?'

'Disobedience,' she confessed candidly. 'I'm told I have a sentimental streak.'

'And was your interview assisted in any way by dragging our trainee investigator from his sickbed despite my ordering you not to?'

'Nope.' She smiled, uncontrite.

Groombridge sighed and went to the bar. Harper strode in, talking loudly with others, including Bryden. When one nodded Stark's way Harper turned and his latest anecdote died on his lips. He turned back to his friends, didn't look at Stark again and left soon after. Fran and Groombridge saw this but said nothing. Most people would've seen through Harper's latest fib but chalked the bad arm up to another domestic. Fran knew better, but Groombridge? For the moment Stark was content just to see Harper go. Only time would tell whether anything could be salvaged there.

Some – including Bryden, Stark was pleased to see – made a point of joining him for a drink, but few lingered long in his company. Stark was not dismayed: he'd been through this before. Even close friends had to find common ground anew. It was just another facet of being a veteran.

'When do your doctors say you can come back to work?' asked Groombridge, sipping his pint thoughtfully.

'Another week, Guv,' admitted Stark, reluctantly. 'Then light duties only.'

'And what do you say?'

'I don't like doctors.'

Groombridge laughed. 'Then sod them. Clearly both you and DS Millhaven here think you're better qualified in medical matters anyway so get your arse in the station first thing Monday, if you must. I'm sure we can find some use for you.'

'Thanks, Guv.'

'A man knows his own limits.'

'And a copper knows when it's their round,' added Fran. 'Get them in, Stark.'

Monday morning shone with a golden sunrise. Fran had offered to pick him up but Stark, keen to reassert his independence, declined. Instead he caught a bus, his first since moving to London. He'd even purchased an Oyster card. The shiny red double-decker dropped him at the bottom of Royal Hill and he managed the short climb at a leisurely limp. He paused across the road from the station, staring at the entrance ramp, the very spot he'd given himself the limp, the very spot he'd arrested Maggs just eleven weeks earlier. It seemed longer. He looked up at the building, ruminating on all that had transpired. In policing terms, at least, there was satisfaction to be drawn from his part in events. A helicopter clattered noisily across London's busy airspace and, for a moment, Stark was transported back to that night-flight into Combat Outpost McKay and the cocksure clarity he'd felt. Suddenly, fleetingly, something of that young fool's surety reached out across the gulf and touched the new Stark, mocking his pride and self-pity with a soldier's laugh. *No fucking sympathy!* Stark chuckled.

He turned his head to let the warm sun kiss his face. Leaning on his cane and closing his eyes, he took deep breaths of warm English-summer air, laced with pollen, car fumes and life. Nearby a small child laughed with his mother. Stark caught a waft of the verdant Helmand river valley, and smiled. He felt a swell of pleasure, that sudden irrational breath of euphoria that fills you sometimes with little apparent cause, or serendipitous overlapping of small causes, real or imagined, of hope, no strings attached. Whatever Maggs said, there was such a place.

Hazel had accused Stark of imbalance. Here and now, redressing that seemed simple. He would fix one side of the scales and raise the other to meet it, merge duty and desire and be whole. If the last few weeks had demonstrated anything, it was that he was no longer a soldier, no longer able or willing to procrastinate behind that. Give it a year, he'd thought. What did he realistically think would be different a year from now? And what did he think he was good for if it wasn't service? Green or blue, he was a man of uniform. His Queen. His country. He was entrusted to protect, keep peace. He'd sworn, and he would keep covenant. That was who he was. And this was where he would do it.

40

It felt good to be back in the office. Everyone did their best to act normally and Stark had high hopes that they'd pull it off, given time, say, ten years or so. Only Fran, Groombridge and, perhaps surprisingly, Maggie remained unmoved by the whole business. He would be for ever grateful to all three. Someone *had* stuck a newspaper cutting of him with his VC on the wall, to which Harper nodded with a snide remark, but Stark wasn't about to let that dampen his spirits. At least Harper had spoken – another start, perhaps. Groombridge had preloaded Stark's small desk with a big stack of files but desk-bound was better than sofa-bound. Light duties beat crushing boredom.

And so it proved for the first week, but as the second ground on, Stark's interest in data-input palled, and watching the rest of the team go about their business made him feel like a spare wheel. Even so, he was pleased to observe people slowly relaxing enough to tease him and make jokes, and even if Harper's were barbed, at least he felt confident enough to make them. Stark was grateful no one had witnessed their one-sided tussle. To confront a bully was one thing but to crush their self-esteem was dangerous. That no one had seen his belittlement allowed Harper room to recover. They might never be friends but Harper had been right in one thing: Stark wanted no man as his enemy.

'Still glad to be back?' asked Groombridge, dumping a fresh stack of files on Stark's desk.

'There's nowhere I'd rather be, Guv,' lied Stark.

'Remember the ancient Chinese curse, Trainee Investigator. "May you live in interesting times."'

'I'll take my chances.'

'Be careful what you wish for. The happiest policeman in the world would be the one with nothing to do.'

'As he queued at the job centre,' commented Stark.

'Good point.' Groombridge laughed. 'Perhaps the honest policemen would prefer *little* to do and a high conviction rate.' He was still chuckling as he closed the door to his office.

The following week Stark settled on the bench in the public gallery of Woolwich Crown Court with relief. It was nearly four weeks since he had ditched crutches for cane, but the better the hip got the more he asked of the muscles. It didn't matter. Today would be a good day. The beginning of an end, and a validation of his new beginning. The gang were back in court, Nikki facing all of her charges and the others the sexual-assault charge, for which the CPS were going after them as joint principals under the common-purpose doctrine.

The clerk entered and required all to stand as the judge took her seat. Judge Penelope Carmichael-Brown – with a name like that, she'd probably convened her first court aged three, wig, gown, teddy-bear barristers, the lot. She had a reputation for severe sentencing. In an ideal world Stark would wish for uniformity but today he felt less pious. So much for ideals.

After brief preliminaries the gang were led in and lined up in the dock behind the tall polycarbonate screen. They presented a miserable conglomerate of fear, shame and denial. Naveen, separated from the rest in his own area, endured murderous looks. Martin Munroe looked like he might vomit. Stark felt little in the way of sympathy. It was believed Munroe was the one heard calling out for Gibbs to stop but there was no evidence of him doing so on the non-sexual assaults. Even Nikki appeared agitated. Stark was not displeased. So much for mercy.

This was the danger Groombridge had warned him of –

the desire to see justice done leading to the desire to see punishment meted out. Goodbye, idealism and mercy; hello, *Schadenfreude?* That way lay darkness, Groombridge said. Stark wasn't unduly worried. He knew his way through darkness well enough.

The clerk of the court called the names one by one and read out the charges against them. She saved Nikki till last. Hers was a long list. Stark watched the jury members' faces darken as it went on and on. At some point he would be called upon to testify. He had been warned that the prosecution would attempt to suggest he had somehow influenced Maggs to identify Nikki's photo in that interview. He might have to endure their whole conversation being shown in court, his insomnia and its cause, his physical and mental decline, his medicinal abuse, all twisted to undermine his credibility. So be it. He was ready.

'*Lies!*' Everyone's head turned. To Stark's right a woman was on her feet. Callie Cockcroft, Nikki's mother. '*You're all liars!*' She gripped the gallery rail, white-knuckled fingers bedecked in gold rings, gold hooped earrings quivering, lank hair scraped back. Shiny gold tracksuit and thin cheeks, gaunt and lined, she was the image of Nikki aged. 'You're all liars! You stole my boy and now you're tryin' t' steal my girl! You're all *liars!*'

'Remove that woman from my court!' ordered the judge.

The door guard, from a private security firm, tried to shuffle along the front row to restrain Callie but she shuffled further away, still shouting. When he did reach her she tried to hit him with her mobile phone, shrieking that she would sue him for assault.

From the corner of his eye Stark caught a movement. Some of the accused were on their feet. Their guard was keeled over. Tyler had cupped his hands together. Nikki put a foot on the makeshift platform and was boosted smartly to the top of the screen. Tyler held up a hand for her to pull him up, but she ignored it and dropped down the outside. He stared in disbelief and fury, then jumped on a chair and leapt for the top of the screen, with Colin Messenger following his lead.

'*Guards!*' yelled the judge.

A rotund guard came to meet Nikki but she lashed out at him with something and dashed past. Stark and Fran were already out of their seats and heading for the door, Fran first with Stark struggling down the stairs behind, cursing.

They were too late. Nikki was already out of the court, heading for the main door at speed. A tall man in dark clothing and baseball cap was running with her. Behind them a guard lay on the floor clutching his eyes and face, gasping. Tyler and Colin were grappling with two more. Colin broke free and took off with Fran on his heels.

Useless in pursuit, Stark stopped and kicked the back of one of Tyler's knees. The boy went down with a guard on top of him.

Stark turned to the downed guard. From his agitation it was obvious he had been the victim of an incapacitant spray, OC, oleoresin capsicum or pepper spray from the smell, rather than CS. '*Water!*' he pleaded.

'No good. It's not soluble,' replied Stark. 'Just keep blinking. It'll wear off. You're going to be okay. It *will* wear off. Try not to rub – that'll make it worse. Just keep blinking and breathe calmly.' He knew from training how hard it was to do so. 'Call an ambulance!' he shouted down the corridor to the front desk.

Tyler was pinned face-down now.

'Are you a medic?' Another guard stood over him.

'Police. Why?'

'Ryan's been stabbed.'

Ryan, it turned out, was the rotund guard. It had been a blade in Nikki's hand, a shiv. It was more slash than stab, a wide, thick cut in the left forearm. The clerk already had a first-aid kit out and was pressing a dressing to the wound. There was little Stark could add. There wasn't enough blood to fear anything arterial. He said so, and that an ambulance was on its way.

'Little bitch!' spat the wounded guard.

Paul Thompson had made it over the screen but was now cuffed to the witness stand.

'Need some help here!'

In the dock, the remaining accused were corralled in one corner under the watchful eye of two guards, while another knelt over his fallen colleague, hands bloody.

Cursing, Stark clambered awkwardly over the tall balustrade, falling on the other side with a pained grunt. He moved the guard aside. 'Hold his arms, keep him still!' He lifted the injured man's shirt. A small circular puncture wound. The dock guard really had been stabbed. Punched in the gut with the shiv. He looked up into the man's panicked expression and remembered the Bastion medics. 'You're okay. You're gonna be fine.' Confident tone, confident smile, sugar-coating. The man was in trouble. Gut wounds were bad news, and if the point had angled up towards a kidney . . . 'Get me that first-aid kit,' he ordered.

He was running low on reassurances and dressings when the paramedics eventually arrived.

Powerless he watched the blood drying on his hands, as the man was stretchered hastily away.

'Stark!' Fran's voice. She stood beckoning from the doorway, mobile pressed to one ear and hung up as he approached. 'Nikki and her accomplice got away in a blue Ford Focus driven by another. I got the plate. Messenger hoofed it on foot. Wantage is being sat on outside.'

'Thompson made it over but no further. They . . .' Stark looked around and realized the room was all but empty. 'I guess they've been taken down.'

Fran noticed him rubbing at the dry blood. 'You hurt?'

Stark shook his head. 'The guard. Nikki used a shiv.'

'We've got Messenger, sir!' said a sergeant, from the door. 'Transport Police picked him up jumping the barrier at Plumstead station and trying to board a train to Dartford, just like you said.'

'Granny's house,' said Fran.

'Never the brightest spark,' added Groombridge. 'Thanks.' There was no sign of Nikki and her accomplices, though. This isn't going to go down as our finest hour, he thought. Despite the private security, the police would shoulder all the blame if the absconders weren't recaptured swiftly. He shook his head, still incredulous. 'Jumped the *bloody* dock.'

'Hasn't happened in a while,' agreed Fran. 'And I doubt they'd have made it out the door without help.'

A poor consolation. Groombridge stared at the paused image on the CCTV monitor in the court's security suite. The accomplice had kept his head down as he entered the building, using his cap and a hand to hide his face. The security firm should've made him remove it but he'd waited in the lobby until the commotion had broken out, then pulled a tube scarf up over his face, vaulted the gates and sprayed the guard before anyone could stop him. A big man but nimble, black jacket, boots and cap.

'Has to be Dawson,' said Fran, standing beside him. 'But what the hell is he thinking? Taxiing her around is one thing, but this?'

'It's a strange move,' agreed Groombridge. 'Get me a list of everyone who visited Nikki inside . . . and Gary.'

'You think big brother had a hand in this?'

'Maybe. Plan B after his failed attempt to silence Maggs. And he's got Her Majesty's perfect alibi.'

They all stared at the paused image. 'How did Dawson know when to make his move?' said Fran.

'Callie Cockcroft had her mobile in her hand when she kicked off, Guv,' said Stark.

'Did she now? Where is she?'

'Uniform have her in a car,' replied Fran. 'Not sure whether to arrest her.'

'Arrest her. Suspicion of assisting escape from custody. Bag her mobile and bring it here.'

'Guv.' Fran disappeared.

Groombridge stared at Stark, wondering if they were thinking the same thing – the ancient Chinese curse. 'I don't suppose it would do much good to remind you that you're still on light duties?'

'You tell me, Guv.'

In other words, it's up to you, Guv, as long as you tell me to stay, Guv. The problem with authority was that it only counted for anything if the other person accepted it. Stark was one of those people who saw through it, knew when to say yes and when to invite you subtly to reconsider. In that, he reminded Groombridge of his younger self, and being on the receiving end had its piquant irony. In other respects he remained an enigma. Officially he was still signed off sick yet here he was in suit and tie, defiant as ever. He'd washed the blood from his hands but there was some on his shirt cuff. 'Sit down at least. You're no use knackered.'

'Guv.' The boy slid into a creaky office chair. It was hard to think of him as a boy now. He'd aged in the short time he'd been around, not just in himself but in Groombridge's perception of him. His deterioration had peeled away the lad with scars and left the man with his past etched on him. Not to mention how hard it was to look at him now without seeing khaki, crimson and bronze. One day Groombridge hoped to sit down over a drink and hear the truth behind the sterile citation and the papers' sensational interpretations of what had happened that day. But he wouldn't try to coax it out. There

419

was little probability of success anyway. Stark was an easy guy to like but a hard man to know. Maybe in time.

'Got it, Guv,' said Fran, when she reappeared. 'She texted another mobile, listed just as L, at eleven nineteen. One word – go.'

Stark rewound the film. 'There.' He pressed play. The accomplice took something from his pocket, looked at it, put it away, got up and jumped the gates. The time on the monitor read eleven twenty.

Groombridge phoned HQ to request a ping on the mobile number's location.

Fran's phone rang. The news was clearly mixed. 'We've got the Ford, Guv. Ablaze on the Abbey Wood flyover.'

The column of black smoke rose high in the windless sky, pin-pointing their destination. It was a short journey, a little over two miles, mostly dual-carriageway, a smart escape route in a busy city. And it was an interesting place to dump the car. The flyover carried an arterial road over a railway line. In the centre of the flyover there were bus lay-bys either side, with staircases and ramps down to ground level either side of the railway. Worse, the car was actually parked at the foot of the flyover where it was less conspicuous and footpaths angled off each side. Uniform were already canvassing pedestrians but it was a futile gesture. Anyone waiting at the bus stops would long since have travelled on. By simply walking under the flyover the suspects could immediately be out of sight of anyone who'd seen them get out of the car; leaving it alight provided a distraction and destroyed evidence. They could flee in several directions and either side of a railway. They might have caught a train or a bus or simply got into another vehicle.

'Smart,' commented Fran.

'They all make mistakes, DS Millhaven,' replied Groom-bridge, looking about him thoughtfully. It makes the mistakes harder to spot when the sodding criminals knew what they were doing, he didn't add. The phone ping had already come back as pay-as-you-go and switched off. Savvy villains knew the tricks. Bloody thing probably had a new SIM card already.

The Fire Brigade had the blaze out and the local SOCO team were waiting for the steaming wreck to cool down. Groombridge chose the first and most obvious of the foot-paths, which turned under the flyover and came out below by a smaller road.

Tucked under the flyover there was a small public car park encircled by security fencing. They crossed to the nearest con-crete staircase, went up on to the flyover and down the far side to the railway station. There was another car park on this side too. Both had CCTV, limited but worth checking, the station, too, and most buses these days. 'Train or bus wouldn't have been smart – too easy to see where you got on and off.'

'The car parks, Guv?' suggested Stark.

'Nice and dark under those flyovers,' agreed Fran.

They checked for signs of broken glass, evidence of break-ing into cars, and found a depressing number in both car parks.

'Guv.' Stark was pointing at the CCTV camera on an eight-foot pole. It had been sprayed out with black paint. A quick scan showed there were no other cameras covering that car park, the surrounding streets or buildings. Stark squinted towards the railway station. 'What about those, Guv?'

The platform cameras were high on a pole. They tramped back up and over to the station side. Stark was noticeably slower this time, his breath laboured when he thought no one was looking. Groombridge shook his head but said nothing. The man in the ticket office reluctantly let them in to see the monitors. They were not of the finest quality, but the relevant camera had sufficient elevation to pick up the distant entrance/exit of the car park.

They rewound to roughly when the Focus had been dumped

and three figures in caps appeared, entered the car park, then disappeared into the gloomy undercroft. A minute later a dark grey saloon exited.

'Ford Mondeo,' suggested Fran.

Groombridge nodded. 'They all make mistakes.'

They returned to the station with all of the footage. The car-park camera had been fine until five forty-five the previous afternoon when a hand had appeared from below holding a spray can. The platform camera showed a man arrive on foot, spray, and leave the way he'd come. A minute later the grey Mondeo came around the same corner and disappeared into the car park. A black Mercedes pulled up outside and what looked a lot like the vandal emerged, got in on the passenger side and the car drove off. Too far for faces or plates.

'Can we enhance it?' asked Stark.

'Not on this,' replied Dixon.

'Email a copy to FSS and see what they can do,' said Groombridge. 'What else have we got?'

'Just spoken to the crime-scene manager, Guv,' said Fran. 'Melted remains of a toothbrush handle found on the floor of the burnt Focus.'

Groombridge nodded. Nikki's shiv — anything a prisoner could grind to a blade on brickwork or a concrete floor. Toothbrush handle was a common choice.

'The car's plates were cloned but the engine compartment serial number showed it was nicked in Chatham this morning. Some prints found on surviving paintwork. Officers have been sent to fingerprint the owner and her family for exclusion. We're collating footage from traffic cams in the area but they're few and far between. We've got incident signs up in case anyone wants to call and uniform are still canvassing.'

Exactly the kind of work Stark didn't miss about uniform. Not that sitting in front of a monitor was much better. He,

Dixon, Williams and Bryden were left to search the traffic-camera footage for signs of the Mondeo and Mercedes under the watchful eye of DS Harper while Groombridge and Fran spread the net nationally.

'Christ, talk about a needle in a haystack!' complained Williams.

'Look for both cars together,' suggested Stark. 'If they were lazy they might've convoyed there.'

Harper huffed. 'Another clever idea from Trainee Investigator Goldenballs. Listen to this one, lads, he's destined for greatness.' Masquerading as a joke, there was enough poison in the sarcasm to raise Stark's hackles. Harper looked to Bryden for laughter but received only a smile of acknowledgement, not a convincing one. Tolerance for his humour was wearing thin. There was a frayed look to the man this week. He hadn't turned up with any new cuts or bruises but he was clearly tired and stressed. It was impossible not to feel sorry for him. Stark had kept his own mental health and family apart; Harper's wife could not do the same and it was important to remember that, even as the man pecked away with his petty revenges.

'Got them, I think,' said Williams, suddenly. 'Here.' His screen showed the Mondeo following the Mercedes turning right. A rear view so no faces, but the licence plates of both were discernible.

'Where is that?' asked Stark. Williams gave the location and they traced the direction towards the nearest camera.

41

'We've got them twice coming and once going, different routes, but both instances we lose them south of Abbey Wood. And traffic cameras are always on sodding poles,' said Fran. 'With caps on . . .' You couldn't see faces.

Groombridge stared at the camera stills, baseball caps and gloved hands. 'Oh, for a distinguishing tattoo.'

'But . . .' She slid a still image on to Groombridge's desk. There was no mistaking Dawson in it. 'From the prison-visit camera, Guv. He visited Nikki four times. Guards say they held hands affectionately.'

Groombridge made a face. 'Doesn't sound like our Nikki.'

'Gives us a motive for Dawson, though, if she's more than just his foot-soldier.'

Groombridge made a face of distaste. 'Just when I thought nothing in this job could make me shudder. Visits to Gary?'

'Just his mother. But Dawson visited Tyler Wantage once.'

'Roping him in,' suggested Groombridge. 'What about the vandal?'

Fran slid another picture in front of him. 'Just after they dropped off the Mondeo. Best FSS can do with the image.'

The grainy enlargement was still inconclusive. Shorter than Dawson, slim, thin-faced beneath his cap: that was about all you could say. Groombridge stared at it thoughtfully. 'The cars?'

'Both on cloned plates. The Merc is the same class and marque as Dawson's but we can't tell the model.'

'Dawson's was de-badged too,' offered Stark, uselessly.

'A Mondeo matching the description was stolen two nights ago in Gillingham.'

Groombridge nodded, still staring at the vandal. 'If I had to guess,' he said slowly, 'I'd say this was Billy Whelan.'

'Guv?'

'My old guv'nor, DCI Darlington, liked Whelan for the getaway driver.'

'For the van heist?'

'Whelan was a usual suspect. Breaking and entering mostly, bit of drugs, but nicking cars was his speciality and he had links to Dawson. I always thought he was too small-time. Anyway, once the case against Dawson fell over, we had nothing on him. But this could be him – he was a skinny little tocrag. Though last I heard he was still driving a cab.' Groombridge sighed. 'I don't know, I'm chasing ghosts today.'

'So where do we start?' asked Stark.

'*That* is a good question. If Dawson is smart he'll be working in his office like nothing happened.'

'With four employees swearing he's been there all day,' added Fran.

'As for Whelan, he hasn't shown up on my radar for a while. Uniform might know him. Work up associates, family, known hangouts and lock-ups.' Groombridge tapped the image of the Mondeo on the pinboard. 'I don't suppose we'll find it parked in plain sight.'

A constable stuck his head round the door and passed a note to Groombridge.

'Okay, the guard is out of surgery and stable. They're confident he'll recover, no thanks to Nikki bloody Cockcroft.' Groombridge crumpled the paper and tossed it into a nearby bin. 'All right, everyone, it's leg-work time.'

'You'll like this, Guv,' said Stark, hanging up the phone. 'Billy Whelan is still a registered private minicab driver. Greenwich

Council tell me they received a cancellation notice two years ago. Whelan re-registered with *Chatham* Town Council. They gave me his mobile, cab registration and home address, two streets from where our silver Ford Focus was boosted.'

Fran smiled. 'Shall we ask HQ to ping the mobile?'

Groombridge shook his head, pained. 'It's all a bit circumstantial. The authorizing officer is a stickler. Let's try this the old-fashioned way first. Call me a cab, would you, Trainee Investigator Stark?'

'Happy to, Guv.' Stark used his mobile so Whelan wouldn't see the area code and put it on speakerphone. It rang but went to answerphone. Stark tried again.

'Hello.'

'Hi, is that Billy?'

'Yeah.'

'Can I order a cab for tonight?'

'Nah, sorry, mate. I'm off.'

Stark thought on his feet. 'Come on, mate, I won't take long. Jonny said you'd sort me out.' He didn't try to modify his accent: his own was just as likely.

'Jonny who?'

'Jonny! Probably didn't use his name – he's a bit cute like that. He got your card from last time, said you sorted him out.'

'I'm off tonight.'

'Come on, man, there's this party. It's not far. I said I'd sort everyone out with tickets.'

There was a long pause. 'What d'you need?'

'Five tickets. And some biscuits, how many can you get?'

'How many d'you need?'

'Twenty.'

'Too many. I don't know you.'

'I can pay.'

Another long pause. It was a delicate balance. It had to be enough to distract Whelan from his current activities, but it

426

was a lot to ask for a first-time contact calling out of the blue. Too much, probably. A ticket was phone speak for a wrap of cocaine, a gram wrapped in a folded square of paper, like the ones he'd pulled from Gibbs's rubbish. A disco biscuit was one of the original ecstasy tablets, *circa* 1988, but was still used as generic slang. Approximately forty to fifty pounds per ticket, and eight to ten per biscuit. Cheaper than getting drunk and prices kept falling.

'Sixty a ticket. Fifteen a biscuit.'

'That's a bit steep!' Stark grabbed his pad, scribbled one word and held it up to Fran – address!

'I don't know you.'

Fran pulled up online maps.

'Oh, come on, mate, this is highway robbery!'

'Take it or leave it.'

Stark paused as long as he dared while Fran searched for Chatham. 'I'll take it.'

'What's your name?'

'Joe.'

'Address?'

Fran zoomed in on a residential area. 'Meet you at the corner of Gordon Road and Portland Street. Nine o'clock.'

'Where's the party?'

Groombridge shook his head. Whelan was fishing. He wanted to drive by and check it out before he made the pickup. Stark wouldn't want to guess a location anyway. 'I'll tell you when you pick me up.'

'Tell me now.'

'So you can leave me standing in the street while you sell direct? I wasn't born yesterday.'

'I'm only asking.'

'Maybe, but I don't know *you,* and you're already overcharging.'

Whelan laughed. 'All right, don't get mardy. If you don't

dick me around tonight we'll talk a better price next time. Bring your tokens. Don't be late. We good?'

'We're good.'

Whelan hung up. Stark let out a long, deep breath.

'Not bad.' Groombridge chuckled. 'Your first undercover work. What made you think of it?'

'You mentioned drugs and his connection to Dawson. We nabbed a handful of Gosport cabbies for dealing, and some doormen.'

'A universally convenient and lucrative sideline to both. But if he's willing to show his face for pocket money he's either stupid or uninvolved. I look forward to asking him. Put out a call on his cab, see if we can pick him up early. Otherwise Stark goes undercover for real.'

Fran shook her head. 'Guv. His face . . .'

Stark said nothing. She was right. His face was too public, his scars too memorable. Undercover work would not feature heavily in his new career.

'Maggie will sort him out. Swing by home for suitable attire on the way. Get on to Chatham for a bit of help.'

There was no sign of the Mondeo or the trio when Stark and Fran set off to Chatham. Whelan was late, probably coasting up and down the local streets to check for uniform cars. It was already ten past nine and Stark had been on the corner of Gordon Road and Portland Street for twenty minutes without his cane. He was beginning to sweat.

A Skoda Octavia minicab appeared at the next junction along. Whelan peered at him for a moment, cautious, then pulled up alongside. 'You order a cab?'

'Yeah.'

'Name?'

'Joe. You Billy?'

'Hop in the back.'

Stark did his best not to fall in.

'I know you?' said Whelan, looking in his mirror.

Stark had on casual clothes, a cap to cover the scars in his hairline and the cunning contents of Maggie's makeup case masking those on his face. Harper hadn't passed up the opportunity to suggest lipstick and a frock. 'Must've used you before. Expect I was mashed.'

Whelan appeared to accept this. 'Where to?' he asked, pulling out.

Fran's car pulled across the street forcing Whelan to stop. 'What the . . . *Oi!*' he shouted out of the window and leant on his horn angrily. Fran waved cheerily. A local unmarked car pulled up behind and both put on their concealed blue lights. In the mirror, Whelan's face was a picture.

'The police station, please,' said Stark, holding up his warrant card. 'Billy Whelan, I'm arresting you on suspicion of possession of prohibited substances.' Better to have him in cuffs before they mentioned assisting an escape. Possession, even in the amounts discussed, was less likely to send him running. The locals had wanted to wire Stark up and go for supply, but once they realized who he was it was obvious his face was too fresh in the public mind. His inexperience clinched it.

Whelan still looked panicked and fit to bolt, but there were already uniforms outside his door. A search of the car showed why. He'd brought extra, a lot extra, obviously hoping to re-supply the party. The Chatham police understandably insisted on charging him at their nick before handing him over. It was gone midnight before Mick closed the cell door on Whelan in Royal Hill.

The buzz of the day had long fizzled out. Two-thirds of the team had been sent home to sleep. Those left looked out on their feet and out of ideas. There had been several public sightings of the grey Mondeo, all mistaken, and nothing on the plate-recognition cameras. Liam Dawson had not turned up at his office or been tracked down at any of the clubs. Stark made himself busy, lest anyone point out that he shouldn't be there. He picked up Whelan's phone in its evidence bag and began copying its numbers into the database. He was tired, and it was several minutes before he thought to scroll down to L.

Keeping a lid on his excitement he double-checked before showing the number to Fran.

'Liam?' Fran looked at him. 'A different phone from the one Callie Cockcroft texted at the courthouse?'

Stark nodded. They could request a ping on the new number's location. 'There's more – that number flagged a connection in the database. Nikki Cockcroft had the same number saved in her smashed phone as D. And it gets better – while Dawson was smart enough to use a separate phone for the escape, Whelan wasn't. His shows calls to and from Liam's courthouse phone and the records might pinpoint locations.'

42

Whelan barely reacted when confronted with his blunder. He listened to their questions, accusations and threats in silence, then uttered just one word: 'lawyer'.

'Well, that was short and sweet,' said Fran, closing the door to the interview room.

'He might be small-time but he's a proper villain.' Groombridge rubbed his temples. 'We won't get anything out of him.'

Stark looked at the clock: ten past one. No wonder the guv'nor was tired.

'Guv!' Dixon came down the corridor, looking like he'd run every step.

'The ping?' asked Groombridge.

Dixon shook his head. 'No current location on the new number, Guv. Either switched off or another burner . . .' He glanced at Groombridge, whose disapproval of cop-show Americanisms was written on his face. 'Sorry, Guv, disposable pay-as-you-go mobile phone.'

'Right. So?'

Dixon rallied. 'I just took a call for Stark from the National Crime Squad – one of the numbers he entered on the database, off Whelan's phone, flagged up against an NCS investigation. They wanted to know everything we had but they wouldn't tell me anything at all.'

Groombridge's hackles rose. 'Is that so? Well, let's see if they'll be any more forthcoming with me.'

They followed the DCI up to the door of his office but he closed it behind him. In the prevailing quiet the door was no

431

match for the raised voice behind it. For the first time Stark heard Groombridge swear. It turned out the DCI was quite proficient.

A few minutes later Groombridge emerged, unruffled. 'Right. NCS immigration crime team have been working jointly with the UK Border Agency, and the number flagged belongs to a fake-passport supplier they're keeping tabs on in deepest, darkest Deptford. They've had his phone tapped for months. They refused my request to pick him up for questioning – they want whoever is supplying him with blank documents but, most importantly, they're keeping tabs on his customers. They're after terrorists or people-traffickers, not small-time crooks like Whelan. After a little persuasion they did agree to email over redacted transcripts of "relevant conversations" for my eyes only.'

It took an hour for the email to arrive. Heads were nodding when Groombridge bustled out of his office holding a sheaf of paper. 'Right, heads up! Nearly four weeks ago Whelan ordered two fake IDs – passport, driving licence, birth certificate, bank account, credit card, the lot – paying in cash. The names on the documents were Nicola Michaels and Steve Baker. Get back on the phones to the airports, ferries, Eurostar, Eurotunnel, shipping companies, private-boat hire, et cetera. Bookings under those names. That means now!'

'Let's hope we're not too late,' said Fran, earning a sharp look from Groombridge.

There were no bookings, past or future. That ruled out airports. Unfortunately all it took to legitimately leave mainland Britain was to be seated in a car booked on to a ferry or into a tunnel by a third party, real or fictitious. On the ferries you had to stipulate in advance how many people would be in the car; for the tunnel you didn't even have to do that. Likewise Nikki Cockcroft might have left by private light aircraft or small fishing boat, though the weather offshore had been rough. Consequence of an island nation. Nikki, a.k.a. Nicola, could already be abroad. Interpol had her alias now but Europe was a big place with vast open borders.

'Okay,' said Groombridge, with energy he couldn't possibly feel. 'If you can't find the person, find the car. Where are we?'

'Nowhere,' replied Fran.

'No ports have a booking for the Mondeo, Guv,' added Williams.

'They're obviously not that stupid. Our Nikki needs a new car.'

'I'll get on to Chatham and see what other cars went missing in the last few days,' suggested Fran.

Groombridge was shaking his head. 'Do that. But they'd be mad to use a hot car. They need a clean one. That's what we should be looking for.'

'Guv.' Stark put up his hand self-consciously. 'One of the numbers on Whelan's phone was a car dealership in Chatham.'

It turned out that three cars had been boosted in the Chatham area in the last two days. But Fran was more interested in what the Chatham police had to say about the dealership.

'It's a small independent owned and run by one of those old-school wide-boys. They suspect he supplies the odd stolen luxury car to an Albanian outfit that ships them off in containers, ruthless bastards. Whelan might supply the occasional car, I suppose. But if you're an iffy type in need of a clean car and you know an iffy car dealer . . .'

Groombridge nodded. 'All right. You and Stark get over to Chatham and shake down the car dealer.'

'Come off it, Guv. We just got back from that shit-hole!' protested Fran.

'So you know the way.'

Fran rolled her eyes. 'Come on, then.' She jerked her head at

Stark with enough of a glare to impart blame. 'If we leave now, you can buy me breakfast and at least three coffees.'

Fran was still *tsk*ing an hour later as they sat in the car outside the dealership, sipping their cooling coffees. Stark's stomach rumbled. A service-station sandwich was not the canteen's full English he'd been banking on. Fran seemed satisfied with her Danish and double espresso. She didn't seem tired, she didn't seem hungry, just angry. Perhaps that was what sustained her. But if she was too angry to be tired he was rapidly becoming too tired to be angry. He wasn't sure how long he could keep this up. He rested his head against the cathartic coolness of the glass.

A punch in the arm woke him. Fran ignored his pointed rubbing and pointed across the street. A man in a Barbour jacket and flat cap was unlocking the heavy padlock on the barrier across the entrance to the yard. Stark got out stiffly. The man looked at them as they approached, uncertain. It was too early for customers unless they were very keen. Fran held up her warrant card and his face defaulted to cagey.

'Douglas Brown?'

'Not a crime, last time I heard.'

'We'd like a word inside, if you don't mind.'

'I do mind.'

'I suppose we could talk out here. We could still be talking out here half an hour from now when your customers start showing up. Stark, go and put on the blue lights so everyone can see who Mr Brown is chatting to so early in the morning.'

Brown looked at the busy passing traffic, clearly unhappy at the suggestion.

'We just want to see a list of recent sales, nothing untoward.' Fran smiled but Brown's distrust was plain. She sighed. 'Listen,' she let her impatience show, 'I'm interested in your legitimate dealings. If you prefer I'll have an officer here in an

434

hour with a warrant. But by then I might decide to take an interest in other dealings. Albanian ones, perhaps.'

'I don't know what you're talking about.'

'Perhaps a quick outing to their yard might jog your memory. They're upstanding citizens like yourself. I'm sure they'll be as happy to help us with our enquiries as they'll be to know you're doing the same. You know how co-operative these Albanians are with the police.'

Brown was in his sixties. Long past the bravado and imagined invincibility of the up-and-coming crook. 'Come in, then.'

He showed them his books.

No Whelan. No Nikki Cockcroft, Nicola Michaels, Liam Dawson or Steve Baker. Fran slid an image of Dawson across the desk: the CCTV still from the prison visit, a dodgy-looking image of a dodgy looking bloke. 'Know this man?'

Brown shook his head. Fran placed Whelan's latest arrest mugshot on the desk. 'This one?' Same reaction from Brown, but his eyes betrayed him. 'You've a lousy poker face, Mr Brown. Billy Whelan is a known associate of yours. And he's in a world of shit. If you don't want to join him, I suggest you start being a whole lot more co-operative. All I want to know is whether he bought a car from you recently.'

It was almost laughable to watch the man's eyes darting as his brain scrambled for options. It was a wonder he eked out a living trading used cars.

'Perhaps we should ask the Albanians,' suggested Fran.

'All right, all right! Billy bought a car, couple of weeks back.' Fran jabbed at the books. 'Which?'

Brown found the entry. 'This one. Silver Volkswagen Golf.'

Fran stared. 'Says here this car was bought by a John Michaels. Whose name is the car registered in?'

'I'll look.' Brown pulled out a ring-binder of ownership slips. 'Here ... Nicola Michaels.' Fran glared at him dangerously and he went on the defensive. 'Billy asked for the slip in that name, said the bloke was a mate. Nothing illegal there, happens all the time. Dad buying his daughter's birthday surprise. It's all legit!' he insisted desperately.

'Look at the address, Sarge,' said Stark. According to the book, Nicola Michaels lived on the Ferrier Estate.

'One of Dawson's flats, maybe.' That wasn't the only detail that piqued her curiosity. 'According to these numbers you sold at a loss. Paid in cash, did he?'

'Win some, lose some,' said Brown, innocently. It was an old trick. Fill in the price on the buyer's slip but not your own. Then fill in a lower number on yours, pocket the rest VAT free and offset the loss. Fran slapped the book shut and took it.

'I didn't do anything wrong!' protested Brown, in rising alarm, as Stark followed Fran across the showroom.

Fran stopped. 'Tell the Albanians you're getting too old for their game. You're retired. Otherwise I'll be back with that warrant.'

'The Golf's registered under Nikki's alias . . .' Groombridge's voice sounded mechanical, Bluetoothed through the car speakers. 'Okay, I'll get someone back on to DVLA to confirm, and have uniform check out the address. In the meantime we've got a shout on the Mondeo. The phone ping still hasn't got a live location but the call history shows multiple calls in the vicinity of a light-industrial site in Welling. We got hold of the manager, who thinks he's seen a grey Mondeo coming out of a unit rented recently by a tall, heavy guy in a black bomber jacket and baseball cap, fictional name, of course.'

'Text Stark the address. We'll meet you there. Good hunting!'

Moments later, Stark's phone beeped and he typed the location into the sat-nav. They were still thirty minutes away and the dull rumble of the road coaxed Stark's eyes closed once more, but the possibility of his colleagues kicking in the right door stopped him nodding off.

'How's it going with Aqua-hottie?' asked Fran, out of the blue.

'Given your recent conspiracy, you could call her by her name.'

'Defensive of her already. How sweet.'

'I hardly think this is the time, Sarge.'

'I'm just making conversation.'

'Try "Nice weather for the time of year."'

Fran tutted. 'You were more fun when you were falling apart.'

'That show's over.'

'I thought you were finished being a secretive bastard now your sordid past is public knowledge.'

She had a point. And he'd decided to make changes. 'She's great, thanks. She's forgiven me for being a secretive bastard.'

Fran glanced at him in surprise. She made little effort to hide her triumph. 'Meaning you think it's about time I did too? After that stunt with the CPS lawyer!'

Stark smiled. 'I can wait. You'll forgive me eventually.'

'What do you mean "eventually", Mr We'll See? You're just trying us out for size, remember?'

'Not any more.'

Fran blinked. 'You're ready to hop off the fence and be a proper copper?'

'I'm ready to try.'

'Wow! Another blistering strap-line for the recruitment poster.'

'At least I'll be learning from the best.'

'Flattery now, is it?'

'I was talking about the DCI.' Stark laughed.

That earned him another punch in the arm. 'Another year in my bad books! Keep this up and you'll never make DC. It's not the DCI who signs your PDP sheets. All right, next question.'

'Come off it, Sarge!'

'What happened with your SAS thing?'

'What SAS thing?'

'Training. Why were you sent home?'

Stark cursed silently. Where had she unearthed *that*? 'They call it "returned to unit". And it's Special Forces Training. You're not SAS or SBS till you've passed.'

'Which you didn't. Why? I asked Captain Wendy but she wouldn't say.'

'Wouldn't admit she didn't know.'

'She didn't? She gave me guff about how these things are "not discussed".'

'They're not.'

'Boy Scout bullshit again. Tell me.'

'Why should I?'

'I'm curious.'

Just that. No threat or dissemblance, just plain, honest curiosity. Was she beginning to work him out? 'Malaria.'

'Malaria?'

'During jungle training in Borneo.'

'They can't fail you for getting *ill*!'

'They can and they do. Malaria, dengue fever, dehydration, infected cuts, blistered feet – it doesn't matter. Whether it's carelessness, susceptibility or plain bad luck, if you're not fit to go on you go home.' They had always been swamped with applicants. For years Special Forces had represented the best hope of genuine combat, until Afghanistan and Iraq had changed everything. Stark had given it little thought until an ex-SAS instructor pushed him to apply. For a while a sand-coloured beret had appealed to his vanity. A proper cap, as Maggs would've put it. Now just another forgotten dream.

'So that's it? All that cock-waving and it comes down to who gets a mozzie bite and who doesn't – that's madness!'

'Maybe.' Of course that wasn't it – not all of it. But Fran couldn't see through him like Groombridge; not yet at least. Stark hadn't flown home early from Borneo. His symptoms

438

hadn't seriously kicked in till weeks later. By the escape-and-evasion he had felt like death but didn't know the cause and sure as hell couldn't let the Directing Staff know.

He'd escaped and evaded, but still had to face the resistance-to-interrogation test, or tactical questioning, as they liked to call it now. Stark had had little fear of it. However real they tried to make it, it wasn't. No matter how tired you were, how humiliated, what stress or discomfort you were put in, they weren't going to pull your nails out or attach electrodes to your balls. All you had to do was wait them out. Or so he'd thought. But three days' E&E in winter sleet, old boots and a Second World War greatcoat had let the malaria take hold. During TQ the fever had spiked and he'd become delirious. They'd eventually tracked him down eight miles away, barefoot and raving.

As the first applicant ever to escape TQ he was credited with demonstrating 'unique resolve', but told that escaping while too ill to evade recapture demonstrated 'flawed strategy'. He was invited to think better next time. So much for the grey man. Stark still felt mildly embarrassed about the whole thing.

The phone rang again.

'Fran!' Groombridge's voice, urgent now.

'Yes, Guv.'

'Where are you?'

'A2 passing Gravesend.'

'Turn around. Head for Folkestone. We just got a call saying the silver Golf is booked on Eurotunnel, midday train. Reservation was made by one Nicola Michaels. DVLA confirmed the Golf is registered to that name and the address is an empty flat, not one of Dawson's. You're closest now. Local uniform have been told to wait for you unless Nikki tries to take an earlier train. The super won't look kindly on us if she's handed back by French Customs.'

'And the Mondeo? Dawson?'

'The car's here. Dawson's not. SOCO are on their way. I'll

439

have to wait around. Get Nikki Cockcroft for me. And be careful, she's a spiteful little cow.'

'Don't worry, Guv. I'll send in Stark to charm her, then cuff her while she's busy chewing his head off.' She gunned the accelerator.

43

Fifty minutes later they cornered into the terminal service road and flashed their warrant cards at the gate. A uniform constable met them in the staff-only area. 'The Golf arrived ten minutes ago. Woman driver.'

'She's early?' Fran clicked her tongue in irritation. No time to set up or direct her car quietly aside.

'Sergeant Riley is waiting upstairs. I'll show you the way.' They followed him up to the police suite, cluttered with monitors that looked like they'd been there since the 1994 opening. A window looked into the central atrium of the terminal, a square, two-storey concourse with a coffee booth, seating in the centre and the typical shops dotted around the outside. The atrium roof was a tensile fabric tent, the going thing in the early nineties; *nouveau* modernism reasserting itself over post-modernist usurpers. Sadly the edifice was dogged by the usual civic underfunding and showed its age. The louvred glass ventilation windows beneath the roof were dirty, their cheap actuators black with grease. The painted walls looked cheap, the sloping, flush, inward-looking first-floor windows made an effort to be modern but were obviously hard to clean. Even the concourse floor showed signs of indifferent repair. On a sunny day like today the sunlight diffused evenly through the roof, reflecting off the white walls and bathing the concourse in an overgenerous, even glare. The one-way mirrored glass of the police-suite window looking in was an adhesive film rather than a factory-applied aluminium coating, an afterthought, now blistering and peeling at the edges.

Stark stared through it despondently, embarrassed by the parsimony, the state disease of post-war, post-imperial Britain. He was knackered and there were no spare chairs in the cramped suite.

Sergeant Riley introduced himself. 'She's at the coffee booth.' He pointed to one screen. The image was several generations short of high definition, but there, sitting among those topping up on hot drinks and pastries, was a girl, short to average height, boyishly skinny, shiny branded tracksuit and baseball cap. Nikki sipped her coffee with her head down and kept checking the phone in her hand.

'She's gone blonde.' Stark pointed at the ponytail.

'She'll be the belle of the jail,' muttered Fran, with a dark smile. 'How long till her train's called?'

'Forty-five minutes.'

'Okay. Safer if we take her in the car away from the crowd.'

Riley nodded. 'I've got Passport Control standing by to pull her car over on the pretext of a spot check.'

A few minutes later Nikki stood and walked into the toilets.

'Odd,' said Riley. 'She went on the way in.'

'I guess the heartless little cow is prone to nerves after all.' Fran scoffed. 'The Ladies Room has never been a sadder misnomer.'

Nikki emerged, towing a small black, wheeled suitcase, and turned towards the exit. Every officer in the suite sat up.

'Are we looking at some kind of drop?' frowned Riley. 'I thought this was a fugitive case.'

'It is,' said Fran, equally puzzled. 'Can you wind this back?'

'There!' Riley pointed at a woman, emerging backwards from the toilets. His officer paused the image. She was pulling a large wheeled suitcase. One of those solid ones with the hard shell, but cheap, unbranded.

Fran frowned. 'What?'

'People don't wheel in cumbersome luggage. They leave it

in the car. Why is this woman trailing around a sodding great case? Rewind a bit more . . . There, play.'

Coming in from the car park the woman approached the coffee booth without looking at Nikki, glanced at the refreshments without buying, then walked back past them on her way to the toilets. Nikki got up and followed her in. The woman re-emerged and went straight back outside. Nikki came out with the smaller case.

Another camera showed the woman lifting the large case into a BMW, getting in and driving off to join the queue for France. Riley was shaking his head. 'Little woman throws a big case into the boot one-handed . . . Rewind it to where she gets out, Thompson.'

The constable complied. The woman parked, got out and lifted the big case out of the boot.

'Two hands, much heavier,' nodded Fran. She turned to stare at the real-time image of Nikki crossing the car park. 'So what's in that case?' she mused aloud. 'Get Passport Control to pull her over.'

Riley radioed the instruction.

'Where's she going?' asked Stark. On screen Nikki had turned right out of the exit and was heading out of the car park.

'The Golf's in the coach park,' explained one constable, operating the CCTV.

The car park swept in a quadrant around one corner of the terminal and gave way to an equally large area crammed with coaches, motor-homes, towed caravans, dozens of cars and hundreds of people milling around and making use of the grassed area and children's playground beyond. 'Where?' asked Stark.

'I haven't got a camera on it. It's back there between those gold double-deckers.' They watched Nikki disappear where the constable was pointing.

Several minutes passed.

'I don't like this,' announced Fran, picking up a pair of radios. 'Let's go round there and get eyes on her.'

They hurried outside to the car and drove back round to the public side. Riley and the constable who'd greeted them came too.

The Golf hadn't moved. It had tinted rear windows and from where they'd parked the police couldn't see in, but the officers in the police suite assured them Nikki had not emerged or gone elsewhere.

Minutes ticked by. 'Something's wrong,' said Stark.

'I thought soldiers were taught to be patient,' sighed Fran.

'They're also taught to be wary.'

'She's getting out,' announced Riley.

But it was the passenger door opening, and Nikki wasn't getting out. Stark stared at the big-framed figure in jeans, navy-blue hoodie with the hood up over a grey baseball cap, and cursed his stupidity. He'd noted the same figure on the CCTV several times. 'He was shadowing her in the terminal. I should've realized. It's Dawson.'

As he said it, the figure glanced around and they saw his face. It *was* Dawson, minus the goatee. 'How did he get here?' asked Fran.

'Could easily have been in the back seats when the Golf arrived,' suggested Riley. 'The automated check-in booth camera wouldn't have seen him.'

Dawson opened the boot of the Golf and lifted out the small black suitcase Nikki had been pulling and walked away. Suddenly he froze. A blue Volvo had cruised into the space in front of him and two men in their late thirties got out, wearing dark suits.

'Yours?' said Riley.

'No,' said Fran. 'If those arseholes at National Crime have decided . . .' The two men walked past Dawson, chatting idly.

444

'I thought he was going to bolt,' said the constable, leaning forward between Fran and Stark for a better look.

Dawson wheeled the case to join a group of people milling around a huge coach with Belgian livery. 'What's he doing?' asked Riley.

'Switching,' said Stark, with sudden certainty. 'Something's wrong.'

Fran was nodding. 'Let's take him. If he gets on that coach this could get ugly.'

In that moment Dawson looked their way. The constable's uniform must've drawn his attention straight to Stark and Fran. Dawson's eyes went wide with shock. Looking around desperately, he shoved a young couple out of the way and set off across the coach park with the suitcase snaking behind him.

'Shit!' hissed Fran, kicking open her door. 'Get Nikki!' she barked at Stark and set off with Riley and the constable at a surprising turn of speed.

Hurrying between the coaches, Stark approached the rear of the Golf. He could see Nikki's white cap in the wing-mirror. Adrenalin coursed through him. He should have been looking forward to this – Nikki had tried to cheat justice, cheat him as she had cheated Pinky and the others of a life without fear, as she had cheated Alfred Ladd of his remaining years, his remaining dignity, as she had cheated Stacey Appleton of her young life – but creeping up the side of the car, he couldn't shake the feeling that something was badly wrong.

He felt for a pulse but knew it was too late.

Nikki stank of booze. There was a bottle of vodka open in her lap, a clear plastic bag of pills too, with more on the floor. The air reeked of cannabis, but something else, something Stark recognized from the pipes of Afghan villagers and Afghan National Army soldiers, but there was no pipe or joint in sight. Then he saw the phone in Nikki's hand. The screen was still awake – a sent text. *Goodbye Mum I'm sorry*.

Dawson.

Slamming the door, he set off after the others as fast as he could, hobbling, almost hopping, on his good leg, using the cane for balance rather than support. 'Nikki's dead,' he shouted, into the radio. 'Get some uniforms out here to the car.'

In the distance Stark saw the eager young constable cut around some cars in front of Dawson but the big man simply dipped his shoulder and slammed through, like a battering ram.

Looking around wildly, Dawson jumped in front of a blue Toyota, forcing it to stop. Then he yanked open the door and dragged the driver out on to the tarmac, the poor man's wife screaming as she climbed out of the other side. Riley caught up and, unlike his constable, had thought to flick out his ASP baton – twenty-six inches of telescopic steel. Mistake, thought Stark. Given Dawson's size and profession, CS spray would've been a safer bet.

Sure enough, Dawson dealt with the baton the old-fashioned way, soaking up the blow with his fleshy upper arm, accepting the pain for the gain. He was inside the weapon's reach now and made Riley pay, smashing him aside like a bull tossing a toreador. Fran was too late to stop herself and arrived just as Dawson hoisted up the suitcase and used it to smash her aside. Stark was relieved to see the big man didn't stop to do more damage, but instead heaved the heavy-looking case into the Toyota.

The constable was curled up in pain, clutching his elbow, fallen badly, broken something perhaps. Riley was struggling to his knees, Fran was still down and Dawson was cramming himself into the car. He planned to ram his way out of the complex and make a break for it. Stark would be damned if he'd let that happen. Riley could help the others. Stark went straight to the far side of the Toyota where he held his cane in both hands, pressed the small indentation under the tiger handle and twisted. There was a quiet *snick*, and he slid out the blade from the shaft. Stiletto thin, double-edged, eight inches of needle-sharp steel. Too short for a true sword-cane – the tiger handle made you hold it more like a pistol anyway – this was a stabbing, slashing, close-quarters weapon. The Duke's valet must've told Pierson about it but she'd judiciously failed to pass on the information, given the timing. Stark had discovered it weeks later. He thrust the blade into the front tyre and withdrew it, hobbled back and did the same to the rear. As a getaway vehicle it was finished. Dawson felt the car dropping on one side and stared out at Stark in furious disbelief.

Don't get out, thought Stark. Dawson was a big man, well over six feet, a little fat over a lot of muscle but fast for his size. He knew his way around a brawl. He'd taken on Riley and his ASP without a second's hesitation. The only advantage a smaller man could have was better training and more speed. Or a concealed knife, the use of which would certainly cost him his career. Stark kept the blade out of sight and slid it away with another precise *snick*. Without it he would fancy his chances on a good day but, as he was, Dawson would make mincemeat of him. He looked very angry indeed.

Don't get out!

Poor impulse control, Stark had been taught, was manifest to a greater or lesser degree in the majority of convicted criminals – that imbalance between subconscious voices and failure to give due consideration to potential negative implications of your deeds, to yourself or others. Of course, Stark had exhibited similar failure in the past. Dawson threw the door open but Stark had already backed out of its arc.

The big man began to climb out, dragging the case with him. He did it all wrong, left himself wide open. When you're kicking in a door you use your boot, not a shoulder. It focuses the impact

447

with less chance of injury and less chance of following through off balance. The same thing if someone's behind the door, or climbing out of a car. Time it right and the window smashes over the head, the leg is trapped, perhaps broken, the arm jarred backwards, wrist possibly broken. Stark couldn't kick the door but he was willing to risk his shoulder.

Instead he backed away. There were cameras. Pre-emptive violence was a soldier's luxury. He immediately regretted his restraint as Dawson's hand reached inside his zipped hoodie. *Don't be a gun!*

Dawson withdrew his fist. In it he held a blackjack, a modern-day club. Not a gun but still a formidable weapon, easily lethal. Illegal too, but less so than gun or knife: an ideal concealed weapon for a doorman. A foot long, probably a plumber's pipe-bending spring originally, grip and lanyard at one end, lead ball at the other, all bound tight in black leather.

The lead ball was oval. If Stark had needed any more confirmation, this was it, but he did not. The moment he'd read Nikki's text message, the enormity of their mistake had struck him: Pinky had seen Nikki and Kyle look down on Stacey Appleton's corpse, but Dawson had been there too, lurking in the shadows. Whoever had hit Stacey with her phone, it was Dawson who'd stove in her skull from behind – with that brutal little club – Dawson who'd tipped the poor girl screaming to her death, Dawson who'd texted the fake suicide note. Stacey had snitched to the police, or was in danger of doing so, and Dawson needed the Ferrier and its Rats silent. That was why he'd helped Nikki look for Pinky: fear that she'd seen him too.

And now Dawson was coming for Stark. It was too late to attack and there was no avoiding the superior force. That left tactical retreat and misdirection. It was time to shift the engagement sideways.

Should've barged the door, thought Stark, gesturing behind

his back to Riley and backing away further. Dawson followed, raising the blackjack with a snarl.

'Hey, big boy!'

Dawson glanced round just as Riley sent a jet of liquid at his face. Police-issue five per cent CS methyl isobutyl ketone solvent propelled by pressurized nitrogen, accurate range four metres. The gesture Stark had used was that of an index finger depressing a spray button. Riley was a fast learner. From behind, Stark seized Dawson's wrist, twisted up and punched the handle of his cane into the man's triceps as hard as he possibly could. Dawson's fingers sprang open, sending the blackjack spinning.

There would've been some justice in seeing Dawson go down clutching his eyes, gasping for breath, as the court guard had, but the man had somehow got one hand in front of his face to ward off the worst, and in attacking one arm Stark had left himself exposed to the other. With a roar, Dawson twisted backwards and round, driving his elbow into Stark's side. Stark rolled with it to preserve his ribs, but it knocked all the wind from his body and sent him crashing across the ground.

It was worth it, though, to see the blackjack roll beneath the nearest car where it could do no more harm. Dawson stood over him menacingly, ready to finish what he'd started, perhaps, but seeing Riley raise the spray once more he grabbed the suitcase and ran towards the terminal building.

Fran was up and staggered after him. Riley came to help Stark. 'I'm fine,' gasped Stark, wincing in pain as he forced himself to his feet, fighting for breath. 'Go!' Ignoring him, Riley helped him lean against a car. Feeling his ribs, Stark decided they were intact. 'Bag that blackjack. It's a murder weapon. And call for back-up.'

'I've got five men waiting inside,' grinned Riley.

The gunshot turned their heads.

*

449

Riley frowned, confused, but Stark was already on the move, hobbling, hopping, cursing viciously. How could he have been so stupid? He should've taken Dawson out when he had the chance.

People were running from the entrance, some screaming, most quiet with flight, ducking as they ran. Instinctive, largely pointless: it made you a slightly smaller target, but a slower one. Still, you couldn't outrun a bullet. One man nearly knocked Stark over as he passed through the doors, sending Stark twisting off balance. A sharp pain shot through his pelvis – not good. He ignored it and hobbled on but could take less weight on his bad leg.

Inside, a policeman lay sprawled on the ground, bloody, with another kneeling over him. But the blood was all from his nose – he wasn't shot. Two others were pressed up against the wall where the entrance corridor opened into the atrium. Panicked people lay flat on the floor or crouched behind shop counters. Beside the wide coffee booth another policeman lay on his back, unmoving.

In the far corner of the concourse, Fran was kneeling with a gun to the back of her head.

44

Now Stark was angry. It struck from nowhere, like a crocodile lunging from murky waters. It seized him, but he seized it back: he would not be dragged under. These were his snapping jaws, this was his thrashing fury: his own, his to direct. He recalled the guv'nor's words: 'Whatever demons and furies pursue us cannot be vented. They must be seized upon and channelled to drive us forward as *we* choose.' A chill calm descended on him. His jaw tightened. He wanted to march straight over and punch Dawson in the face but he wouldn't. He couldn't beat him that way. All was silent, bar the tapping of his cane on the hard, polished floor as he walked towards them.

Fran looked frightened. Angry too. With herself. She set the bar high. The sight of a pistol to her head made Stark's stomach twist.

'Open this door, Sparky,' Dawson ordered, jerking his head towards the staff-only door behind him. If he got to the service side of the building where Stark and Fran had not long ago arrived he could jack a car and be gone. His eyes were red and streaming from the CS.

Stark didn't advise him not to rub, to keep blinking, that it would wear off. Instead he shook his head. 'You know I don't work here.'

'Get one of your pals to open it.'

'Then what?'

'She drives. When I'm safe I'll let her go.'

Safe? 'Put the gun down,' said Stark, hobbling forward, cane clicking.

'Stay back!' Dawson jabbed the pistol into the back of Fran's skull.

Fran winced in pain, then anger. Stark could see her contemplating a move. Dawson was being stupid, giving in to the inner bully. A gun is a range weapon: pressing it against the target might thrill the ego but you might just as well have a knife. A trained person could have that gun off him, standing so close. Fran was a trained person. Stark could see her thinking it through. He shook his head. It was too high-risk, the option of last resort. Stark would already have done it, and not with restrained police methods. 'It's over, Liam.'

'Door! Now!' Dawson stared, defiant, almost triumphant. Was he so deluded he thought he'd won? Did he think this was a game? If Stark had had his rifle the fool would already be dead. As it was, Armed Response were doubtless on their way. Forget impulse control or lack thereof, this was something else altogether. Dawson believed himself untouchable; even now he hadn't grasped that it was over, his zenith was passed. Just like the girl he'd pushed off a building, he was about to slam into the ground.

In pre-deployment training, Stark had been shown footage of an Iraqi suicide bomber at a checkpoint. Torso wrapped in explosives, he had stood with his hands raised as three American troops crabbed towards him, shouting, weapons pointed. His eyes darted back and forth between them but there was something in his expression, fear, yes, but also a kind of mad certainty. It was hard to describe but unmistakable. The Americans had seen it. They had stopped, shouted, screamed at him to get face down on the tarmac. When he didn't comply, they shot him. There followed independent interviews with all three soldiers. None could say why but they'd each opened fire within a millisecond. It was just in his eyes, they said. The bomber was found to have a pull-cord trigger tied round one wrist. All he'd had to do was wait till they were close and straighten his arm. The video finished with a zoom of his face as the soldiers approached. If Stark had believed in the devil, that would have been his disguise: the malignant madness of the zealot, the selfish, ignorant shit who saw the world in one way only and the rest be damned. It hadn't been long before Stark had seen that look for himself. Now, behind Dawson's darting eyes and imperious glare, he saw it again – the same inhuman selfishness, the same psychopathy. Hazel would probably call it antisocial personality disorder or something equally colourless. Stark just knew he was looking into the eyes of the enemy once more. 'How do you think this is going to end?' He took another three steps. 'Where do you think you can go? France? We have European arrest warrants now. Switzerland? You'll never make it.' He winced and limped forward again.

'Stay back, Sparky!'

'I'm hardly likely to try anything,' said Stark, pausing, weight all down one leg, holding up the cane as evidence. 'I can hardly stand.' He gave a suitable grimace and wobble.

'Tell them to open that door!'

Stark shook his head, as he tapped slowly across the floor to the fallen constable.

'Sparky!' warned Dawson.

Stark crouched and felt for a pulse. Alive. No blood. Marks to his face suggested Dawson had simply punched his lights out. Stark glanced up, looking for a telltale pinprick of sunlight. There it was. Dawson had fired into the air, not at anyone, for show not effect. Not an imitation gun, though. He could see now it was a Glock 17, one round used; that still left sixteen. A nine-millimetre bullet fired straight up takes about forty seconds to hit the ground. Chance dictated it would not have hit anyone, but it was a busy day outside, and who was Dawson to place that bet?

Gripping the shoulder of the unconscious man's utility vest, Stark tugged past the initial friction.

'*Sparky!*'

Ignoring Dawson, he towed the man behind the booth, wincing in pain with each step. Standing straight, stars danced for a second – not good. Dawson was staring at him, incredulous and angry. 'You're pushing your luck, Sparky.'

He's right! Wait for response. That's what they do. The Judas thought, the fear. *No!* Stark squashed it aside with his searing anger, his cold clarity. If response intervened, this would end badly. It was in the eyes. Dawson was deluded, unstable and cocksure behind his little gun, his lethal fistful of power. He wouldn't lie down on command, like a dog. He wasn't the little bitch but the alpha male, used to cowing the other dogs with vicious brutality. To back down was to be torn down, ripped apart with feral savagery. It wouldn't even occur to him. He had to be put down or broken, re-domesticated.

First he had to be muzzled.

Another three steps. Fran was staring at him as if he was insane. Perhaps he was. Hazel was certainly going to have observations on this if he survived to the next session. Stark was pushing this beyond luck. He was five metres away now. Between his hip and Dawson's gun it might as well have been fifty. He and Dawson locked eyes. Eye contact was good. Let the dog know you see it for what it is. Do not cajole: it is beyond reason. Do not plead: it is without compassion. Let it feel your contempt.

'I won't go with you, Liam, not willingly, and neither will she.' Stark nodded at Fran. 'We know how this kind of thing ends – you arrested, or you dead.'

'Or me killing you both,' sneered Dawson, mockingly.

He could do it. He was both willing and proficient. As Maggs had said, the key to violence was the readiness to act without hesitation or restraint. Dawson would not be restrained by fear or consequence. The only hope was that he might hesitate: he was used to operating in the shadows.

'Did you know Nikki liked to film her attacks on the homeless – post them online for her own titillation?' Stark gestured at the CCTV cameras. 'You'll go viral. Millions of hits of you losing or you dying. Armed police are on their way. They're not harmless cripples like me. They'll shoot you before you know they're here. They might just wound you but if you hurt either of us, or they believe you might, they'll shoot you in the head. They might be aiming at you right now.'

Dawson glanced around, scanning the upper windows.

Stark sneaked in an extra step. 'They're not here yet. Won't be long, though. Have you ever been shot?' he asked. 'I have. To start with you're not sure what's happened. It hurts like hell but you can't really feel it. Sounds weird, I know. Ow.' He winced and wobbled. 'Bollocks to this, I'm going to sit down while we wait. I've been up all night and this really hurts.' Without waiting for permission, he turned to a nearby café chair and dragged it over slowly, hobbling backwards towards them, the metal chair screeching across the floor in the echoey space. From the corner of his eye he saw Dawson tense, wondering if he would try to hit him with the chair and unsure how to deal with his approach. He might just shoot him, of course. Switching the cane to his right hand, he turned to lower himself into the chair, at least two metres away.

Dawson stared blankly at his lunacy. Was some of the big man's certainty crumbling? Would that make him less dangerous, or more? 'Car, Sparky! *Now!*'

'The best you can hope for is to make it out the back and spend the next twenty-four hours on the run in sunny old Kent. Frankly I doubt you'll last that long.'

'*I'll cap this bitch!*'

'And then what? Who will you take as hostage? Me? I'm famous. I'm worth more.' Fran glared. If she ended this in a body-bag he'd never forgive himself. If she caught a bullet and lived she'd never forgive him. 'We know your face. We know about your fake ID. Liam Dawson or Steve Baker, you're going nowhere.'

Something in that hit home. Dawson's face fell, then darkened. Did he finally understand his empire had fallen?

Then Stark saw it, pale in the uniform brightness, one small red dot high on Dawson's chest above Fran's head. Damn. It was elliptical, angled. The shooter was in the shop behind, to the left. They'd done well to get into position without being seen, made use of his diversion. There was a Heckler & Koch MP5 semi-automatic carbine trained on this rabid dog now. One more snarl and it was finished. Stark would not allow it. Dawson had cheated him of Nikki but he would not cheat justice. Stark would see him live to pay his debt, to face the consequences of his actions. For the lives he had taken or blighted, Dawson would feel Groombridge's finger on his collar.

But, first, Stark needed a trigger. 'Time's up, Liam. Let's see if you're ready to play with the big dogs.'

Dawson's eyes went wide with comprehension. Glancing wildly around for armed police, his gun hand drifted away from Fran.

Stark's cane whipped over into one all-or-nothing, full-stretch lunge from the chair. The option of last resort. Inelegant. Expedient. It smashed down on Dawson's gun arm with a loud crack.

Hopelessly off balance, Stark crashed down on his bad shoulder with a grunt but saw the gun clatter and skid away. Dawson howled in pain, cradling his arm. Fran rose like an avenging angel and kicked him between the legs. As he fell to his knees she shoved him sprawling across the floor. Two firearms officers materialized, weapons trained, shouting, shock and awe, '*Stay down! Don't move!*' Another patted Dawson down for further weapons. Fran held out her hand and Riley handed her his speed-cuffs.

For a moment Stark thought she might actually cuff

Dawson's injured wrist but instead she knelt on the back of the gasping man's knees and cuffed his ankles. 'Liam Dawson, I'm arresting you for assisting escape from lawful custody, unlawful possession of a firearm with intent . . .'

Stark stopped listening. It was over. His heart was pounding in his chest. His hands were shaking. He felt sick. He felt like laughing. This was life! This was survival, red in tooth and claw! Fran would be furious with him but he didn't care. She would expect him to give a militaristic explanation when all he could offer was bloody-minded anger. It didn't matter. This was victory.

Riley helped him to his feet, handing him his cane. It was whole. Stark was pleased. For all he hated the incapacity it represented he would have been sorry to see it broken. It was an exquisite example of its craft. Snakewood was among the hardest of timbers. Harder than bone, it seemed. Dawson's face was white with pain. Stark felt no pity. He was glad.

'Here.' Riley pressed a café knife into his hand. An everyday stainless-steel implement, dull-edged and long bereft of shine. 'The knife I used for my breakfast. The one you picked up on the way out of the police suite, the one you used to stab the tyres,' he said. 'Forward thinking that, you should be proud.' A knife inside a cane was still a knife. It wasn't a folding pocket-knife and its blade was definitely not less than three inches. The law was quite specific. 'Keep it as a souvenir.'

'Thanks. Your man outside?'

'Jarred elbow. Needs an X-ray but I reckon he's fine. How about you?'

'Intact,' grunted Stark, rolling his sore shoulder.

Riley held up an evidence bag containing Dawson's black-jack. 'We've got the BMW taped off, SOCO and pathologist en route. And we've got the woman who delivered the suitcase. Latvian, won't say a word in English.'

'Hold on to her. Organized Crime are going to want a word.

And search around the BMW, under vehicles and in bins for a smoked joint.'

'A joint? Here?'

'Spiked with heroin,' said Stark. Riley looked at Dawson in understanding. 'And you're going to need some guards for that,' added Stark, indicating the black suitcase.

'What's in it?'

'Eight million and change, minus laundry and storage.'

Everyone around fell silent. Even Fran stared. Grabbing a pair of gloves from a uniform, she knelt and unzipped the case.

Riley whistled appreciatively.

'That's mine!' shouted Dawson, from the floor. 'That's *mine*!'

Epilogue

'DS Millhaven?' asked Superintendent Cox.

Groombridge considered his words carefully. 'More stirred than shaken, sir.'

'Good show. And our irrepressible trainee investigator?'

'Fine.' That was Stark's line and Groombridge was his guv'nor.

Cox accepted the lie with a smile. 'Stabbed the tyres with cheap canteen cutlery?'

'Sir.' Groombridge adopted Stark's other line of choice. The CCTV from the terminal car park showed little to arouse suspicion, but little to allay it. The sooner Stark could manage without that cane the better.

'Shows initiative,' nodded Cox. He'd watched it too. 'I must remember to pass on our gratitude to the chaps down there. Sergeant Riley, you said?'

'Yes, sir.'

Cox smiled. 'Liam Dawson?'

'Broken radius and ulna, both bones of the left forearm. He's claiming brutality.'

Cox rolled his eyes. 'Stark again, tut-tut. He does seem to prefer . . . direct methods. Will it stick?'

'I emailed the CCTV to a chap I know in IPCC. He just laughed and said there should be a law against wasting Complaints Commission time.'

Cox seemed to appreciate the joke but it was no laughing matter and they both knew it. An officer willing and able to do violence, however justified or efficacious, might one day cross the line. 'Reasonable force again?'

'Reasonable force,' nodded Groombridge. 'FSS are testing Dawson's blackjack for Stacey Appleton's blood or DNA. It's leather, porous, so they're quietly confident.'

'Good. Now, tell me about the money.'

Groombridge slid his report across the desk. 'Seven million, nine hundred thousand euros, in five-hundred-euro notes. The going rate for this kind of laundry is fifteen per cent. Add that back in and it exchanges to roughly eight million Great British pounds, plus change.'

'The SecuriGroup van heist,' grinned Cox.

'And I'm willing to bet Ballistics will match the bullet that killed the guards to the pistol Dawson was waving around today. DS Millhaven says when she cornered him Dawson produced it from the suitcase, inside a plastic bag in which we subsequently found a pair of black rubber gloves like the ones used in the heist.'

'Stored with the money? Why?'

'After he was convicted Gary Cockcroft pleaded that killing the guards was never part of the plan. My theory is that Dawson got carried away, and that the gloves will have his DNA inside, gunfire residue outside. When Gary felt the long arm of the law closing in he hid the money along with the gun and gloves as insurance against Dawson.'

'Which explains why Dawson and Whelan never got their share.' Cox nodded.

'Gary uses this leverage to get Dawson to watch over his sister. But when things get serious, Dawson makes him an offer. He and Whelan help Nikki escape if Gary releases their cut. Though the fact that Whelan was willing to risk a small drugs deal with us suggests the idiot didn't know the big money was back in play.'

'But Gary wouldn't let them shift his share abroad too,' said

Cox. 'Not without him, not with every copper in Britain after them. Too risky.'

'But the fool trusted his little sister, gave her the laundry ticket not knowing she'd use the familial name to get all the money released. My guess is Nikki and Dawson have been at it for a while. Maybe Dawson began it as a little private revenge, or maybe she seduced him, or both. Either way it looks like they planned to rip Gary and Whelan off and abscond into the sunset with the lot.'

'But Dawson was just using her to get to the money and evidence.'

Groombridge nodded. 'Nikki was smart enough to have the courier deliver the money to her at the terminal, just in case Dawson couldn't be trusted, but not smart enough to say no to one last joint before they embarked on their new life of luxury together. SOCO found it in a nearby bin, half smoked. They're testing it for heroin – the pills found were opiate-based painkillers and would've hidden it from blood toxicology. With it they found a shot glass and a small bottle of GHB – gamma-hydroxybutyrate. It's used by some body builders instead of anabolic steroids because it occurs naturally in the body so is less obvious in blood tests. Hidden in vodka it would work a lot like Rohypnol, the date-rape drug. Either joint or shot would've rendered Nikki helpless. Dawson probably sold it as a celebration, then poured pills and more vodka down her before she passed out. And if she didn't fall for it, he always had his blackjack.'

'And Stark worked all this out?'

'Enough to add two and two and get eight million.'

'We shall have to watch that young man.'

'He's perhaps not as young as his years, sir.'

'No, perhaps not. And DS Millhaven's name on the arrest sheet – you're not miffed, I hope?'

'My team, my collar. Dawson knows – that's all that matters.'

'Still,' Cox grinned, 'worth a little gloat.'

Groombridge allowed himself a smile. 'I might drop in on the arraignment, sir, if workload permits.' The fatal heist had left a bitter aftertaste for six years. It had soured DCI Darlington's retirement – it had been his last case. Now they had the money, the murder weapon and the remaining perpetrators. The old boy would enjoy this a great deal more than his cheap gold retirement watch.

'You owe Millhaven and Stark a drink, I'd say.'

'They're aware of that, I think. And it gets better, sir. Dawson had a coach ticket from London to Brussels. It was a neat plan – miss the first leg but join the coach at the terminal and pretend he'd been on it all along. Travelling as Steve Baker, he had paperwork for a Swiss bank account in that name and a train booking from Brussels to Basel. SCD7 say the account is linked to an offshore shell company to which Dawson Security sold all its property title deeds for one pound just two days ago. They're going to take his empire apart. Criminal Gains will confiscate everything.' Which meant the government would now own seventeen flats on the doomed estate. There was no hope for the Ferrier but demolition. Maybe this would prompt a swifter resolution.

'Has the courier said anything?'

'Claims she doesn't know what we're talking about. But I sent her photo to NCU and they came straight back with an ID – Brigita Ulmanis. Latvian, with connections to organized crime, trafficking, laundering. They're keen to have a word with her.'

'What about Gary Cockcroft?'

'An illicit mobile phone was seized in his cell last night. Recent calls to his mother, Dawson, and to some unknown mobiles we're running past NCU, the Latvians hopefully. CPS think they can tie him to assisting escape. Whatever happens, he'll be behind bars, knowing his nest egg is gone and that his sister betrayed him.'

'What about their odious mother?'

Groombridge shrugged. 'Had a hand in the escape. Again, CPS think they have it.'

'Good show,' said Cox.

'It's not all good news, sir. Now Nikki can't be convicted it's harder to pin joint principal on the rest for the killing of Alfred Ladd and the sexual assault on Paula Stevens. CPS are going to offer them accessory instead, so long as they all plead guilty. When it comes to sentencing they'll claim duress and blame the whole thing on Nikki and Kyle.'

Cox waved a hand. 'The judge'll still throw the book at them. And it saves the taxpayer the cost of the trial.'

'And their victim, Paula Stevens, the trauma of giving evidence and cross-examination,' added Groombridge. The silver lining. 'CPS say she's agreed to plead guilty to manslaughter due to provocation and they're dropping the murder charge. They reckon she'll get two to three years suspended with some counselling thrown in.'

'So Stark's man Maggs gets his wish, after all,' said Cox, levelly.

'Indeed. Stark seemed to enjoy the irony.'

Cox clearly enjoyed it less. 'I might've preferred fewer man-hours wasted.'

'Sometimes these things just have to play out, sir,' suggested Groombridge.

Cox sighed. 'I suppose. You'll send Stark home?'

'Just as soon as the CPS have finished interviewing him. DS Millhaven was quick to point out to them the benefits of a prompt, extensive debrief.'

'I'll bet,' agreed Cox wryly. Stark's stunt was now station legend.

'I do have another piece of bad news, sir. DS Harper has requested leave of absence. Three months. His wife is having health problems.'

'I'm sorry to hear it,' said Cox, though Groombridge knew his efforts to cover for Harper's absences were unlikely to have escaped notice. 'I'm sure we can scrape together some paid time.'

'Thank you, sir. He's a decent copper.'

'Well, then,' said Cox, gathering his papers, 'we'll not let one grey cloud spoil our parade. It's not often we get to break good news to the press. I rather think the honour should be yours. Well done, Michael.' He stood, and held out a hand.

Groombridge shook it warily. Cox hadn't called him Michael since he'd promoted him into Darlington's shoes. It was no secret that Cox fancied himself for advancement. Groombridge had a nasty feeling he might be being groomed as replacement. If Alison got wind of this, he'd never hear the end of it. Twenty years a policeman's wife, it was no wonder she longed to see him safe behind a desk.

'Don't frown, Mike. I'll be standing right behind you. Can't let you take all the glory. Think we should have Millhaven and Stark there?'

'Definitely not, sir.'

'I suppose you're right. Come on, then, our adoring public awaits . . .'

Fran watched from the canteen window as Stark limped across the road. He'd taken the rear exit to avoid the media circus outside the station's main door. The guv'nor seemed to have them at bay. She'd watch it later on the news. Stark waited on the far pavement with his back to it all, leaning on his cane.

'Café knife, my arse.' Fran chuckled to herself. 'Thanks,' she'd said to him as he left; they'd seen little of each other during the busy afternoon.

'Any time.' He'd nodded wearily.

That was it.

On reflection, 'thanks' didn't quite say it all either. When she was less angry, when she was less tired, when she'd forgotten the fear a little, she would have a few questions to add. Like, how did you know Dawson wouldn't shoot? *Did* you even know? And how the hell dare you be so bloody reckless?

He would have smug answers, couched in desiccated army-speak, no doubt. She would have to wait until she was a lot less tired and a lot less angry. It was a good job he'd decided to stick around because that might take a while.

A blue VW Polo pulled up, Aqua-hottie at the wheel. Stark got in. Fran sipped her coffee and smiled.

Kelly leant over and kissed him, then wrinkled her nose. 'You need a shower!'

Stark chuckled. 'It's the Spandex. Crime-fighting is hot work.'

'Get the bad guys?' She laughed.

'The citizens can sleep safe in their beds.'

Kelly grinned, pulling the little car out into the traffic. Stark looked out of the window as a beautiful sunny afternoon flickered by. He felt hollowed out, spent, happy – the fading afterglow of victory. There might be criticism, praise, gratitude, anger; there would certainly be misunderstanding. None of that mattered. He had done what he could, what he should, what every police officer would, and that was that.

Kelly glanced at him. 'Tired?'

'Tired,' he agreed.

'It's been a long couple of days.'

Stark wound down the window and leant his face into the wind while Kelly steered for his flat. 'It's been a long year,' he said quietly.

Acknowledgements

One never dares believe this day will come. Publication of a debut novel is a golden milestone and culmination of the time, effort and patience of more than the author alone. In recognition of this I offer heartfelt thanks to my family and in-laws for their love and support, friends for never doubting, all those who read early drafts with encouragement and kindness, my agent for his guidance and toil, my publishing-editor for his faith and enthusiasm, my copy-editor for her kind words and rigour, Penguin Books for taking the leap and above all, my wife and three sons, for all of the above and so very much more.

dead good

*For all of you who find
a crime story irresistible.*

Discover the very best crime and thriller books on our dedicated website – hand-picked by our editorial team so you have tailored recommendations to help you choose what to read next.

We'll introduce you to our favourite authors and the brightest new talent. Read exclusive interviews and specially commissioned features on everything from the best classic crime to our top ten TV detectives, join live webchats and speak to authors directly.

Plus our monthly book competition offers you the chance to win the latest crime fiction, and there are DVD box sets and digital devices to be won too.

Sign up for our newsletter at www.deadgoodbooks.co.uk/signup

Join the conversation on:

He just wanted a decent book to read ...

Not too much to ask, is it? It was in 1935 when Allen Lane, Managing Director of Bodley Head Publishers, stood on a platform at Exeter railway station looking for something good to read on his journey back to London. His choice was limited to popular magazines and poor-quality paperbacks – the same choice faced every day by the vast majority of readers, few of whom could afford hardbacks. Lane's disappointment and subsequent anger at the range of books generally available led him to found a company – and change the world.

'We believed in the existence in this country of a vast reading public for intelligent books at a low price, and staked everything on it'
Sir Allen Lane, 1902–1970, founder of Penguin Books

The quality paperback had arrived – and not just in bookshops. Lane was adamant that his Penguins should appear in chain stores and tobacconists, and should cost no more than a packet of cigarettes.

Reading habits (and cigarette prices) have changed since 1935, but Penguin still believes in publishing the best books for everybody to enjoy. We still believe that good design costs no more than bad design, and we still believe that quality books published passionately and responsibly make the world a better place.

So wherever you see the little bird – whether it's on a piece of prize-winning literary fiction or a celebrity autobiography, political tour de force or historical masterpiece, a serial-killer thriller, reference book, world classic or a piece of pure escapism – you can bet that it represents the very best that the genre has to offer.

Whatever you like to read – trust Penguin.